Richard Laymon was born in [illegible] He grew up in California and has a BA in English Literature from Willamette University, Oregon, and an MA from Loyola University, Los Angeles. He has worked as a school-teacher, a librarian, a mystery magazine editor and a report writer for a law firm. He now works full-time as a writer. His novel FLESH was named Best Horror Novel of 1988 by *Science Fiction Chronicle* and also shortlisted for the prestigious Bram Stoker Award, as were FUNLAND and his short story collection, A GOOD, SECRET PLACE. Richard Laymon is the author of many acclaimed works of horror and suspense, including THE STAKE, SAVAGE, AFTER MIDNIGHT and the three novels in the Beast House Chronicles: THE CELLAR, THE BEAST HOUSE and THE MIDNIGHT TOUR. He lives in California with his wife and daughter.

For up-to-date cyberspace news of Richard Laymon and his books, contact Richard Laymon Kills! at: http://rlk.cjb.net

'In Laymon's books, blood doesn't so much drip drip as explode, splatter and coagulate' *Independent*

'Stephen King without a conscience' Dan Marlowe

'A gut-crunching writer' *Time Out*

'An uncanny grasp of just what makes characters work . . . readers turn the pages so fast they leave burn marks on the paper' *Horrorstruck*

'Incapable of writing a disappointing book' *New York Review of Science Fiction*

Also by Richard Laymon

The Beast House Series

The Cellar
The Beast House
The Midnight Tour

The Woods are Dark
Night Show
Beware!
Allhallow's Eve
Flesh
Resurrection Dreams
Funland
The Stake
One Rainy Night
Darkness, Tell Us
Blood Games
Dark Mountain*
Midnight's Lair*
Savage
Out Are The Lights
Alarums
Endless Night
In the Dark
Quake
Island
Body Rides
Bite
Fiends
After Midnight
Among the Missing

*previously published under the pseudonym of Richard Kelly
Dark Mountain was first published as Tread Softly

Come Out Tonight

Richard Laymon

First published in 1999
by HEADLINE BOOK PUBLISHING

First published in paperback in 2000
by HEADLINE BOOK PUBLISHING

10 9 8 7 6 5 4 3 2 1

All characters in this publication are fictitious and any resemblance to real persons, living or dead, is purely coincidental.

ISBN 0 7472 5828 7

Typeset by Avon Dataset Ltd, Bidford-on-Avon, Warks

Printed and bound in Great Britain by
Mackays of Chatham, Chatham, Kent

HEADLINE BOOK PUBLISHING
A division of the Hodder Headline Group
338 Euston Road
London NW1 3BH

www.headline.co.uk
www.hodderheadline.com

THIS BOOK IS DEDICATED TO
STEVE AND ADDIE GERLACH

'RICHARD LAYMON KILLS'
YOUR WEBSITE
KILLS

THANKS SO MUCH
FOR ALL YOUR SUPPORT

Chapter One

On his knees, Duane braced himself up with one arm. With the other, he reached out past Sherry's face. She heard his clock radio scoot on the shelf of the headboard.

'Putting on some music?' she asked.

'Getting this,' he said.

She looked up at the plastic packet and said, 'Ah. Good thinking.'

As he ripped it open, Sherry gently glided her hands up and down his wet thighs. Only a few minutes earlier, she had toweled him dry after their shower. But now he was sweaty – and so was she. Her hands made soft wet sounds as they slid against his skin.

We must be nuts, she thought, doing this on the hottest night of the year. And at *his* place. But she supposed the heat was probably what had brought them to this. On all those other nights, she'd managed to control herself and call a halt before it went this far.

Tonight, she had no intention of stopping.

She *wanted* him. Wanted him all over her, hot and wet and slippery, wanted him *inside* her.

Maybe the heat had something to do with that.

Maybe a lot.

The unusually hot night. And Duane's apartment building without air conditioning.

His windows were wide open. The hot Santa Ana winds blew in, caressing her, filling the room with the acrid aromas of brush fires somewhere in the distance.

It was the sort of night that made you feel restless and vulnerable and maybe a little frightened . . . the sort of night that stirred desires.

'Here we go.' He slipped the rubber disk out of its wrapper, then waved it at Sherry with a crooked smile. His face was red and sweaty. 'Now if I can just figure out what to do with the damn thing . . .'

'Allow me,' Sherry said.

'Really?'

'Sure.'

'Okay.' He handed it to her. 'I never . . . used the things with . . . you know, with Bev. She was on the pill and . . .'

His voice stopped as Sherry took hold of him with one hand.

'I'm not so good at this sort of thing myself,' she said. 'All I know is, you don't unroll them first.'

'You're probably right.'

Still holding Duane's penis with her left hand, she used her right to push the disk against its head. Fingers encircling the rubbery ring, she started to roll it down. The latex felt sticky. It crackled.

'Is it supposed to be like this?' Duane asked.

'I don't think so.'

'It feels . . . awfully tight.'

'You're too big for it.'

He laughed softly.

With little more than an inch of him covered, it suddenly stopped unrolling. 'Looks like we've got a problem,' Sherry said.

'Oh, great.'

'How old *is* this thing?'

'Twenty-eight.'

Sherry laughed. 'Not this thing,' she said. '*This* thing. This *rubber*.'

'Oh. I don't know. A few years, I guess.'

'A few *years*?'

'I never had much use for them, so . . .'

Sherry used force. Instead of coming unstuck, it split. The rubbery ring slid all the way down, leaving him capped with a flimsy, pale toque.

She laughed, shook her head and said, 'Shit.'

Duane laughed too. Then he sighed. 'Maybe it's a sign.'

'A sign, all right.' Still laughing, she plucked off the latex cap.

The laughing stopped as she rolled the ring up his thick erection.

'I guess it's not *that* funny,' she whispered.

Leaning forward, he took hold of her shoulders. He stared down into her eyes. 'I want you so badly,' he said.

'I want you, too.' Trying to smile, she said, 'The sooner, the better.' She tossed the remains of the condom aside. 'Maybe we'll have better luck with the next one.'

He grimaced. 'I don't have any more.'

'You're kidding.'

'Afraid not.'

'That was *it*?'

'I'm sorry.'

'Ah, that's all right,' she said. She resumed caressing his thighs.

'Do *you* have any?' he asked.

'I wish.'

'Can we . . . you know, do it anyway?'

Sherry shook her head. 'I don't think that would be such a good idea.'

'I'm perfectly healthy. I won't give you anything. I mean, I haven't . . . Nobody since Bev. That was two years ago, and I've had regular checkups, so . . . I won't give you AIDS or anything.'

'I know,' she said.

But she didn't know. Not for sure.

I'm not going to risk my life, she thought.

She said, 'You wouldn't want me to get pregnant, would you?'

'That's not very likely, is it?'

'Likely enough, tonight.'

He shook his head slowly from side to side.

'There's always tomorrow night,' Sherry said.

'But I don't want to wait.'

'The anticipation will make it all the better.'

'I've *already* been anticipating it for weeks.'

'I know, I know. Me, too.'

If we'd just done a little advance planning along with all that anticipation . . .

'Just go to the store tomorrow,' Sherry said, 'and pick up a good supply of the things. Then come over to *my* place tomorrow night. I'll make us a nice dinner and we'll try again. How does that sound?'

From the look on his face, she knew that it didn't sound great.

'Just one more night,' she said. 'It won't kill us to wait.'

'I know, I know, but . . . Whoa!'

'What?'

He suddenly laughed. 'I'm so stupid.'

'What?'

'I'll go to the store *now*! The Speed-D-Mart must carry condoms, don't you think so?'

'It probably does.'

'And it's open all night.'

'You don't want to go over there at this hour,' Sherry said.

He glanced at his clock radio. 'Only five after ten.'

'*Eight's* too late to be going to *that* place.'

'I'll just run in, run out. Be back in ten minutes.' He ducked down and kissed her on the mouth. Then he crawled backward, pausing along the way to kiss her naked body half a dozen times before climbing off the bed. 'You just wait right here,' he told her.

He hurried into the living room.

'Don't forget your clothes,' Sherry called after him.

'Thanks for the reminder.'

She crawled out of bed. Standing in the doorway, she watched Duane hop as he pulled a sock onto one foot.

'Don't fall and hurt yourself,' she said.

'Time is of the essence.'

'I'm not going anywhere,' she told him. 'Unless you want me to go *with* you.'

He snatched his shirt off the floor. Darting an arm into one sleeve, he said, 'You aren't dressed.'

'I could get dressed.'

'Wouldn't want you to do that.' Into a sleeve shot his other arm. The shirt flapping behind him, he ran to the end of the couch and plucked his underwear off the cushion.

'I could just throw something on real fast,' Sherry said.

He ducked and stepped into the briefs. 'No, no, don't. Whatever you do, don't throw something on. Stay just like you are.'

Leaning sideways against the door frame, Sherry put her weight on one leg and let her hip shift out. She smiled and shook her head as Duane sprang into his shorts.

So cute, she thought. Just like an overgrown kid.

Though the air was hot, her skin suddenly grew crawly with goosebumps.

What if something happens to him?

'You really don't have to do this,' she said. 'It's not a good idea. Things *happen* at night.'

Done buttoning his shorts, he jerked the zipper up. 'I'll be fine.' He fastened his belt.

'Why don't you just take everything off and we'll both get back into bed?'

'Nope.' He looked around, frowning, then gasped 'Ah!' as he spotted his other sock. It was on the floor near a leg of the coffee table, half hidden under Sherry's skirt. He rushed over to it. As he pulled it on, he said, 'I'll be back before you even know I'm gone.'

'Right. Unless you get creamed by a drunk driver or shot in a stick-up or mugged by one of those bums that's always hanging out in that parking lot.'

'Not gonna happen.' He dropped onto the couch and started to put his shoes on. 'Want me to pick up anything else while I'm there?'

'No, thanks.'

'Potato chips? Jerky?'

'Why don't you just stay here? Forget about the condoms, okay? Let's just go ahead without them.'

He made a face at her. '*Now* you tell me.'

She shrugged.

Shaking his head, he stood up. 'I'm already dressed.'

'That's easily corrected.'

She eased away from the door frame and walked toward him.

He watched her breasts, then met her eyes. 'I'd better go ahead and pick 'em up,' he said.

'You don't have to.'

'We might regret it if I don't.'

'I'll take my chances.' She reached out and began to unbutton his shirt.

He took hold of her wrists. 'It'll be better this way,' he said, then pulled her forward, raising and spreading her arms until her body pressed against him. He kissed her on the mouth. 'Back in ten minutes,' he whispered. 'If I'm late, just start without me.'

As Sherry grinned and shook her head, he let go of her and turned around and hurried to the door.

Chapter Two

It's silly to worry, Sherry told herself. He *will* be back in ten minutes.

Maybe fifteen.

Hordes of people go to convenience stores day and night. Most of them never run into anything worse than an annoying beggar.

He was right to go.

Thank God I didn't talk him out of it, she thought. My luck, I probably *would've* ended up pregnant.

Probably?

She let out a humorless huff.

Thirsty, she stepped over to the coffee table. She picked up the glass that she'd used for her Pepsi. The ice cubes had melted, leaving half an inch of amber-hued water at the bottom of the glass. She drank it. Though the mixture looked somewhat repulsive, it tasted cool and sweet.

Keeping the glass, she bent down and picked up the popcorn bowl. It was empty now except for two or three dozen unpopped kernels and a scattering of puffy white crumbs – all that had remained by the time they finished watching the video of *GI Jane*.

In the kitchen, Sherry set the bowl on the counter. She ran a fingertip across its slick, grainy bottom. Her finger came out coated with congealed butter and salt. She licked it clean, licked her lips, then stepped to the sink and filled her glass at the faucet.

The tap water was neither sweet nor cold.

She stepped over to the refrigerator, opened its freezer compartment and took out a handful of ice cubes. She dumped them into her glass and shut the freezer.

Stirring the cubes around with her forefinger, she stepped out of the kitchen.

How long has he been gone? she wondered.

Probably two minutes.

Just about time enough to get downstairs to the building's parking lot.

This is going to be a long wait.

She took her finger out of the water and slipped it into her mouth. It felt very cold. After a few seconds of sucking, however, it was warm again.

She took a long drink.

Lowering the glass, she sighed.

Now what? she wondered.

She stepped around to the front of the couch, sat down, took another drink, then leaned forward and eased her glass down on the coffee table. She picked up the clicker and turned the TV on.

Flipping from channel to channel, she found that most of the local stations had dropped their regular programming to cover the brush fires.

They *oughta* cover them, she thought; they *started* them.

She doubted that any of the local newscasters had actually applied matches or lighters to the dry hillsides, but she was *certain* they'd put the idea into the heads of the firebugs. Every year, they never failed to announce when conditions were ripe for blazing disasters. And the fires would start immediately, as if every pyromaniac in southern California had been biding his time in front of the TV, patiently awaiting the official word to begin.

Ready. Set. Gentlemen, start your fires!

Now the local news shows had what they wanted – what they'd begged for.

Every station seemed to have a helicopter circling over bright rows of flame. And crews on the ground standing dangerously close to assorted infernos, interviewing fire-fighters or people who'd just lost their homes or anyone else who might have a story to tell. And anchor teams safe in the studio, eagerly expounding on every aspect of the 'worst firestorm ever to hit the southland'.

She doubted that.

She had learned, long ago, that LA newscasters were masters of hyperbole.

The fires were certainly bad this year. It was inevitable, after all the rain from last season's *El Niño* storms. Listening to these people, though, you'd think the Apocalypse had arrived.

'Get some perspective,' she muttered to the television.

A map filled the screen. She checked the locations of the fires, found them in Malibu, Pasadena, up near Newhall, and several in Orange County. None within ten miles of Duane's building or her own. Nor were there fires anywhere near her parents' home.

The clock on the VCR showed 10:18.

Sherry was glad to see that so much time had passed.

He's probably in the store by now.

Should be back in five minutes or so.

Though watching television would help the time pass quickly, she didn't want Duane to walk in and find her sitting naked on the couch, gaping at the boob-tube.

How about a little atmosphere? she thought.

She turned off the television, then wandered through the rooms, switching off every light. Duane kept a candle in the bathroom. She lit it, then carried it into the bedroom and placed it on the nightstand.

In the living room again, she picked up her glass and took a drink of the ice-cold water.

10:22

Any minute now.

She returned to the bedroom. It looked wonderfully romantic in the glow of the candle – golden light fluttering, shadows dancing, the curtains bellowing like wispy windblown nightgowns.

As she sipped more water, she noticed her reflection in the mirror above Duane's dresser.

She turned and looked at it.

A corner of her mouth tilted upward.

Not bad for an old broad.

The 'old broad,' approaching her twenty-fifth birthday, knew that she appeared more like nineteen.

Nineteen, and a guy.

With her slender build and very short hair, she was often mistaken for a boy – especially when seen from a distance.

Watching herself in the mirror, Sherry figured nobody would likely mistake her for a boy at the moment. The gold hoop earrings wouldn't count for much – LA was *full* of guys wearing earrings. But she clearly had breasts. The mounds were small, but nicely round. Her nipples were dark and smooth.

'What a babe,' she whispered. Smiling, she added, 'A babe in heat.'

Her sweaty body glistened golden in the candlelight as if she'd been rubbed with melted butter.

She took another drink of water, then slid the dripping glass against her left breast. Its icy touch made her gasp and arch her back. As her nipple grew hard, she glided the glass over her other breast.

She rubbed her face with it, then drank the last of the water and filled her mouth with the remnants of the ice cubes. She set her glass down on the nightstand beside the candle.

Bending over the bed, she narrowed her eyes at the clock radio.

10:25

Any second now.

She crawled on to the bed, flopped over and sprawled out.

'Come and get it,' she muttered. Squirming, she raised her knees and spread her legs wide. Then she huffed quietly. 'Right,' she muttered.

She lowered her knees, sat up and reached beyond her feet for the top sheet. Holding its edge, she eased down onto her back. Then she swept the sheet high and let it float down. It settled lightly, covering her body almost to the shoulders.

'Ready when you are,' she said.

She listened for the sounds of Duane's approach.

She stood no chance of hearing his car. From here in the bedroom, she probably wouldn't be able to hear his footsteps in the hallway, either. She might hear his keys when he unlocked the front door. If not, the sounds of the door shutting behind him ought to reach her.

Unless he gets sneaky about it.

I probably *will* hear him come in, she told herself.

But when?

For a long time – or what seemed like a long time – Sherry lay still and listened for him. She heard mostly noises made by the blowing wind. While the curtains lifted and flapped in near silence, the wind outside sounded like a tribe of demented phantoms roaming the neighborhood – moaning, hissing and howling. Wind-grabbed objects bumped and clattered and shook, while others rolled along walkways or streets. Car alarms beeped and tooted. From nearby and far away came the cries of sirens.

What a night, Sherry thought. Sounds like all hell is breaking loose out there.

Why isn't he back yet?

Rolling onto her side and pushing herself up with an elbow, she looked at the clock.

10:31

She flopped down again.

She stared at the ceiling. It shimmered in the candlelight.

What time did he leave, anyway? Ten after? Something like that.

He's been gone more than twenty minutes.

Sherry suddenly felt too hot. Her head was half-buried in the pillow's moist heat. Her back and buttocks were sticking to the bottom sheet. The top sheet, resting lightly atop her body, walled her away from the caresses of the wind.

She cast the sheet aside and sat up.

And sighed as the wind drifted over her skin like warm, dry hands.

She crossed her legs and straightened her back and rested her hands lightly on her thighs.

I'll just sit like this till I hear him come in.

She sat there and waited. The roaming wind dried her sweat. She felt almost cool – except for her rump, which was pressed against the hot, moist bottom sheet.

After a while, she longed to look over her shoulder at the clock.

She resisted the urge.

She kept on resisting the urge.

He'll be here any second, she told herself.

Finally, she looked.

10:41

She grimaced.

He's been gone half an hour, she thought. The damn store's only two blocks away. He could've *walked* and gotten back ten minutes ago.

Something went wrong.

He was in a wreck or walked into a hold-up or . . .

Wait!

She suddenly huffed out a laugh.

I know what went wrong, she told herself. He got to the Speed-D-Mart all right, no trouble, but found out that they didn't carry condoms. So he headed off for some *other* all-night store. LA was *jammed* with convenience stores, mini-marts and even grocery stores that remained open twenty-four hours a day.

Some guys might give up and come back empty-handed, but not Duane.

He won't come back till he has them.

This might be a very long wait, she thought.

To free her buttocks from the moist heat, she dropped forward. She caught herself with stiff arms. On hands and knees, her rear end stroked by the soothing wind, she resumed her wait.

Thing is, she thought, he knows I expected him back in ten or fifteen minutes. Would he really take off for another store? At the very least, wouldn't he call and let me know what's going on?

Maybe, maybe not.

He's not always the most considerate guy in the world.

Not very long ago, he'd shown up at her apartment almost an hour late. His excuse? He'd been stuck in traffic on the way home from work.

Thing is, he had a car phone. He could've called, told her not to expect him on time.

She hadn't bothered to get on his case about it.

I'm his friend, not his mother.

Was tonight just another example of such thoughtless behavior?

Maybe it's more than that, she thought. Maybe he's late on purpose to punish me, teach me a lesson. *This is what happens when you send me out in the middle of the night for condoms.*

He wouldn't be that low, would he?

You never know.

Duane's not like that.

If he *is* like that, she thought, it's better to find out now.

He *probably* decided to try one more store. What's five or ten more minutes? But maybe that store was farther away than he thought . . .

From somewhere outside, somewhere a block or two blocks or maybe even five blocks away, came a bang.

It might've been a door slamming.

It might've been the backfire of a car.

It might've been a large firecracker.

But Sherry thought it sounded mostly like a gunshot.

Chapter Three

Though this neighborhood on the west side was fairly safe by Los Angeles standards, a day rarely went by without Sherry hearing a few mysterious bangs. If they seemed to come from nearby, she might look out a window. If *very* nearby, she might hurry away from the windows and duck with her back against a wall. Usually, however, she did nothing.

For the most part, the bangs were simply background noise. Like sirens and car alarms and police helicopters and screams, they were of little importance unless they happened in front of your face.

Or unless your boyfriend was out there on an errand.

And late returning.

Had the blast come from the direction of the Speed-D-Mart?

Sherry couldn't tell. *All* outside noises seemed to be entering through the open windows on the other side of the bedroom.

It probably wasn't even a gunshot, she told herself. And if it was, it might've come from just about anywhere. The chances of Duane being the target were enormously slim.

But where is he?

On her hands and knees, Sherry turned her body until she could look back and see the clock radio on the headboard.

10:47

Time sure flies when you're waiting for someone.

Especially when you're afraid he might've gotten killed or something.

'He's fine,' she muttered. He'll come waltzing in with a perfectly reasonable explanation.

Maybe reasonable to him.

How can he do this to me?

He'd better *have a good explanation.*

She turned around completely, crawled to the corner of the bed, leaned forward and puffed out the candle. The room fell dark except for the ambient light from the windows. She climbed off the bed and made her way to the door.

In the bathroom, she stepped to the sink. She turned on the cold water, bent over, and splashed her face. It felt very good, so she ducked lower and cupped water onto her head.

Maybe I should take a shower.

A nice, cool shower would feel great – and she could easily make it last fifteen or twenty minutes. By the time she finished, Duane would certainly be back from the store.

Or wherever the hell he went.

But she had already taken a shower tonight – with Duane after watching the *GI Jane* video. Taking another so soon . . .

She suddenly found herself thinking about the look and feel of Duane as he'd stood with her under the hot spray. She remembered the longing in his eyes, the taste of his open mouth, the slippery caresses of his urgent hands, the stiffness of his penis pushing against her, rubbing her, nudging her, prodding her as if hoping to endear itself and find a snug home.

We should've just done it there in the shower, she thought.

But I had to insist on the bedroom.

And a condom.

And now he's gone.

Sherry turned off the faucet. She stepped away from the sink, found her towel and pulled it off the bar. It was still damp. She used it on her dripping head and face, then stood in the near darkness and mopped the sweat off the rest of her body.

As dry as she was likely to get, she hung up the towel.

In the living room, she turned toward the television.

The red numbers of the VCR looked very bright.

10:53.

Gone about forty minutes.

By the faint light from the windows, Sherry made her way toward the kitchen. The carpet ended. The tiles of the kitchen floor felt a little slippery under her bare feet. Careful not to fall or bump into anything, she stepped over to the wall phone.

Call information, maybe. Get the Speed-D-Mart's number. Maybe somebody over there can tell me what's going on.

She took hold of its handset and raised it to her ear.

Silence.

It's dead?

Oh, great.

What if somebody cut the lines?

She'd seen that sort of thing countless times in movies and TV shows – but she supposed it rarely happened in real life.

With the Santa Anas howling outside, the probable culprit was the wind. Falling branches must've taken out some phone lines.

Duane might've tried to call.

But where is he?

Sherry hung up.

Phone or no phone, his destination was only two blocks away.

She returned to the living room.

10:56.

She turned on a nearby lamp. The brightness hurt her eyes and made her squint. Not waiting for her vision to adjust, she squatted between the couch and coffee table and picked up her panties. She pulled them on.

Next, she put on the short, pleated skirt that Duane had given to her last week. 'In case you ever feel like dressing like a woman,' he'd told her. To which she'd responded, 'Looks like you want a cheerleader.'

To which he'd said, 'It'll sure cheer *me* up.'

This was the first night she'd worn the skirt for him.

And now I'm stuck with it, she thought as she slid its zipper up.

She found her blouse on the floor behind the couch, right where she'd tossed it. Normally, she wore T-shirts and jeans when she wasn't at work. But you can't wear a T-shirt with a bright yellow cheerleader skirt, so she'd bought a special blouse for tonight. Lightweight and slippery, it was gaudy with scenes of jungles and lagoons and tropical birds.

As she fastened its buttons, she hurried around the couch. She picked up her socks and sneakers, then sat down long enough to put them on.

Her denim handbag was on the seat of a nearby chair. She grabbed it by the strap and hurried to the door.

She paused at the door.

Have I got everything?

Clothes, purse, what else is there?

That should about be it.

She looked at the clock.

10:59.

Standing there, she waited for 11:00.

Did I blow out the candle?

Yes.

11:00.

Sherry opened the door and stepped out into the hallway. The entire length of the corridor was deserted. She eased the door shut until it latched, then tried the knob.

Satisfied that the door was locked, she headed for the stairway. All the doors along the way were shut. No sounds of people or televisions or music came from inside the rooms, but she could hear the wind howling and battering things outside the building.

What if nobody's here?

What if everybody *has vanished?*

'Oh, that'd be a hoot,' she muttered.

And extremely unlikely.

This is real life, she reminded herself. Everybody doesn't vanish in real life.

Not often enough to worry about.

Besides, she told herself, I heard sirens. And a gunshot. Maybe. They require the presence of people. So I'm not the last person left on Earth, or even in Los Angeles.

Maybe just in this building.

Smiling and shaking her head, she hurried down the stairway. In the lobby, she opened a side door and trotted down a flight of stairs to the underground parking lot.

Most of the spaces were occupied by cars and sport utility vehicles.

Duane's assigned space was empty. His van was gone.

Okay, Sherry thought. He hasn't made it back, but he got away from the building all right.

Probably.

From where she stood, she saw the security gate blocking the driveway to the street. She had no way to activate it, so she returned to the lobby.

As she pushed open one of the front doors, the wind caught it and tried to rip it from her grip. She held on tight, got outside, and leaned her back against the door to force it shut.

This isn't good, she thought.

But it's not exactly the end of the world, either. She'd been in strong winds before. To one extent or another, this sort of thing happened almost every year.

Pushing away from the door, she lowered her head and hunched over and started out. She trotted down half a dozen stairs and headed for the sidewalk. As she hurried along, the wind shoved at her, shook her skirt and blouse and threw grit against her.

When she reached the sidewalk, she looked both ways. There was no traffic on the street. Several cars were parked along the curb.

Too bad mine isn't one of them.

Normally, for a dinner and evening at Duane's, she would've driven herself. But her Jeep was back in the repair shop for the umpteenth time – this time for major, expensive transmission work. (Turns out the supposedly all-American Jeep secretly had a Japanese transmission.) So Duane had picked her up and brought her over in his van.

Her apartment building was about three miles away.

She supposed she could walk the distance in less than an hour.

It'd probably be a very exciting hike, she thought.

If I don't get jumped, robbed, raped or shot, a tree'll probably land on my head.

But she had no intention of making such a hike.

Not with Duane unaccounted for.

Turning to the right, she headed for the Speed-D-Mart.

This is probably not the smartest thing I've ever done, she thought.

Hell, it's only two blocks. What's the alternative, sit around and wait for him?

As she walked along, the wind pushed against her and flapped her clothes. Every so often, it flipped her skirt up. A couple of times, it hoisted her blouse as high as her breasts. She stopped and tucked her blouse snugly down the waistband of her skirt. Then she shifted her purse strap to her other shoulder so the strap crossed her chest. That took care of half her problem; the wind continued to fling her skirt.

And each time it did so, it threw debris against her bare legs.

Just before the end of the block, she came to an alley. She knew this alley well, having walked it often with Duane. Decently lighted, it passed behind several small shops, a couple of private schools, and finally the laundromat and Speed-D-Mart. On the other side of the alley were the back fences, carports and garbage bins of several houses and apartment buildings.

Pausing, she studied the alley. Wrappers and leaves were tumbling along its pavement. Pages from newspapers were performing low-level aerial acrobatics. A black cat scurried out of the shadows, raced across the alley and scooted underneath a parked car.

She saw no people.

Between here and the mini-mart, however, were a great many places where someone might be lurking.

The alley was a lonely place.

If she ran into trouble . . .

'Not a chance,' she muttered, and continued on to Robertson Boulevard. A major north-south route through west Los Angeles, Robertson usually had heavy traffic. Tonight, only a few cars were rushing by.

Still a lot better than the alley, Sherry told herself.

She turned right. Hands against her thighs to hold her skirt down, she followed the sidewalk past the fronts of a carpet shop, an antique store, a pawn shop, a Jewish girls' school – all shut for the night.

The errant page of a newspaper blew against her left shin and stayed. After taking a few steps, she reached down and plucked it free and it flew off down the sidewalk.

Each time headlights approached, she looked over at Robertson to see if they belonged to Duane's van. And to make sure they weren't from a car packed with gangbangers.

At the corner, she stepped off the curb. The street to her right was littered with half a dozen palm fronds as large as human bodies. No cars were coming. She hurried to the other side, then walked past an auto-repair shop, a place that sold exercise equipment, a flower shop, and a private pre-school. All were closed for the night.

As she passed the pre-school, the Speed-D-Mart's parking lot came into sight.

Chapter Four

The lot provided parking for the Speed-D-Mart and the all-night laundromat that shared the building.

It had spaces for at least a dozen vehicles.

All were empty except four.

Duane's white van wasn't there, but Sherry knew that he liked to park in one of the two spaces around the far side of the convenience store. Those spaces couldn't be seen from here.

Eyes fixed on the area beyond the corner of the Speed-D-Mart, Sherry continued up the sidewalk.

And saw the right rear corner of a van.

Her heart lurched.

Picking up her pace, she cut across the parking lot. With each stride, more of the van came into sight.

A dealer in collectable books, Duane used his van for business but left it unmarked. The side of this vehicle was plain white, the same as his.

The bumper sticker would tell the tale.

Duane's van sported a single sticker: I'D RATHER BE READING.

So far, Sherry couldn't see whether this van carried such a slogan.

Finally, she stepped behind it.

I'D RATHER BE READING.

His, all right.

Now we'll find out what's going on.

Hopeful but nervous, Sherry hurried to the front of the van and peered into the driver's side window.

The seats were empty.

He must still be in the store.

She stepped around the rear of the van and headed for the

Speed-D-Mart's entrance. As she neared the door, a man came shuffling toward her from the area in front of the laundromat. In spite of the heat, he wore heavy clothes, a toque and boots. His clothes looked filthy. His face and hands were mired with grime. His dirty hair and beard were so stiff that the powerful wind hardly moved them.

'How 'bout a quarter, lady? Ain't had me a bite t'eat in two days.'

Shaking her head, she muttered, 'Sorry,' dodged him and rushed into the store.

It was brightly lit, strangely silent.

She glanced back to make sure the beggar wasn't coming in after her. He was wandering toward the laundromat.

Maybe he should try making use of it.

Sherry felt ashamed of herself for thinking such a thing. But she resented being confronted by such people. You couldn't go anywhere in Los Angeles without having them creep out of shadows to accost you for money. From investigations she'd seen on the TV, she knew that plenty of the beggars were fakes. Some of them made a lot more money than she did.

And many of them were dangerous.

At the counter, the clerk was busy ringing up a sale. The husky customer getting ready to pay him wore curlers in her hair.

Turning slowly, Sherry scanned the store. Its rows of shelves were only chest-high. She saw the heads of four customers.

No Duane.

But she couldn't be sure he wasn't somewhere in the store – maybe crouching to study items on a bottom shelf – so she began to walk up the nearest aisle.

The shelves to her left carried toiletries.

Curious, she stopped and studied the selection: combs, toothbrushes, toothpaste, deodorants, razors and shaving cream, bandages, antiseptics, condoms.

Condoms.

Half a dozen varieties, in neat little packages, hung from a rack on the top shelf.

They're right here, she thought. Duane *must've* found them.

But where is he?

She resumed her search, walking slowly up one aisle and down the next. It didn't take long. When she finished, she knew for certain that Duane was not in the store.

She walked back to the first aisle.

Though the store was nearly deserted, a guy had stationed himself in front of the toiletries section.

Terrific, Sherry thought.

Just ignore him.

She stepped around him, turned, reached out and plucked a pack of condoms off the rack.

The stranger paid no attention.

Blushing, she hurried away and headed for the checkout counter.

A customer was already there, waiting while the cashier bagged a six-pack of Budweiser.

Sherry opened her purse and pulled out her billfold.

Picking up his bag, the customer headed for the door.

Sherry stepped forward and placed her box of condoms on the counter.

The cashier looked at it. Then he raised his brown eyes to Sherry and smiled. 'Will that be all, my friend?' he asked, his voice lilting like a native of India.

'That'll be it.'

He punched a few keys on his cash register and mumbled the total. Sherry handed over a ten-dollar bill. As she took her change, the cashier asked, 'Would you perhaps like a bag for that?'

'No, that's all right. You mind if I ask you something?'

'Oh, not in the least. Please do ask.'

'I'm looking for a guy who probably came in here about an hour ago. He might've bought some of these, too.' She picked up the box of condoms and held it in front of the cashier.

'I see,' he said.

'Were you here an hour ago?'

'Oh, most certainly.'

'Do you remember him? He would've been wearing a blue shirt and tan shorts.'

'Oh, yes, I remember him well. He was most amusing. I think you must be the lucky girl he spoke of. Am I right?'

Blushing, she said, 'Maybe. Do you know what time he left?'

'Oh, some time ago.'

'He never came home. His van's still in your parking lot.'

Somebody stepped up behind Sherry. She looked over her shoulder. It was the guy from the toiletries area. He smiled a polite greeting. Sherry nodded to him, then faced forward.

'Was anyone with him?' she asked.

'Who?'

'The guy we were talking about. Did you see him with anyone?'

'Oh. I shouldn't think so, no. No, I saw him with no one.'

'Nothing funny happened?'

'Funny? No. I'm afraid not.' He glanced at the waiting customer.

'Thanks,' Sherry said. Stepping away from the counter, she slipped her billfold and condoms into her purse.

Okay, she thought. Duane was here. By himself. He bought condoms and left, and the clerk didn't notice anything strange.

Whatever happened must've been *after* Duane left the store.

If the clerk's telling the truth.

Why should he lie?

He might have reasons, she told herself. But let's just assume for now that he told the truth.

Sherry pushed open the door and stepped outside.

No sign of the bum.

Thank God for that, anyway.

She turned to the left and followed the walkway to the laundromat. Through its glass front, she saw eight or nine people. Some were busy at the machines, but most were just waiting for their loads to finish. Some leafed through magazines, one read a paperback, another talked on a cell phone, and a few were chatting.

Duane had no reason to be in the laundromat.

But he was a friendly, talkative guy. Someone from the laundromat might've asked him for change, for a helping hand, and maybe they'd started talking . . .

And he let an hour slip by?

Duane had done that sort of thing before.

But he wouldn't do it tonight, Sherry told herself. Not with me waiting like that.

He didn't seem to be in the laundromat.

Maybe somebody saw him.

She started toward the open door. As she stepped past the front of a parked car, its horn tooted.

She flinched.

Jerking her head to the right, she saw a kid in the driver's seat. He smiled and waved at her through the windshield.

Do I know him?

He opened the door and climbed out. 'Hi, teacher!'

'Hi.'

He was a tubby, cheerful-looking guy, maybe seventeen or eighteen years old. His brown hair was shaggy and windblown. Like so many guys his age, he wore a T-shirt underneath an open, long-sleeved shirt. The open shirt blew behind him as he came toward Sherry.

'Didn't you sub for Mr Chambers last week?' he asked.

Sherry nodded. 'You must've been in one of his classes.'

'Third period. Hope I didn't scare you with the horn.'

'Just a little.'

'Sorry. I was just so surprised to see you. It's so *weird* when you run into a teacher in real life.'

'We're just people, too.'

'But it's weird, though. Do you live around here or something?'

'Not too far away.'

'I can't think of your name,' he said.

Smiling, she held out her hand. 'Sherry Gates.'

'Ah! Right! Miss Gates! Now I remember!' He shook her hand and said, 'I'm Toby Bones.'

'*You're* Toby Bones. I remember your name from the roll book. It's a very unusual one.'

'Thanks. Everybody . . . uh . . . sure has a lot of fun with it.'

'Envy.'

He shrugged his heavy shoulders.

'Have you been here long, Toby?'

'Where?'

Sherry spread her hands. 'Here.'

'Oh, I don't know. I came over to do my wash.'

'Have you done it yet?' she asked.

'Just finished. I was all set to leave, but then I saw you come out of the store.'

'So you've been here for an hour, maybe?'

'Something like that.'

'The reason I'm asking, I'm looking for someone. A friend of mine. He came over about an hour ago to pick up something at the Speed-D-Mart, and now I can't find him.'

Toby's brow furrowed. 'What do you mean, you can't find him?'

'He was only supposed to be gone for ten or fifteen minutes, so I finally got worried and came over to look for him. His van's still here. He apparently showed up a *long* time ago and bought his cigarettes and left the store. But he never drove away. His van is still here, but he isn't.'

Frowning, Toby studied the parking lot. 'I don't see no van.'

Any van, she thought. But she didn't correct him.

'It's around the side,' she explained.

'Ah.' He nodded.

'You might've been here at the same time he was. I'm just wondering if maybe you saw him.'

'I don't know. What's he look like?'

'He's about twenty-eight, six feet tall, slender, good-looking. Brown hair.'

'Long or short?'

'His hair? It's longer than mine . . . a little shorter than yours. He was wearing a blue shirt and tan shorts.'

'Oh, yeah, I saw that guy.'

'You *did*?'

'I don't know about any van, though. When I saw him, he was walking off down the street.' He nodded toward the corner of Robertson and Airdrome. 'He crossed over to the other side and went on down the road there.'

'Down *Robertson*?'

'Yeah.'

'He walked *south*?'

'Is that south? Yeah, I guess so. Anyhow, that's which way he went.'

'But he lives the *other* way.'

Toby shrugged. 'I'm just saying what I saw.'

'He went that way on *foot*?'

'Yeah.'

Sherry scowled toward the street corner.

Why on earth would Duane walk in the wrong direction?

'Maybe it wasn't him,' she said.

'Maybe. I don't know. You know what he looked like? Sort of like Han Solo. You know? Like Harrison Ford back then.'

Sherry felt her stomach sink.

'That's him, all right,' she said. 'But I don't get it. He leaves his van here and walks in the wrong direction?'

It broke down so he set off to find a service station?

That made no sense at all. If it broke down, he would've walked back to his apartment. Besides, what service station could he possibly go to? Nothing like that would be open at this time of night.

'I just don't get it,' Sherry said.

'Well . . .' Lowering his eyes, Toby shook his head.

'What?'

He grimaced. 'The guy I saw? Your friend? He didn't exactly walk off by himself.'

Chapter Five

'He left *with* someone?' Sherry asked. 'Who?'

'I don't know,' Toby said. 'Some other guy.'

'What sort of guy?'

'What do you mean?'

'Maybe you should just tell me what you saw. Just describe it all to me from the time you first saw Duane.'

'Is Duane your friend's name?'

'Yeah.'

'Well, I guess I first saw him when he was coming out of the Speed-D-Mart. I was out here. You know, waiting for my stuff to get done in the washing machine. I don't like to sit around inside there very much. These people look at you, you know? Sometimes they're pretty weird. And a lot of them smoke. I don't like to smell that stuff.'

'Sounds like you're an old hand at doing the laundry.'

'Yeah, I been doing it a while. To help out my mom, you know? I didn't want her coming here anymore, not after she got attacked that time.'

'Attacked?'

'Yeah. Last year. A couple of guys came in and . . . you know, assaulted her. Raped her.'

'My God.'

'It was pretty bad.'

'Right here at *this* place?'

'Yeah. Right inside there. Well, more toward the back. She was all alone and these guys came in . . .' He shook his head, then said, 'Anyway, ever since then I've made her stay home and *I* come over and do the wash.'

'That's a really nice thing to do for her.'

He shrugged.

'Brave, too.'

'Yeah, well . . . I can take care of myself.' A smile spread across his pudgy face. 'Anyway, nobody's gonna rape *me*. You don't even gotta worry about fags when you're a fat slob like me.'

Trying to smile, Sherry said, 'Oh, you look fine.'

'Yeah, sure.'

'Anyway, it's awful what happened to your mother. Is she all right now?'

'Sort of. Except she's scared all the time. Like she's afraid it'll happen again, or something.'

'It must've been terrible for her.'

'Yeah. So anyway, that's why I do the wash.'

'And you were standing here when Duane came out of the store . . .?'

'Yeah. I guess he'd bought something. He was carrying a little bag.'

'His cigarettes,' Sherry said.

'Yeah. You said his van's over there?'

She nodded.

'That's which way he started to go. But then this other guy came along and they started talking.'

'Where did he come from?'

'Inside the store, I think. Yeah. He came out right after Wayne . . .'

'Duane.'

'Oh. Duane. Okay. The way it happened, I thought maybe they were together and the other guy was just slower at coming out.'

'You got the impression they knew each other?'

Toby nodded. 'Yeah, like they were friends.'

'Did you hear what they said?'

'Nah. It was too noisy. The wind and everything. Cars going by. And it wasn't like they were yelling.'

'How long did they talk?'

'I don't know. Couple of minutes. Then they walked over to the corner and crossed the street and kept on going and that was the last I saw of them.'

'You thought they looked like friends?' Sherry asked.

'Yeah. You want to know the truth, I sort of figured they were *boy*friends.'

'What made you think that?'

Toby shrugged. 'I don't know. Two guys together. This time of night. And the other guy, he *looked* sort of faggy.'

This kid could really use some sensitivity training, Sherry thought.

'What do you mean?' she asked.

'You know. The way he walked, and stuff. Swishy. And he was wearing this shirt that looked like it was made out of a basketball net. You could see right through it. He had . . .' Toby grimaced, shook his head, then said, 'Rings. Through his nipples. And he wore these tiny little shorts. And sandals.'

'You must've gotten a pretty good look at him.'

'You see a guy like that, it's sort of hard not to stare.'

'How old do you think he was?'

'I don't know, twenty-five or thirty. He had white hair, but it was probably a bleach job.'

'He was a white guy?'

'Oh, yeah.'

'What about his height and weight?'

'He was a little taller than Duane. I don't know about the weight. He was *big*, though. Like a body builder. Had these huge muscles everywhere.'

'Doesn't sound like anyone *I* know,' Sherry said.

'Duane seemed to know him, though. I mean, the guy put his hand on Duane's shoulder when they were walking away.'

'What'd Duane do?'

'Nothing. Sort of smiled at him.'

Sherry stared at Toby, vaguely aware of frowning and shaking her head.

Duane walked off down the street with a gay boyfriend?

'It's crazy,' she muttered.

'You okay?' Toby asked.

'Yeah. Fine. Just . . . a little shocked.'

'I'm sorry.'

'That's all right.'

'Maybe the guy I saw *wasn't* your friend. Maybe he just *looked* like him or something.'

'I don't know. Maybe. Is it possible that what you saw might've been some kind of abduction?'

'You mean like when aliens—?'

'Like a kidnapping. Maybe this guy was forcing Duane to go with him.'

'Sure didn't look that way.'

'Did you see any weapons?'

'Huh-uh.'

'But a big guy like that, he might not *need* a weapon. If he was a huge, muscular guy like you said.'

'Oh, yeah, he was. But it didn't look like any kidnapping. I mean, your friend was all smiling and stuff.'

'It's insane,' she muttered.

Toby suddenly raised his eyebrows. 'You know what? Maybe we can find them. I mean, they went off on foot. If they're still walking and we take my car, we might catch up with them.'

'How long ago did they leave?'

'I guess forty, forty-five minutes ago.'

'That's a long time.'

Toby shrugged. 'I'm all done with my stuff. If you want, I'll drive you around for a few minutes before I go home.'

'Thanks, but you don't have to do that.'

'I don't mind. You want to find him, don't you?'

'Sure, but . . . You should probably be getting home.'

'It's okay. No school tomorrow.'

'We don't want your mother to worry.'

'Ah, she's asleep by now, anyway. She won't know *what* time I get home.'

'Well . . . If you're sure you really want to do this . . .'

'Sure. Hop in.'

'Okay. Thanks.' Sherry hurried to the passenger door. It wasn't locked. She opened it and climbed into the car while Toby went around to the other side and dropped down behind the steering wheel.

The doors thudded shut.

Toby smiled at her and started the engine. 'This'll be cool,' he said.

'I really appreciate your help.'

'No big deal.' He put on his headlights and backed out of the parking space. 'I just hope we can find him for you.'

'Me, too.'

Toby turned his car around, drove across the parking lot, swung out onto Robertson and stopped for a red light. 'This Duane, is he like your boyfriend or something?'

'We've been seeing each other for a while.'

'You think he's . . . you know, a fag?'

Politely, she said, 'That's not a very nice word, Toby.'

'Oh. Okay.'

'Just say "gay".'

'Gay. Sure.'

'Anyway, I don't think he is. Gay.'

The light changed to green. Toby accelerated through the intersection. 'That'd be like a real bummer,' he said, 'having a boyfriend and it turns out he's more interested in guys.'

'Right now, I'm just interested in finding him. Which side of the road did they go down?'

'That.' Toby nodded to the right. 'You watch that side,' he said, 'and I'll watch this.'

'Good. Thanks.'

Peering out the windshield, Sherry gazed at the walkway along the right side of the boulevard. It led past a branch of the public library, then past the fronts of apartment buildings and stores. A few cars were parked along the curb, but they weren't large enough to obstruct her view. Vans and trucks *were* large enough, but there weren't many of them.

It's too soon to find Duane, anyway, she told herself. He's had time to walk a couple of miles by now.

Unless maybe he's on the way back.

Where the hell did he go?

With a guy?

She felt squirmy and hot inside.

He's not gay, she told herself. No way. Not a chance.

As they passed through an intersection, Sherry peered down the sidestreet, quickly checking for pedestrians. The sidewalks looked empty.

'Maybe it was some kind of emergency,' she said.

'Huh?' Toby asked.

'The reason Duane went off with that guy. Maybe it was an emergency.'

'I don't know. Maybe. Only they didn't act much like anything was wrong.'

'It has to be *some*thing. Duane knew I was waiting for him. He wouldn't just . . .'

I told him to forget about going for the condoms, but he insisted on going anyway.

To meet someone?

To avoid having sex with me?

No, that's crazy, she told herself. If the rubber hadn't broken . . . and *I'm* the one who broke it . . . he never would've left at all. He didn't *plot* any of this. That's ridiculous.

She looked down another sidestreet as they rushed by it. The sidewalks appeared to be empty.

'What?' Toby asked.

'He wouldn't just go off with someone. Not unless there was an awfully good reason. Like maybe the guy needed his help. Or forced him to go along.'

'I don't know,' Toby said. 'Maybe.'

'I *know* he's not gay.'

'There!' Toby blurted. 'That them?'

Chapter Six

Sherry noticed the direction of Toby's gaze, looked ahead and to the right, and saw two figures striding past the front of a lighted display window on the next block.

Toby sped up.

Sherry took a quick look down a sidestreet, then fixed her attention on the couple.

They were walking away, holding hands. The guy, powerfully built, had curly, bleached hair. Instead of a net shirt and skimpy shorts, however, he wore a tank top and cut-off jeans.

His partner, long black hair blowing in the wind, wore a tank top and cut-off jeans and white cowboy boots. Though only able to see the brunette from behind, Sherry was pretty sure she must be a woman.

As they drove alongside the couple, she got a side view and saw the brunette's large breasts swinging and bouncing unrestrained inside the tank top.

'Guess it's not them,' Toby said.

'Doesn't look that way,' said Sherry.

'The *guy* looks a lot like the one I saw. Not exactly the same, but . . . I mean, the one with Duane wasn't dressed like that.'

'This *isn't* the man you saw, is it?'

'No. Huh-uh.'

'Are you sure?'

'Positive.'

On the next block they drove past a hunched, filthy man steering a train of three heavily loaded shopping carts down the sidewalk.

Sherry wondered if this was the beggar who'd accosted her in front of the Speed-D-Mart.

They all looked so much alike, bundled up in their soiled clothes, hair and skin dark with grime.

This guy's bigger than the other one, she thought.

As they came up on Hamilton High School, Sherry sighed.

'I'm not sure this is accomplishing much,' she said. 'They could be anywhere.'

She saw the freeway underpass just ahead.

'I can't imagine Duane would've gone much farther,' she said. 'He'd have to deal with that weird mess of intersections and off-ramps and everything. It's bad enough in a car. He wouldn't try to walk through it.'

'Guess not. But you know what they might've done? They might've gone down National. I mean, they were heading in this direction . . .'

Toby flicked his turn signal and pulled into the left-hand turn pocket for National. Stopping at the red light, he said, 'We can just take this over to Venice Boulevard.'

'Why would we wanta go there?'

'Maybe it's where *they* went, you know? Duane and that guy were walking down Robertson. If they kept going, they might be heading for someplace on Venice.'

The signal changed to a green arrow. Toby stepped on the gas and turned left onto National.

'If they *did* go this way,' he said, 'we oughta spot 'em pretty soon. We're sure going a lot faster than they are.'

'That's true,' Sherry said. 'But I have my doubts that they came this far. For all we know, maybe they only walked down Robertson for half a block and climbed into a car. Or went into a building or down a sidestreet. They could've gone just about anywhere.'

'I know,' Toby said. 'But if they kept going south, maybe they're on the way to someplace on Venice and we'll run into them pretty soon.'

Approaching the intersection, he steered to the right.

'I guess it couldn't hurt to look,' Sherry admitted.

'I know it's a long shot,' Toby said, and made the turn. Ahead of them, Venice Boulevard was brightly lit. 'We'll start back if we don't find them in a few blocks.'

'Yeah. 'Cause I don't think we're going to find them along here.'

'A lot of places are open,' Toby said.

Sherry nodded.

'Maybe they went in somewhere to rent a video or get a bite to eat or something.'

'I doubt it,' Sherry said.

'Yeah, me too. But you never know. Hey, know what? I'm starving. You wanta stop and get a little snack or something?'

'I don't think so.'

He turned his head and smiled at her. 'My treat.'

'I'd rather get back to the Speed-D-Mart.'

'Do you mind if *I* get something?'

She did mind, but she hated to say so. After all, Toby had gone out of his way to help her look for Duane. And this was his car.

'I guess we could stop somewhere,' she said.

'Great. We'll make it real quick. Where you wanta go?'

'It's up to you.'

'You like tacos?'

'Sure.'

'Me, too. I like 'em a lot. How about the Nacho Casa? We can get 'em at the take-out window, you know? That way, we won't be wasting time.'

'Sounds good,' she said.

'Hope it's still open.'

As Toby drove west on Venice Boulevard, Sherry kept her eyes open for Duane. Not that she expected to find him this far from the Speed-D-Mart.

By now, wherever he'd gone, he might've even returned to his van and driven back to his apartment. He might be standing in his bedroom at this very moment with a bag of condoms in his hand, thinking, *Where's Sherry?*

Now *I'm* the missing one, she thought.

Serve him right.

She doubted, however, that he *had* returned to his apartment.

It'd be nice, but didn't seem very likely.

The longer I stay away, she thought, the more likely he'll be there when I get back.

'Are you going to be subbing again pretty soon?' Toby asked.

'I don't have anything lined up.'

'How does that work, anyway?'

'Well, I'm on the district's list of substitutes. If they want me to work somewhere, they phone me in the morning and tell me about it. Then I can either accept the assignment or turn it down.'

'You like it?'

'Oh, it's not so bad.'

'Everybody craps all over the subs.'

'It can be a little hairy sometimes. Usually, though, I get along okay.'

'I guess a lot of 'em take it easy on you because you're so beautiful.'

She let out a quiet laugh. 'Think so?'

'Yeah. Guys, anyway. I bet they do. I mean, they'd all want to get on your good side, you know?'

'I suppose that might happen sometimes.'

'Anybody ever . . . you know, put moves on you?'

'Oh, sometimes.'

'I bet. Oh, here comes the Nacho Casa. Looks like it's still open.'

'I think it's open twenty-four hours.'

'Yeah, maybe so. Sure you don't mind if we stop?'

'No, that's fine.'

Signal blinking, Toby eased over to the right-hand lane then made a turn into the Nacho Casa's driveway. 'How about if we go in?' he asked. 'I sort of need to make a pit stop.'

'That'll be okay.'

'Sorry,' he said, and swung into a parking space.

'No problem. I don't suppose five or ten minutes is going to make much difference one way or another. For all I know, Duane might be gone for hours.'

He might be gone for ever.

Dead.

I might never see him again.

The thoughts gave her a hot, squirmy feeling.

Don't be an alarmist, she told herself. He's probably fine.

Then where is he?

'Maybe I'll wait for you in the car,' she told Toby.

He grimaced. 'If you want to. But . . . I don't know how safe it'd be. I mean, it's getting pretty late and this isn't the greatest neighborhood. Somebody comes along and sees you by yourself . . .'

'You come back and *I'm* missing,' she said.

'I'd hate to have that happen.'

'Me, too. Hey, maybe I'd end up in the same place as Duane.'

Toby laughed. 'That's a good one.'

'I'll come in with you,' she said.

As she climbed out, the wind flung her skirt up. She shoved it down. Holding it against her thighs, she met Toby behind the car. 'I hate skirts,' she said.

'You look nice in 'em, though.'

'Thanks.'

They walked across the parking lot to the door. Toby hurried ahead and opened it for her.

She entered the Nacho Casa and was glad to be out of the wind. Toby pulled the door shut.

The small restaurant was well lighted. Air conditioning chilled the air. All but two of its tables were empty. A gray-haired man sat alone at a corner table, his eyes checking out Sherry as he bit into a burrito. At another table, a teenaged couple sat across from each other. The way the guy was staring at his girlfriend, Sherry figured he must be madly in love.

Do I ever look at Duane that way?

She was pretty sure she didn't.

When was the last time I looked at anybody that way?

It had been a very long time.

'You want to go ahead and have something, don't you?' Toby asked.

'I don't think so.'

'Are you sure?'

She remembered the bowl of popcorn she'd eaten on the couch with Duane. Though she'd devoured a lot of it, she now had a vague, empty feeling in her stomach. It probably had to do with missing Duane, not with hunger.

But maybe a snack would help.

'I guess I could use something,' she said.

Standing beside Toby, she tilted back her head and studied the elaborate display of menu items above the counter area.

'Can I help you?' asked the teenaged girl behind the cash register.

They never give you a chance to look at the menu.

'Just a second,' she said.

As she frowned at the menu and tried to make up her mind, she realized Toby was staring at her.

Thinks I'm beautiful.

Sure is checking me out.

Feeling herself start to blush, she smiled at him and said, 'I guess I've made up my mind.'

Side by side, they stepped up to the counter.

'Have you decided?' the girl asked.

'You first,' Toby said to Sherry.

'Okay. I'll have one hard-shell shredded beef taco and a small Pepsi.'

'Give me a medium Pepsi,' Toby said, 'and two of those tacos like she's getting.'

'Will that be for here or to go?' the girl asked.

Toby looked at Sherry.

'Either way,' she said. 'They might be messy, though. Maybe we'd better eat them here.'

'Are you sure?'

'Sure.'

'Great.' Looking very pleased by her decision, he said, 'For here.'

The girl repeated their order. As she rang it up, Sherry opened her denim purse to look for her billfold. 'My treat,' she told Toby.

'Oh, no, I'll get it.' Toby reached for a rear pocket of his shorts.

Sherry caught hold of his wrist.

He gasped and looked at her, his mouth drooping, his face turning crimson.

'I'm paying,' she said.

'But—'

'You've been nice enough to help me look for Duane. I really appreciate it, too. I don't know what I would've done if I hadn't run into you. So let me pay. Okay? Please?' She squeezed his wrist.

'Well . . . okay.'

Chapter Seven

'I guess I'll use the john while we're waiting,' Toby said.

'Okay. I'll be right here.'

He hurried away, and Sherry remained standing near the front of the counter.

On the other side, the girl filled cardboard cups with ice and Pepsi while a young man was busy behind her preparing the tacos.

The girl snapped plastic lids onto the drink containers. 'Your tacos'll be ready in a just a minute,' she said, and pushed the drinks across the counter.

'Thanks. I'll come right back for them.'

Sherry picked up the Pepsis, grabbed a couple of straws and went looking for a table. The gray-haired man stared at her.

Pick a table nice and far away from him.

She smiled at the young couple as she stepped past them, but they didn't seem to notice. Their eyes were locked on each other.

Not wanting to intrude, Sherry picked a table a fair distance away from them. It looked clean except for the small wadded ball of a straw wrapper. She set down the drinks, placed a straw across the top of each, then returned to the counter for the tacos.

The man kept staring at her.

Finished with his burrito, he sucked on a straw as his eyes followed Sherry.

Not a bad-looking guy. Slim and rugged-looking.

But creepy, the way he wouldn't quit staring at her.

Don't choke on your drink, jerk.

At the counter, she found two plastic plates. One held a

single taco wrapped in white paper. On the other were two tacos. Each plate was piled with tortilla chips.

She picked them up carefully and headed back for the table.

The guy was still watching her.

She frowned at him and he smiled.

A creepy smile, as if he had secret, nasty plans for her.

She looked away from him.

The way she was dressed, she supposed she shouldn't blame him for staring. Not every night you get to see a gal wandering around in a cheerleader skirt and Hawaiian shirt.

I must look like a refugee from a pep squad luau.

On second thought, her costume probably didn't matter to this guy: he seemed to be looking straight *through* her clothes as if he had x-ray vision.

She set the plates on the table, then turned her back to the man and sat down.

Maybe it'd be better to keep an eye on him.

Why bother? she asked herself. It's not as if he's going to try anything. Not inside a place like this.

I hope.

She tore the paper wrapper off her straw. As she poked the straw through the crossed slits in the lid of her drink, Toby stepped past her. She felt as if the troops had arrived. She smiled up at him.

'Everything okay?' he asked.

'Everything's fine,' she said.

Toby sat down across the table from her. Unwrapping his straw, he leaned forward and whispered, 'You wouldn't believe what just happened to me in the john.'

'Oh, I'd probably believe it.'

'Something happen to *you*?' he asked.

'No. Not really. Just some guy in the corner who can't seem to take his eyes off me.'

Toby sat up straight and gazed past Sherry's left shoulder. 'Him? The gray hair and blue shirt?'

'Yeah, but don't stare.'

'What'd he do?'

'Nothing. Just sits there and . . . you know, watches

me. Like he's never seen a woman before.'

Blushing, Toby said, 'He's probably never seen one who looks like you.'

'Right. I'm one of a kind. My clone moved to Alabama.'

Toby laughed softly and sipped his drink. Then he said, 'Want me to get rid of him?'

'No. Are you kidding? Just ignore him. Unless he tries something. Then you can wrestle him down and I'll kick him.'

Laughing, Toby unwrapped one of his tacos. 'I guess you're kidding, huh?'

'Sort of.'

'You like to kid around, don't you?'

'Sometimes.'

'Everybody in class thought you were hilarious.'

'Well, I try to keep things interesting.'

'You should've heard them telling Chambers about you. He'll probably ask to have you back, next time he's out.'

'Hope so.'

'Anyway, I'll take care of this guy if he causes any trouble.'

'Let's not think about "taking care" of people, okay? Let's just enjoy our meal.'

With that, she unfolded the white paper around her taco, lifted the dripping concoction to her mouth, and took a bite. Her teeth crunched through the corn tortilla shell. Inside was a mixture of cool shredded lettuce and cheddar cheese, hot sauce and hot, spicy, shredded beef. She moaned with pleasure as the flavors filled her mouth.

The shredded beef was springy. After a lot of chewing, she swallowed and took a long drink from her Pepsi.

Then she said, 'You were going to tell me about a restroom adventure?'

Toby chewed and nodded. As he swallowed, he glanced around as if afraid someone might overhear him. Then he leaned forward. Speaking quietly, he said, 'There was a *girl* in the john.'

'In the *men's* room?'

'Yeah. She came out of a stall while I was . . . you know, *going*.'

Sherry grinned. 'Holy Toledo,' she said. 'You were at a urinal?'

He blushed. 'Yeah. With my *thing* out and everything.'

'Jeez.'

'She came up behind me and put a hand on my rear end and asked me if I wanted her to . . . uh, you know . . . give me a blow job.'

'You're kidding.'

Eyes wide, he shook his head. 'I swear to God.'

'Wow.'

'Yeah. Never had *that* happen before.'

'So, did you take her up on the offer?'

He looked shocked. 'No! Are you nuts?'

Smiling, Sherry shrugged. 'What'd she look like?'

'I don't know, she looked pretty good. She looked a lot like you, but not nearly as pretty. And she didn't have short hair like yours. Hers was down to her shoulders. I like it a lot better your way.'

'So, what else? What was she wearing?'

Toby grimaced and shook his head. 'Nothing.'

'*Nothing?*'

'I'm not kidding. She was starkers. Totally.'

'You were in the men's restroom, a naked girl came out of a stall while you were peeing, put a hand on your butt and asked if you wanted a *blow* job?'

'Yeah. That's what happened.'

'And she was *good*-looking?'

'She was *great* looking.'

'And you turned her down?'

'Sure.'

'Why?'

He shrugged, said, 'I'm not that kinda guy,' then took a large bite of taco.

Smiling, Sherry shook her head. 'That's amazing.'

He shrugged again and chewed.

'Did she ask for money?'

He shook his head.

'What did she want?'

After swallowing, Toby said, 'I don't know. She didn't say.

Just that she'd like to . . . you know, *do* that to me. She had that hand on my rear end, you know? And then she reached in front of me with her other hand and . . . took hold of my, uh . . . thing.'

'Lord.'

'I was sort of like done going by then. But she was holding me and she said, "Your cock's wet, honey. Want me to blow it dry for you?" '

'You've gotta be shitting me,' Sherry whispered.

Face red and twisted into a half-smile, Toby said, 'I couldn't believe it myself.'

'So then what happened?'

'I pulled her hand away and said "Thanks anyway, but I'm saving myself for the woman I love." '

'You said *that?*'

'Sure. Why not? It's just the truth.'

'So then what happened?'

'She said, "If you change your mind, you know where to find me." Then she went back into the stall.'

Astonished, Sherry shook her head. 'You think she's still in there?'

'I guess so. I don't think she can leave without coming out through there.' He nodded toward the passageway behind Sherry.

'Tell me if she comes out. I'd like to get a load of her.'

'I'll let you know.'

They continued eating for a while. Then Sherry said, 'Weren't you tempted?'

'Huh?'

'To let her *do* it?'

Toby swallowed, took a drink, then said, 'Not really.'

'Most guys I've ever known, they'd *kill* for a chance like that.'

Blushing, he shrugged. 'Maybe if I was by myself. But not with *you* sitting out here waiting for me.'

'A couple more minutes wouldn't have hurt.'

'It's not *that*. It would've been an insult to you.'

'Not if I didn't know about it. Even if I *did* know . . . no reason for me to be insulted.'

'Anyway,' Toby said, 'it just seemed like a really crummy idea. And dirty. I wouldn't want to mess around with someone like her.'

'Well, I can't knock that. Good for you.'

'Oh, hey.'

'What? Is she coming?'

'Huh-uh. But it looks like there's a guy on his way to the john.'

Twisting around, Sherry glimpsed the teenaged boy as he walked beneath the *BANOS* sign. A moment later, he disappeared down the passageway.

'Oh, shit,' she muttered.

'What's wrong?'

'I suppose she'll try *him*.'

'Sure she will.'

What'll *he* do? Sherry wondered. He was obviously madly in love with the girl at his table. But how many guys would be able to resist such temptation?

'You want to do me a favor, Toby?'

He met her eyes. 'Anything. Just name it.'

'Go back in there. She probably won't try anything if there're *two* people in the john.'

'You want me to, like, *save* that kid from her?'

'Couldn't hurt to try.'

'Okay.' Toby wiped his mouth with a napkin, then left the table and headed for the restrooms.

Sherry watched him hurry into the passageway.

Then she turned forward and resumed eating her taco.

Wait till I tell Duane about all this. A naked babe grabbing guys at a urinal and . . .

She remembered that he was missing.

It made her feel sick.

What if I never see him again?

What if he's dead?

He's probably just fine, she told herself. Might even be wondering what happened to *me*.

Chapter Eight

Toby came back to the table, smiling and shaking his head.

'What happened?' Sherry asked.

'Nothing.'

'Is she gone?'

'I think she was still in the stall. *Somebody* was. But she didn't come out. I went ahead and pretended to use the urinal.'

'What about the kid?'

'He wasn't in there to go. He was trying to buy rubbers out of the vending machine.'

Buy rubbers?

'You're kidding,' Sherry muttered, shocked.

What is this, the Night of the Condoms?

'They've got this vending machine in there,' Toby explained. '*Two* of 'em. One has stuff like cologne and aspirin, and the other has nothing but different kinds of rubbers.'

She shook her head.

'So the guy, like, bought some while I was at the urinal. He left before I did. And the girl stayed in the stall the whole time.'

'Good deal.'

Smiling, Toby said, 'I guess he's gonna score with his girlfriend tonight.'

'Apparently he hopes to.'

With a shrug, Toby picked up his remaining taco. 'Guys like that *always* score,' he said.

'Scoring isn't what counts,' Sherry said. 'But I think you already know that, having recently turned down a rather amazing offer.'

He almost smiled. 'I guess so.'

'It's finding the right girl.'

'Yeah,' he said, then bit into his taco.

'It's being in love.'

Chewing, he nodded. 'You in love with Duane?' he asked, his mouth full.

Sherry almost said, 'Sure.' Instead, she tilted her head, smiled and shrugged. 'I don't know if it's *love*, exactly. We certainly care a lot for each other. I know I want to *find* him.'

Toby swallowed and said, 'But you don't really *love* him, huh?'

'I *sort of* love him.'

'And you sort of *don't*?'

Sherry forced herself to smile. 'You practising to be a shrink?'

He took another bite, shrugged and chewed.

'Anyway,' Sherry said, 'we haven't been seeing each other for very long. It's only been three weeks. He's a terrific guy and we get along really well for the most part.'

Toby took a drink of Pepsi and said, 'Must be something wrong with him.'

'Not really.'

'If you don't always get along, must be *something* wrong with him.'

'The only thing wrong with him right now is that he's missing. Or maybe he isn't, anymore. He might be he back by now and wondering where *I* am.'

'Guess we'd better get going,' Toby said.

'You can finish . . .'

He stuffed the remains of the taco into his mouth, wiped his bulging lips with a napkin, wrapped a hand around his drink and started to stand up.

Sherry waved him down. 'Take it easy. I'm not in *that* big of a hurry.'

Toby settled back down in the seat.

Sherry thought about making a trip to the restroom herself. She felt a need to go, but it wasn't urgent.

Maybe I'd better wait. They've got a naked gal ambushing guys in the men's john, no telling what I might find in the ladies.

Twisting around in her seat, she looked for the gray-haired

man who'd spent so much time staring at her.

He was no longer at his table.

She couldn't see him anyway.

Maybe he left.

Maybe he's waiting for me in the john.

He'll have a long wait, she thought.

Done chewing and swallowing the taco he'd shoved into his mouth, Toby sucked Pepsi up his straw. After a few seconds, the straw made sputtery sounds. 'I'm ready,' he said.

On the way out, Sherry saw the young lovers still sitting across from each other. They were holding hands in the middle of the table and gazing deeply into each other's eyes.

Deeply, searchingly, sincerely.

Sherry figured the guy was at least sincere in his desire to screw her.

Can't blame him for that, she told herself.

Just hope all the goo-goo eyes stuff isn't a big act.

She tossed her garbage into a container near the door, then followed Toby outside. The wind grabbed her and shoved her. She stumbled and almost fell before regaining her balance. Toby hurried over to her. He put an arm across her back. Hand firm against her side, he held her steady.

'You okay?' he asked.

'Yeah. Thanks. I'm fine.'

'I'll help you over to the car.' Keeping his arm around her, his hand planted just below her armpit, he walked her across the parking lot. By the side of his car, he let go of her and unlocked the passenger door. He put a hand on her shoulder as she climbed in. Then he swung the door shut.

Glad to be out of the wind, Sherry set her purse on the floor, then drew the seat belt across her chest and lap.

Toby hurried around to the other side. 'Wild out there,' he said, dropping into the driver's seat.

'You're not kidding.'

'Hey, thanks for the tacos and Pepsi.'

'Thanks for helping me look for Duane.'

'Oh, that's okay.' He fastened his seat belt, started the engine and put on the headlights. 'Know what? Maybe it's true what they say about the Santa Ana winds.' He drove out of his

parking space. 'You know, that they make people crazy.'
'Wouldn't surprise me,' Sherry told him.
'Maybe that's how come there was a naked gal in the john.'
'Right,' Sherry said. 'Or maybe the wind blew her clothes off.'
Toby turned his head and smiled. 'Yeah.'
'And the Santa Anas might easily be the reason she was so eager to go around and *blow* people.'
He laughed. 'Like the wind!'
'Yep. Turnabout's fair play.'
Shaking his head, Toby eased to a stop at the driveway's exit. 'Anyway,' he said, 'it might've made her nutty enough to do something like that.'
'Could be.'
Toby waited for a few cars to rush by, then pulled forward onto Venice and turned right.
Toward the ocean.
A center divider prevented any left-hand turns, but Sherry reminded him, 'We do need to go the other way.'
'I know. I'll find a place to turn around pretty soon.'
Sherry nodded. 'I guess you might as well take me back to the Speed-D-Mart.'
'What'll you do?'
'See if the van's still there.'
'What'll you do if it is?'
She thought for a few moments, then said, 'I don't know. I've never had anybody . . . disappear before. I'm not sure what to do. At some point, if he doesn't show up, I guess I'll have to call the police. But that seems like it ought to be a last resort. Especially since I don't know what happened to him. Wouldn't want to get him in trouble.' She huffed out a laugh. 'There we go,' she said, 'a real-life catch-twenty-two.'
'Huh?'
'Since I don't know what's going on with Duane, I can't call the police. If I *did* know, I wouldn't *have* to call because I'd already *know* what happened to him. Catch-twenty-two.'
Toby looked at her. 'I don't get it.'
Sherry shrugged. 'Doesn't matter. Just sort of a teacher thing.'

'Oh.'

'Anyway, it's a bad idea to get the cops involved in anything unless you really *have* to. You can end up getting the wrong people in trouble. Even yourself.'

'Guess so.'

'We're still going the wrong way, Toby.'

'Oh? Yeah, you're right. I got so busy listening to you.' Laughing softly, he shook his head. 'I'll turn us around next chance I get.'

'Maybe you can pull a U at the next light.'

'Right.'

'Left,' Sherry said.

Toby laughed again. 'Trying to confuse me?'

'Nah.'

Nearing the deserted intersection, he eased into the left-hand turn pocket. He pulled up to the crosswalk and stopped for the red light. Then he said, 'Uh-oh. No U-turn.'

Sherry scowled at the sign.

'Should I make one anyway?' Toby asked. 'Nobody's around.'

'You'd better not. You never know. We don't want to get pulled over. Anyway, it's always better to play by the rules.'

'Another teacher thing?'

'I suppose.'

'What'll I do?'

'Go ahead and turn left. Then we can just circle the block and come back to Venice.'

When the traffic signal changed to green, Toby swung through the intersection and headed up the sidestreet. This was a residential neighborhood, a mixture of homes and apartment buildings, both sides of the street lined by trees that shook wildly in the fierce winds.

Slowing down, Toby said, 'Why don't I just turn us around here?'

'That'd be fine.'

Though there was no traffic, he drove slowly past the first driveway. It was wide and well lighted. He drove past two more. Sherry wondered if he'd changed his mind; maybe he planned to circle the block, after all.

Then he swung to the left, crossed the empty lane and steered up the driveway of a small, stucco house. The driveway was narrow and dark and had a thick hedge close to the driver's side.

Toby shut off his headlights.

Then he shut off the engine.

Chapter Nine

'What're you doing?' Sherry asked.

Had she missed something? He was supposed to back the car out, not shut it off.

He turned his head toward her. Here in the driveway, so little light came into the car that Sherry could only make out the vague shape of him. His face was a dark oval surrounded by shaggy hair. He seemed to have no eyes, no nose or mouth.

'Is it okay if we just sit here for a minute?' he asked. He sounded hesitant, a little sad.

'What's the matter?'

'Nothing.'

'Toby?'

'Please?'

'What is it? What's wrong?'

'I don't know.'

'Come on. What is it?'

'It's just . . . if I take you back, it'll all be over. Maybe I'll never see you again. I don't *want* to never see you again.'

'Hey,' she said gently. Shaking her head, she reached out and patted his knee. 'We're friends now. We'll see each other.'

'Nah. I don't think so. I think . . . after tonight, you won't wanta have anything to do with me.'

'Sure, I will.' She gave his knee a squeeze.

'Nah. You won't. You wanta know what'll happen? You're gonna find out I lied about Duane, then you'll be mad at me and—'

'What do you mean, you lied about Duane?'

'Well . . . I never saw him go off with that guy.'

'*What?*'

'That queer guy in the net shirt I told you about? I made him up.'

'*You made him up?*'

'Yeah. I'm sorry.' He sighed. 'I figured I'd . . . you know, if I told you a story about Duane walking off with some guy, maybe you'd let me drive you around to look for him.'

'You're kidding,' Sherry muttered.

'I'm sorry. I know it was a dumb thing to do.'

She realized her hand was still on his knee. She took it away. 'You lied about the whole thing?'

'Pretty much.'

'Did you see Duane *at all*?'

'Yeah. I saw him.'

'Saw him do what? If he didn't walk off with the guy you told me about, where *did* he go?'

'I'm not so sure you want to know,' Toby said.

'Believe me, I want to know.'

'It's pretty bad. It's another reason why I lied and wanted to take you for a drive – to get you away from it. I guess . . . I sort of wanted to protect you.'

'Protect me from what?'

Toby shook his head.

'Tell me.'

'Are you sure?'

'I'm sure. Come on, I want to know what happened.'

'When he came out of the Speed-D-Mart, he ran into this woman. He called her Grace.'

'Grace?'

'Do you know her?'

Sherry shook her head.

'Duane knew her *real* well. First they kissed, right there in front of the store. Then they went over to his van and got in. But the van didn't leave. And they didn't come out. Grace was still in there with him when *you* came along. That's why I made up the story about the queer guy. I mean, I wanted to save you from *finding* him that way.'

She gazed at Toby, stunned.

'I'm sorry I lied,' he said. 'The thing is, I thought the truth would *hurt* you.'

'My God,' she muttered.

Duane goes to the Speed-D-Mart for condoms, then has to try them out on this Grace woman? So he's in the back of his van, having a merry old time with her while I'm worried sick about him, searching high and low, half-figuring he's dead or something.

What sort of bastard . . .?

Hang on, she told herself. Maybe it didn't happen. All I've got is Toby's say-so, and he lies.

Would Duane *do* something like that? she wondered.

Might. Who knows what a guy'll do, you wave a hot babe in front of him?

'Are you all right?' Toby asked, sounding very timid.

She shook her head.

'I didn't want to tell you,' he said.

'I . . . It's all right. It's something I . . . I'm glad you told me.'

Gotta find out if it's true, that's the thing.

'I don't want to say anything bad about your boyfriend,' Toby said, 'but he must be a real jerk. You know what I mean?'

'Oh, yeah.'

If he did it . . .

'To do that to you. I mean, he was so lucky to *have* you, and then to treat you that way . . .' Toby shook his head. 'Not just a jerk, but nuts.'

'I'm just glad I found out now. Before things went any further with him.'

'Yeah. I'm really sorry.'

'Not your fault. But I wish you'd told me the truth in the first place.'

I could've taken a look in the van right then and there, she thought.

'I couldn't,' Toby said. 'Huh-uh. "Oh, yeah, I saw him, all right. He's over there in his van doing it with some *other* gal." ' Toby shook his head. 'No way. I couldn't tell *you* that. I like you too much. I couldn't stand the idea of hurting you like that. And, like I said, I got this idea about the two of us driving around to *look* for him. I thought you were so terrific when you were subbing for Mr Chambers, and this'd be my big chance to spend a little time with you . . . I know it was wrong to lie . . . But also, I figured by the time we'd get done searching around, maybe Duane would be finished with this other gal. So then you might never have to find out what a horrible cheating creep he really is. That's also one of the reasons why I wanted us to stop and have a snack – so he'd have more time to get done screwing around in his van. So maybe you wouldn't catch him at it. But then when it came time to turn around, I got to thinking what if they're *still* doing it? I couldn't just take you back to the Speed-D-Mart and have you find them in the van like that. So . . . now you know. I guess I can take you back, now, if you want.'

She nodded. 'Might as well.'

'To the van?'

'Yeah. Please. If it's still there.'

'What'll you do?'

'Find him, for starters. Then I'll listen to what he has to say for himself. Maybe it wasn't what it looked like.'

And maybe it didn't happen at all, she reminded herself. Grace might be no more real than the guy Duane supposedly walked away with.

'What do you think it was?' Toby asked.

'I don't know. But I want to reserve my judgement till I've talked to him. It's just . . . hard to believe he could do anything that rotten.'

'I'm pretty sure he did, though. I mean, you should've seen how he kissed her. Their mouths were open. And she was sort of squirming against him, and he had a hand on her rear end. He was, you know, rubbing her butt while he kissed her.'

Thanks for telling me that, Sherry thought. It gave her a heavy, sick feeling.

'She was wearing this really short skirt,' Toby went on. 'And nothing under it.'

'What?'

'No panties.'

'How do you know that?' Sherry asked.

Why is he telling me these things?

'The wind kept blowing her skirt up,' he said.

'Wonderful,' she muttered.

'I'm sorry. I just don't want you to get your hopes up, that's all. I *know* it wasn't just some innocent thing. They went in the van to . . . finish what they'd started.'

'If that's really what happened.'

He raised his right hand. 'I swear to God.'

'Well, I'll have to make up my own mind about it – see what Duane says.'

'He'll probably just lie to you.'

'Let him try. He'll have a tough time getting away with it. Anyway, I'm about ready to go. How about you?'

'I guess so.'

Instead of starting his car, however, he continued to stare at her.

'What is it?' she asked.

'You sure you wanta go back to the van?'

'Pretty sure.'

'What if he's still in there with Grace?'

The thought of it made her feel sick inside. 'Meet the competition,' she muttered. 'Not that there'll *be* any competition. If Duane's got a woman with him . . .' She shook her head. 'That'll be the last he ever sees of me.'

'Won't it hurt an awful lot?'

'It already hurts an awful lot.'

'Why don't you *not* go back to the van? You know? Just forget about it. I'll take you home, instead.'

'Home? You mean back to Duane's place?'

'You don't want to go there, do you?'

If Duane's not back yet, she thought, I can pretend I never went out looking for him. Say I fell asleep, find out what he has to say about his disappearance.

'I don't know,' she said. 'Maybe it wouldn't be a bad idea.'

'It'd be an *awful* idea. You don't wanta go to *his* place, not after what he's done.'

'So you think I should just go back to *my* place and . . . what, wait for him to get in touch with me?'

'*My* place,' Toby said.

'Your place?'

'Sure. That way, Duane won't know where you went. Neat,

huh? He disappeared on you, so now you disappear on him. Make *him* do the worrying.'

With a grim laugh, Sherry shook her head. 'Not sure he'd worry too much, not if he's spent the past hour or two screwing someone in the back of his van. Probably be glad I'm gone.'

'How about it, though? We've got a really nice guest room. It'll be fun. Anyway, you shouldn't really be by yourself on a night like this. Things are kind of crazy. The wind . . .' He shook his head. 'The power's already out in some places. You wouldn't want to be all alone in your apartment and have the lights go out, would you?'

'Oh, I think I could survive that.'

'And the fires . . .'

'They're all pretty far away.'

'But you never know. What if all of a sudden you needed to evacuate?'

'Guess I'd evacuate.'

'How *could* you with your car in for repairs?'

'Oh, I'd manage somehow,' Sherry said.

When did I tell him about my car trouble? she wondered.

In the silence, she heard the wind howling and hissing outside the car.

'Anyway,' she said, 'west LA doesn't have brush fires. Everything's paved. But if I *did* have to get away, I'm sure I could talk someone into giving me a ride.'

'So, you don't want to spend the night at my house?'

'It's nice of you to invite me, Toby. Maybe I can see your house some other time.'

'Oh, okay.'

'For now, I guess I just want to go back to the Speed-D-Mart and see about Duane's van.'

'You *sure* that's what you want?'

'I think so.'

'Okay.' He reached for the ignition and put his hand on the key, but didn't turn it. Looking at Sherry, he said, 'I bet you're wondering how come I knew your car was in the repair shop.'

'I must've mentioned it.'

'No, you didn't.'

'Then I guess I *do* wonder.'

'I know because I followed you there.'

'Huh?'

She felt a sudden squirm of apprehension.

'I've been following you *everywhere*.'

'What're you—?'

His arm swung out and the back of his fist crashed against Sherry's brow. The impact jolted her head backward. As it bounced off the headrest, Toby clutched the nape of her neck. He jerked her toward him, dragging her out from under the chest harness.

The lap belt was too loose to keep her up.

She fell sideways, landing with her shoulder on the driver's seat and her head on Toby's lap.

He pressed her head down with his left hand.

Then he let go of her neck, leaned toward the passenger seat, raised his arm high and brought his fist down like a hammer. It sledged Sherry in the side, pounding deep into the soft area below her ribcage and above her hip.

Pain erupted through her body. Her breath exploded out.

Chapter Ten

As his left hand kept Sherry's head pressed against his lap, his right clutched the side of her blouse and yanked it out of her skirt. Then he slid his hand under her blouse. It felt cold as ice.

Though stunned by the blows, Sherry clamped her right arm against her side to block his way.

'Get your arm outa there,' Toby said.

She didn't move it.

'Okay.'

As his right hand gently patted her bare flank, his left ripped the earring from her pierced lobe.

With a squeak of pain, Sherry flinched and grabbed her torn ear.

Her arm no longer barred Toby's way.

As his hand glided up her side, goosebumps swarmed over her skin.

She brought her arm down fast. Just as it trapped his forearm against the side of her ribcage, his cold hand cupped her breast.

He moaned.

Sherry felt movement under the side of her face. Movement under the fabric of Toby's shorts.

A blunt hardness rose out of his soft lap. It pushed against her cheek as if trying to raise her head, then tilted away. She felt the solid length of it from her jaw to her temple.

Squirming, Toby drifted his hand over her breast as lightly as a breeze. She felt her skin crawling, her hard nipple tingling and aching.

He fingered her nipple, gave it a gentle squeeze.

Then suddenly he clutched her breast, kneading it and

squirming and making sounds that were almost sobs as the stiffness under Sherry's face jumped and throbbed. She tried to raise her head, but Toby shoved it down tight against the jerking front of his shorts. He thrust up against her. In his frenzy, he squeezed her breast so hard that she cried out.

And it ended.

He let out a long, trembling sigh. His left hand stopped shoving her head. His right hand relaxed its grip on her breast. He settled down in the seat and panted for air.

Under her face, Sherry felt moist warmth spreading across the fabric of his shorts.

She felt a trickle down the side of her neck and figured it must be blood from her ear lobe.

She didn't move. She said nothing.

Toby slowly calmed down. After a while, he whispered, 'Wow.' Then he took his hand out from under Sherry's blouse and drew the blouse down to her hip. 'You're so great,' he said.

Thanks a heap, you sick fuck.

'Thanks,' she said.

'Did I hurt you?'

What do you think?

'A little,' she said.

'I'm sorry. I'm so sorry.' His left hand, still resting on Sherry's head, began to caress the side of her face. 'The last thing I wanta do is hurt you.'

Could've fooled me.

'I guess I got carried away,' he said.

'It's all right,' Sherry told him. 'I understand.'

I understand plenty.

'Do you hate me?' he asked.

'No, I don't hate you,' she said softly. 'You just got . . . too excited, that's all.'

'That's for sure.'

'It could happen to anyone.'

'You're just so beautiful and . . . I haven't been able to get you out of my mind.' As he caressed her face, his other hand gently rubbed her upper arm. 'I've been thinking about you night and day . . . dreaming about what it might be like to . . . to *be* with you.'

'Can I sit up now?' she asked.

'I like you like this.'

'Okay.' She stayed down. The front of his shorts now felt sticky under her face.

'We've gotta figure out what to do,' Toby said.

'Whatever you want is okay with me.'

He caressed her cheek. 'You're so wonderful.'

'What do you want to do?'

'Take you to bed.'

Big surprise.

Though the idea of it disgusted her, she said, 'I'd like that, too.'

'Really?' he asked.

'Sure. I think it'd be wonderful.'

He gave her arm a gentle squeeze. 'The question is, where?'

'How about my apartment?' Sherry asked.

'Nah, I don't think so. You're too friendly with everyone over there. If they saw me show up with you, they'd figure something was wrong.'

'Not necessarily. I can say you're my kid brother or something.'

'No good. Anyway, I can't have anybody seeing me.'

'What about *your* place?' Sherry asked.

'No way.'

'I thought you *wanted* to take me there.'

'Huh? Oh, yeah. That was just talk. I can't take you there.'

Let it go, she warned herself.

'Then how about a motel?' she asked.

'How am I gonna check in at a motel without somebody seeing me?'

'I could check us in.'

'By yourself?'

'Sure. It'd be easy.'

'Yeah, and easy to tell on me.'

'Why would I tell on you?'

'Why *wouldn't* you?'

'I wouldn't. I like you, Toby. I like you a lot.'

'Sure you do.'

Don't push it.

'I won't tell on you,' she said. 'You pick the motel. I'll get us a room . . . I have credit cards. We'll go up and spend the night together. How would that be?'

'It'd be great. Only thing is, you'd tell the desk clerk you're a prisoner and I'd be up to my asshole in cops.'

'I wouldn't tell.'

'Yes, you would. I know you, Sherry. I know *exactly* what you'd do.'

I doubt it.

But he was right in this case; left alone with a desk clerk, she would either blurt out the truth or call the police herself.

Phones aren't working.

Maybe they are by now, she thought.

'There's Duane's place,' Toby said.

'What about it?'

'He has a bed, doesn't he?'

'Yeah.'

'Nobody knows *any*body in that building,' Toby explained. 'We could just walk in. Even if we got seen, nobody'd be suspicious of us. They'd just think we live there.'

'They might get suspicious when they hear us kicking open Duane's door.'

'Haven't you got a key?' Toby asked.

'No.'

'That's okay. I can get us in.'

'Okay. Duane's place sounds great to me.'

'Good.' Toby gave her arm a pat, then took his right hand away and started the engine. He pushed the gear selection lever to reverse. 'I guess you can sit up now,' he told her. His other hand went away, and the car started to roll backward.

Sherry pushed herself up, gritting her teeth but making no sounds. On her way up, the chest harness rubbed across her sore right breast. She pulled the strap away.

'Leave that alone,' Toby warned, swinging on to the street.

She eased the strap down against the middle of her chest. 'It was hurting me,' she said.

'Just keep your hands away from your seat belt.'

'Fine.'

He stopped the car, shifted to drive, then stepped on the gas. Ahead of them, the traffic signal at Venice Boulevard was red.

The pavement just in front of Toby's car was dark with the shadows of windblown tree limbs.

He hasn't got the headlights on.

She resisted an urge to tell him.

No headlights is reason enough for cops to stop us.

Like *that's* gonna happen, Sherry thought.

It might, she told herself. This time of night, there're plenty of cops around and not much traffic. A car without headlights might actually get noticed.

Toby flicked on his signal for a right turn.

In front of the car, an amber glow lit the darkness, went off, came on, went off . . .

Toby put on his headlights.

Terrific.

Just before he reached the intersection, the traffic signal changed to green. He glanced to the left, then pulled out and made his right turn.

Venice Boulevard was bright with streetlights.

And nearly deserted.

Toby turned his head and smiled at Sherry. 'You know what?' he said.

'What?'

'We're gonna have a really great time.'

Nodding, she tried to smile. 'Yeah,' she said.

'Only it won't be so great if you do anything to ruin it.'

'I won't.'

'Like try to get away.'

'I'm not gonna try to get away.'

'You'd better not.'

'I won't.'

'If you *do*, you'll be really sorry.'

'I told you . . .'

'I'll hurt you a *lot*.'

'I thought you *liked* me.'

'I like you. I *more than* like you.'

'Then you shouldn't *hurt* me. And you shouldn't *threaten* me. That's not stuff you do if you like a person.'

'But I *have* to.'

She almost asked 'Why?' But she was afraid of the answer he might give. Instead, she told him, 'No, you don't. You don't have to do any of this.'

'Yeah, I do.'

'You could just stop it all right now.'

'Stop it?'

'Let me go.'

'I can't. I've already . . . done stuff to you. It's too late to stop.'

'No, it isn't.'

'Yeah.'

'Everything so far can just be our secret. I don't have to ever tell *anyone* what you did.'

'But you would, though.'

'I won't. I promise. Just let me go. Nothing else has to happen.'

Toby turned his head and frowned at her. 'I thought you wanted to go to bed with me.'

'I did. I really did, but that was before you started with all these threats.'

'So now you *don't* wanta?'

'I don't know. You've got me scared.'

'You don't gotta be scared.'

'I don't want to get hurt.'

'You won't. Not if you don't deserve it.'

'I already told you I won't try to run away. Will you promise not to hurt me any more?'

'Okay,' Toby said. 'I promise.'

Sighing, he eased his car to a stop at a red light. There were no other cars nearby – except for a few in the parking lot on the other side of Venice Boulevard.

The parking lot of the Nacho Casa.

'How about another taco?' Sherry asked.

Toby turned his head for a look at the restaurant.

Sherry snapped open her seat-belt buckle, flung the straps aside and threw open her door.

'*No!*' Toby yelled.

As he reached for her, she dropped sideways and tumbled out of the car.

Chapter Eleven

Sherry flung up an arm. The street pounded her elbow and crashed her arm against her head. Still half inside the car, she felt as if she were being thrown upside down.

Toby grabbed her right ankle.

She kept falling.

Toby's hand slipped. The shoe was jerked from her foot and he lost his hold.

Her legs came flying out of the car and slammed against the pavement. Grunting with the pain, Sherry flipped herself over. She rolled and rolled, then pushed herself to her hands and knees.

The passenger door stood wide open.

Toby, still behind the wheel, was twisted sideways, one arm stretched out as if frozen in the act of reaching for her. 'Get back in here,' he said, his voice not loud but hard and clipped. 'Right now!'

Sherry got to her feet.

Except for Toby's car, the four eastbound lanes of Venice Boulevard were empty. She saw the headlights of three cars, but they were still far away.

On the other side of the divider, a car rushed by.

She saw the shapes of people inside the Nacho Casa. She'd probably be safe if she could get there. But the restaurant was on the other side of the boulevard.

Running across all those westbound lanes would be easy – no traffic to worry about for a while – but Toby's car was in the way.

'Sherry!' he snapped. 'Come back here!'

'Go away and leave me alone!' She broke into a dash for the area behind his car.

The back-up lights flashed on.

The car shot backward.

She wondered if she could beat it.

Then she saw that she had no choice. She might have time to dodge away and avoid the rear of the car – but the wide open passenger door would nail her for sure.

Go for it!

She sprinted for all she was worth.

Go-go-go!

Now she was directly behind the backward-rushing car.

Quick!

It roared toward her legs.

She pictured herself crumpled on the road, her legs shattered, Toby hurrying back and scooping her up and loading her into the car.

His tires screamed.

Nothing hit her.

I made it!

The driver's door flew open and raced toward her.

No!

She dived for the center divider.

In midair, she felt something bump against the edge of her right foot. The door? It knocked her foot sideways. Her legs smacked together, turning her, flipping her over.

On the far side of the concrete divider, she hit the pavement of the westbound lanes. She skidded and rolled, then scurried up and ran.

Her right foot hurt, but not much.

Though most of her body seemed to be ringing with pain, it worked. She supposed she was no more injured than if she'd taken a bad spill with her bicycle.

A little battered and skinned.

I'll live.

Dashing for the far side of the road, she swung her head around and saw Toby's car speeding forward, racing for the intersection.

He's gonna make a U!

But other cars, approaching from the east, were nearing the intersection – three of them in a wedge formation like fighter jets coming to her rescue.

The turn arrow for Toby was red.

His brake lights came on. He squealed to a halt.

The other three cars kept coming.

As Sherry ran for the curb, she wondered if she should try to wave down one of them.

First get out of their way.

She barely made it to the parking lane before the first of the cars whizzed by. As she turned around, the others rushed past her.

Didn't it cross anyone's mind I might need help?

Toby's car lurched into the intersection. Tires whining, it started into a tight U-turn.

Sherry ran for the Nacho Casa.

As his car roared closer, she rushed to the restaurant's nearest door.

Made it!

She grabbed the handle and pulled. As the door swung toward her, Toby's car lurched to a stop at the curb.

She stepped inside.

Out of the wind and heat, into air-conditioned brightness and tangy aromas of Mexican food.

Standing just inside the doorway, she stared through the wall of windows. Toby's car remained at the curb, headlights on. But he didn't get out.

He's afraid to come in.

Of course he is, she told herself. He tries to come in after me, all these people are going to see him.

All these people?

Forcing her eyes away from Toby's car, she scanned the restaurant.

Most of the tables were empty.

Him!

He'd moved to a different table, but Sherry was certain this was the same man she'd seen in here earlier – the creepy, gray-haired guy who'd spent so much time staring at her.

He was staring at her now.

Staring and frowning.

Sherry looked away from him.

At one of the other tables sat a filthy old woman jibbering to herself.

At another were a couple of husky, tough-looking bikers. The one facing her was a woman with a black patch over one eye. The other had wild black hair and a thick beard. He wore a sleeveless denim jacket with *Hounds of Hell* on its back.

Glad *they're* here, Sherry thought.

Far down near the other end of the restaurant, two guys and one gal were seated at a table. They were probably in their early twenties, and seemed serious as they talked quietly and sipped coffee. Several books were piled on the table.

Probably college students, Sherry thought.

She liked them at first glance.

Maybe they'll give me a ride.

Turning her head, she saw Toby's car still sitting by the curb. Its headlights were now off.

He's still in it, isn't he?

She crouched slightly and narrowed her eyes and made out a vague shape in the driver's seat.

As she straightened up, aches and pains made Sherry grit her teeth. She looked down at herself. The right sleeve of her gaudy, tropical blouse, ripped at the seam, drooped off her shoulder, which was skinned and shiny with blood.

A single button, just above her navel, was all that held her blouse shut. Completely untucked, the blouse draped over her yellow skirt. The skirt was filthy in front, but didn't seem to be torn.

Leaning forward, she pressed the pleated fabric against her thighs and looked at her knees. They were both scraped raw.

The shoe was missing from her right foot.

Deedle-deedle dumpling . . .

Her white sock, now dirty, was half off.

Balancing on her left leg, Sherry raised her right and pulled up the sock.

Then she checked both her arms. Aside from the skinned shoulder, she had an abrasion on the underside of her right forearm.

She wondered what *else* was wrong.

Torn ear lobe.

Maybe bruising in the face from the first punch.
Damage to her side from the second.
Probably a bruised breast.
She thought about going to the restroom. She could take a better look at wounds, clean herself up a little, use the toilet . . .
She needed it badly, now.
But what if Toby decides to come in?
He'd have me alone.
She looked out the window, crouched and saw the dim shape of Toby behind the wheel of his car.
Planning to wait me out?
She glanced toward the creepy, gray-haired man. He was still staring at her.
She turned her back, then looked down at her blouse, hoping to fasten the rest of her buttons. They were gone, leaving behind tufts of broken thread.
All over the street, she supposed.
Along with bits of my skin.
Holding her blouse shut and not looking back, Sherry hurried into the alcove under the *BANOS* sign. The short hallway led past several doors. She glanced at the signs on them: *Employees Only*, *Private*, *Hombres* . . .
She stopped and frowned at the *Hombres* door.
Was the naked girl still in there, hiding in a stall?
Maybe I can borrow her top. She isn't using it anyway. Or buy it from her. Give her ten bucks, let her have mine to wear home . . .
MY PURSE!
Sherry let go of her blouse and raised her arms away from her sides and looked down at herself, turning her head from side to side, double-checking, checking again, hoping her purse was there after all, hanging from one shoulder or the other – that it was somehow simply escaping her attention.
She whirled around.
It wasn't on the floor.
It didn't swing by its strap and bump against her rear end.
It was really gone.
Sinking inside, she tried to remember losing it. Had it been torn from her shoulder when she hurled herself out of Toby's

car or when she dived over the center strip – torn off and left on the pavement of Venice Boulevard like her buttons and her skin?

Abandoned there, waiting for someone to grab it and take it?

If they haven't already.

I've gotta go get it!

With quick, jabbing hands, Sherry started to tuck her blouse into the waistband of her skirt.

Toby's out there. He'll nail me for sure if I make a try for my purse. It isn't worth getting killed over. Or raped over. Or . . .

But what if he gets it?

Blouse tucked in, she still had a strip of bare skin down to her belly. As she pulled the edges of her blouse together, she remembered where her purse was.

And groaned.

He already has it.

Chapter Twelve

It's right where I left it, Sherry thought. On the floor of Toby's car, just in front of the passenger seat.

Dazed and sickened, she pushed open the door to the *Hombres* restroom.

Nobody stood at the sink or urinal. The stall door was shut. She glimpsed the two vending machines on the wall. Just as Toby had told her, one was a condom dispenser.

She remembered the pack of condoms in her purse.

Toby, out in his car, had probably already discovered it.

That and everything else. My money, my credit cards, my driver's licence, my keys. If he wants, he can go over to my place and let himself in.

The awful possibilities seemed overwhelming.

She pushed the stall door. It squeaked open, revealing a toilet full of unflushed paper and brown water. But there was no girl.

She turned away quickly and didn't breathe again until she was safely on the other side of the *Hombres* door.

The alcove was deserted.

She hurried into the *Senoritas* restroom. Nobody at the sink. There were two stalls, both empty. One of the toilets looked fairly clean and had a supply of toilet paper.

She shut the door and slid the latch across to lock it.

The latch would give her some privacy, she hoped. But it was too flimsy for real protection. It wouldn't stop anyone determined to get at her.

If an assailant *did* have trouble with the latch, he could climb over the top of the stall or slide in through the gap at the bottom.

Just get it done and get out.

She took a step backward toward the toilet. Cool liquid suddenly soaked through the bottom of her right sock.

She moaned.

Feeling desperate and disgusted and about ready to cry, she bent over and reached under her skirt and lowered her panties.

The moment she squatted over the seat and started to go, she expected Toby to burst into the restroom.

And I won't be able to stop, she thought. I'll be stuck here, peeing my heart out with my undies around my knees and he'll come sliding under the door, smiling up at me.

Too much Pepsi.

I've gotta get out of here. I'll be trapped . . .

At last, she finished.

On her way from the stall to the sink, she left wet sock-prints.

At the sink, she balanced on her left foot and pulled off the sock, being careful not to touch the wet part.

She tossed it into a trash container.

Then she swung up her leg and put her foot in the sink and turned on the hot water. There was greenish-yellow liquid soap in the dispenser. Straining forward, she pumped some into her hand.

As she lathered her foot, she saw herself in the mirror.

Her short hair, dark with sweat, was clinging to her temples and brow. Her forehead had a reddish hue from Toby's punch. Her face was shiny. Her eyes had a haggard, blank look as if she were only half conscious.

Turning her head, she stared at her right ear. The bottom half of the lobe was split open. The edges looked as if they'd been glued together with old blood. Just below her ear, the side of her neck was painted with red streaks.

She rinsed her foot, then looked for the paper towels.

She saw only air blowers.

'Just great,' she muttered, and lowered her wet foot to the floor. The tiles felt gritty.

At least there's probably no pee over here.

She shut off the hot water and turned on the cold. Bending low over the sink, she cupped her hands under the faucet. She splashed the chilly water onto her face and head. Using her fingertips, she rubbed at the blood stains on the side of her neck. Then, with some soap on her thumb and forefinger, she gently cleaned her earlobe. She rinsed off the suds.

Nervous about how much time was going by, she glanced at the restroom door.

So far, so good.

Maybe he won't be coming in at all. Why should he risk it?

Leaning close to the mirror, she inspected her skinned right shoulder. Without a cloth or paper towel, it would be awfully hard to clean. The same with her other abrasions.

She supposed she could use toilet paper.

Go back into the stall?

With one bare foot?

'No way,' she muttered.

Then she realized she could use her left sock.

Is there time for all this? she wondered.

Why not? Maybe Toby'll give up waiting and go away.

'Sure he will,' she said.

But she still had the restroom to herself, so why not stay and tend to her injuries? As a Girl Scout, she'd learned that open wounds should be cleaned with soap and water as soon as possible to prevent infection. And in recent years, thanks to television news, she'd developed a terror of the 'flesh-eating bacteria.'

Standing on her bare right foot, she pulled off her left shoe and sock. The lower part of the sock was sweaty, but the area from around her ankle seemed dry and clean. She held it under hot water until it was soaking wet, wrung it out, then applied soap and gently swabbed her shoulder abrasion.

When this is all over, she thought, I'll take a nice, long bath. I'll soak in the tub for an hour . . .

He's got my keys!

When this is all over, she told herself, he *won't* have them. Obviously, it won't be over until I've got everything back . . .

Including Duane?

She supposed she didn't want *him* back. He'd gotten her into this, testing the damn rubbers on a slut in the back of his van.

How could he *do* a thing like that? she wondered. Knowing

I was waiting for him in bed? What kind of miserable bastard *is* he?

I thought he *cared* about me.

The slut probably has bigger boobs.

Like who doesn't?

'Fuck him, anyway,' she muttered.

Tears filled her eyes.

Stupid me, she thought. I should've just stayed in bed. But no, I had to get all worried and go *looking* for him and run into my pal Toby.

I'm getting my ass abducted 'cause Duane's a back-stabbing piece of shit . . .

Sobbing, tears running down her face, she finished cleaning her shoulder, then soaped and rinsed her other abrasions, and finally wrung out her sock. Still crying, she hopped on her right foot and pulled the sock on. Then she struggled into her shoe.

Duane wasn't that great in the first place, she told herself. I oughta be glad it's over. And be *really* glad I didn't find out what a lying cheating bastard he is *after* he put it to me. This was my lucky night.

She laughed and shook her head.

It *is* my lucky night, she told herself. I got away from *two* dirty rotten bastards. A little the worse for wear, but nothing that won't heal.

A sadder man, but wiser.

'Woman,' she muttered.

No longer crying, she stared at her face in the mirror and shook her head.

'What a wreck,' she said.

Bending over the sink again, she splashed her face with water. Then she straightened up and turned off the faucet. And stood there, looking at herself.

Her face was dripping.

Her blouse, splashed with water and clinging to her, was open an inch or so all the way down to the single remaining button at her belly. She pulled its edges together, then sighed.

Then flinched as someone knocked on the door.

'Are you all right in there?' a man asked.

'Fine,' she said.
'You can come out any time.'
'The men's room says *Hombres* on the door.'
'Yeah, I know. What I'm saying is, you can stop hiding in there. He's gone.'
'Huh?'
'The chubby guy. He drove off a few minutes ago.'
She shut her blouse all the way, pressed her left hand against it, and opened the restroom door.
The man met her eyes.
You!
She felt herself shrivel inside.
'Just thought you might want to know,' he said.
'Thanks.'
'Looks like you've been having a rough time.'
'Yeah. A little bit.'
'Maybe I can help you.'
'Oh, I don't know.' Shaking her head, she said, 'But thanks.'
'I tell you what,' he said. 'Come on over to my table and sit for a while. I'll buy you a cup of coffee. You look like you could use some time to recover and sort things out.'
Out of the frying pan, into the fire.
But the man didn't seem quite so creepy, now that he'd spoken to her. He still had very intense eyes and a hard face. Nothing about him, however, suggested that he might intend to do her harm.
If he wanted to attack me, she thought, he could've done it when I was in the john.
'I guess I wouldn't mind a cup of coffee,' she said.
'Good.'
She followed him out of the alcove. With a glance toward the windows, she saw that Toby's car was no longer at the curb. She quickly scanned the restaurant. The bikers had left, but the crazy woman and the college kids remained at their tables. A gawky-looking man in glasses was leaving the pick-up counter with a tray in his hands.
No sign of Toby.
'That's my table over there,' said the gray-haired man, nodding toward it.

'I know,' Sherry said.

'I know you know,' he said. 'I'll get the coffee. You can go on and have a seat. I'll be right over.'

'Okay.'

As he headed for the counter, Sherry walked to his table. His old coffee cup was still there, along with a few wadded napkins. The other side of the table was clear. She sat down, turned to the window and peered out.

Turning her head from side to side; she looked again for Toby's car.

The entire length of the block, nothing was parked at the curb.

He seemed to be gone, all right.

But Sherry didn't like it.

Better, by far, to be able to look out the window and see his car, see him waiting behind its wheel . . . and know where he is.

Chapter Thirteen

The man came to the table carrying a tray. On it were two large styrofoam cups of coffee, a couple of small plastic tubs containing creamer, several paper packets of sugar and sugar substitutes, two red plastic stirrers and some napkins. He set down the tray in front of Sherry.

'Help yourself,' he said.

'Thanks.'

He sat down across from her, reached out and took one of the coffees. 'They've got good coffee here. Good food, too.'

'Yeah.'

Though he didn't quite smile, the corners of his eyes crinkled. 'You've got nothing to worry about.'

'I don't?'

'Not from me you don't. You've been looking at me like I'm Charlie Manson.'

Was it that obvious?

Blushing, she said, 'Well, the way you were staring at me . . . You made me nervous.'

This time, he laughed. 'I make a lot of people nervous.' He took a creamer off the tray, peeled back its top and dumped it into his coffee. 'I don't mean to,' he said. 'But I like to keep my eyes open. You never know what you're going to see.'

Keeping her blouse shut with her left hand, she reached out with her right and lifted her coffee off the tray.

'My name's Jim, by the way.'

'I'm Sherry.'

'Sherry. As in "Sherry Baby"?'

'That's it.'

'Named after the song?'

She nodded. 'My parents loved it.'

'Great song. The Four Seasons. They had a lot of great songs. Before your time.'

'I've got their CDs.'

Jim tore a packet of sugar and dumped it into his coffee. 'I've got 'em on vinyl. That's 'cause I'm an old fart.' He grinned and crinkled his eyes.

Sherry huffed out a laugh. 'How old's that?' she asked.

'Fifty-two.'

'That *is* old.'

'You're telling me.'

'Shouldn't you be in bed by now?'

He laughed. 'I *should* be. You're right about that.' He twirled a stirrer in his coffee. Still half smiling, he looked into Sherry's eyes. 'You want to talk about your situation?'

'I don't know.' She took a drink of coffee. It was hot and bitter. 'I thought you said they had *good* coffee here.'

'You've gotta doctor it up.'

'Guess so.' She took a creamer off the tray.

As she peeled away its top, Jim said, 'I saw the two of you in here earlier.'

'I know,' Sherry said.

'I know you know.'

She poured the creamer into her coffee. 'He was helping me look for someone. That's what I thought, anyway.' She stirred, and the coffee changed color from nearly black to tan. 'But then it turned out to be a trick. After we left here, he started getting funny with me.'

'Put moves on you?'

'Yeah. Well, first he hit me a couple of times. And he tore my earring off.' She turned her head to give Jim a good look at her ear. 'Then he . . . messed around with me. He was trying to take me somewhere to spend the night with him. That's when I got away.'

'Who *is* this guy?'

'His name's Toby. Toby Bones.'

'Toby *Bones*?'

'Yeah.'

'What is he, a pirate?'

She almost laughed. 'I think he's a mental case. But I don't really know much about him.' She picked up a sugar packet, ripped it, and emptied it into her coffee. 'I didn't really know him at all until tonight, but apparently he was a student in one of my classes a few weeks ago. I remember his name from the role book.'

'That'd be a hard name to forget.'

'And I didn't.'

'You're a teacher?'

Nodding, she said, 'A sub. I guess Toby developed an interest in me.' She took a stirrer off the tray and twirled it in her coffee. 'Sounds like he's been following me around. He knows stuff about where I live. And where my boyfriend lives.'

Former boyfriend, she thought.

'And now he has my purse. I managed to leave it in his car when I jumped out. Smart me.'

Frowning, Jim nodded. 'So he now has your keys and so forth.'

'He's got *everything*. And I'm here with nothing. Just the clothes on my back. What's left of them.'

'And me.'

'Huh?'

'You're here with me,' Jim said. 'I'll do what I can for you.'

'Well, thanks.'

'First things first. How badly are you hurt?'

'Just scrapes and bruises, I guess.'

'There's an emergency room a few blocks from here. I'd be glad to drive you over.'

She shook her head. 'I don't think so.'

'Are you sure?'

'I'll be okay. Besides, I can't spend the next two hours sitting in an ER. I've gotta *deal* with all this.'

'Deal with it how?'

'I don't know.' She picked up her coffee and drank some. With the cream and sugar added, it tasted almost like warm cocoa. 'Toby's out there someplace – God knows where – and I somehow doubt he's decided to call it quits for the night. Plus, my boyfriend's missing. Or maybe not. I've gotta find out for sure about him. But I don't want to get nailed by Toby in the process.'

'I can protect you from Toby,' Jim said.

But who protects me from you? she wondered.

He *seems* like a good guy, she told herself. But so did *Toby* right up to the instant he whacked me in the face.

Who's to say Jim isn't *worse* than Toby?

'I'm not sure what to do,' she said.

'You could call the police.'

'Last time I tried a phone, it wasn't working. But I'm not sure I want cops involved in this, anyway. They'd have to know *everything*. Some of the stuff . . . it'd be so damned embarrassing . . .'

As she sipped her coffee, she imagined how things might go with the police. *See, my boyfriend had to make an emergency run to the Speed-D-Mart for condoms.* It would have to be that or a lie, and she didn't like the idea of lying. Especially to the police.

Any guy hearing the truth would immediately picture her naked. From there, he'd start thinking about what it might be like to screw her.

And that would only be the start of the humiliation. The cops would figure she was an idiot for accepting a ride from Toby. *You don't know this guy from Adam, but you go off in his car in the middle of the night?*

Then their imaginations would start running wild again when she told them about the sexual assault.

'They might even think I was asking for it,' she told Jim. 'I mean, nobody forced me to get in the car with Toby. And the way I'm dressed . . . They'll probably book me as a suspected hooker, or something.'

'You look fine. It's too bad your blouse got ruined.'

'I'm barely decent,' she said.

'That's not your fault.'

'Anyway, I'd rather not get the cops involved in this. It'd just be opening a can of worms. Even if they catch Toby . . .' She shook her head. 'I want it to be *over*. I don't want the whole world to find out about all this. I don't want to get questioned or give statements or *testify*. And if Toby ends up in prison, I don't want to spend years worrying about what he'll do to me when he gets out. I just want it to be over.'

'How do you plan to manage that?' Jim asked.

'I'm not sure. But I *do* know that I've got to keep the authorities out of it. This has to stay between me and Toby.'

'Well, I'll stay out, too, if that's what you want. But I'd be happy to give you a hand. Right now, you're stranded and Toby might be out there waiting for you. I don't think you want to go walking off by yourself. Do you?'

Sherry turned her gaze toward the window. The broad, well-lighted pavement of Venice Boulevard reminded her of an airport runway – a runway in the middle of the night with no flights coming in or going out.

Leaves and litter hurried by, leaping and diving in the wind.

On the other side of the road, trees were shaking.

Toby's car was nowhere to be seen.

She saw nobody on the sidewalks.

She met Jim's eyes.

'I guess you're still afraid of me,' he said.

'I don't *know* you. That's how I got in trouble with Toby. I mean, you seem like a really nice guy, but . . . how do I know you're not some kind of maniac *pretending* to be a nice guy?'

He frowned as if giving deep thought to the matter. Then he said, 'I suppose you can't know for sure. You'll just have to trust your own judgement.'

'My judgement hasn't been so great lately. Not where men are involved.'

He suddenly grinned. 'I've got just the solution.' Leaning sideways, he reached into a front pocket of his trousers. Sherry heard jingling sounds. Then his hand came out with a key ring. He unclipped a small, black plastic device and slid it across the table.

'What're you doing?'

'That's the remote for my car. Controls the alarm and door locks.'

'What am *I* supposed to do with it?'

He unclipped a key. 'This is for the ignition.' He slid it over to her.

'Jim?'

'Take my car,' he said.

'*What?*'

'It's just outside in the parking lot. A blue Saturn. Take it. I'll walk home. It's not that far.'

'Are you saying I can take your car *without* you?'

'Sure. Do whatever you need to do. I can get by without it for a while.'

'You're not serious.'

'You can drop it off at my place when you're done. My address is in the glove compartment.

'I can't take your car.'

'I want you to.'

'*Nobody* lets a stranger drive off with his car. You don't even know me. What if I decide to keep it?'

'You won't,' he said.

'How do you know?'

'You're not a thief.'

'You can tell by looking?'

He tipped his head to one side and squinted at her, his eyes twinkling. 'I think so.'

'Tell you what,' Sherry said. She pushed the remote and ignition key back to his side of the table. 'You drive.'

Chapter Fourteen

'Wait here,' Jim said. 'I'll check the parking lot and make sure the coast is clear.' He shoved open the door and went out into the night.

Sherry stayed just inside the Nacho Casa.

Jim returned in about fifteen seconds and opened the door for her. 'No sign of him. Ready to go?'

'Ready.'

Hunched over and leaning into the wind, Jim hurried across the parking lot. Sherry followed him, holding her blouse shut with one hand, pinning her skirt down with the other. The hot wind blew against her. It hurled grains of debris that bit at her bare skin and raw wounds.

Jim stopped at a low, dark car. Ducking, he pulled open the passenger door. Sherry climbed in, and he shut the door. It closed with a quiet solid thud, sealing out the wind and grit and noise.

She reached for the seat belt, then stopped.

Let's just leave it off, she thought. I might need to get out of here fast.

Not that I don't trust him.

Jim dropped into the driver's seat and shut his door. 'Where to?' he asked.

'How about the Speed-D-Mart over on Robertson?'

Jim started the car. 'What's the main cross-street?'

'Airdrome.'

He backed out of the space, pulled forward to the lot's exit, then turned right.

This has happened before, Sherry thought. It made her uneasy, even though she knew that a left turn onto Venice would've been illegal.

'It's the other way,' she said.

'I know.'

'I realize you can't *go* that way.'

'I could. If you don't mind a few bumps.'

'That's all right.'

At the first intersection, he turned right. This wasn't the route Toby had used. Plus, they were now heading in the proper direction. Sherry felt some of her tension slip away.

'This is awfully nice of you,' she said.

'I like your company.'

'Lucky for me you were there.'

'I'm there most nights.'

'Why is that?' she asked. 'I mean, if you want to tell me.'

'I'm a people person.'

A laugh jumped out of her.

Jim turned his head and smiled. 'I don't mean that the way you probably think.'

'You mean you're *not* a "touchy-feely" kind of guy?'

'Right. I just like to watch people. From a distance. So I go where they are. Late at night, that limits my choices. A place like the Nacho Casa is perfect. Open all night. Different people coming in all the time. Most of them sit down and stay a while so I have plenty of time to observe them.'

'So . . . you sort of *spy* on everyone who comes in?'

'That's about it.'

'That's a wee bit strange, Jimmy.'

He looked over at her and laughed softly. 'Keeps me out of trouble,' he said.

'I'd think it might get you *into* trouble.'

'Doesn't usually.' Not signalling, he suddenly cut hard to the left and swung onto a sidestreet.

Alarm slammed through Sherry. 'What're you doing?'

He swerved, stopped at the curb and shut off the engine and lights.

'Jim!'

'I want to see if we're being followed.' He turned his head to the left, apparently to watch the side mirror.

'Are we?' Sherry asked.

'We'll know pretty soon.'

'I didn't notice a car behind us.'

'Neither did I. But it'd be hard to see if its headlights are off.'

A sensible precaution, she thought.

Or is this just an excuse to stop? This is just the sort of thing Toby pulled. What's he gonna do next, pound me and start feeling me up?

Why did I get into the car with this guy? What am I, a moron? Don't I ever learn *from my mistakes?*

Good going, Sherry. They can put it on your tombstone. HERE LIES SHERRY GATES. SHE NEVER LEARNED.

'Looks like we're in the clear,' Jim said. He started the car and pulled away from the curb. 'I'm a little surprised. I figured Toby would probably hang back, keep an eye on things, and follow us.'

'Guess he didn't.'

'Guess not. Makes me wonder what he *is* doing.'

'Maybe waiting at *my* place,' Sherry said. 'He knows where I live and he has a key.'

'But he knows you know that,' Jim pointed out. 'He might figure you'll be expecting to find him there, so he'll avoid it. At least for tonight.'

'Maybe,' Sherry said. 'Or he might think, since I expect him to be there, he'd be an idiot to stick around, and I'd realize *that*, so I won't really think he'll be there, so that's where he goes.'

Jim turned right, and they were again moving in the proper direction. Looking at her, he smiled. 'If Toby thinks you think *that*, he'll stay away.'

'But if he thinks I think he'll stay away . . .' She groaned.

'I tell you what. We'll expect Toby *everywhere*. And we'll deal with him when we have to.'

'Okay.'

'It'll be less confusing that way.'

'Planning to stick with me for a while?'

'Let's just see what happens.'

'What do you do, hang out at the Nacho Casa waiting for damsels in distress?'

'Not exactly,' he said.

'I'm the first, huh?'

'Not exactly,' he said.

She was surprised to feel a small pull of disappointment. 'Oh, you do this sort of thing all the time?'

'I do stuff. But not often. Mostly, I just watch.'

'When do you do *more* than just watch?'

'Seldom.'

'That's not what I meant,' she said.

'I know.'

'I know you know.'

Jim laughed.

'Why me?' she asked.

'You looked like you could use a hand. I saw what happened to you out in the street. You almost didn't make it.'

'You just sat there and watched?'

He nodded. 'It only lasted a few seconds. Then you were on your way over here, so I just stayed put. And kept an eye on things.'

'Would you have stopped Toby if he'd come in?'

'He didn't come in.'

'What if he *had*?'

'Hard to say.'

'You like to be evasive, don't you?'

'Do I?'

'What do you *do*, anyway?'

'In terms of what?'

'For a *living*, for starters. Or do you just hang *around* places day and night staring at everyone and looking for babes to rescue?'

'I do this and that.'

'You're a bank robber.'

'Nope.'

'A private eye.'

'I'm just Jim, okay?'

'Jim . . . ? Oh, my God, you're James Bond!'

'Afraid not.'

'What *is* your name? Your last name. Or is that a state secret?'

'It's Starr. With two r's.'

'Jim Starr?'

'Yep. And yes, I was born with it. And no, I'm not a stripper. And yes, I *am* the star of my own life.'

'Does everyone give you the star treatment?'

'I get the treatment, all right.'

'And you made fun of a guy named Bones?'

'What's your last name?' he asked.

'Gates.'

'Sherry Gates.'

'Want to make something of it?'

'Any relation to the Chief?'

Surprised, she said, 'No.'

'Hell of a guy.'

'Ah-ha! You just gave yourself away, buster. I now know that you're not a criminal or shithead. Anyone who still calls Darryl Gates the Chief after all these years . . . Oh, my God! You're a cop!'

Suddenly remembering what she'd said about staying away from the police, she felt herself go hot with embarrassment.

'Oh, man,' she muttered. 'I should've known. It should've been so *obvious*.'

'I'm not a cop,' Jim said.

'A *former* cop.'

He stopped for a red light. Sherry realized that the road in front of them was Robertson Boulevard.

'I was never a cop,' he said.

'Liar. I bet you quit the force like all those others back when Gates retired . . .'

'And they replaced him with a park ranger? No. But I probably would've quit if I'd been in the department.' The light changed to green. He eased forward into the intersection, then turned left.

'You *were* LAPD,' Sherry said. 'Come on, admit it.'

'Nope.'

'Come on, Jim. We're going to be there in a couple of minutes. Tell me.'

'I've never been in law enforcement.'

'Then what *are* you?'

'Just a regular citizen.'

'How do you earn your living?'
'Haven't we already gone over that?'
'Come on, tell me. What are you?'
'I am what I am.'
'You're Popeye the Sailor Man!'
'Toot toot,' he said.
She laughed. 'Come on, Jim!'
'It doesn't matter,' he said.
'Then why won't you tell me?'
'Then you'd know.'
'You're a *therapist!*'
'Good guess.'
'Are you?'
'Do you *think* I am?'
She flung out her arm and whacked him on the thigh.
'Here it comes,' Jim said.
Turning her face toward the windshield, Sherry saw the Speed-D-Mart just beyond the next intersection. From here, she had a full view of Duane's parking space by the side of the store.
His van was gone.

Chapter Fifteen

'Do you want me to pull in?' Jim asked as they neared the Speed-D-Mart.

'No, don't,' Sherry said. 'It's not there anymore. Duane's van. It was parked right there.'

'The van of the guy you were looking for?'

'Yeah. Duane. My boyfriend.'

Maybe my *former* boyfriend, she thought, depending on what he's been up to.

'What now?' Jim asked.

'I'm not sure. Maybe you can drive me over to his apartment. I need to find out for sure if he's back. And what was going on. Can you make a left?'

'Here?'

'Yeah.'

No cars were coming, so Jim hit the brakes and swung to the left. As the tires sighed quietly on the pavement, Sherry felt her body sway toward the passenger door. Jim straightened out the car.

'It's just up the block a little. The third building on the left. Maybe you could pull in.'

Slowing down, he steered into the driveway. Then he braked to a halt. Just down the ramp, the path was blocked by an iron gate. 'I'd better back us out of here,' he said, and reached for the gear selection lever.

'Wait. Let me take a look.'

She climbed out. Holding her blouse shut as the wind whipped against her, she hurried down the driveway. She stopped just in front of the gate and peered through it. The interior of the parking area was well lighted. Most of its spaces were full. She spotted Duane's white van in its usual space.

Ducking against the wind, she returned to Jim's car.

She pulled open the passenger door and leaned inside. 'It's there all right. He's back. I guess I might as well go on up. Thanks an awful lot for—'

'Why don't you climb in? We'll find a parking place on the street.'

'It's not really necessary.'

'I can't leave my car here,' Jim said. 'I'm blocking the driveway.'

'Well, *I* can just go on up.'

'I'd like to stick with you till we're sure everything's okay.' He patted the passenger seat. 'Come on. We'll park on the street and I'll see you safely to Duane's door.'

'Okay,' she said. 'If you're sure you want to. It probably isn't necessary, though.'

'Can't be too careful.'

She climbed into the car and pulled the door shut.

'Thanks,' Jim said. He backed out of the driveway and pulled forward on to the street.

'Are you planning to be my *permanent* bodyguard?' Sherry asked.

'You won't need one if you don't get through tonight.'

He drove slowly up the street, turning his head from side to side.

'It's tough to find parking places along here,' Sherry said. 'Too many driveways. And most of the apartment buildings don't even have enough spaces for their tenants.'

'We'll find a place,' Jim said. He stopped at the corner, then drove across the intersection. Halfway down the next block, he added, 'Sooner or later.'

'If we don't find one pretty soon,' Sherry said, 'we'll end up at *my* place.'

'Would you rather go there?'

'It's actually a few miles.'

'No problem, if that's where you'd like to go.'

'That's where Toby is.'

'Maybe. But I'll go in with you and . . .'

'I'd rather not have to deal with him again tonight. Or ever, for that matter.'

'*I'll* deal with him.'

'Or maybe he'll deal with you. No thanks. I've had enough excitement. I can just stay at Duane's tonight. Even if he *did* . . .' She imagined him in the back of his van with Grace underneath him, both of them naked, Grace gasping as he thrust into her. 'Whatever he did,' Sherry said, 'he won't throw me out. Tomorrow, I'll go back to my place and have someone change the locks.'

'Here we go.' Jim slid his car into a stretch of open curb between two driveways. 'It's a little bit of a hike.'

'That's okay.' She swung open her door. As she climbed out, the wind blew under her skirt and hurled it up. She let go of her blouse to battle it, so the wind jerked her blouse wide open. The only button came undone. The blouse started to fly off her shoulders, but she quickly caught it and pulled it shut.

Looking over her shoulder, Sherry saw that Jim was making his way, hunched over, toward the front of the car. He'd probably seen nothing of the wind's attempt to strip her.

Quickly, she tucked her blouse down the waistband of her skirt.

'A blustery night!' she called to Jim.

He smiled and shook his head. His hair was a wild, blowing tangle. His clothes flapped.

Sherry waited for him on the grass strip beside the curb. The grass felt soft and warm under her bare right foot. As Jim approached, she stepped over to the sidewalk. The concrete didn't feel good, but at least she could watch its flat gray surface and avoid kicking a sprinkler head or putting her foot down in broken glass or a dog pile.

Jim came to her on the sidewalk. 'I forgot about your bare foot,' he said, speaking loudly to be heard over the moans and howls of the wind.

'It's okay,' Sherry told him.

'Are you sure? Maybe we should get back into the car. I can go ahead and park in Duane's driveway. If I'd remembered about your foot . . .'

'No. It doesn't matter. It's not that far, anyway.'

'Want to wear one of my shoes?' he asked.

She looked down at Jim's feet. He wore high-top leather

hiking boots. Large ones. 'What are they, size fifty?'

'Twelves.'

'I think I'll pass. But thanks for the offer.'

'I'd be more than glad to *carry* you.'

Sherry huffed out a laugh. 'I wouldn't want you to hurt yourself.'

'I'd risk it.'

'Well, I'll keep it in mind. Thanks.'

As they hurried down the sidewalk, Sherry felt the gusts flinging her short hair every which way. It blew its hot breath against the nape of her neck. It snapped the sleeves and sides of her blouse while it pasted the center against her back. It pressed her skirt against her rump and legs. Sometimes, it gave her a rough shove as if it hoped to throw her sprawling on the concrete.

'Your boyfriend picked a great night for his disappearing act,' Jim said.

'I shouldn't have let him go out. It was my fault.'

'Did you get an urge for a snack?'

'Huh?'

'Did you send him to the store for a *snack*?'

'Not exactly.'

'How long was he gone?'

'About an hour. Then I went looking for him. Another big mistake. I should've waited.'

'Maybe so.'

'What do you mean "maybe"?'

Bumping gently against her, Jim said loudly into her face, 'You met me, didn't you?'

'Is that supposed to be the silver lining?'

He laughed.

Holding her blouse shut with one hand, Sherry used the other to point across the street. 'That's his entrance,' she said.

Jim nodded. 'Let's go.'

They walked down a driveway to the street. No traffic was coming, so they rushed to the other side. There, Sherry took the lead. She waded through the wind to the foot of the stairs, then trotted up them to the building's front stoop.

She tried to open the glass doors, but they were locked.

Beyond them, the lobby and ground-level corridor were dimly lighted. And deserted.

She stepped over to the call box. Leaning in, she thumbed the button for Duane's apartment. Then she put her ear close to the speaker.

'Yeah?' she heard.

'It's me.'

'Sherry?'

'Yeah. Let me in.'

Through the noises of the wind, she heard a faint buzzing sound.

Jim, standing by her side and ready, pulled open the door.

While he held it wide, she rushed into the lobby. Turning around, glad to be out of the wind, she watched Jim struggle to pull the door shut.

'Wow,' she said.

Jim smiled slightly. 'Nice and quiet in here, isn't it?'

'Almost peaceful.'

He stared into her eyes. 'I guess you're probably safe now.'

'Looks that way.'

'Do you mind if I go up with you, anyway?'

'It really isn't necessary.'

'I'd hate to bring you this far and lose you at the last moment.'

'Lose me?'

'Have you get hurt.'

'You're the one who said it's safe.'

'*Probably* safe. We can't be positive.'

'I suppose not.'

'If you don't have any major objections, I'd like to go up to the room with you.'

'Okay. Why not? You've come this far, might as well go the rest of the way.'

'I concur,' Jim said. Smiling, he crinkled his eyes at her. 'Don't worry, I'll be out of your hair as soon as I've delivered you safely into the arms of your beau.'

'Let's go.' She headed for the stairway, Jim walking close by her side. 'You probably just want to check him out,' she said, starting up the stairs.

'Now that you mention it.'

'You'll be nice to him, won't you?'

'I'll be charming.'

'You'll probably scare the hell out of him.'

'I do tend to sometimes have that effect on people. Through no fault of my own.'

'Maybe I should keep you around till I find out what he was up to. Maybe I'll want you to hurt him.'

'Oh, you wouldn't want that.'

'Don't count on it. He might've been with another woman.'

'When? Tonight?'

'Yeah. Right there in his van in the parking lot of the Speed-D-Mart.'

'With you *waiting* for him?'

She nodded.

Jim shook his head. 'No way.'

They reached the top of the stairs. 'This way,' Sherry said.

Side by side, they walked down the silent corridor.

'No man in his right mind,' Jim said, 'would mess around with some other woman when he's got *you* waiting for him.'

The heat of a blush rushed through Sherry. 'I don't know about that,' she said.

'He'd have to be nuts.'

'Well . . . thanks.'

'What makes you think he was with this other woman?'

'Toby saw him with her. They kissed, then Duane took her into his van.'

'Maybe Toby lied.'

'I don't know,' Sherry said. 'I don't think I've ever completely trusted Duane. Something like that wouldn't really surprise me.'

'If you felt that way, what were you doing . . . ?'

'Shhhh!' She suddenly hushed him.

Duane's door, only a few more paces down the corridor, stood partway open.

Holding her blouse shut with one hand, she reached out with the other and took hold of Jim's forearm. 'Be nice to him,' she whispered. 'But maybe stick around for a while. I might want you to drive me home if things don't go well. Okay?'

'I'll do whatever you want.'

'Thanks.' She gave his arm a gentle squeeze. Still holding it, she stepped up to Duane's door.

Chapter Sixteen

She leaned toward the opening. The room inside was lighted. Though she couldn't see Duane, music was playing. Some sort of sad, haunting . . . she realized it was the soundtrack from *Titanic*.

'Duane?' she called.

An answer came, but she could barely hear it through the music. One of the words sounded like 'bedroom'.

'What'd he say?' Jim asked.

'I think he said he's in the bedroom.'

'Oh.'

'Come on in.' Sherry swung the door wide open and entered the living room of Duane's apartment. Jim came in behind her and shut the door. 'You'd better wait here,' she whispered. 'He might not be decent.'

Jim's face twitched slightly. 'Go on,' he said. 'Yell if you need me.'

Sherry walked down the passageway, glancing into the dark bathroom on her way to Duane's bedroom.

His door stood open. She took a step inside, then halted. The room was lit by a single candle on the nightstand – probably the same candle that she'd put there earlier. It cast a shimmering, mellow glow across the bed.

She saw Duane's head on the pillow.

Staggering sideways, she reached out and flicked the light switch. The bedside lamps came on, flooding the room with brightness.

Is it real?

It's real.

And it's Duane.

It looked as if someone had eaten his nose and lips and part of the right side of his face. Sherry could see his teeth, all bloody, through the gap where his cheek should've been.

Blood was dripping slowly from the pulpy red stump of his neck.

'Jim!'

She heard quick, heavy footfalls behind her. Turning sideways, she saw Jim running toward her.

A moment after he ran past the bathroom, someone leaped out behind him.

A naked, tubby guy with butcher knives in both hands.

'*Look out!*' Sherry yelled.

In midstride, Jim started to twist around.

Toby – she could see his face now in the light from the bedroom – sprang at Jim and pounded the knives into his back. Jim's mouth twisted. He grunted and fell, Toby on top of him.

'*No!*' Sherry cried out, racing toward them. '*Stop it!*'

Toby stabbed him again, then stopped and looked up. His face was spattered with blood. As his eyes latched on Sherry, his heavy lips curled into a smile.

Sherry aimed a kick at them.

With her left foot. The one with the shoe.

Toby dodged the kick.

Sherry's leg flew high. Too high. Balance gone, she waved her arms and fell backward and slammed against the floor. The impact jolted her, hurt her, but she shoved at the floor and started to sit up.

'*Yeeeeee!*' Toby keened. He crawled off Jim's back and scurried toward her on his knuckles and knees, a knife in each fist, a grin on his bloody face. '*Yeeeeee!*'

'*No!*' she cried out, shoving at the carpet with her heels and elbows, sliding on the seat of her skirt, scooting herself away from him but not fast enough.

Not *nearly* fast enough.

I've gotta get up!

The back of her head bumped against Duane's bed.

Toby suddenly let go of the knives and lunged forward, reaching for her feet.

He missed her left foot, but caught her right with one hand.

Then he had both hands around her ankle. Thrashing, she kicked at him with her other foot. He lurched backward and stood up, lifting and pulling her leg.

She twisted and writhed, kicking at him, trying for his naked groin though she couldn't see it, her own high legs in the way.

The heel of her shoe struck him. He grunted, then let go with one hand and caught her *left* ankle.

He jerked both her feet wide apart.

And stared down at her, grinning and gasping, his naked body dribbling with blood and sweat.

She knew her blouse was wide open. He wasn't staring at her breasts, though. His gaze was latched on her groin. With her skirt rumpled around her waist, she could see the panties herself – the black string across her pale skin, the narrow panel of transparent black fabric between her legs.

'Toby,' she gasped.

His eyes went to her face.

'I'll . . . make you . . . a deal.'

'Huh?'

'We'll . . . go someplace. I won't . . . fight you. I won't try . . . to get away.'

Shaking his head, he sank to his knees. He let go of her ankles. With both hands, he grabbed the waistband of her panties. He tugged it away from her right hip and tried to break it. The elastic stretched but didn't pop. Gritting his teeth, he pulled harder.

Sherry clutched his wrists.

'Not here,' she said.

'Wanta bet?'

'What if the cops come?' She panted for air. 'We've made . . . a lot of noise. Somebody might've heard us and . . .'

'Phones don't work, remember?'

'Cell phones do.'

'I don't care. Let go.'

She released his wrists.

He jerked hard, breaking the waistband and yanking the panties halfway down her left thigh.

'We leave now,' Sherry said. She squirmed as his fingers

explored her, but she didn't resist. And she kept on talking. 'Duane's got a cell phone in his van. We call and get 'em to send an ambulance for Jim. Maybe they can save him.'

'Shut up.'

'I'll go with you. I'll *do* whatever you want.'

The hand went away. He slipped his fingers into his mouth and sucked them.

'Please,' Sherry said. 'I don't want Jim to die. I'll go with you. But we've gotta go *now* and . . .'

Throwing himself forward, Toby grabbed her shoulders and dropped onto her. He grunted and rammed, shoving at her but not into her, missing her center, sliding against the crease of her groin and suddenly throbbing, spurting out warm fluid. Making little whimpery sounds, he kept shoving, prodding her, rubbing her through the slippery gush as he pulsed out more and more.

Done, he sagged on top of her.

Sherry put her arms around him and held him gently.

He panted for breath.

'I . . . didn't make it in,' he gasped.

'That's okay,' she said. She felt as if he'd poured glue onto her. It was rolling down her groin and into the crevice between her buttocks. 'Next time, I'll help you. But not here. Right now, we've gotta get going before the cops show up.'

'Cops?' He raised his head and blinked down at her. He had a dull look in his eyes.

'Do you want the cops to get you?'

He shook his head.

'Then we've gotta leave as fast as we can. Okay? We'll go somewhere else. But I'll stay with you. I won't try to get away anymore.'

He pushed himself off Sherry and stood up. Then he stared at her.

Her blouse was wide open, her skirt rumpled up around her waist, her panties hanging around her left knee. Squirming inside, she resisted an urge to cover herself.

'You need a shower,' Toby said.

She looked up at his sweaty, blood-smeared body. 'We both do,' she said.

He turned away from her, crouched and picked up the knives. Facing her again, he said, 'Get up and come here.'

She stood, but remained where she was.

'Come here,' he said again.

'What're we gonna do?'

'Anything I say.'

She had a sudden urge to look over her shoulder and see if Duane's head was really there on the pillow. And was it really *eaten*?

I don't wanta see that!

She kept her head straight forward, but looked past Toby at Jim's sprawled body.

Is he still alive?

She pulled her blouse shut, took a deep breath and said, 'I'll do anything you want, but not till an ambulance is on the way for Jim. Come on. Please. He doesn't deserve this. He was just *helping* me.'

Toby stepped around to the side of Jim's body and stomped on his back.

Jim let out a low groan.

'I guess he's alive.' Toby grinned at Sherry. Then he crouched over Jim and raised one of the knives.

Sherry shrieked.

It hurt her ears, but it stopped Toby. His mouth dropping open, he gaped at her and yelled, '*Shut up!*'

Shoving her hands against her ears, she shrieked again.

Toby leaped up and rushed at her.

Knives in both hands.

She whirled around and ran from him. In front of her was the bed. When she leaped onto its mattress, Duane's head tumbled off the pillow and rolled toward her.

She swung around in time to see Toby dive toward her legs.

She kicked him in the face.

The blow knocked his head sideways. It didn't stop him, though. The momentum of the dive kept him flying toward her. Sherry tried to jump out of the way, but he crashed through her legs. She fell across his back, tumbled down his buttocks and legs and rolled onto the floor behind his feet.

Sprawled on her back and gasping for breath, she heard quick, hard pounding sounds.

They came from somewhere outside the bedroom.

Somewhere down the passageway.

Somewhere, maybe, out near the living room.

Duane's front door!

Chapter Seventeen

Sherry flipped over, scrambled to her feet and ran from the room.

Glancing back, she saw Toby shove himself off the bed.

Ahead of her, knuckles pounded furiously on the door.

She dodged Jim's body on the floor, raced past the bathroom and poured on the speed.

Behind her back, the thuds of Toby's bare feet pounded after her.

In front of her, a fist knocked on the door again and again.

She dashed into the living room, ran toward the door.

'What's going on in there?'

It was the urgent voice of a woman.

Skidding to a halt, Sherry grabbed the doorknob. She twisted it and jerked the door open. On the other side stood a woman no older than herself, slim and dressed in a pink bathrobe and frowning first with annoyance but then with concern.

Sherry crashed the door shut in the woman's face.

'Get help!' she shouted. 'There's a mad—!'

Coming up behind her, Toby clenched her hair, jerked her away from the door, swung her sideways and let go. She shuffled over the carpet, trying to stay on her feet. A lamp table got in the way. Her thigh rammed the table against the side of the couch. Her shoulder hit the lamp. As the lamp flew, she tumbled across the top of the table and fell over the padded arm of the couch. She felt a cushion underneath her body, but only for a moment. The lamp crashed and the room went half-dark as Sherry fell off the couch. Her weight shoved the coffee table away and she landed on the floor.

Through the melancholy strains of the *Titanic* soundtrack,

she heard thudding sounds. A woman yelled, 'Help!'

Sherry sat up.

'*Someone! Please!*'

The door was wide open.

Shoving at the couch and coffee table, Sherry got to her feet. On wobbly legs, she stumbled over to the door and staggered out.

Halfway down the hallway, Toby had caught the woman.

His back to Sherry, he was sitting on the woman's rump and pounding his knives into her back. Right, left, right, left, right. Her legs were twitching, her feet thumping against the floor.

Except for Toby and the woman, Sherry saw nobody in the corridor.

She saw no open doors, either.

Where is everyone? Don't they hear anything? Are they hiding in their rooms?

Toby kept driving his knives into the woman's back.

The woman didn't stand a chance. Toby must've already stabbed her a dozen times or more.

He'll be done any second . . .

What'll I do?

Shut the door. That's for sure. Shut it and it'll lock and he hasn't got a key on him. He'll be locked out. At least for a while.

But what about me?

I shut the door, but where am I?

Inside or out?

The frenzy of stabbing came to an end. Toby jerked the knives out of the woman's back and started to climb off her.

Don't just stand here!

He stood up and turned around. The front of his naked body was crimson. Grinning, he raised both arms high like a knife-crazed Rocky Balboa and did a little victory dance.

Midway down the stretch of hall between Sherry and Toby, a door eased open a few inches.

Then it bumped shut.

Grin slipping away, Toby lowered his right arm and pointed the dripping blade of his knife at Sherry's face. 'Stay,' he said.

She lurched sideways and slammed the door.

Toby's eyes widened. 'You fucking *nuts?*' he blurted.

She tested the knob.

Locked.

'*No!*'

She whirled away from the door – away from Toby as he broke into a run – and raced for the stairway.

She had a good head start.

But she heard Toby chasing her and she suddenly felt that she'd made the wrong choice. She should've locked herself in the room, not tried to flee.

But she'd had no time to *think!*

Maybe this *is* better, she told herself. At least I'm not trapped. All I've gotta do is outrun him.

If I can get outside, I'll be all right.

Nearing the stairs, she skidded and grabbed the banister. She looked back. Toby hadn't gained on her, but he was still coming, arms pumping, knives in both hands, heavy legs chugging out. His mouth drooped. His chest heaved. His fat jiggled. His half-stiff, bouncing penis pointed at her.

He's about had it, Sherry thought.

She bounded down the stairs.

He's *screwed*, she thought.

No clothes, no keys, no nothing.

But my God, he *killed* that woman. And he killed Duane and . . .

I've gotta do something about Jim!

Three stairs from the bottom, she leaped. Her blouse lifted behind her like a cape. Her skirt billowed up. The way the air felt underneath her, she remembered her panties were gone. She felt the wetness from Toby, too.

But you didn't make it in, you bastard!

Her bare foot slapped the tile floor of the lobby while her shod foot landed with a soft bounce. Lurching forward, she threw out her arms and rushed at the glass door straight ahead of her.

What'll I do about Jim?

She rammed the door open. It let in the noises of the windy

night: hisses and roars, bams, rumbles, car alarms and distant sirens.

Twirling around, she glanced up the stairs.

No sign of Toby yet.

Instead of running outside, she scurried back toward the stairs.

I've lost my mind, she thought.

She ducked into the space behind the staircase. Squatting in the shadows, she tried to stop panting for air.

He'll hear me!

She heard him thumping down the steps, heard him huffing for breath.

And heard the glass door finally bump shut, muffling the outside noises.

Will he think I ran out?

Not a chance.

But he might, she told herself. He'll know it's an old trick, but he'll also know I'd have to be nuts *not* to run away.

I should've. I'd be safe now.

She heard Toby's bare feet slap against the lobby floor as he trotted to the doors.

Glass doors, she reminded herself. He's now standing stark-naked and bloody behind glass doors in a lighted foyer. With butcher knives in his hands.

How about a cop car driving by?

How about anybody *driving by?*

Isn't anybody out there jogging? Walking a dog?

Come on, somebody! Open your eyes and get on your cell phone!

She heard a quiet, metallic sound.

Toby pushing against a door's crossbar.

He's going out?

The door squeaked. The noises of the rushing, howling wind rushed in.

Is he leaving?

He doesn't dare, Sherry thought. The door'll lock behind him and he won't be able to get back in. He needs to get back to his clothes. And his keys.

Come on, you bastard, do it! Go out!

Sherry suddenly imagined herself sneaking out from under the staircase, rushing Toby from behind, ramming him in the back with both hands and *shoving* him out the door. He'd go diving headlong down all those concrete stairs.

Major injuries.

Maybe he'll land on his knives.

Even if he doesn't get demolished in the fall, I can make sure he's locked out.

Squatting under the staircase, sore all over, sweat pouring down her body, Sherry knew that a shove might put an end to her ordeal.

If I've got the guts . . .

But the shove was movie-heroine stuff, and she knew it. A tough little starlet would pull it off without a hitch.

But if *she* tried it . . .

In real life, Toby would hear – or *sense* – her approach. Before she could get close enough to shove him out the door, he would turn around. And then he would kill her.

She'd seen him pound those knives into Jim and watched him drive them in a wild frenzy again and again and again into the back of the woman.

She could almost feel them ripping their way deep into her own body.

And she knew that she *would* feel them – no doubt about it – if she tried to creep up on him.

The door shut.

Its lock tongue snapped into place.

Did he go out, or . . . ?

She heard his quick, ragged breathing, but no footsteps.

What's he doing?

Listening?

She held her breath.

She didn't move, except to blink her eyes. When she blinked, her lids made quiet, wet clicking sounds. Certainly Toby couldn't hear *that.*

But what about the soft plips of sweat drops hitting the floor underneath her?

What about the wild pounding of her heart?

He can't hear any of that, she told herself. Not the way he's huffing and puffing. And not with all the noises from outside.

Why doesn't he go away?

Maybe he knows I'm here.

Her chest ached from holding her breath.

From times she'd spent swimming underwater, she knew she could go without air for much longer than this. Maybe for another minute or so.

But what if I hold it and hold it till I can't stand it any more, and he's still here?

The first breath would be a loud one.

Afraid to risk it, she parted her lips and slowly exhaled. Then she slowly inhaled.

Not bad, she thought. Almost silent. This'll work fine.

Why doesn't he go away!

How *can* he go away? He's naked. His clothes and car keys are locked in Duane's apartment.

Probably his wallet, too.

I shafted you, you dumb prick.

She almost wanted to smirk. But the amusement she felt over putting Toby in such a predicament was smothered beneath heavy layers of fear and horror and sadness and discomfort.

Toby's bare feet patted the tiles.

Here he comes!

Gritting her teeth, Sherry turned her head to watch him crouch and look in at her. He would probably smile. Maybe he would make a crack – '*Lose a contact lens?*'

She wondered whether he would try to drag her out . . . or just waddle in and start slashing.

Chapter Eighteen

Hearing Toby start to climb the stairs, Sherry lowered her head and shut her eyes.

Thank God, she thought.

Her eyes suddenly stung, and tears spilled out. She struggled not to sob or sniffle.

That'd be rich, she thought. He hears me weeping, comes back down and butchers me.

What'll I do now? she wondered.

What's *he* doing now?

Going upstairs.

Maybe it's a trick so I'll come out.

The pounding sounds of Toby's footsteps diminished as he continued to climb the stairs. Then Sherry couldn't hear them anymore.

Is he gone? she wondered.

Or is he sitting on the top stair, eyes on the lobby?

He's gone, she told herself. He *has* to get back into Duane's room. He's screwed without his stuff.

Unless he's got a key up his butt, he'll have a tough time getting in.

When I hear him trying to break the door down, I'll know where he is. That's when it'll be safe to make my move.

Staying crouched under the stairway, she listened.

What if he *doesn't* try to break in? she wondered.

He has to.

But maybe he'll be afraid to make so much noise. Sooner or later, someone other than that one poor woman might decide to get involved.

They can't all be deaf or yellow.

Somebody must have a gun, for godsakes. A gun and a

smidgen of guts. That's all it would take to stop him, folks!

Sherry suddenly realized that Toby'd had plenty of time to reach Duane's door.

What's he doing?

Come on, give it a kick!

Maybe he already did, she thought. Maybe he bashed the door open already and I just couldn't hear it.

Whatever made me think I would be able to hear it from all the way down here?

He might be inside the apartment right now . . .

Or rushing down the back stairway to sneak up behind me.

Sherry's hot, sweaty skin tingled as goosebumps scurried up her body.

On hands and knees, she eased her head out from under the stairway. She looked at the deserted lobby and glass doors, then swiveled her head and looked down the corridor.

Nobody. And no open doors.

She pictured herself hurrying through the corridor, hammering every door with her fists.

If she tried a stunt like that, the commotion might bring Toby running.

Would anyone open up and let her in?

Maybe.

Fast enough to save her from Toby?

The way things had gone so far, she doubted it.

And if someone *did* let her in, she'd still be a long way from helping Jim unless the phone service had been restored or the person kept a cell phone handy.

Nearly everyone in LA seemed to have a cell phone.

At least in their cars.

Or vans!

Sherry scurried out from under the stairway. On her feet, she twirled for a scan of the stairs. No Toby. Crossing the lobby, she looked toward the glass doors. Instead of seeing outside, she saw little more than a reflection of the lobby, the lower stairs, and herself: the torn sleeve drooping off her shoulder, her open blouse hanging outside her skirt, her one foot wearing a crew sock and sneaker while her other foot was bare.

'Cute,' she muttered.

Perky cheerleader survives bus accident.

Or gangbang, more like it.

At the other side of the lobby, she jerked open the door to the parking lot. She eased it shut behind her, then trotted down the stairs. They were made of corrugated metal. They felt cool under her bare foot, and made soft ringing sounds as she pounded her way down.

There was no door at the bottom. She hurried out of the stairwell. The underground parking lot was well lit. Though crowded with vehicles, she heard no engines and saw no people.

She glanced up the driveway. Its gate was shut, just as it had been when she'd stood on the other side and peered in.

Felt like hours ago.

How long ago *had* it been? she wondered as she ran toward Duane's van. Half an hour ago? Fifteen minutes? Ten?

How long since Jim was stabbed?

Five minutes?

Is he still alive?

If only he'd just dropped me off and gone home . . . too damn much of a man to do that and now look what it got him.

She trotted into the space between Duane's van and a blue BMW.

It's gonna be locked. I'll need a way to break the window.

She tried the driver's door anyway.

It swung open.

'*All right!*' she gasped, and climbed up.

She dropped into the driver's seat, took a deep breath and almost gagged at the foul odors that suddenly filled her nostrils.

Who the hell crapped in here?

She suddenly knew who, and it wasn't only crap but also urine and blood and vomit and a gamey odor like raw hamburger.

Her eyes watered.

She shut the door. She didn't *want* to shut the door and close herself inside with the stench, but she *had* to. Had to make the overhead light go off so it wouldn't give away her position.

Open a window!

She pressed a switch on the door, but nothing happened.

Of course not, she thought. Gotta have the ignition on.

They make it so you can't put down the window!

Just to be sure Toby hadn't left the key behind, she glanced at the ignition. No key. Of course not.

So forget the stink. Grab the phone and get outa here!

Determined not to look over her shoulder and see the carnage – the headless wreckage of Duane that had to be somewhere in the rear of the van – Sherry reached down to the console beside her seat. She swung its lid up.

Inside the console was Duane's cell phone.

She snatched it out, then realized she'd better not just run away with it; she might need to use the power cord.

She flipped the phone open, raised its antenna and thumbed the red power button. The phone beeped once, and the screen glowed green. Blinking on and off was the message, *Battery Low*.

Maybe it still had enough juice to work.

The phone made musical beeps as she tapped 911, then beeped again when she pushed the green send button.

At her ear, the phone made hissy, crackling sounds.

Then it went silent.

She looked at the phone. Its screen had gone dark.

She whispered, 'Shit,' then dropped the phone onto her lap and reached into the console again. She whipped out the cord. She plugged one end into the phone, then plucked out the cigarette lighter and jabbed the other end into the socket.

She'd seen Duane do this once.

Does the engine have to be running?

She thumbed the power button. The screen lit up, showed her the blinking Battery Low sign, then went dark again.

'Fuck,' she muttered.

Without the ignition key—

The passenger door swung open and Toby clambered in, wearing the dead woman's pink bathrobe. His face was bloody and he held a butcher knife in his teeth.

Sherry shoved her door open.

On his knees on the passenger seat, Toby lunged at her.

She tried to throw herself through the open door, but he grabbed her with both hands. One clutched her neck while the other wrapped around her upper arm.

He jerked her toward him, let go of her arm and snatched the knife out of his teeth. Still squeezing the back of her neck, he pressed the flat of the blade against her chest just below her left breast.

'I'll slice it off for you,' he hissed. 'Want me to?'

'No.'

'Drive.'

'I can't.'

'Key's under the seat.' He took the knife away from her breast and thrust her head down.

Face against the steering wheel, she spread her knees and reached down and fingered the floor mat.

'Come on, come on.'

'I'm trying.' She swept her fingertips back and forth over the rubber mat. 'Are you sure it's here?'

'Yeah, I'm sure. It's just the ignition key, not the whole bunch.'

As she reached further back, she brushed the key with a fingertip. It slid away, but she found it again and peeled it off the mat. 'Got it,' she said.

Toby let her sit up, but didn't release the back of her neck.

'Get us out of here,' he said.

She tried to fit the key into the ignition slot, but her hand trembled too much.

'Nervous?' Toby asked.

She got it in, twisted it and gave the gas pedal a push. The engine roared to life.

'Let's go.'

She put on the headlights, released the emergency brake, and backed out of the space.

'Figured you were long gone,' Toby said.

Saying nothing, she headed for the driveway. As she approached the gate, it began to rise automatically. She drove out, and up the slope. At the edge of the road, she stopped the car. In the side mirror, she saw the gate begin to lower.

'Go left,' Toby said.

She kept her foot on the brake.

'Come on, move.'

'Let me make a call first. Okay? Just let me call so they'll send an ambulance for Jim. Then I'll go with you.'

'You'll go with me, all right.'

'Please. What's it going to hurt?'

'What *good's* it gonna do me?'

'Let me call, and *I'll* be good.'

'Sure.'

'I'll cooperate with you.'

'Right. You think I'm a moron?'

She turned her head and looked at him. 'If you *don't* let me call, it ends here.'

'Yeah?' He squeezed the back of her neck, reached across with his other hand and pushed the long edge of his knife against the underside of her breast.

'Go ahead and do it,' she said. 'Kill me and throw me in the back with Duane. I'll be a lot of good to you then.'

The blade slit her.

Chapter Nineteen

Sherry winced and arched her back and felt blood start to slide down her skin. The cut burned. It felt very shallow, two or three inches long. Though she wanted to grab it, Toby's knife was still there. She kept her hands on the steering wheel as blood slid down to the waistband of her skirt.

'Drive,' Toby said.

'No.'

'You wanta *die* for that bastard? Isn't he the creep from the taco joint?'

'He's not a creep.'

'He's probably dead by now.'

'Let me make the call and I'll drive us anywhere you want.'

He took the knife away and rested it on his thigh. 'Go on and call.'

'Thanks,' she muttered. With one hand, she bunched up the left front side of her blouse. She pressed the wadded fabric against her cut.

The phone cord was still plugged into the dash. The phone itself had fallen to the floor. Toby kept hold of Sherry's neck as she bent down and picked it up with her right hand.

Needing both hands for the phone, she used her left wrist to hold the wad of blouse against her wound. Then she flipped open the phone and thumbed the power button. With a beep, the screen came to life, glowing pale green. She tapped in 911, then pressed send. Holding the phone to her ear, she heard ringing.

'Start to drive,' Toby said.

She drove onto the road, turning left.

'I hate assholes who talk on the phone while they

drive,' Toby said. 'Oughta be against the law.'

A recorded voice said, 'You have reached the nine-one-one emergency dispatch number. If you are calling to report an emergency, please remain on the line. Our first available operator will answer your call.'

'What's going on?'

'I'm on hold.'

Toby chuckled. 'Good thing this ain't an *emergency*.'

She kept driving. The recorded voice kept repeating itself.

'Still on hold?' Toby asked.

'Yeah.'

'Pull over and stop.'

As she stopped the car in front of a driveway, she heard ringing again. There were clicks as a connection was made. A woman's voice said, 'Nine-one-one emergency, Mable speaking. What's the nature of your emergency?'

'We need ambulances,' Sherry said, and quickly gave the street address of Duane's apartment building. 'There's an injured man in room two three six.'

'And what is the nature of his injury?'

'Multiple stab wounds. A woman's in the hallway, too. Stabbed and . . .'

Letting go of Sherry's neck, Toby snatched the phone out of her hand. He jabbed the power button. The phone beeped and went dead. He dropped it to the floor in front of him, then reached out and plucked the cord out of the cigarette lighter. 'You're welcome,' he said.

She glanced at him. 'Thanks.'

'I let you make the call, right?'

She nodded.

'So now you gotta keep your word and cooperate.'

'I will,' she said.

'You better.'

'Where do you want to go?' she asked.

Toby was silent for a few seconds. Then he said, 'I've gotta think.' After another pause, he muttered, 'What'd you wanta go and shut the door for?'

'Duane's door?'

'Yeah, Duane's door. My *clothes* were in there.'

'Your wallet, too?'

'Yeah, my wallet.'

'Too bad,' Sherry said.

'I had twenty bucks in there.'

'And your driver's license?'

'You wish.'

'Your license *wasn't* in your wallet?'

'Shit, no. You think I'm stupid? I read about this serial killer – Greenwood? – he lost his wallet at the scene of a crime and that's how the cops got him. I didn't have *nothing* in mine. Just the twenty bucks.'

'Well,' Sherry said, 'that's lucky.'

'They can't get me from any of that.'

'What about your keys?'

He suddenly punched her in the upper arm.

'*Ow!*'

'That's for my keys.'

Rubbing her arm, she said, 'I'm sorry.'

She thought, *fantastic.*

'Sid's gonna kill me.'

'Sid?'

'None of your business.'

'Did you try to get back into the room?' Sherry said.

'You locked the *door*!'

'Well, I shut it. It locked automatically.'

'Same difference. You locked me out. Man, *all* my keys are in there. The car, the house . . .' He punched her again, his fist slamming against her arm just below where he'd struck her before.

'I'm *sorry!*'

'You oughta be!

'Did . . . did you have an ID with your keys?'

'Hate to disappoint you.'

'That shouldn't be so bad, then. I don't think some *keys* will tell the cops who you are.'

'I should've burnt the fucking place to the ground.'

'Why didn't you?'

'With what? My lighter? It's in my shorts, and they're in your lover-boy's bathroom. And the *door's* locked!'

I really *did* screw him up, Sherry thought. But not nearly bad enough. If only he'd had his driver's license in his billfold . . .

'Get moving,' he said.

'Where?'

'Never mind. Just drive. I'll tell you when to turn.'

She checked the side mirror, saw no traffic, and swung into the lane. She steered with her right hand, using her left to hold the wadded blouse front against her cut.

'Thanks to you,' Toby said, 'We're stuck with this stinky van.'

'Where's your car?'

'None of your business. But it's no good, anyway, without the keys.'

'Can't you hot-wire it?'

'Yeah, sure. *You* know how?'

'No. Don't you?'

'You gotta be kidding. How am I supposed to know how to do that?'

'I don't know. I thought guys like you *knew* that sort of stuff.'

'Guys like me?'

'Yeah.'

'You think I'm some kind of experienced criminal?'

'Aren't you?'

'You gotta be kidding. I've never done shit like this before. Didn't plan on doing it tonight, either. Things just happened.'

'Things *just happened*? You murdered Duane and . . . ?'

'Like, one thing led to another, you know? I was just following you the same as I *been* doing. All I wanted was just to *watch* you. Never figured I'd get a chance to . . . *be* with you, you know? Didn't plan to waste anybody, either. Stuff just worked out that way.'

'Your lucky night,' Sherry muttered.

'Thing is, I was parked across the street when lover-boy's van came up the driveway, and I couldn't see through his windshield too good. So I thought you were *both* in there. That's how come I followed it. I was just hoping to *see* you, you know? So I follow it to the Speed-D-Mart, and he parks it around the side, but he's the only one that gets out. Come to find out, *you're* not even there. He must've left you back in his apartment. And that's when I start to think. Just suppose he doesn't come back? You just gonna wait for him all night? With the Speed-D-Mart only a couple of blocks away? Huh-uh. I figure, give you a while, you're gonna start wondering what happened to him. An hour or two, maybe you'll walk over to look for yourself.'

'Guess you had *me* figured,' she muttered.

Toby chuckled. 'Turned out just like I hoped. The first part, anyhow.'

'Did you have to *kill* him?'

'That was the fun part. Only thing is, now we've gotta dump his body.'

'Why do we have to dump it?'

'You happen to notice it doesn't exactly smell like lilacs in here?'

'Wouldn't it be better to get rid of the whole van?'

'Yeah, sure. And that's *just* what we'd do, only you screwed me out of my car keys. So how're we gonna get home if we ditch the van?'

'Home?'

'Yeah, home.'

'You want to take me home?'

'That's what I said. And we can't exactly *hike* there, can we? Maybe if you hadn't locked up my *clothes* . . .' He punched her arm again.

'*Ouch! Shit!* Would you *stop* that?'

'I'll do whatever I want. You're lucky I haven't killed you.'

'I won't be nearly as much fun if I'm dead.'

'Who says so?'

Sherry turned her head and glared at him.

Toby smiled. 'When you're dead, I'll *eat* you. If you give me any shit, I'll eat you *before* you're dead.'

Her insides seemed to turn cold and shrivel.

'I *liked* it.'

'Huh?'

'The taste. *Duane's* taste.'

I'm gonna be sick.

'What I figured, I'd chew the skin off his fingertips so nobody'd be able to get prints off him. Only thing is, I *liked* it. So I kept on eating. After his fingertips, I worked on his face for a while.'

'Shut up.'

He punched her arm again.

'I sampled him all over. Know the best part?'

Gritting her teeth, she shook her head.

'The weenie.'

She slammed on the brakes. As the van skidded to a halt, she threw open the door and leaned out.

'*No you don't!*' Toby yelled, grabbing her arm.

She choked and gagged, wracked by heaves, but not much seemed to come up except thin, hot fluid. Her throat burned. Her eyes watered. She felt as if her lungs and heart were being wrenched from her body.

Behind her, Toby laughed.

Then he said, 'Just kidding about the weenie. You really think I'd bite a guy's *dick*? No way. What do you think I am, some kinda pervert?'

The moment Sherry finished vomiting, Toby pulled her arm. She sat upright and shut the door.

'Get any on you?' Toby asked. He sounded merry.

'I . . . don't think so.' She'd forgotten about the wound beneath her breast, but now she felt blood trickling out of it and dribbling down her midriff. She looked down. Her breast was bare. She drew the blouse over it, then pressed her left hand against the wet fabric.

'Get driving before somebody comes along,' Toby said.

He still clutched her right arm.

'Let . . . go of my arm.'

He released it.

Sherry wiped the tears from her eyes. Then she wiped her wet mouth and chin.

'Let's move it!'

She put both hands on the steering wheel and stepped on the gas.

'See that alley up ahead? Let's give it a try. Maybe we can find a nice home for Duane.'

'In an *alley*?'

'In a dumpster.'

Chapter Twenty

Sherry steered into the alley. The straight, paved lane was bordered by block walls, fences, and the doorless carports of apartment buildings. Each building seemed to have four to eight carports in a row, with a couple of dumpsters near one end or the other.

Though patches of darkness were scattered down the length of the alley, the areas near the dumpsters were mostly well lighted.

Nothing moved except windblown scraps of paper and foliage, and, far ahead, an empty shopping cart that drifted toward them as if steered by an invisible derelict.

Sherry saw no people.

But most of the apartment buildings had second storeys with windows – and sometimes balconies – overlooking the alley. Not many of the windows were illuminated.

Toby, hunched forward in the passenger seat, twisted his head this way and that as if searching for snipers. 'I don't like this,' he said. 'Somebody picks the wrong time to look out a window . . .'

'Everybody's probably asleep.'

'Not everybody. No telling who might be watching us.'

'So what do you want to do?'

He was silent for a few seconds. Then he said, 'See if you can find an empty place in one of these garage things.'

'Then what?'

'Pull in. Gonna let that thing hit us?'

'Guess not,' Sherry said, and veered right to avoid the shopping cart. As it clinked and rattled past her side of the van, she saw that it wasn't entirely empty. It held a single, white sneaker.

A sneaker very much like the one she had lost.

But that was miles from here.

It can't be mine, she told herself.

'Did you see that?'

'Huh?'

'A *shoe* in the shopping cart.'

'So?'

'*I'm* missing a shoe.'

'So?'

'Can we get it?'

'You outa your mind?'

She stopped the van.

'Keep moving.' Toby grabbed the back of her neck. 'You don't need a shoe. You're lucky you've got *one*. Look at me. Thanks to you, I haven't got *shit*.'

'Should've kept your clothes on.'

'You're the one locked the door.'

'I didn't *lock* it. I just *shut* . . . *Ow!*'

'Get moving.'

She took her foot off the brake and drove slowly forward.

'Oughta make *you* wear this shitty robe, see how you like it. The bitch got her blood all over the back of it. Makes me itchy.'

Not wanting to be punched again, Sherry kept her mouth shut.

Near the end of the block, Toby pointed through the windshield and said, 'There!'

At first, the space appeared to be empty. As Sherry drove closer to it, however, the rear end of a tiny sports car came into view.

'Keep going,' Toby said.

They came to the end of the block without finding an empty carport.

Sherry stopped at the cross-street. No cars were approaching from any direction.

'Keep going,' Toby said.

She drove across the street and entered the alley on the other side. It seemed no different from the alley they'd just left behind.

But this one had an empty carport – one of four stalls in a row beneath the second apartment building on the right.

'All *right!*' Toby blurted.

Sherry swung in and stopped the van.

'Kill it,' Toby said.

She shut off the headlights and engine. 'Now what?' she asked.

'I don't know. I gotta think.'

They sat quietly in the darkness.

What *I've* gotta do is get away from him, Sherry thought.

Right, and get how many more people killed?

In her mind, she saw Duane's severed, partly eaten head rolling off the bed pillow. Then she saw Toby hunched over the woman in the hallway, slamming his knife into her back.

She saw the look on Jim's face when Toby pounced on him and stabbed him.

And she wondered if Jim was still alive.

She pictured him on a gurney being wheeled out of the building into a chaos of police cars and flashing lights and into the rear of an ambulance.

I'll never find out about him till I get away from Toby.

If I don't get away, he's gonna kill me. Sooner or later. He sure can't let me go.

Wants to eat *me?*

Take it easy, she told herself. He isn't about to kill *or* eat me. Not for a while. He hasn't even made it *in* yet. He'll want to keep me alive till after he's done that, at least.

Unless I try to escape again and he rips me up with that knife.

Next time I make a break for it, she thought, I'd damn well better do it *right.*

I sure can't try it here.

'What're we going to do?' she asked.

After a few more moments of silence, Toby said, 'I want to take you home. But I don't know how.'

'Where's home?'

'None of your business.'

'Do you want my help?'

'You'll just try to mess me up.'

'I owe you, Toby. You let me call the ambulance for Jim.'

'After *I* stabbed the shit out of him.'

'You didn't have to let me call. But you did. I *told* you I'd cooperate if you let me do that. I can't be much help, though, if you won't discuss it with me.'

'Thing is,' Toby muttered, 'I just don't know about driving home in this thing. Even if we get rid of the body, it's still *his* van, and it's all fucked up inside with his blood and everything . . .' Toby shook his head. 'I can hide it in our garage so the cops won't find it, but then Sid's gonna see it and start asking questions.'

'So the thing is,' Sherry said, 'you want to take *me* to your house but you don't want Sid to see the van?'

'Yeah.'

'Why not?'

'Are you kidding? He'd go apeshit.'

'What'll happen when he sees *me*?' Sherry asked.

'That'll be okay. I've got that all figured out. I'll just tell him I found you. I'll say you were in an accident and I brought you home to take care of you.'

'And he'll believe that?'

'Sure. Why not?'

For godsake, don't argue!

'No reason,' she said. 'Sounds good to me.'

'Only what about the van?' Toby asked.

'You could tell Sid it's mine. You and I had a collision. I was driving the van and crashed into you, how's that?'

'I don't know,' Toby mumbled.

'*Your* car was knocked out of commission, so I was nice enough to drive you home in my van.'

'How come you don't just drop me off?'

'Because I'm hurt. I *am* hurt.'

'Yeah,' Toby said. 'You are, all right.' Though Sherry couldn't see more than the dim shape of him in the darkness, she was sure a smile must be lurking at the corners of his mouth. He was probably thinking about the slit below her breast.

'I'm hurt and I don't have anyone to look after me,' Sherry explained. 'You felt sorry for me and offered to let me stay at *your* place till I get better.'

'How come I didn't take you to *your* place?'

'Because . . . I can't go home. Because . . . I've *got* it! Spousal abuse! My *husband's* the one who beat me up and ripped off my earring and cut me! I ran away from him tonight. I jumped in the van and sped away . . . Next thing you know, I crashed into *you.*'

'So you've gotta stay with us because you're hiding from your husband?'

'Exactly.'

After a small silence, Toby said, 'That's pretty smart. No wonder you're a teacher.'

'Do you think Sid'll buy it?'

'Sure. It's a *great* story.'

'To make it work,' Sherry said, 'we'll need to do a few things.'

'Like dump the body?'

Grimacing, she nodded. 'That's number one. Next, we've got to really crash the van into something.'

'So it'll have dents and stuff,' Toby said.

'That's right.'

'You really *are* smart.'

'Can you guess what else we need to do?'

'Clean all the blood and shit outa the van?'

'Sooner or later, yeah. Come on, think. You read books about serial killers, don't you?'

'Yeeeahh. *I know!* Get rid of the license plates!'

'That's it!'

'Switch 'em with some other car.'

'Right.'

The excitement draining out of his voice, he said, 'Only I'd need to have tools or something.'

'A screwdriver is all,' Sherry said. 'Then just switch the plates with any car that's handy, throw away Duane's registration or whatever, and Sid'll never have any reason to think the van isn't mine.'

'That'd be *so* great. But where'm I gonna get the screwdriver?'

'Speed-D-Mart.'

'You mean like walk into a *store*? In my robe?'

'I'll go in,' Sherry said.

'Oh, sure. You oughta see what *you* look like.'

'I can clean myself up a little . . .'

'Besides, how do I know you won't *tell* on me?'

'Take my word on it?'

'Oh, sure. Anyway, we can't buy anything even if we *did* go in. How much money have *you* got on you?'

'None.'

'Same here,' Toby said. 'Wanta take a wild guess at where *my* money is?'

'Locked in Duane's apartment?'

'That's about the size of it, thanks to you know who.'

'Sorry about that.'

'Sure you are.'

'But I might know an easy way to lay our hands on some cash.'

'Yeah?'

'Unless you already did something with it, there should be a wallet back there.' She jabbed her thumb toward the rear of the van.

'Huh?' Toby asked.

'Has Duane still got his clothes on?'

'*Yeah!* Told you, I ain't a pervert.'

'When he left his apartment tonight, he had a wallet in the back pocket of his shorts. It probably has *lots* of cash in it.'

'Holy shit,' Toby said.

Chapter Twenty-one

'You gonna stay put?' Toby asked.

'Whatever you want,' Sherry told him. 'Do you need me to help with something?'

'Just don't try running away.'

'I won't.'

'Maybe you better stay here.'

'All right.'

'Put on your seat belt.'

Sherry pulled the seat belt down across her chest and lap and snapped its buckle into place.

Toby plucked out the ignition key. With the key in one hand and his knife in the other, he climbed between the seats. He stepped behind Sherry and said, 'I'm just gonna put this around you.' A strap of some sort dropped past her eyes, fell onto her shoulders for a moment, then closed softly around her neck.

It seemed to be a cloth belt. Probably from the robe Toby was wearing.

'I'm just gonna tie it to the headrest,' he explained. 'It's for your own good. 'Cause if you try and run away again, I'll have to kill you.'

'I won't try to run. But if this makes you feel better, fine.'

'There. How's that?'

'Fine.'

'Not too tight?'

'No.' Leaning forward slightly, she felt the belt press against her throat. She settled back in her seat and the pressure went away. 'It's okay,' she said.

'Good. I don't want to hurt you.'

Oh, that's obvious.

Toby's hand came over the top of the seat back and patted her right shoulder. Then it moved downward, pressing her gently through her blouse, until his fingers covered her breast.

Sherry wanted to shove his hand away.

She resisted the urge.

I try to stop him, he'll do something worse.

He slid her blouse to the side and his hand drifted over the bare skin of her breast.

The feel of it gave Sherry gooseflesh. As the bumps crawled over her body, her nipples grew hard and stiff. Her right nipple prodded Toby's hand. Moaning, he rubbed it between his thumb and forefinger.

She grabbed his wrist. 'Stop it,' she said.

'Let go.'

'*You* let go.' She tried to pull his hand away.

He twisted her nipple and she yelped with pain, but then he let go and she released his wrist and he swatted the side of her face.

Not saying a word, he went away.

The pain quickly subsided from Sherry's nipple and face, leaving them hot and tingly. She blinked tears out of her eyes. As they slid down her cheeks, she took deep, trembling breaths.

Stupid! What'd I try to stop him for? All it did was give him an excuse to hurt me.

He probably liked it, she thought. Hell, he probably *loved* it.

Next time, just let him do what he wants.

'All *right*!' Toby blurted from the rear of the van. 'Got it!'

'Go to hell,' Sherry said.

Idiot! Don't piss him off!

'What's wrong with *you?*' he asked.

'Nothing,' she muttered.

'Want me to come up there?'

No!

Afraid to answer his question, she asked, 'How much money did you find?'

'I don't know. I can't see. But there's *some*.'

'What about his clothes?'

'What about them?'
'Are they okay to wear?'
'Wear? Who?'
'You.'
'No way. You gotta be kidding. It's like he *exploded* in 'em.'
What did you do *to him?* She almost asked, but didn't dare. She didn't want to know. She knew too much, already.
'I'm gonna try and get him outa here,' Toby said. 'Stay put.'
Eyes forward, Sherry heard the rear doors squawk open. The van shook slightly. Then she heard quiet, sliding sounds, a little like a wet mop, but heavier.
Duane.
She supposed that Toby was standing behind the van, dragging Duane's body out by the ankles.
The van lurched.
Then she heard a heavy, moist *whop!* Duane's body hitting the concrete? She expected the *whop!* to be followed quickly by the *thunk!* of his head.
The *thunk* didn't come.
Oh, yeah, Sherry thought.
She suddenly felt very much like screaming.
Don't! For godsake, don't!
The van's rear doors squawked and banged shut.
In the side mirror, she saw Toby behind the van. He wore the pink robe. Without the belt, it hung open like an overcoat. He was walking backward, bent over, dragging Duane by the ankles. Duane's legs were bare, his shorts rucked up high around his thighs. The lap of the shorts was soaked with blood. The belt was unfastened, the waist open, the zipper down.
Sherry turned her head away and shut her eyes.
What did *he do?*
Her mind suddenly shrieked, *I'VE GOTTA GET OUT OF HERE!!!*
She reached down and clawed open her seat-belt buckle, then hooked both hands under the cloth belt at her throat. She tugged it. The cloth stretched and made quiet sounds like groans, but didn't break.
STOP IT! DON'T DO IT!

She quit straining at the belt.

I've gotta be smarter than this. If I just leap out and make a run for it, he'll nail me.

She released her grip on the belt and lowered her hands to her lap.

What I've gotta do, she told herself, is go along with everything. Stop fighting him. Stop trying to get away.

She drew down the seat belt and snapped its buckle into place.

Stay calm and wait for the right time.

She turned her head and again looked at the side mirror. Toby and Duane were no longer in sight.

How long have I got? she wondered.

No way of knowing.

Enough time to make a call?

But Toby had jerked the phone's plug out of the cigarette lighter and thrown the phone to the floor. It was probably in front of the passenger seat somewhere. In the darkness, it would be hard to find.

And she couldn't even *try* without freeing herself from the belt around her neck.

And if she *did* manage to find the phone and plug it in, the damn thing wouldn't work *anyway* without the engine going – and Toby had taken the ignition key.

Forget it, she thought.

What about honking the horn?

With the engine off, it might not work, either. But even if it let out a blast loud enough to wake the dead, it'd probably do her more harm than good.

In an area like this, people learn to ignore such late-night sounds as car horns, burglar alarms, gunshots, shouts and screams. The chances of anyone coming to the rescue were slim to none.

More than likely, *Toby* would be the first to respond.

The hell with that, Sherry thought.

She checked both the side mirrors, then opened the console to the right of her seat. She knew it was where Duane liked to store his cell phone. She also knew he kept a coin purse, a few maps, and some napkins inside it.

But what else?

She took out several napkins and dropped them onto her lap. Then she thrust her hand into the deep compartment and felt around.

Ever since the '92 riots, a lot of LA people carried handguns in their cars. Sherry did. So did most of her friends. It was illegal, but they figured they would rather face a jury than a funeral. So they hid a firearm in their glove compartment, in their console, under their seat, or even in a special holster secured out of sight beneath the dashboard.

Not that Duane'll have one.

Unless he's the biggest hypocrite on the face of the earth.

Was.

He used to call Sherry a 'gun nut' and argue, 'A gun never solved anything.'

Doesn't mean he hasn't got one, Sherry told herself as she rummaged through the console. Every so often, it turned out that some of the biggest anti gun activists in the country were packing firearms in secret. They wanted to take away everybody's guns except their own.

If Duane had one, though, he wasn't keeping it in his console. Not a gun, no weapon or tool of any sort. Not even so much as a can opener.

Sherry lowered the lid.

With the belt around her neck, she couldn't reach the glove compartment. She couldn't reach under her seat, either.

Nothing to find, anyway, she thought.

Thanks for killing me, Duane.

She suddenly felt glad that she'd never made love with him.

Then she felt sick about thinking such a thing.

I got him killed, and I never even let him have me. Always put it off, made excuses . . . as if we had all the time in the world. And now he's dead.

Is this his way of getting back at me? she wondered.

For what? For not making it with him? Or for sending him out to buy condoms? Or for bringing a homicidal lunatic stalker into his life and getting him murdered?

He's got plenty of reasons to hate me, Sherry thought. But they had nothing to do with depriving her of the means to save her own life.

Blame that on dumb, misguided idealism. You didn't believe in guns, Duane, so I pay the price.

She wished this was her Jeep Cherokee.

She carried a .380 in the console. By now, she would have it in her hand . . .

It's not in my Jeep *now*, she realized. She'd removed the automatic and left it in her apartment before taking her car in for the transmission repairs.

What if I can get Toby to take me there?

Earlier, not even thinking about her gun, she'd tried to talk him into it. The idea was so they could use the bed. For some reason, he'd been against going there.

Oh, yeah. Because I'm friendly with my neighbors.

Good old friendly me, she thought.

Using one of the napkins, she dabbed at the cut beneath her left breast. It no longer seemed to be bleeding. She wiped the area below it all the way down to the waistband of her skirt. Then she gently touched the wound with a fingertip. The sting made her wince, but she eased her finger along the length of it. The cut seemed to be a curving line about three inches long, but very shallow.

Wherever we go, she thought, I'd better try to put some antiseptic on it. And a bandage. He must have some first-aid supplies . . .

Sherry suddenly remembered that, during the same earlier discussion about where to find themselves a bed, Toby had spoken up *against* taking her to his place. But even earlier, he'd mentioned *wanting* to take her there.

Can't make up his mind about that.

Probably has something to do with Sid. Whoever the hell *Sid* is.

Sid's the guy who kills Toby for losing the car keys.

So he's living with his mother *and* this Sid?

Maybe Sid's his stepfather.

Keeping her eyes on the side mirror, Sherry picked up a fresh napkin and gently wiped her face. The soft paper's dryness felt good, rubbing through the sweat and grime – and probably blood.

Whoever Sid is, she thought, it sounds as if he's strict with

Toby. Maybe he'll take my side. Or maybe the mother will.

On the other hand, the gun's at *my* apartment.

I know damn well it'll *take my side.*

Toby's reflection rushed across the side mirror. He was running up the alley, naked from the shoulders down, the beltless robe flowing behind him in the wind, the butcher knife waving in his right hand.

Chapter Twenty-two

Toby climbed into the van and closed the door. He was panting for breath. Lowering the knife against his bare thigh, he slumped low in the passenger seat.

'Did it,' he gasped.

'Where'd you put him?' Sherry asked.

Toby shook his head. 'Just . . . Couldn't pick him up. Too heavy. So I . . . hadda just drag him.'

Though Sherry had seen him drag Duane past the rear of the van, she decided not to mention it. If she told about seeing the body, Toby might suspect she'd noticed Duane's open, bloody shorts.

She didn't want to go where that might lead.

'So you *didn't* put him in a dumpster?' she asked.

'Huh-uh.'

At least Duane had been spared *that*.

'Where did you leave him?'

'Found a . . . laundry room. Unlocked. Just off the alley. You know, like what they have . . . for apartment people. Dragged him in.' Toby let out a couple of gaspy laughs. 'Almost did a load. His stuff. Figured . . . we wait here till it's clean.' He shook his head. 'Too much mess. I just . . . left him on the floor and got outa there.'

Thank God, Sherry thought. She hated to think what Toby might've wanted to do if they'd had to wait for the clothes to get done.

'Are we ready to go?' she asked him.

'Go where?' he asked.

'It's up to you. We can go to my place or yours.'

'Why not . . . stay here a while?'

Sherry cringed. 'Here?'

'We can go in the back of the van. You know? And lie down. There's blankets. We can rest and stuff.'

And stuff.

'Just for maybe like an hour,' Toby added.

'Isn't it *messy* back there?'

'Sort of,' he admitted. 'But it's nothing that won't wash off.'

'You ever try to wash blood out of clothes?'

'We'll leave our clothes here on the front seats.'

Oh, this is getting better and better.

'It sounds like a pretty neat idea,' Sherry said. 'But you know what? Wouldn't you rather wait till we're someplace safe? Where we'll have privacy?'

'We got privacy here.'

'Right now, we do. But this is somebody's regular parking stall, Toby. They might come back any minute.'

'Well, yeah.'

'Also, there's no telling when somebody might go into the laundry room and find Duane. If *that* happened, we could have cops up the ying-yang.'

'I guess,' Toby muttered. 'But I bet nobody's gonna find him till morning.'

'We shouldn't take a chance like that. Not when it'd be so easy to drive somewhere else.'

'I don't mind staying here.'

I do!

Sherry turned her head, feeling the soft rub of the belt against her neck, and looked at Toby. 'Anyway, there's no bed here. Didn't we already agree that we wanted to wait and do it on a bed?'

In the darkness, she saw the vague shape of his shoulders rise and fall. 'I don't know.'

'And we wanted to take a shower first. Together.'

'Yeah?' He sounded a little confused, but pleased.

'Yeah. We agreed, didn't we? To take a nice long shower together before we get in bed? We'll soap each other all over till we're squeaky clean. You want to do that, don't you?'

'Yeah.'

'Well, we can't do that here.'

'We can do it at my house.'

'Or at my apartment. If we go to *your* house, Sid might not *let* you take a shower with me. He might not let you do *anything* with me. At *my* place, there'd only be the two of us.'

He moaned with indecision then said, 'I don't know.'

'If we go to my place,' Sherry said, 'we can skip that stuff about crashing the van and . . .' An idea struck her. '*I've* got screwdrivers.'

'Huh?'

'If we need to take the license plates off the van, *I* have screwdrivers. Which means we won't have to buy one at the Speed-D-Mart.'

'We got money now,' Toby pointed out.

'Yeah, but look at how we're dressed. Neither of us can go in a store like this. Now we won't have to. *And* we can change into some clothes so we don't look . . .' She shook her head. 'Face it, anybody who sees us is going to *know* something is wrong.'

'That's for sure,' Toby muttered.

'At my place, we can put on some decent clothes.'

'You got *guy* stuff?'

'We'll find you something to wear. I mean, just about anything would be better than that bloody robe, don't you think?'

'Guess so.'

'And we can do whatever we want and we won't need to worry about Sid bothering us.'

'Yeah, okay.' Toby put the key into her hand.

'Before we go,' she said, 'you'd better take this belt off me. If we happen to drive past a cop and he happens to look over this way . . .'

'Good idea.' Toby clamped the knife between his teeth, then climbed through the space between the seats. Standing behind Sherry, he started to untie the belt.

She slid the key into the ignition.

'Don't start it yet,' Toby said.

'I won't'

I could!

She saw herself twist the key and gun the engine and plow through the wall.

That'd sure catch somebody's attention, she thought. But how's it suppose to save me? I'd still be stuck in the van with Toby. He'd have plenty of time to kill me before anyone came along to see who'd wrecked the carport.

And then he might kill some of them.

Besides, she told herself, it'd be incredibly stupid to do anything risky at this point.

Save the risky stuff for when we get . . .

'Got it,' Toby said. He slipped the cloth belt away from her neck.

But he didn't come back to his seat. A few seconds after removing the belt, he reached down from behind Sherry with both hands. He spread her blouse wide open and cupped her breasts.

Sherry gripped the steering wheel.

Toby's hands moved gently. She could feel them trembling. They caressed her slowly, lightly, as if studying the texture of her skin. 'So smooth,' he whispered.

'Thanks.'

'These're my first.'

Wonderful to hear it.

'Really,' she muttered.

'Yeah. Nobody else has ever let me. Just . . . never mind. She doesn't count.'

Whose breasts don't count? Sherry wondered. And *why* not?

'Oh, now they're getting goosebumpy.'

That's 'cause you make my skin crawl.

'That's because it feels so good,' she said. 'The way you're touching them.'

'Yeah?'

'Yeah,' she said.

His thumbs glided in circles around her nipples. The feel of them made her want to shudder.

Just take it easy, she told herself. Go along with it. Go along with everything. Let him do whatever he wants. The only thing that matters is getting out of this alive.

Unraped, if possible – but alive, that's the main thing.

Behind her, Toby moaned.

Sherry began to writhe in her seat.

When his hands tightened on her breasts, she moaned as if lost in pleasure.

Don't overdo it.

I'm his prisoner and I've gotta act like it or he'll figure I'm up to something.

'We'd better stop now,' she said.

Toby squeezed her right breast so hard she gasped and flinched rigid.

'We stop when I *wanta* stop,' he said.

'I know. I wasn't . . . I just meant . . . we don't want to get *caught* here, do we? Don't we want to go over to *my* place?'

'Maybe, maybe not.'

'I thought we agreed . . . *Ow!*' She twitched with pain as he drew a fingernail along her cut.

'We didn't agree on nothing.' He took his hands away from her breasts and slapped her face, whapping the right side, then the left, then the right, then the left, his open hands taking turns, striking her just hard enough to make each side of her face sting, then burn.

Soon she began to cry, but she kept her own hands on the steering wheel, knowing she would only make matters worse if she tried to resist.

He'll pay for this!

He'll pay for everything!

He kept slapping the sides of her face.

Then, through her sobbing sounds and the quick claps of the blows, she heard Toby start to laugh.

Thinks this is funny?

Sherry suddenly realized that she was wrong about the strange, gaspy sounds. They weren't laughter.

He's crying!

He gasped and sobbed and choked as he smacked her.

Sherry twisted the ignition key. As the engine grumbled to life, Toby's hands went still. 'What're you . . . doing?' he blurted.

'Getting us out of here.' She shoved the shift lever to reverse and backed the van out of the carport. 'You'd better take your seat.'

His two hands clutched her neck.

She swung the van into the middle of the alley and eased it to a halt.

He still had her by the throat, but he wasn't squeezing very hard.

'I'm not trying to pull anything, Toby. But we'll be in trouble if we don't get away from here.'

'What do *you* care?'

'I don't want to be caught in the middle.' She put on the headlights, took her foot off the brake, and started driving slowly up the alley. 'Why don't you get back into your seat before you fall down? I'll drive wherever you want me to.'

'Promise?'

'I promise.'

'No tricks?'

'No tricks.'

'Better not be.'

Sherry eased the van to a halt.

Toby took his hands away from her neck. When he climbed into the front and sank into his seat, his robe hung open. He held the knife in his right hand. With his left hand, he wiped his eyes.

'Are you okay?' Sherry asked.

'Yeah.' He sniffed.

'What the hell were you crying about? I was the one getting hit.'

'They were . . . tears of joy.'

Chapter Twenty-three

'Did you decide we'll go to my place?' Sherry asked, starting the van forward again.

'Yeah. Yeah, I guess.'

She stopped at the end of the alley, took a few seconds to pull her blouse shut, then turned onto the street. 'We're not very far away,' she said.

'I know. I been there, remember?'

'Oh, yeah.'

'I been there a lot.'

Obviously, he'd been there often enough to notice that Sherry was on friendly terms with quite a few of the other tenants.

But had he been inside?

Maybe not. He could've made those observations by catching glimpses of her through the courtyard gates. Or by watching her arrive or depart.

Her building didn't have a subterranean parking lot like Duane's: just rows of parking stalls at the front and back. Her space was in front. Toby might've easily watched her leave the building with a neighbor, chatting as they went to their cars.

'How we gonna get in?' Toby asked.

Sherry felt a sudden collapse inside.

Oh, my God!

'You got keys?' Toby asked.

'No. I . . . They're in my purse.'

'And where's that?'

'In your car, I guess.'

'That's where it's at, all right.' He laughed or sobbed quietly, sniffed and rubbed his eyes. 'Looks like every damn thing you or me own is locked up someplace.'

'Where's your car?'

'None of your business.'

'All we have to do is go to your car and get my purse out. Then I'll have my keys and we can drive on over . . .'

'How we gonna get *into* my car? I locked it up and took *my* keys with me – and you locked *them* up in Duane's room. Which probably has cops in it by now.'

'Can't we get my purse, anyway?'

'How?'

'Maybe your car isn't locked. Maybe one of the back doors, or something . . .'

'It's locked, all right. It's got one of those remote-control dealies where you push a button and it locks *all* the doors. Sets the alarm, too.'

'Your car has an alarm?'

'Sure does. So if we go fooling around trying to break in, we'll set it off.'

'Nobody pays attention to those things, anyway. Especially not on a night like this. They'll just think the wind set it off.'

'So what do you wanta do, bust a window?'

'It's an idea.'

'Forget it,' Toby said. 'It's Sid's car. I take it home fucked up, he'll kill me.'

'He doesn't have to know *we* did it. You can tell him a branch blew off a tree, or . . .'

'No way.' Toby shook his head. 'You think he's gonna care *how* it got busted? He'll say it's my fault, no matter what.'

'That doesn't sound fair,' Sherry said.

'Nothing fair about Sid.'

'Why do you put up with him?'

'I got no choice.'

'There's always a choice.'

'Think so, huh? That shows how much *you* know. Teacher or not.'

'Is Sid your father?' she asked.

Toby shook his head.

'Stepfather?'

'Brother.'

'He's just your *brother*? The way you talk about him, I

thought he must be your mean old stepfather or something.'
'He's my older brother.'
'And you let him run your life like—?'
Toby punched her in the upper arm. Yelping, she grabbed it with her left hand.
'He don't run my life,' Toby said. '*I* run my life.'
'Sorry.'
'Just shut the fuck up.'
Clutching her arm, she steered with her right hand, blinked tears out of her eyes and kept her mouth shut.
'I guess we don't go to your place after all,' Toby said. He sounded disappointed. 'Fuck. I been wanting to see what it's like inside. See your stuff, you know. I've tried to look through your windows, only the curtains are always shut too tight.'
'What windows?'
'The big ones in front.'
Her apartment, on the second story, could only be reached by climbing stairs to the balcony that overlooked the courtyard and swimming pool. Her front door faced the balcony – and so did the two big windows of her living room and bedroom.
'You've gotten into the courtyard?' she asked.
'Oh, sure. It's not so hard. Know what? I've even used the pool a few times. Know what else? You've *seen* me down at the pool.'
'You're kidding,' she muttered, feeling her gooseflesh return.
'Yep. You even said hi to me once. I was down by the pool in my swimming suit and sunglasses and hat and everything. Had a towel with me, and I was pretending to read a book. I looked just like I belonged there.' He chuckled. '*Every*body thought I belonged there.'
'Terrific,' she muttered.
'You can get away with all kinds of stuff if you play it right.'
'Could you get us inside the courtyard tonight?' she asked.
'Yeah, but so what?'
'If you can get us that far, I can probably get us into my apartment.'
'Yeah? How? Bust a window?'

'The bedroom window's just an old piece of crap with a broken lock. And there isn't any screen on it.'

'You kidding me?' Toby asked.

'I'm surprised you never noticed – what with all your snooping and peeping.'

'I never *tried* to bust in,' he said, sounding offended. 'All I wanted to do was look.'

'Oh really?'

'Yeah. I never wanted to *do* anything to you.'

'I guess that changed tonight,' Sherry muttered.

'Yeah. Well. What can I say? Opportunity knocked.'

That was me sending Duane to the store. I triggered the whole damn thing. Sent him to his death.

We get into my apartment, she thought, and I'll trigger *Toby*.

'Should we go ahead and give my place a try?' she asked.

'Yeah. Why not? If you think you can get us in.'

'I'm pretty sure I can.'

'Okay, then. We'll give it a try. But you better remember a couple of things. Like how you gave me your word you'd cooperate.'

'I'm cooperating, aren't I?'

'So far. But you better remember something else, too. Remember what I do to people. If you don't want to get anyone else killed, you better do everything I tell you.'

'Everything,' she said. 'I promise.'

Midway down the next block, they came to her apartment building. Sherry slowed down, then turned onto the broad driveway.

'What're you doing?

'We might as well park in my stall,' she said.

'I don't know if that's such a hot idea.'

'This is *Duane's* van,' she reminded him, steering into the sheltered slot. 'People are used to seeing it around here. Not that anybody's likely to be up and around at this hour, anyway.'

Toby nodded and mumbled something.

Sherry stopped. She shut off the lights and engine, then pulled out the ignition key.

'Put it on the floor. We don't wanta be losing that, too.'

She unfastened her seat belt, eased the straps out of her way, reached down between her legs and dropped the key to the floor.

'Stay put,' Toby said. 'I'll come around to your side.' He threw open the passenger door, eased it shut and walked toward the rear of the van.

Is this a test? Sherry wondered.

She sat still and waited for him.

With the point of his knife, he tapped against the window of her door.

She opened the door and climbed out.

'You go first,' Toby said.

Walking through the narrow space between Duane's van and the Mazda parked beside it, Sherry pulled her blouse shut and tucked it under the waistband of her skirt. She felt bare skin down there where her underpants should've been.

'Front gate?' she asked, stepping out into the light and wind behind the parking spaces.

'Yeah.'

She turned toward the main entrance. The wind huffed in her face, flapped her blouse and skirt, tossed leaves against her legs. She clenched her blouse shut with one hand. With the other, she pressed her skirt against her thigh.

Toby, walking beside her, leaned into the wind and tried to keep his robe from flying open. He could use only his left hand; his right was hidden inside the robe, keeping his knife out of sight.

Sherry saw no cars coming. She saw nobody out for a stroll or a jog, nobody walking a dog. No bums were skulking about or trudging along behind shopping carts.

Fine, Sherry told herself. It's just as well. I might be tempted to make a break, yell for help . . .

It *would* be nice, she thought, for a cop car to come along right about now.

That happens, I'll take the risk.

She stepped into the recessed area of her building's entryway. Sheltered from the wind, she leaned back against the stucco wall.

Toby walked past her. At the gate, he tried the handle.

'It locks automatically,' Sherry said.

'I know. Just thought I'd check.'

He came over and stood in front of her. 'Hold this,' he said. He took off his robe and handed it to her. But he kept the butcher knife.

'What are you going to do?' Sherry asked.

'Go over the top.'

She frowned at the double doors of the gate. Between the iron top rails and the ceiling of the entryway, she saw a narrow space. 'You can't get through that,' she said.

'Wanta bet?'

'Is *that* how you sneak in?'

'Sometimes. When nobody's around. I've got lots of ways.'

Up on top, it would be a tight fit for Toby. Sherry supposed it was possible for him to squeeze through – if he really sucked in his gut – but the struggle was bound to take him a while.

If she waited till just the right moment, she could probably make a clean getaway.

Run like hell for the van. I know right where the key is.

'Let's see you do it,' she said.

Toby grinned strangely. 'You know what?' he said. 'When I'm up top trying to get through, I bet you'll try and run off.'

'I won't,' she said. 'I promise.'

'Know what?'

'What?'

'Two-eight-three-two Clifton.'

Once again, she felt herself collapsing inside.

'Know who lives there?'

She nodded.

'So do I.'

'My God,' she muttered.

'What do you guess I might do to your mommy and daddy and little sister if you run off and leave me?'

Stunned, she muttered, 'I won't go anywhere.'

'I almost hope you do,' Toby said. 'Your mom's almost as pretty as you, and Brenda . . . Mmmm, Brenda.' Still grinning, he spread his arms and looked down at himself. 'Look at that! That's what happens just thinking about her.'

You'll never get the chance, you sick fuck.
'Just shut up and climb the damn gate,' Sherry said.

Chapter Twenty-four

Here came his left hand. It clutched Sherry's throat and shoved her head against the stucco wall. Down low, the knife punched through the front of her skirt then hit the stucco. He pulled it straight upward between her legs, the point scraping the wall, her skirt rising.

Sherry flinched and dropped the robe when the steel edge touched her.

'Say you're sorry,' Toby whispered.

'I'm sorry.'

'How sorry?'

'*Very* sorry.'

The knife moved upward. Gasping, Sherry tried to rise to her tiptoes but the hand at her throat kept her pinned to the wall.

'Are you ever gonna tell me to shut up again?' Toby asked, grinning.

'No.'

'You ever gonna try and *order me around*?'

'No.'

'You ever gonna try and run away?'

'No.'

'How would you like me to give it to you with my knife?'

'I wish you wouldn't. But . . . whatever you want.'

'Good! You get an A-plus!' He lowered the knife away from her flesh. Then he jerked downward. Sherry felt a tug at her waistband, heard the rip of fabric, felt another tug as the knife tore through the hem of her skirt. Still clutching her throat, Toby said, 'What're you gonna do when I climb the gate?'

'Whatever you want.'

'I want you to just stand here. Don't move a muscle.'

'Okay.'

He released her throat, then turned away and walked to the gate. Squatting, he reached between two of the horizontal bars and set down his knife on the concrete.

Sherry felt warm dribbles trickling down her inner thighs.

Blood?

Toby straightened up. Head tilted back, he seemed to be studying the top of the gate.

Sherry slipped a hand through the slit in her skirt. Though she felt no cut between her legs, wetness smeared her fingertips.

Reaching high, Toby grabbed the top rail with both hands. He jumped, pulling himself up, and slammed against the gate. It clanked with the impact. The fat of his naked body shimmied. He jerked up his left leg and managed to plant his foot on the knob.

Sherry took her hand out and looked at it. Her fingers were shiny, but not red. Just perspiration, she supposed.

With the knob as a foothold, Toby pulled himself up. He ducked headfirst through the narrow opening above the gate. His shoulders followed. Then all Sherry could see of him were his thick legs and a pair of sweaty, jiggling buttocks.

He squirmed sideways and swung his right leg up and hooked his thigh over the top.

He's gonna make it, Sherry thought.

She latched her eyes on the butcher knife.

Though on the other side of the gate, it was near enough to grab if she crouched and reached through the bars.

Toby now had one leg on each side of the gate, his belly and chest pressing into the top rail, his back against the stucco ceiling of the passageway. He groaned and squirmed, struggling to squeeze through.

Do it! Grab the knife . . .

Or run and get the hell away from him!

Then he goes after Brenda?

Just stay put, she told herself. Don't move a muscle. Not unless you're *sure* you can kill him.

In her mind, she saw herself make a mad dash for the gate

as Toby, straddling its top, squirmed in a frenzy and shouted curses and threats. She ducked and reached through the bars and grabbed the knife. Then she sprang up. But even as she drove the blade toward Toby's bare flank, he dropped out of reach. He fell to the pavement on the other side of the gate and yelled, *'Now you're gonna get it! Now you're* all *gonna get it! You and your whole fucking family!'*

'Easy as pie,' Toby said.

The chance was gone.

He'd made it over the top of the gate and now stood on the other side, arms stretched high, hands still clutching the top rail. He was panting hard for breath. His body ran with so much sweat that he looked as if he'd just stepped out of a shower. But he seemed very pleased. His face, between two bars, grinned at Sherry. Lower, his penis jutted out, rigid and pointing at her face.

'Don't forget my robe,' he said. He let go and backed away from the gate. 'You were a very good girl, Sherry.' He squatted and picked up his knife. Then, swinging open the gate, he said, 'Come on in.'

She followed his orders.

After easing the gate shut, Toby took the robe from her. He put it on, but allowed it to hang open. 'You go first,' he said.

She headed for the stairway. In front of her, the swimming pool was dark but its surface shimmered with the reflections of several porch lights. She saw no one. She saw no lighted windows.

Is *everybody* asleep? she wondered. That hardly seemed possible. Even on a good night, some people probably had trouble sleeping, got out of bed to use the toilet or watch some television or read a book – or look out the windows. Tonight, with the wind moaning and squealing and slamming things about, plenty of people must be wide awake.

But she saw no evidence of it.

Let's keep it that way, she thought. The last thing I need is anyone else getting involved.

She walked to the stairway. With Toby just behind her, she began to climb. The steps felt rock-hard under her bare right foot, soft and springy through the shoe on her left. Neither footfall made any sound that might be heard through the raging wind.

The surrounding walls sheltered her from the wind until she reached the balcony. There, she felt it swoop down and muss her hair and huff against her face. It fluttered the front of her blouse. It spread her ripped skirt and flew in, hot and dry against her wet skin.

She didn't bother trying to hold her clothes together. There was nobody to see, and the wind felt good.

Every window she walked past was dark.

And shut.

The doors were all shut, too.

She heard no sound from inside any of the apartments.

Everybody *must* be asleep, she thought.

And then she walked past a picture window and saw deep into a moonlit living room.

The curtains are open!

She glimpsed the dim shapes of furniture and a few tiny bright red numbers at the far side of the room. A clock or VCR, she supposed.

She looked away quickly.

Was anyone *in* there? she wondered.

Ronnie, maybe? Or Chris?

They were both flight attendants and worked unusual hours. One or the other of them might very well be awake.

Sitting in the dark, looking out, seeing us walk by?

What a sight *we'd* be, she thought. We must look like something from a nightmare.

If you saw us, just stay out of it. Please.

Maybe they're not even home, Sherry told herself. They might be away on flights, or on overnight dates, or on vacation somewhere.

If they're home, Sherry thought, they probably would've closed the curtains after dark.

The picture window was now behind her. So far, Toby hadn't mentioned it. He must've noticed it, though.

Just a few paces past Chris and Ronnie's door, Sherry came to her own bedroom window. Set higher in the wall than the picture windows, its bottom sill was level with her chest.

Looking around, she saw only Toby.

'Go on and open it,' he whispered.

She turned toward the window, pressed both hands against the glass and tried to slide it sideways. Her hands slipped. The window stayed put. Reaching out with her left hand, she pulled at the edge of the frame while trying again to thrust the glass sideways with her right.

It still refused to move.

'You sure it's not locked?' Toby whispered.

'It's just a little stuck. Maybe you can get it started with your knife.'

He stepped in, shouldering her out of the way. With the tip of his knife, he delved into the crack at the window's edge. He worked the blade sideways. The crack suddenly spread open wide enough for fingertips.

'That ought to do it,' he said. He stepped back.

Sherry dug her fingertips into the narrow gap. As she skidded the window toward the center, a gust flung the curtain inward and bells jingled. She cringed.

'What's that?'

'Christmas bells.'

'Huh?'

'I hung some sleigh bells on the window. You know, so I'll know if somebody tries to get in.'

'How come you didn't just get the lock fixed?'

'I've had to get in this way a couple of times. And the landlord's a creep. I don't ask him for *any*thing.'

'I could take care of him for you.'

She forced herself to smile. 'Thanks, Toby. I might just take you up on that.'

'My pleasure,' he said. He switched the knife to his left hand, then gave Sherry a pat on the rump. After the pat, his hand cupped her buttock through the fabric of her skirt. 'Go on and climb in. But don't forget what happens if you try to pull something.'

'What do you want me to do after I'm inside?'

'Nothing. Just wait. I'll come in right behind you.'

Sherry thought about her pistol. Before taking her Jeep in for repairs, she always removed it and left it on the bookshelf just inside her front door.

'If you'd like,' she whispered, 'I could just walk through and open the front door for you.'

'Thanks anyway.'

'Just trying to make things easier.'

'Don't bother.' He gave her rump a couple of gentle pats, then said, 'Climb on in.'

'Okay.'

Sherry planted both hands on the windowsill, jumped, thrust herself up and caught the edge of the sill with her right knee. She brought up her other knee. Perched precariously, she raised her arms and found handholds – her left hand clutching the frame, her right hand gripping the side of the open window itself.

As she knelt there, the curtain deflated. It drifted in, brushed against her face, then sailed off.

Though she *had* climbed in this way a few times, she wasn't exactly sure how she'd maneuvered herself from this point. It seemed that she needed to bring one leg forward and get her foot on the sill. But which leg would be better to start with?

She flinched as Toby touched her.

His hand was underneath her skirt, an open curve against her thigh. Slowly, it drifted upward between her legs.

The curtain settled against her face. She turned her head aside.

She wanted to yell. She wanted to clamp her legs together. She wanted to reach down and stop Toby's hand.

But any quick moves might make her fall.

And if she tried to stop him . . .

Just let him.

Kneeling on the sill, she remained motionless except for her breathing and the quivering of her muscles as Toby's fingers stroked her, spread her, delved.

The curtain rubbed her cheek.

She felt Toby's thumb.

The gun's on the middle shelf, she told herself, trying not to think about what he was doing. I oughta just make a run for it. It's all set to go. One up the chute, five or six more in the magazine. All I've gotta do is pull the trigger.

Chapter Twenty-five

Toby took his hand away, but he didn't say anything. Twisting her head around, Sherry looked down at him. He was licking his fingers. As he slid his thumb into his mouth, he noticed her watching. He slowly pulled his thumb out. 'Go on in,' he said.

Though every muscle in her body seemed to be trembling, she struggled off her knees and managed to get both feet on to the windowsill. The curtain, briefly blown inward, came silently back at her. It slipped between her thighs, brushed against her face.

She couldn't see. The darkness was bad enough, but the curtains blinded her completely.

Reaching out with her left hand, she swept the curtain out of her way.

And lost her balance.

Left shoulder first, she started falling forward into the darkness.

Toby grabbed her skirt. She felt a rough tug at her waist. Her fall almost stopped. But then came a pop and a rip. The skirt went loose.

Loose but not gone, it snared her feet and kept them high as she plunged toward the floor.

On the way down, she struck nothing. She was apparently dropping into the narrow space between her bed and the side of her desk.

With her hands, she tried to break her fall.

They were bashed out of the way and her head struck the floor. For a moment, she felt as if she'd been propped upside-down and crooked against the wall. Then her legs started to drop. Her rump and back followed them toward the floor.

Shit!

She bent her back and jerked her knees toward her chest.

Instead of slamming down with a stunning crash, she rolled quietly to a sitting position.

She jerked her head around.

The blowing curtain let her see Toby as he boosted himself onto the windowsill. When his body blocked the wind, the curtain swept toward him.

Sherry struggled to her feet. Her bedroom doorway was straight ahead, its opening darker than the walls. She staggered over to it. In the hallway, she dodged to the right and broke into a run for the living room.

From behind her came a heavy thud – Toby hitting the floor?

The people under us must think . . .

No, they'd moved out a few days ago. There *isn't* anybody under us.

'*Sherry?*' Toby's voice was a harsh whisper. '*Sherry!*'

She suddenly heard his footfalls.

Here he comes!

After the deep darkness of the hallway, the living room seemed almost bright. The curtain across the picture window looked like a dimly glowing wall. It cast a gray luminescence over the couch and the coffee table, but it left the front door in utter blackness.

Sherry couldn't see the bookshelf at all.

She raced for it, anyway, dashing past the coffee table then turning toward the door.

Toby sounded as if he might already be in the room.

She hurled herself against the door, reached out past its jamb and slapped the light switch. The room filled with light. She heard Toby gasping, running, but she didn't look at him.

Instead, she twisted away from the door and lunged for the bookshelf.

The place near the front edge of the middle shelf, where she'd left her pistol, was empty.

No!

As Toby pounded toward her from behind, she raced her eyes up and down the whole bookcase.

It has *to be here!*

She suddenly remembered Duane.

Because her Jeep was in for repairs, Duane had come here to pick her up for their evening together. But she hadn't been quite ready to leave, so she'd left him alone for a few minutes. Coming out of the bathroom, she'd found him in front of the bookshelf with the pistol in his hand. 'You really shouldn't leave something like this out in plain sight, Sherry. You shouldn't have one at all, but that's beside the point. What if a kid came in and—?'

'Kids don't *come* in.'

'You should at least keep it somewhere out of sight.' With that, he'd reached up to the top shelf, pulled out a handful of hardbacks, placed the pistol at the rear of the shelf, then returned the books to their place. Looking pleased with himself, he'd said, 'Now some stranger won't come in and end up shooting somebody with it.'

Not wanting to begin their evening with an argument, Sherry had nodded and smiled. 'Good idea,' she'd said. She would be away from the apartment, anyway.

Gotta make sure I take it out of there when I get back.

The moment she remembered what Duane had done, she reached for the highest shelf with both hands. The books were in her way. She clawed at them. Seven or eight flew forward, falling, some of them hitting her face and shoulders and chest.

Fingernails suddenly scratched the nape of her neck and she was jerked backward by the shoulders of her blouse. As she stumbled away from the shelves, Toby swung her to the right. A corner of the couch clipped her leg out from under her. She slammed down sideways on her coffee table, skidded across it and tumbled off the other side. Her back struck the floor.

She tried to raise her head off the floor, but couldn't work up the strength.

What's he doing?

Pretty soon, the coffee table slid out of the way. Then Toby loomed over her. Standing on his left foot, he rested his bare right foot on her belly. His robe was gone. Sweat was spilling down his body as he huffed wildly for breath.

He held the butcher knife in his left hand, Sherry's semi-automatic pistol in his right.

'You were . . . gonna kill me,' he gasped.

Blinking sweat and panting for air, she stared up at him and didn't try to answer.

'I . . . warned ya . . . what'd happen.'

'Go to hell,' she said.

He gazed down at her and shook his head. 'Now you're . . . in for it.'

'Fuck you,' Sherry said.

'Huh-uh, fuck *you*.'

He stomped on her belly.

As her breath exploded out, her knees jerked up. Hugging her belly, she rolled onto her side and curled up.

'That's for starters,' Toby said.

She felt as if she'd been caved in. She couldn't breathe at all, just hugged her knees and struggled to drag air into her wide-open mouth – but couldn't.

Then something crashed against the side of her head.

Her brain seemed to detonate with a brilliant flash.

He shot me?

Chapter Twenty-six

What's going on?

Sherry's head throbbed with fiery pain and her scalp, just above her right temple, was stiff and wet. She felt something moving under the back of her head. Under her *whole* back. It was flat, rubbing her, making her burn.

The carpet?

She realized she was being dragged by her feet.

I'm still alive.

She thought about trying to open her eyes, but decided against it. Without her lids down, her eyes would burst into flames.

They won't, she told herself.

But they felt as if they might.

Anyway, let him think I'm out cold.

Maybe I *am*, she thought.

Or maybe I'm dead. Dead and dreaming that he's dragging me by my feet.

What if I'm dead and it all keeps going on?

Scared, she opened her eyes. They felt raw and hot, but she kept her lids open long enough to see that she was being dragged down the hallway by Toby. Apparently, the lamps were still on in the living room. They cast a dim glow on her elevated legs and on Toby. Both her feet were bare, now. Toby was clutching her ankles together out in front of him, leaning backward and towing her along like a bag of rocks.

He seemed to be staring at her breasts.

Sherry could tell by the feel that her blouse wasn't just wide open, it was gone.

She shut her eyes.

She wondered what to do.

What *can* I do?

Go with it. Just let it happen.

She wondered what Toby had done with the knife and pistol. He didn't have them with him, that was for sure.

Had he left them somewhere in the living room?

I'll just run right in and find them.

Sure.

Toby lowered her legs to the floor.

She heard his footsteps alongside her. They moved past her head and kept going. Opening one eye slightly, she saw her bedroom windows high on the wall beyond her feet. The windows were pale in the darkness and one side of the curtains was sailing high, flapping and shaking.

The desk lamp came on.

Sherry shut her eyes.

Toby walked up behind her head. He shoved his hands under her shoulders. As he lifted her into a sitting position, she let her head sway and flop. Staying limp, she felt him reach under her armpits, wrap his arms around her chest, and hoist her off the floor. In a tight hug, she was swung sideways. She landed on the mattress, Toby still clinging to her, heavy on her back.

He loosened his hold, but didn't climb off.

His hands, pressed between her body and the bed, moved around until they were underneath her breasts. He began to flex his fingers. His mouth opened against the side of her neck. He kissed her there, sucked and nibbled, while his hands plied her breasts and his body began to writhe.

He felt soft and hot and slimy on her back and buttocks. Soft except for his penis. She could feel it back there, big and rigid and sliding against her.

He's gonna get me this time, she thought. Nothing I can do to stop him.

Thanks for moving my gun, Duane.

In her mind, she heard him answer, *Thanks for sending me out for the condoms, Sherry.*

It's not Duane's fault, she told herself. Don't blame him.

It's Toby.

All Toby.

Gasping for air, Toby pulled his hands out from under Sherry and climbed off her. She could suddenly feel the wind rubbing against the sweaty skin of her back and buttocks.

Toby lifted her legs onto the bed. Then he turned her over. Shoving and pulling, he arranged her body so that she lay flat on her back with her arms down straight against her sides and her legs spread wide.

The wind blew down on her.

It felt good.

But she knew things were about to get very bad.

Here we go.

Keeping her eyes shut, she felt the mattress shift. Then there were hands on her thighs. She could feel them trembling as they slid upward. When they reached her groin, she heard Toby moan. Then she felt his mouth, his tongue.

His teeth.

Though she tried to remain limp, her body flinched with the sharp, sudden pain. Though she tried to stay silent, a quiet squeak escaped from her throat.

'Told you I'd eat you,' Toby said.

She raised her head off the mattress.

Toby raised his head and smiled at her. He had blood on his lips.

He went down again and thrust in his tongue, then took it out and began licking his way up her body. As his tongue lapped and probed, his hands glided up to her breasts. They squeezed her, pinched and pulled. Then his hands moved up to her shoulders and held her down while his mouth latched on to her right breast, pulled at her nipple, opened wide and sucked hard. She felt as if her whole breast were being drawn into his mouth.

She felt the edges of his teeth.

No!

Just when she was sure he would bite, he pulled his head back. Her breast popped out of his mouth with a sucking, slurpy sound and he planted his wet lips against her mouth and thrust in his tongue.

She thought about biting it.

But he could've chomped off half my breast and maybe he will if I bite his tongue.

She decided not to do it.

A moment later, Toby rammed his penis up deep into her and his mouth caught her outcry of pain and despair.

He turned off the lamp, then came back to the bed. He lay down beside Sherry. She hadn't changed her position, still lay sprawled on her back, arms at her side, legs spread. She supposed she *could* move, but she wasn't sure of it. She knew, however, that she didn't *want* to. She hurt everywhere. And if she moved, Toby might do something to make it worse.

He rolled toward her. His belly pushed against her side. Reaching across her chest, he curled a hand over her left breast. He eased his upper leg forward and rested it on the top of her right thigh. Then he squirmed, rubbing his penis against her hip. It felt soft and sticky.

'You know what?' he whispered.

Sherry didn't answer.

Toby stopped squirming, but she felt one of his fingertips slowly circling her nipple. 'You're the greatest.' He went silent. He hardly moved at all except for his belly pushing at her as he breathed, his fingers drifting lazily over her breast. She had goosebumps and her nipple was sticking up straight and rigid. Toby's fingers kept returning to it. 'Know what?' he whispered. 'This is the best night I ever had.'

She didn't say anything.

She could hardly even *think*; she felt too hurt and tired and defeated.

She closed her eyes. Tears slid out and trickled down toward her ears.

'I never . . . never even had a girlfriend before. Never did *any* of this stuff. Good news, huh? I mean, you're probably worried, me not using a rubber. AIDS and stuff. But I haven't got it. I'm a hundred percent healthy.'

'I've already got it,' she heard herself mutter.

Now *you've* got it, she wanted to add, but the words didn't come out.

Had she really spoken the first part?

Must've. And Toby must've heard it, too, because his hand was no longer fiddling with her breast.

She hadn't *planned* to say such a thing, hadn't given it any thought at all – it had just grumbled out. Apparently, her mind wasn't totally wrecked, after all.

Good going, she told herself.

Give him something to think about.

'You do not,' he said. 'Duane had to go out and buy rubbers. I bet it was you who made him . . .'

'Didn't want . . . him . . . to catch it.'

'Bullshit.'

'You . . . should've left me . . . alone. Now you're . . . gonna die.'

'Fuck you.'

'You *did*. And . . . bit me.'

He shoved himself back. Braced up on an elbow, he stared down at her.

'Got *blood* in your mouth. *My* blood. You got AIDS now.'

'No I don't.'

'Yeah.'

'Lying bitch.'

'Sorry.'

'Take it back.'

'*Not* sorry.'

'Say it's a lie.'

'Sorry.'

'You're dead,' he muttered.

'You, too.'

His right fist shot out and bashed the side of her face, knocking her head sideways and throwing spit from her mouth.

Then he climbed onto her.

'Say it's a lie,' he said.

She couldn't say anything.

But she soon found that she could scream.

By the time Toby tore the scream out of Sherry, she had a pillow over her face.

Chapter Twenty-seven

An hour before dawn, Toby stopped the van on an empty stretch of Mulholland Drive. He could see the orange glow of the Malibu fires in the distance. But the glow was very far away. The fires would probably be stopped long before they got this far.

But if they came here tomorrow or the next day, so much the better.

There were trees on one side of the road, a drop-off on the other.

No cars were in sight.

He opened the rear doors of the van, leaned in, and dragged the rolled blanket toward him with both hands.

He wrestled it onto his shoulder.

Staggering under the weight, he made his way to the side of the road and stepped up to the guard rail.

In front of him, Los Angeles was a distant vista of bright lights.

Leaning over the guard rail, he let go of the blanket.

It dropped.

He leaned over some more. The blanket was slightly darker than the earth and bushes of the hillside. He thought he could see it falling, then bouncing.

It was only a vague black blur down there.

As he watched, its shape seemed to change.

The blanket seemed to be growing.

It's coming unrolled, he realized.

And then Sherry emerged from the blackness.

Her wonderful, pale body left the blanket behind as she dived and tumbled on her wild journey to the bottom.

Chapter Twenty-eight

'Sid. Sid, wake up.' Dawn was shaking him by the shoulder.

He rolled onto his back, turned his head and blinked at her. She looked worried.

'Somebody's at the door.'

'Huh?'

'He keeps ringing the doorbell.'

'He? Who?'

'I don't know. Somebody. He keeps *ringing* it.'

The doorbell rang.

'See?'

'Shit,' Sid muttered. He turned his head the other way and saw the clock on the nightstand.

6:50.

'Shit,' he said again.

The doorbell rang once more.

'Aren't you gonna see who it is?' Dawn asked.

'I'm gonna see who it is, all right.' He swept the top sheet away from his body and sprang out of bed. His father's blue silk robe lay in a pile on the carpet. He snatched it up and put it on.

The doorbell rang again.

'Do you think something's wrong?' Dawn asked.

'Whatever it is, I'll take care of it.'

'Should I like . . . hide?'

He swiveled around, scowling. But he lost the scowl when he saw the way Dawn was braced up on her elbows, naked down to where the sheet draped her lap, her skin tawny against the white of the sheets. Smiling, he shook his head. 'What do you wanta hide for?' he asked.

'I don't know. You tell me.'

He suddenly felt a small, squirmy chill deep inside. 'No reason I can think of. But you're welcome to hide if you—' Knuckles knocked hard against the door. Flinching, Sid gasped out, 'Shit!' Then he said, 'Okay, I'm gonna go kick some ass.'

'Be careful.'

'Sure.' He hurried out of the room. On his way to the door, he closed his robe. The front edges barely met. As he tied the belt, he remembered how large the robe used to seem. His father had been a big guy – a real lard-ass. In the past couple of years, however, Sid had outgrown him.

With Sid, the bulk was all muscle.

Soon, if he kept up with the weights, he wouldn't be able to shut the robe at all.

Dawn'll love that.

Whoever was on the other side of the front door kept pounding.

What if it's the cops?

It's not, he told himself. No way.

Then who is it?

He stepped up to the door, leaned forward and put his eye to the peephole.

Toby?

Toby, all right, but looking weird.

Sid unlocked the door. By the time he could swing it open, Toby had taken a few steps backward and put a nervous smile on his face.

'Greetings, bro,' Toby said.

His hair was a tangled mess, his face filthy and battered. He seemed to be wearing nothing except a red nightshirt with Winnie the Pooh on the front. Winnie wore a sleeping cap and carried an oil lamp. Sid had never seen the nightshirt before.

It was much too small for Toby. It hugged his body, bulging around his midsection and butt. It didn't reach very far down his thighs.

'Get in here,' Sid told him.

Toby entered the house.

Sid shut the door, then turned around and said, 'You look like shit.'

'Yeah, I know. I got jumped. Some guys . . .'

'You got *jumped*? What're you talking about? Where *were* you?'

'Out.'

'Out where?'

'It's a long story.'

'Yeah, sure. Well, I got lots of time. I mean, who needs any sleep?'

'Sorry.'

'You're sorry, all right. Sorriest dumb fat-ass tub of shit I've ever known.'

'It's not my fault.'

'Yeah, sure. Nothing's *ever* your fault.'

'I didn't *do* anything. They were just looking for a guy to nail, you know? And there I was.'

'*Where*?'

'I stopped at this Speed-D-Mart to get me some nachos . . .'

'Oh, yeah. Always gotta feed your face.'

'Anyway, they had the car surrounded when I came out.'

'The Mustang?'

'Yeah.'

'Shit. You better not tell me they stole it.'

'They didn't. That's the thing. The way they were hanging around it, I could tell they were gonna jack it. I mean, they were real bad-ass types, you know? I think they were probably Crips or Bloods or something.'

'Yeah, sure.'

'So anyway, I come out of the store and see 'em, so I don't go for the car. I act like it ain't mine and just keep on walking, you know? But they come after me. One of 'em says, "All we want's your car, man. Just give us the keys 'n nobody's gonna hurt you." So you know what I do?'

'What?'

'I run like hell, and all these guys chase me, but I make it to the road and throw the keys down one of those storm drains.'

'You *what?*'

'I threw 'em down a storm drain. You know, one of those big holes under the curb . . .'

'I know what a storm drain is, asswipe. You threw your *keys* down one?'

'Yeah.'

'Smart move.'

'Kept *them* from getting 'em. The *house* keys, too.' A smile lifted one side of Toby's mouth. 'Guess I saved *your* ass, huh?'

'Yeah?'

'You know what's in the car? Like the registration? It's got our address on it. I bet they would've paid you a visit last night. You and Dawn. She's here, right?'

'She's here.'

'They would've eaten her alive.'

'*Who* would've eaten . . . My God, Toby! What happened to you?' Dawn strolled into the foyer, her bare feet silent on the marble. She'd put on her cut-off jeans and the top of her lime-green, string bikini.

'I'm okay,' Toby said. 'I got jumped by some guys, that's all. They wanted to steal the car and—'

'You look awful!'

He smiled and blushed and shrugged his shoulders. 'I kinda pissed 'em off when I threw away the keys, so they let me have it.'

Looking concerned, Dawn stepped up to him. She put an open hand gently against the swollen side of his face. 'You poor darling,' she said.

'I'm okay,' he told her. 'But they took everything. All my clothes, my wallet . . .' Meeting Sid's eyes, he said, 'But they didn't get the car.' To Dawn, he said, 'I was afraid they'd come over here. They would've . . . done awful things to you, Dawn.'

'That was so brave of you.'

'My ass,' Sid said. 'You know what was going on? Little brother here, he was out driving around in the middle of the night . . . Doing what, Tubby? Looking in windows?'

'I was on my way home from a movie, as a matter of fact.'

'Sure.'

'I *was*.'

'If you say so.'

'Be nice, honey,' Dawn said.

'Oh, he's such a fuckin' loser. Don't believe a word out of him. He probably lost his clothes while he was jackin' off in somebody's back yard or something.'

'Did not. Those guys *stole* my clothes and beat me up and left me in an alley. They knocked me *out*. That's how come it took me so long to get home. I must've been out cold for *hours*. And then I woke up and had to find something to wear.' He plucked at the front of his nightshirt. 'I found this hanging up to dry on somebody's clothes line. And then I had to walk all the way home in it. I had to hide every time a car came along.'

'So where's *my* car?' Sid asked.

'Over by the Speed-D-Mart on Robertson. At least that's where it *was*. I figured we could go and get it this morning.'

'You lost it, you go get it.'

'I'll drive you over,' Dawn said.

'That's what you think,' Sid told her.

'I will if I want to,' she said.

'You better not *want* to.'

She pushed her lower lip out at him. 'You know, Toby *is* your brother. You could stand to treat him a little better.'

'Never mind,' Toby said. 'I'll just walk over and get it. I don't need a ride.' Facing Sid, he asked, 'Can I at least borrow your keys?'

'You gonna throw 'em down a drain?'

'No. I'll go somewhere and get duplicates made.'

Sid thought about it for a moment, then said, 'You're not going anywhere with *my* keys. *I'll* go and get dupes made. Then you can walk over and pick up the car this afternoon.'

'I'd sort of like to get it over with,' Toby said. 'You know? The car's not very safe over there.'

'Yeah, well. If it made it through the night, I guess it'll be okay for a while longer. I'm going back to bed. You better take a shower or something. Let's go, Dawn.'

He started toward the bedroom, Dawn walking ahead of him.

'What time are we gonna go?' Toby asked.

'When I say so,' Sid said. 'Now shut up and leave us alone.'

'Creep,' Toby muttered.

Sid swung around. 'What'd you say?'

'Nothing,' Toby said, shaking his head and backing away.

'You call me something?'

'No.'

'I'll kick your fuckin' ass!' Sid lurched forward, stomping the marble floor with his bare foot.

Toby whirled around and ran for the other end of the house, his fat butt bouncing under the nightshirt.

Sid laughed and came back to Dawn.

'That wasn't very nice,' she said, frowning slightly.

'He called me a creep, the fat fuck.'

'Sometimes you *are* a creep.'

He slugged Dawn on the upper arm. The blow knocked her stumbling away from him. Clutching her arm, she started to cry.

'When I want your opinion,' Sid explained, 'I'll ask for it.'

Chapter Twenty-nine

Brenda, seated on the living-room floor for her breakfast of toast and milk, thumbed a remote button to mute the television. 'Hey, Dad,' she said, 'does Sherry know about the car wash?'

Her father, seated in his usual armchair, looked up from the book he was reading. 'I don't know if she does or not. I don't think *I've* mentioned it to her.' He picked up his coffee mug and took a drink. 'Couldn't hurt to give her a call, I suppose.'

'Did they get the phones working again?'

'Forgot about that. Let's see.' Dad set down his mug, reached across the lamp table and picked up the phone. After listening for a moment, he said, 'Well, we've got a dial tone.'

'Good deal.'

'Want to try her now?'

Brenda glanced at the bright red numbers of the television clock.

8:22.

'I'd better wait, maybe call her just before we're ready to leave. She'd kill me if I woke her up.'

Brenda shut off the television. Then she finished her glass of milk and stood up. Bending over the coffee table, she picked up her plate. It was smeared here and there with jelly, littered with crumbs and the crusts of her toast. 'Want my crusts?' she asked.

'Have they got spit all over them?'

'They're all the better that way.'

Her father laughed.

'I *cut* them off. I *always* cut them off. You really pay attention.'

'You *want* me to study your eating habits?'

'Anyway, do you want the crusts or not?'

'I think I'll pass. Mom and I are probably going to stop somewhere for a nice breakfast after we drop you off.'

'Okay. We're leaving at ten till, right?'

'Sounds good to me.'

Nodding, Brenda left the living room. She turned at the stairway and carried her glass and plate down the hallway to the kitchen, where she set them in the sink. She hit them with water for a few seconds, then hurried back down the hallway to the foot of the stairs.

Her mother was on the way down. 'Morning, honey,' Mom said.

'Hi.' Brenda stepped out of the way, backing toward the front door to wait. She absolutely *hated* it when people crowded the stairs.

Mom was wearing her fuzzy pink robe and slippers.

'We're leaving at ten till nine,' Brenda informed her.

'Fine,' Mom said.

'Are you going to be ready?'

'Oh, I can probably manage it.'

'I don't want to be late.'

From around the corner in the living room, Dad called, 'When have we ever made you late?'

'Always a first time!' Brenda called back.

Mom stepped down off the last stair. 'All clear,' she said.

Brenda smirked at her. 'Very funny.'

As Mom turned away to head for the kitchen, Brenda remembered about Sherry. 'Oh, hey, Mom, does Sherry know about the car wash?'

'I don't think so. Not unless you mentioned it to her.'

'I guess I'll give her a call.'

'You don't want to wake her up.'

'I'll do it last thing before we leave.'

'You should've told her about it when she was here Sunday.'

'I would've, but we weren't sure yet when it'd be. We didn't know till Tuesday.'

'Well, it couldn't hurt to give her a call. She'll probably drop by for a wash.'

'God knows,' Dad called, 'that Jeep of hers could *use* one.'

'Good, Dad,' Brenda called. 'From a guy who gets his car washed once a year.' Climbing the stairs, she added, 'Remember, everyone, ten till nine.'

In the upstairs bathroom, she used the toilet. Then she washed her face, brushed her teeth and rolled deodorant under her arms.

Finished, she hurried to her bedroom and pulled off her pajamas. She tossed them onto her bed, then stepped over to her dresser and took her bikini out of a drawer. After putting it on, she opened another drawer and looked through a stack of neatly folded T-shirts.

She chose a pink shirt with Piglet on the front. Sherry had given it to her for Christmas a few years ago. It was one of her favorites. She'd worn it so often that it looked more white than pink, and Piglet had almost faded away. He looked ghostly. Eventually, he might vanish entirely.

That'll be okay, Brenda thought. We'll still know you're there.

She pulled the T-shirt over her head. It was limp and didn't come close to being large enough. The material was so thin that she could almost see through it. There was a hole near the right shoulder.

Looking at the mirror, she smiled at Piglet's ghost.

Then she hunted for her cut-off blue jeans, found them under a pile of clothes on her desk chair, and put them on. They were loose and faded, but hardly ragged at all. She had a pair of really *good* cut-offs, tattered and patched, but she couldn't wear them anymore – couldn't fit into them.

For footwear, she decided to go with her old white sneakers, no socks.

She put them on, then brushed her hair. There wasn't much of it to worry about. For most of her life, she'd worn it straight and long, but she'd really liked how Sherry looked with a short, boyish cut, so she'd changed her own style a month ago.

It was sure a lot less bother this way.

She liked the tomboy look of it, too.

The only drawback – it apparently made her look younger.

Bad enough to be sixteen without people mistaking you for a *thirteen* year old.

But that's *their* problem, she thought.

All done, she looked at the clock by her bed.

8:40.

She really hated to phone Sherry before nine o'clock, but she needed to be at the car wash by then.

Sitting on the edge of her bed, she picked up the phone. It had a dial tone, all right.

She tapped in her sister's number. After three rings, she heard some electronic clicks. Then came Sherry's voice on the answering machine, 'Hello. I'm unable to answer the phone right now. If you'd like for me to get back to you, please leave your name and number after the sound of the beep.'

A moment later, the beep came.

'Hey, Sher, it's Brenda. Are you there? Are you up yet? Yoo-hooo! Time to rise and shine!' She paused, waiting for Sherry to pick up. Then she said, 'Okay. Whatever. I just called to tell you we're having a car wash over at the high school today – *today and today only!* We're trying to raise money for a new computer for the journalism class. A very worthy cause, even if I do say so myself. So anyway, we're doing it in the parking lot from nine till five, so I hope you'll come over if you feel like it after your night of drunken revelry or whatever. So long.' She hung up.

Then she grabbed her purse, left her room and trotted downstairs. Nobody else was around. Ready to go, she put on her sunglasses, slipped the purse strap over her shoulder, and leaned back against the front door to wait.

Soon, Dad came down the stairs. 'Are you going to call Sherry?' he asked.

'Already did. I left a message on her machine.'

Dad frowned slightly. 'She didn't answer?'

'Would I have left a message on her machine if she'd answered?'

He gave her a look. 'Not necessarily.'

She shrugged.

'It's funny that she didn't pick up,' he said.

'Maybe she was in the can.'
'What's going on?' Mom asked from the top of the stairs.
'Sherry didn't answer her phone,' Dad explained.
'Hmm,' Mom said. 'I can't imagine her being out this early on a Saturday.'
Smiling, Brenda said, 'You never know, maybe she shacked up with some guy last night.'
'I doubt that very much,' Mom said, starting down the stairs.
'You and me both,' Brenda added. 'The Virgin Sherry.'
'Cut it out,' Dad said.
'Well, I bet she is. A virgin.'
'I certainly hope *you* are, young lady,' Mom said.
'I'm sixteen. I'd better be. Right, Dad?'
'Can we not talk about this stuff?' he suggested, grimacing slightly.
At the bottom of the stairs, Mom said, 'Anyway, if she *is* shacked up with someone, it's her own business.'
'She *has* been going with that guy,' Brenda said.
'What guy?' Dad asked, looking surprised.
'You haven't heard?'
'Nobody ever tells me anything.'
'I don't think she's terribly serious about him,' Mom explained.
'*You* knew about him, too?'
'Oh, Sherry's mentioned him a couple of times.'
'Who is he?'
'I think he sells used books or something,' Mom said.
'Out of a van,' Brenda added.
'*What?*'
'He travels to book fairs and stuff.'
'How come *I* never heard about any of this?'
'Maybe you just weren't listening,' Mom suggested.
'You're *never* listening, Dad.'
'It only seems that way because I'm so good at tuning out all the crap.'
'Can we go now?' Brenda suggested. 'I don't want to be late.' She opened the front door.
'I'd like to hear more about this guy.'

Ignoring him, Mom asked, 'Did you want to take a towel or something, honey?'

'Nope.'

'You'll probably get wet,' Dad pointed out.

'Which is why I'm wearing my swimsuit.'

'Which is why you might want a towel.'

'I'll drip dry,' she said, and stepped outside.

'Sun-screen?' Mom asked.

'Got it.'

As they walked toward the driveway, Mom asked, 'Do you have a quarter so you can call home in case . . .?'

'I've got a quarter.'

'What about some money for lunch?'

'Got it.'

'Anything you *don't* got?' Dad asked, coming along behind them after locking the house.

Brenda smirked over her shoulder at him. 'Let's see now, Dad. I don't got a bellybutton ring, tattoos, a drug habit, a criminal record or a sexually transmitted disease.'

'For which you have our undying gratitude,' Dad said.

'You're welcome.'

Brenda stepped out of the way and waited while he unlocked the car's passenger door.

'Why don't you let your mother sit in the front seat?' he asked. 'You'll be getting out in five minutes, anyway.'

'No problem. No problem at all.'

'I don't mind the back seat,' Mom said.

Brenda raised her arms and shook her head. 'No, no, it's all right. You go ahead and sit in front. No problem.'

When they were all in the car, Dad removed the Club from the steering wheel. He put on his seat belt, started the engine, and said, 'So who *is* this guy? Why is Sherry keeping him such a big secret?'

'She didn't keep him a secret from *us*,' Brenda said.

'Why hasn't she brought him by?'

'I told you, Al, I don't think she's very serious about him.'

'How long has this been going on?'

'A couple of months, I think.'

'You know all those Charles Willeford books she gave

you for your birthday?' Brenda asked. 'Well, she bought them from him at the Burbank Book Fair. *That's* when she met him.'

'Buying those books for *me*?'

'Yeah.'

'And nobody even tells me.'

'We're telling you now, Pops.'

'What's his name? How old is he? He isn't already *married*, is he?'

Mom shook her head.

'You don't *know?*'

'I think she mentioned his name once, but . . .'

'It's Duane,' Brenda said. 'But I don't know how old he is or anything.'

'What's his last name?'

'I don't know,' Brenda said.

'I don't either,' said Mom.

'Is he white?'

'I don't know.'

'Me neither,' said Mom.

'A name like Duane . . .'

'Jeez, Dad.'

'Well . . . And the fact that she's keeping him this big, dark secret. What's she trying to hide?'

'She's not trying to hide anything, dear.'

Brenda huffed out a laugh. 'She's *probably* trying to hide from a wildman interrogation by *you*.'

'I'm not a wildman.'

'Yeah, right.'

'She'll be coming over tomorrow,' Mom said. 'Why don't I give her a call? Maybe she'd like to bring Duane with her.'

'Good idea,' Dad said. 'Excellent idea. I want to meet this guy.'

'She might not be too happy about the idea of bringing him over,' Brenda said. 'He's got this terrible skin condition. A rash. It's all over his body, actually. I guess it's sort of runny and gross. If you want to know the truth, that's why she's been so secretive about him.'

Mom looked over her shoulder, frowning at Brenda.

'The good news,' Brenda said, 'is that she hasn't slept with the guy so far. Apparently, this rash is *really* contagious. She can't touch him at all, or she'd catch it.'

Mom said, 'I hope you're making this up, young lady.'

'Huh-uh. He got the rash from being around all those old books. And the thing is, it's gotten so bad he can't even wear clothes anymore. He just hangs around his apartment all day, bare-ass naked, with this slimy, dripping rash all over his body. And Sherry stays there to keep him company But she has to stand in a corner so she won't get any of the goo on her. He leaves like snail trails everywhere he goes. And when he sits *down* . . .'

'That'll be enough, Brenda,' Dad said. 'Your mother and I are planning to have breakfast in a few minutes.'

'Oh, right. Sorry.'

'*Is* there something wrong with Duane?' Mom asked.

'How should I know? I've never met the guy. Sherry hasn't really told me much, either. But I *don't* think she's in love with him. You know? And I'd bet a buck they haven't *done* it. I think she'd have to be in love to do something like that.'

'I sure hope so,' Mom said.

'Also, I happen to know she's pretty scared of getting AIDS.'

'I hope you are, too, young lady.'

'I always insist on a health certificate before I let a guy bang me.'

'*Brenda!*' Mom blurted.

Brenda laughed.

'You're a real comedian,' Dad said.

'I try.'

'You try too hard sometimes,' Mom told her.

'Nah.'

'Do *you* have a secret boyfriend?' Dad asked.

'Me?'

'Yes, you.'

'Nope. Not that I know of. If I have a secret boyfriend, he's a secret to me. And I hope he's *unknown* to me, because frankly every guy I know is either a jerk or a moron.'

'That's my gal,' Dad said.

'Including you.'

He let out a wild laugh.

Chapter Thirty

It was a great morning, sunlit and windy and no school.

And no parents.

Pete's parents were off to spend the weekend playing golf in Palm Springs, so he had the entire house to himself until Sunday night.

Freedom!

Stretched out on his bed, he folded his hands behind his head and smiled. Above him, his window was open. Wind blew in, filling the curtain, lifting it toward the ceiling and letting sunlight slant down on him. The sunlight felt warm. The wind rubbed softly against his body.

Like the caress of a lascivious woman.

That's pretty good, he thought.

Good. Right. If I want to write garbage.

Still, though, caress and lascivious sure sounded good together. Sibilance.

He decided the combination was worth remembering, so he climbed off his bed and walked over to his desk. From a side drawer, he removed a spiral notebook. On the front cover was written, in bold marking pen, RUMINATIONS AND OTHER CRAP, Vol. 1. He opened it, flipped through a dozen pages until he found an empty one, then picked up a ballpoint and wrote, 'The summer breeze was like the caress of a lascivious woman.'

Caress of a lascivious slut.

That had a *lot* of sibilance, but he decided not to write it down. No telling who might lay hands on this notebook, someday. His mom or dad, maybe. Especially if he got shot or hit by a car or if he dropped dead of an aneurism or whatever.

Maybe his girlfriend would read the notebooks someday – if he ever had one.

Or his wife.

Or his biographer.

Like *that's* ever gonna happen.

You just never know, he told himself. So you've gotta make sure you don't put stuff down that'll make you look too much like an idiot or a creep.

Screw that, he thought.

He wrote, 'Sighing, the lascivious slut caressed her breasts.'

Too much sibilance.

And come to think of it, lascivious is a lousy word.

He scratched it out. Then he scratched out 'the slut' and scribbled 'she' above the line.

His sentence now read, 'Sighing, she caressed her breasts.'

Not bad, he thought.

But what if somebody reads it?

He considered scratching out the whole sentence, then decided to leave it.

Nobody's got any business reading my stuff anyway.

He closed the notebook, returned it to the drawer, then opened the bottom drawer of his dresser. He had about ten swimsuits in there. He took out a pair of old, faded blue trunks, stood up and stepped into them. The trunks hanging low on his hips, he pushed the drawer shut with his foot. Then he left his room.

He walked down the hallway, the Spanish red tiles cool under his bare feet. In the kitchen, he started a pot of coffee.

It would take a few minutes to brew. He spent the time in the bathroom, using the toilet, washing his face, brushing his teeth and spraying his armpits with Right Guard. Then he went out the front door and brought in the *LA Times*.

The plastic bag enclosing the newspaper was wet from the lawn sprinklers. On his way to the kitchen, he tore it off. He stuffed it into the wastebasket, then tossed the newspaper onto the table.

It flopped open.

He read the headline: KILLER WINDS BLAST SOUTHLAND

Killer winds? Hyperbole, or had a tree fallen on someone?

Either way, he didn't feel like reading about it.

He glanced at a few of the smaller headlines.

School Board . . . Racial Quotas

Murder Spree . . . West LA Apartment Complex

New Charges . . . Clinton . . . Sex Scandal

'Same old shit,' he muttered.

Leaving the newspaper on the table, he opened a cupboard and took down his Bigfoot coffee mug. He filled it with coffee. Then he carried it into the living room. His paperback copy of *A Moveable Feast* was on the lamp table where he'd left it last night. He tucked it under his right arm. The cover felt slick and cool against his skin.

He picked up a red ballpoint pen and put it sideways between his lips.

Then he stepped over to the back door. With his left hand, he unlocked it and rolled it open. Then he skidded the screen door out of his way and stepped onto the patio.

A warm wind blew against him. The sunlit concrete felt warm under his feet.

But the brilliant glare on the pool's surface made him squint.

Forgot my sunglasses.

Keeping his eyes turned away from the pool, he walked over to the glass-topped table. He set down his coffee mug and book and pen.

The table was in shadow, so he figured he could do without his sunglasses.

He pulled out a chair and sat down with his back to the pool. Then he raised the mug to his lips. Instead of taking a drink, he watched the way the steam swirled and drifted just above the coffee's dark surface.

How do you describe something like that? he wondered. How do you do it so everybody who reads about it can *see* the steam, the way it just sort of hovers low over the coffee and you can just barely see it at all, and how the coffee is trembling and shiny, reflecting the sky, and then the way you can feel the heat and moisture of the steam against your upper lip and the bottom of your nose when you go to take a drink?

He took a drink and noticed that he could feel the steam *inside* his nostrils, too.

The coffee tasted good and hot.

Maybe you *can't* write about this stuff and make it completely real.

Hemingway can.

God, Hemingway.

Pete set down his mug, sighed, then picked up *A Moveable Feast* and opened it to his bookmark and began to read. Soon, he could smell the rain, feel it blowing against his face, see it slanting down through the gray Paris morning, splashing in puddles and bouncing off sidewalks.

God, this guy can write, he thought.

Nobody else can make it this real.

It made Pete wish he were in Paris on such a day, walking through the rain, going into a café to write.

Though *this* ain't bad, he thought, looking up from the book and glancing over his shoulder at the pool and the hillside beyond it.

I should be writing, not reading.

But you've gotta read, he told himself. Especially great stuff like this. See how it's done when it's done right.

He read on.

The reading made him excited and a little sad. He wasn't sure why, but he thought it had something to do with wanting to *be* there – *in* the scene. Not just reading about it, but living it. And knowing that he couldn't, and feeling the loss.

It happened mostly when he read Hemingway.

He *ached* to be there. He wished he could be Hemingway in a Paris café, Nick Adams camping by a woodland stream or walking down a railroad track, Robert Jordan with Maria naked in his sleeping bag, Harry Morgan steering his charter boat through the waters off Key West on a quiet, early morning with no sounds other than the putter of his motors and the squeals of the seagulls.

With Hemingway, he wanted to be there so badly that it made him ache. And it also made him ache with a need to write that well, himself.

God, to be able to do that to people!

But he knew it was too much to hope for, and *that* made him sad, too.

At least I can try, he told himself.

Then he realized that his eyes had been moving over the lines of the book but he'd been daydreaming, not reading.

He picked up his coffee mug.

Holding it close to his face, he couldn't find a trace of steam anymore. The dark surface of the coffee still trembled and flashed reflections of the sky, but now Pete could see subtle swirls of rainbow colors, as if someone had slipped a dab of gasoline into his coffee. He supposed it was caused by oil from the coffee beans.

He hoped so.

It wasn't very appetizing to look at. He needed to remember it, though, so he could use it sometime in his writing.

I should put it in the notebook before I forget about it, he thought.

But he didn't feel like fooling with the notebook again. He wanted to work on his novel.

He sipped the coffee. It had lost most of its heat and didn't taste so good. He set the mug down on the table.

Maybe I should toss it out and get a refill, he thought. And bring out my book and try to get some writing done.

So he took his mug into the kitchen. He dumped the remains of the coffee down the sink, then left the mug on the counter and hurried to his bedroom.

He found his sunglasses on top of the dresser. He put them on, but the tinted lenses made his room too dark. He took the glasses off and slid one of the stems down the waistband of his trunks.

With the glasses hanging at his side, he stepped over to his desk. The two spiral notebooks containing his novel in progress were hidden under stacks of papers at the bottom of a desk drawer. He pulled them out, shut the drawer, then took a black ballpoint pen out of the top drawer. He slid the pen under the band of his trunks, next to the stem of his sunglasses. Then he hurried back to the kitchen.

He filled his mug with fresh, hot coffee from the pot. Mug in one hand, notebooks in the other, he hurried outside. As he put them on the table, he felt excitement in the pit of his stomach.

It wasn't always there when he was ready to start writing, but sometimes it was. Especially if he'd just been reading something really great.

He began to sit down, but stopped when he felt the stiffness of the pen and sunglasses stem inside his trunks. He pulled them out, put on the sunglasses, and dropped onto the lawn chair.

He opened PART 2 and flipped through pages until he came to the end of what he'd written so far. It was two pages into a chapter. He went to the start of the chapter and began to read.

'Who do you think it is?' Shana asked, a tremor shaking her voice.

Ralph darted his eyes again to the rear-view mirror and squinted into the glare of the headlights of the car behind them.

Pete frowned.

Of the headlights. Of the car.

That didn't seem too good, having both those *of* phrases one after another.

He needed to get rid of one.

'Ah!' he said.

He scratched out the first *of the* and changed *glare* to *glaring*.

. . . squinted into the glaring headlights of the car behind him.

Not bad, he thought and resumed reading.

'Whoever it is, he's been on our tale for the past ten miles. I think maybe he's after us.'

'Oh God, Ralph. I'm scared.' With that, Shana reached across through the darkness. Her hand came to rest on Ralph's knee.

On his *knee*? Way down there? Why not have her put it on his *ankle*?

Pete scratched out knee and wrote *thigh*.

That sounds like a chicken part, he thought. Something you'd pick up at KFC along with your drumstick and wing.

He scratched out *thigh* and wrote *leg*.

And heard the doorbell chimes. The sound of them sent a squirm through his stomach.

Somebody's at the door?

He muttered, 'Crap.'

Why don't I just not answer it?

The chimes rang again.

Maybe it's something important, he thought. Maybe it's a cop. Mom and Dad were in an accident . . . Maybe the neighborhood's being evacuated. None of the fires seemed near enough for anything like that, but . . .

I'd better find out.

Grimacing, he shut his notebook and set down his pen and pushed his chair back.

The chimes rang again and again as he hurried through the house.

It's either an emergency or somebody's a real pest.

Stopping at the front door, he leaned forward and looked through the peephole.

The latter.

Chapter Thirty-one

Pete opened the door. 'Hey, Jeff,' he said.

Jeff raised a hand in greeting, lifted his sunglasses so they rested atop his brush cut, and walked in. He was wearing a white T-shirt, faded jeans and cowboy boots. Though he was short and skinny, he walked with a tough-guy swagger.

'Come on in,' Pete said.

'You alone?'

'No, I've got a hot babe in my bedroom.'

'You wish.' He turned his thin, freckled face to Pete. 'Did your folks go to Palm Springs like they planned?'

'Yep.'

'Cool. Wanta do something?'

No, Pete thought. I just want to be left alone.

But Jeff was his best friend.

And Pete was Jeff's *only* friend.

'I guess we could do something for an hour or two,' Pete said. 'Then I have to work.'

'On that book you're writing?'

'Yeah.'

'Christ, you gotta do that on *Saturdays*?'

'Yeah, I sure do. But it can wait a while. What did you have in mind?'

'How's the pool looking? Didn't get wrecked last night, did it?'

'I think it's okay.'

'Any trees land in it?'

'Not that I noticed.'

'Have you *looked* at it today?'

'Not closely.'

'Okay if we use it?'

'Use it for what?'

Jeff let out a bray of laughter. 'Good one!'

'Wanta go for a swim?' Pete asked.

Jeff *always* wanted to go for a swim unless the weather was terrible. In awful weather, he preferred the hot spa. He lived in an elaborate house just down the road, but it had no pool or spa. Not anymore. They'd been removed a few years ago and replaced with a tennis court.

'Why'd your parents want to do that?' Pete had once asked.

'Ah, my stupid sister.'

'What sister?' Pete had asked, unaware that Jeff had any.

'The one that drowned. You ask me, if they were gonna take out the pool, they should've done it *before* she drowned. How smart is *that*? Now *I've* got no pool and I *hate* tennis. Only thing is, I can watch Mom's friends play. Couple of 'em are pretty decent babes. But shit, if we still had the pool, they'd be frolicking around in their bikinis or something.'

'I'm sorry about your sister,' Pete had said.

'Yeah, well . . . Shit.' Jeff had shrugged his thin shoulders, tried to smirk, and added, 'That's the way the ball bounces, you know?'

His attempt to make light of her death with the old, childish saying had brought tears to Pete's eyes.

From then on, Pete could never hear anyone say, 'That's the way the ball bounces,' without remembering how Jeff had said it that day about his sister.

And he never again used the adage himself.

'How about it?' Jeff asked. 'Can we go swimming?'

'Did you bring a suit?'

'Got it on,' Jeff said, and patted the hip of his jeans.

Whenever Jeff came over to visit, he *always* wore his swimsuit underneath his jeans.

'Be prepared,' Jeff said. 'That's my motto.'

'I thought your motto was, "Kill 'em all and let God sort 'em out." '

'That's my other motto.'

'Anyway, I guess we can go swimming if you want to.'

'And then we can, like, lay around and catch some rays for a while, okay?'

'Sure.'

Jeff led the way through the house. In back, he set down his sunglasses on the table next to *A Moveable Feast*. Then he peeled off his T-shirt. 'How about that wind last night?' he asked, hopping on one foot as he struggled to pull off a boot.

'Pretty strong.'

'Killed like nine people, you hear about that?'

'Huh-uh.'

'Yeah. Shit.' With one boot and sock off, he switched feet and started pulling at his other boot. 'Got mashed by trees, most of 'em. But there were a couple of electrocutions, too. Plus a fireman got cooked in a brush fire over in Orange County. Pretty bad shit.'

'It didn't seem that bad around here,' Pete said. 'We never even lost our power.'

'No, but the phones went dead.'

'They did?'

'Oh, yeah.' Barefoot, Jeff pulled down his jeans and stepped out of them. 'Phones were dead all night. Some places had their power knocked out, too. You know, like about half the valley was in the dark.'

'Glad that didn't happen here.'

'Yeah. You all alone in the house. That would've been the pits, huh?'

'Yeah.'

Jeff pulled up his drooping trunks. They were the red, faded ones he always wore. 'Maybe you could've gotten a story out of it, though. You're always looking for *experiences*. That would've been a good one, huh?'

'Would've made things interesting.'

'You could, like, have a killer break into your house. And you can't call anyone for help 'cause the phones don't work. And you haven't got any guns 'cause your parents are a couple of . . .' Jeff's eyes widened. 'Hey!' he blurted. 'Whoa! Did you hear about those killings last night?'

'I saw something in the paper. Some sort of murder spree in West LA?'

'Yeah. They don't know *what* the hell went on. Somebody must've gone berserk with a knife, nailed these people in some apartment building over there. I guess the guy's in a stable condition, but the woman bought it. Stabbed to death. But get this, they found a severed fuckin' head in the room.'

'You're kidding.'

'And no body to go with it. Cool, huh?'

Pete laughed and shook his head. 'Guess it's cool if you happen to be a bloodthirsty maniac.'

Jeff grinned. 'That's me.' He stepped to the edge of the pool and frowned at the water. 'It ain't exactly pristine, pardner.'

Pete wandered closer to the pool. Squinting, he saw quite a few leaves and twigs scattered across the glaring surface. Other debris, waterlogged, seemed suspended partway down. Even the tile bottom of the pool was littered here and there with crumbs of sunken foliage.

'Damn wind,' he muttered. 'I had the pool spotless yesterday.'

'Should've closed the cover.'

'I meant to. Oh, well, it's not *that* bad.'

'Considering the wind,' Jeff said, 'you got off lucky.'

'Yeah. Well, the wall usually keeps out most of the junk.' He nodded toward the six-foot high cinder-block wall at the far side of the pool area. Then he looked at the steep hillside beyond the wall and shook his head at the sight of all those weeds, all those leafy bushes and trees. 'Too bad the wall isn't about twice as high. I'd only have to clean the pool half as often.'

'What you oughta do is defoliate the hillside.'

'Good idea.'

'Hit it with some Agent Orange.'

Pete shook his head and suggested, 'How about nuking it?'

'Get real.'

Pete gaped at his friend for a moment, then cracked up.

'What's so funny?'

'You,' Pete said, and shoved him.

Jeff yelled, '*Yah!*' and went off the edge. In the next instant, he grabbed control of his body, streamlined it and turned his fall into a dive. He entered the water with hardly a splash. Below the surface, he darted the width of the pool. When he came up and twirled around, he shouted, 'You're goin' down.'

'Think so?'

'I *know* so.' Jeff swung around and climbed out of the pool.

Grinning, Pete warned, 'Don't get carried away, Jeffrey.'

'They're gonna carry *you* away.' He started running toward the corner.

'No running,' Pete warned.

'All rules are off! You're a dead man!'

'Yeah, right.'

'I'm gonna waste your ass.'

'You and what army?'

'No army!' Jeff yelled, rounding the near corner and racing straight toward Pete. 'Just takes one bad-ass mother like me!'

'Don't loose your trunks.'

'You'd like *that*, fag.' But Jeff must've been able to feel that they were on their way down. Not breaking stride, he grabbed them with both hands. As he hoisted them up, Pete dived into the pool.

In midair, he heard Jeff shout, '*Chicken!*' Then he plunged into the water. The cold of it jolted him. It made him want to cry out in pain. A moment later, though, it didn't seem so bad. A moment after that, he began to like the way it slid along his skin.

Like cold, liquid silver.

Liquid silver would have to be molten, but he liked the image anyway and hoped he could remember it.

When his fingertips bumped against the tiles, he lunged to the surface.

He turned around.

Jeff, standing by the table, picked up *A Moveable Feast* and faced him.

'Hey!' Pete yelled. 'Put that down. You're wrecking it! You're all wet!'

Grinning, Jeff raised the book overhead. 'Come and get it.'

'I'm serious. Put it down and dry it off.'

'Come on out and make me.'

'Man! You don't mess around with a guy's books!'

'Should've thought of that before you pushed me in.'

'Put it down, Jeff. Come on.'

Clutching the book by one corner, Jeff cocked back his arm and whipped it forward like a knife-thrower. But he didn't let go.

'That's not funny! What if it'd slipped?'

'Guess your book might've gotten a little wet. Just like *I* got a little wet.'

'You were going in the pool anyway, dipshit. All I did was speed things up.'

Grinning, Jeff said, 'Dipshit? You called me a *dipshit*? Is that supposed to win me over?'

'This is not funny, Jeff.'

'*I'm* having fun.'

'If that book's wrecked . . . if it has so much as a *water spot* on it . . .'

Jeff lowered the book to eye level. He frowned at its cover. '*A Moveable Feast*,' he said. 'Do you s'pose it's also a *floatable* feast?'

Pete shoved off and swam fast across the pool at an angle, straight for Jeff.

Who waited by the table, holding the book high and grinning.

Until Pete started to climb out.

Then Jeff dodged around the table and ran away, waving the book overhead.

'Damn it! Get back here!'

'Kiss my ass!' Jeff yelled. It was mostly bare at the moment. He reached down with one hand to hoist his drooping trunks.

As water spilled down his body, Pete stood on the warm concrete and pulled up his own sagging trunks. 'I'm not going to chase you. Just bring the book back, okay?'

'Come and get it.'

'No.'

'Then I can't be responsible for its fate.'

'You *will* be responsible. I'll knock the crap out of you!'

'Oooo, big talk.' Jeff hurried the rest of the way to the cinder-block wall at the side of the pool area. He reached up and slapped the book onto its top. Then, hands free, he climbed the wall.

'Real cute,' Pete called.

'Ain't that the truth?' With his usual agility, Jeff picked up the book and rose to his feet. He waved the book at Pete. 'Don't you want it?'

'Get down from there.'

'You come up.'

'Yeah, right.' Pete had no intention of climbing the wall, but he did start walking toward it. 'Just come on down. I know you're God's gift to the world of gymnastics . . .'

'I'm no gymnast. They're a bunch of fags.'

'Then stop trying to act like one.'

'I'm not. I'm a Great Wallenda!' With that, he started hurrying along the top of the wall, arms wide for balance.

'Wallendas fall and die, you dork.'

'Just once!'

'Get down from there!'

When Jeff reached the rear corner, he stopped. He used one hand to yank up his drooping trunks. Then he spread his arms again, stepped around the corner, and began to walk along the top of the far wall.

'I'm so impressed,' Pete called, striding past the end of the pool.

'Let's see *you* do it.'

'You're the show-off around here.'

'Have you *ever* climbed up here?' Jeff asked, continuing along the wall and not looking back.

'A few times.'

'Then let's see you.'

'I don't feel like it.'

'Tell you what, you come up here and I'll give you the book back.'

'Screw you.'

He stopped and grinned over his shoulder at Pete. 'If you *don't* come up, maybe I'll see how far up the hill I can throw it.'

'You do and you'll be sorry.'

Jeff turned toward the hillside and cocked back his arm as

if ready to hurl the book. But then his body seemed to stiffen slightly. He lowered the book, not even bothering to fake a throw.

'What's wrong?' Pete called.

His friend stood there as if shocked into stillness.

'Jeff? What is it? What's going on?'

Jeff swung his head to the side and called out, 'I think you'd better climb up here and take a look at this.'

Pete ran to the wall. Leaping, he boosted himself up. Instead of trying to stand on the narrow top, he swung a leg over and straddled it.

'Right there,' Jeff said, and pointed his finger toward the hillside in front of them, his arm almost straight out.

For a few seconds, Pete saw only brown weeds and green bushes.

Then he spotted the body.

Chapter Thirty-two

It was slightly lower than Pete's eye level, near the bottom of the slope and only about twenty feet away.

'See it?' Jeff asked.

'Yeah.'

'Wow.'

'Yeah.'

'Looks like a stiff.'

'Yeah.'

The body was sprawled face-down, arms and legs spread out like a skydiver. But it wasn't wearing a parachute.

It wasn't wearing anything at all.

It looked filthy and bloody and battered.

'I think it's a gal,' Jeff said.

'I don't know. Look at the hair.'

The hair was very short. It seemed to be pale blond, but the head was turned away and most of the hair that Pete could see was matted down flat with blood.

'Look at the butt,' Jeff said. 'That's a gal butt.'

'I don't know.'

'I do. Let's take a look.'

'We'd better call the cops.'

'*You* call the cops, *I'm* gonna see what we've got here.' He switched the paperback book to his left hand and held it toward Pete. 'This yours?'

Pete took it. 'You're not . . .?'

Jeff sprang from the wall. His leap carried him out toward the hillside as he dropped. He landed a small distance below the body. Knees bending with the impact, he fell forward and caught himself with both hands. Then he stood up and turned around. 'Come on, man. Don't you wanta see her?'

'You're not supposed to go near a crime scene. You'll screw up evidence.'

'This isn't any crime scene.'

'You think she got like that in an *accident*?'

'Shit, no. Someone probably raped and murdered her. But not here. This is just where she got dumped.' Jeff turned sideways and pointed toward the top of the bluff. 'From up there on Mulholland, I bet.'

'Maybe.'

'Coming?'

'No. And you . . .'

Jeff started climbing the slope toward the body.

'Get back here!' Pete yelled.

Jeff ignored him.

Pete muttered, 'Damn it.' He set down his book on top of the wall, then swung his leg over, shoved off, and dropped to the ground. 'Wait up,' he called.

Jeff stopped, looked back at him, and smiled.

Pete chugged up the slope toward his waiting friend.

He felt very strange: shocked and disgusted and a little frightened at having a murder victim left behind his home, annoyed by Jeff's refusal to leave it alone, dreading a closer look at a dead body but also excited because he'd never before seen one close up and he'd never before seen a naked woman in the flesh.

I don't want to see this, he told himself.

But he trudged the final distance and halted beside Jeff. They stood side by side, huffing for breath, staring at the body sprawled in the weeds just above their feet.

'She's got a nice bod on her,' Jeff said.

'Hey, shut up.'

'Well, she does. Too bad she's so wrecked up.'

Afraid someone might be watching them, Pete scanned the hillside. He saw nobody. The road, high above him, was hidden from sight by the slope and scattered trees. There were no houses directly overhead. Those Pete could see were so far away and off to the sides that even someone up there with a telescope would have a tough time seeing much, especially with so many trees and bushes nearby.

Turning toward his house, Pete found that he could look down over the top of the block wall. If Mom or Dad were home, they would be able to view him standing here – maybe from the chest up – but not the naked body at his feet.

His house stood at the rear of a cul-de-sac. The homes on both sides were a fair distance away and set at angles that gave them almost no view at all of the area behind Pete's house. Also, the house on the right was up for sale. Nobody had lived in it for weeks.

'The coast clear?' Jeff asked.

'I think so.'

'Good deal.' Jeff sank to a crouch beside the body.

'What're you doing?'

'Nothing,' he said, and patted a cheek of the rump.

'Christ, Jeff.'

'Still warm,' he said.

'Probably the sun.'

'Let's turn her over.'

'Are you out of your mind?'

'Come on, give me a hand.'

'You're nuts.'

'You telling me you don't wanta check her out?'

'She's *dead!*'

'So who's gonna find out we looked her over? *She's* sure not gonna tell on us.'

'The cops'll know if we move her.'

'Yeah? So what? We'll just say we didn't know she was dead and figured she might need some first aid.'

'We'd better not.'

'You *want* to, man. I *know* you want to. Don't be such a chicken.'

'It wouldn't be right.'

'Gimme a break. A, who gives a shit? B, what's so bad about looking her over? Who's it gonna hurt? Now come on and help me.'

'You want to turn her over, *you* turn her over. I'm not touching her.'

'Okay, don't.' Jeff shrugged and smiled. '*I'll* do it.' He lifted her left arm off the ground and moved it in against her side. 'No rigor mortis,' he said. Dropping to one knee, he leaned over her, placed a hand on the small of her back to brace himself up, and reached out for her right arm. He hooked his fingers over it and drew it down against her side. 'Loose as a goose,' he said.

'I can't believe you're doing this,' Pete muttered.

'Do you believe you're watching?'

'I'm not about to leave you alone with her.'

'Ha! Good one!' He moved sideways and leaned over the backs of her thighs. Using both hands, he pulled her right leg in against her left. 'Guess we're all set,' he said. 'So get ready.'

'Ready for what?'

'Who knows? Maybe her guts'll fall out or something.'

'Terrific.'

'I mean, she might have a nasty old wound somewhere.'

'Why don't you just leave her the way she is?'

'Because she's here, man.' He smiled over his shoulder at Pete. 'You sure you don't want to help?'

'I'm sure.'

'Scared to touch her.'

'I'm not *scared*.'

'Yeah, you are.'

'That's what you think.'

'Prove it.'

'Screw you.'

'Aren't you the guy with the big plans to *experience* everything? How're you gonna write about a thing like this if all you do is stand there and watch?'

'I've got an imagination,' Pete said.

But maybe Jeff was right. He *should* touch the body – not only to find out how a corpse feels, but to learn how it would make *him* feel.

I owe it to my art.

Right, he thought. That'd give me an excuse to do *anything*, no matter how rotten.

He stood there and shook his head.

'You'll probably never get another chance like this,' Jeff said.

'Why do *you* care?'

' 'Cause you're my best friend. I don't want you missing out on something this big. You know? You'll end up regretting it. I mean, shit, you've got a murder victim at your feet and you won't even *touch* her! Not to mention she looks like she might be a major babe.'

'I'm not touching her.'

'Hemingway would've.'

'Hemingway did lots of crummy stuff. I want to *write* like him, not act like him.'

'You are *such* a chicken.' With that, Jeff stood up and stepped over the body. He turned around, knelt by its right side, jammed his hands underneath the hip and thigh, and heaved upward.

The woman tumbled onto her back. The jolt turned her head toward Pete, flung out her right arm and leg, and sent a tremor through her breasts. She slid downslope a few inches, then stopped.

Her eyes were shut.

Her guts didn't spill out.

Now that her head was turned, Pete couldn't see any major wounds at all. But she seemed to have countless nicks and scratches and abrasions. Her face was puffy and her lips were split as if she'd been punched senseless. She had a thin, curving slit underneath her left breast. Most of her front was smeared and streaked with blood. Clinging to the blood were bits of weeds and leaves, powdery dust and grains of dirt. So much of her body was a mess that the few clean, uninjured areas of skin seemed strangely out of place.

She was a ruin.

But she was naked.

Pete could see *everything*.

Jeff, staring down at her, murmured, 'Wow.' He sidestepped and crouched and peered between her legs.

'Don't be disgusting,' Pete said.

Ignoring him, Jeff sighed and kept on staring.

'Stop that.'

'You ever seen one of these? You better take a good look. Never know when you'll get another chance.'

'I'd rather see a live one.'

'Know what I'd *really* like to do?'

'No. And I don't want to hear about it. I think it's about time we go back to the house and call the cops.'

'What's the big hurry?'

'We've seen her, okay? You turned her over. We've seen both sides, and—'

'I'm still looking,' Jeff said.

'Yeah, and you're starting to get funny ideas.'

'Don't know how funny they are.'

'Come on, let's go.'

'What we really oughta do,' Jeff said, 'is wash her off, see what she looks like underneath all this blood and crap.'

'You're out of your mind,' Pete said.

'Maybe hose her down.'

Pete found himself wondering if the backyard hose would reach this far. Probably.

'Even if the hose *is* long enough . . .' Grimacing, he shook his head. 'No way. We're already gonna be in trouble with the cops. As it is, they'll know we were hanging around back here. All these trampled weeds. They might even think we had something to do with killing her. All we'd *need* is to drag the garden hose back here and—'

'Who says they even have to find her here?'

'What?'

'Suppose her body gets found someplace else? Say, a couple of miles from here? Say, tomorrow?'

Pete gaped at him.

'We do it right, we'd be completely in the clear, wouldn't have to worry about getting blamed for *anything*.'

'You've completely lost your mind.'

'It'd be easy, man. Your mom and dad aren't coming home tonight, are they?'

'Not supposed to, but . . .'

'We can clean her up, hide her in your house, then take her for a ride sometime really late tonight. Find a nice, empty stretch of road and dump her out. Then she's somebody *else's* problem.'

'No! My God! If we got caught trying to pull a thing like that . . .'

'Who's gonna catch us, man? This ain't an episode of *Homicide*, this is real life. In real life, people get away with shit all the time.'

'We wouldn't. We'd get nailed. Anyway, the whole idea is *sick*. You just want to keep her around all day so you can . . . I don't know, look at her and stuff.'

'And you *don't* want to look at her *and stuff*?'

'No!'

'Yeah, sure. You know damn well you'd *love* to. You're just chicken.'

'I want to do what's right, that's all.'

Shaking his head, Jeff let out a sigh. 'Okay, you win. We'll call the cops. Of course, they'll probably haul our asses in for questioning . . .'

Pete suddenly felt squirmy in his bowels.

'Might even charge us with her rape and murder,' Jeff added. 'But we'll do it your way.'

'I think we *have* to. Really. Otherwise, we might get in deep trouble. They'll know we didn't do this.'

'Oh, we probably won't get *convicted*. Not me, anyway. I know she hasn't got *my* semen in her. Has she got yours?'

Pete scowled at his friend. 'What do you think?'

'I don't know, man, we found her behind *your* house. You had the place all to yourself last night. Who's to say you're not the guy that did all this to her?'

'Up yours.'

'Well, then, long as you're innocent, we'll *both* be in the clear once they've run some tests. DNA tests only take a couple of months.'

'You're *not* talking me out of this, Jeff. We're gonna call the cops right now.'

'Fine. If you insist.'

'I do.'

'But we'd better *not* leave her alone. Somebody has to stay behind and make sure she's okay.'

'She's not okay. She's very *un*-okay. She can't *get* more un-okay than she is right now.'

'Don't count on it. We could go off to make that call of yours and come back and find her getting chewed on by a coyote. Or some stray dogs or something.'

'We'll only be gone a couple of minutes.'

'Longer than that, man. The wind, the fires. Not to mention the phones were dead all night. Nobody could even *call* the cops till a couple of hours ago. You could be on hold for half an hour before they even let you talk to someone. A lot could happen to a stiff in half an hour. *Vultures* . . .'

'You just want to be left alone with her,' Pete said.

'I know *that's* not gonna happen. But I still don't think we should leave her by herself. Seriously. So maybe *you* should stay here and *I'll* go call the cops.'

The suggestion took Pete by surprise.

Alone with her!

'Okay,' he said. 'I guess that'll be all right. But hurry.'

Jeff rushed down the slope and climbed the wall. Standing on top, he turned around and grinned. 'Don't do anything I wouldn't do,' he called.

'You're a riot.'

Jeff laughed, turned his back, and leaped.

Chapter Thirty-three

Alone on the hillside with the body, Pete scanned the area again. He saw no one. Nor did he see any roaming coyotes or dogs.

He didn't suppose the body was actually in danger of being eaten by such animals. Especially in daylight. The risk would've been much greater last night. If she'd made it through the darkness . . .

Who says she did?

Pete didn't think he'd seen any bites.

Doesn't mean there aren't any.

He stepped closer to the body. Staring down at it, he searched for bite marks.

The breasts were bloody, dirty, abraded and scratched. Bits of skin were rucked up here and there, but no chunks were missing. Neither breast looked as if it had been ripped by teeth.

To Pete, they looked wonderful in spite of the mess.

He wanted to touch them, put his hands on them and squeeze them gently.

What if Jeff sees me?

He looked over his shoulder at the wall.

Then he stared down at the woman's breasts.

I'd get blood on my hands. And she'd end up with my hand prints on her. How would I explain that to Jeff? Or to the cops?

He didn't care. They were tattered and filthy but lovely and he *ached* to feel them. They glistened with drops of sweat or dew that slid down them through the blood. They would be warm and slippery.

But she's dead! You can't feel up a corpse! Talk about perverted!

I shouldn't even be staring at her like this, he told himself. It's sick.

Maybe I oughta check out the rest.

Excited by the idea, he looked back at the wall again. Then he hurried alongside the body and crouched between its feet.

If Jeff catches me . . .

I'm only looking for bite marks, he reminded himself. To see if a coyote or something got to her last night.

Is it supposed to look like this?

Pretty much, he thought. It resembled drawings and photos he'd seen, but . . .

Something hissed.

A snake?

Pete started to turn his head, yelped as an icy blast of water struck him, then saw Jeff standing on the wall, a huge grin on his face, a wild gleam in his eyes, and the garden hose in his right hand.

Breathless, Pete scurried away from the girl. The water, shooting out of the nozzle like a shiny silver pole, struck him hard in the chest and splashed off as if exploding. 'Stop it!' he yelled.

Jeff lowered his aim.

The water drove into Pete's belly, then smacked the jutting front of his trunks, soaking him with frigid liquid, the powerful stream whapping against his erection.

Pete turned his back to Jeff and hunkered down.

The tight rod of water poked the seat of his trunks, soaked them, pounded against his buttocks, probed between them. 'Quit it!'

Suddenly, it went away.

Looking over his shoulder, Pete saw the silvery liquid slant down and strike the body's right breast. On impact, the tube burst into glistening spray that was pink for a moment, then clear and sparkling. The breast was suddenly clean and pale and shiny. It shook as the water battered it.

Then it stopped shaking.

The water no longer smashed against it, but pounded instead against the woman's right hand, which was raised off the ground to block it.

'My God,' Pete muttered.

The hose jerked aside.

The woman's arm sank to the ground.

Pete looked up at Jeff, who stood atop the wall with his smile gone, his jaw hanging, the hose sending its hard shaft into the ground a short distance from the woman's head.

'What the hell was *that*?' Jeff asked.

'I guess she . . .'

Jeff swung the hose toward her again. The strong jet of water jabbed her shoulder and ricocheted into her face.

'Don't!' Pete yelled.

As the water pelted her face, she grimaced slightly and turned her head.

'Stop it! She's alive, you idiot!'

The tight, hard tube of water suddenly loosened, spreading out. Pete glanced toward the wall and saw Jeff twisting the nozzle. When he looked again at the woman, the blood and filth was being rinsed from her body by a broad, heavy shower.

She raised an arm to shield her face.

Her front was nearly clean, now. The ruddy blotches and cuts and scratches and abrasions stood out in sharp contrast to the areas where her skin was undamaged.

Her cloak of blood and grime stripped off, she suddenly seemed much more naked than before.

And now she's alive!

She was alive before, Pete told himself. Alive while we were inspecting her, talking about her.

Jeff had patted her butt.

Pete had come very close, himself, to reaching for her breasts.

Thank God I didn't do that!

But what did I say? he wondered. Did I say anything raunchy?

He wasn't sure.

He *was* sure, however, there'd been some discussion about keeping her body in the house, getting rid of it after dark.

And what else?

Jeff had talked about the semen in her.

What did *I* say? he wondered. Maybe nothing too awful.

But I sure looked her over. What if she knows?

She doesn't, he told himself. She was out cold. She might've *heard* stuff, but she sure didn't see me inspecting her.

Why did we assume she was dead? We should've checked! How could we be that stupid?

This is gonna be so damn embarrassing.

Maybe she won't even survive.

No, I don't wish that.

But who's to say she hasn't already been fatally injured? Maybe she'll only last a few more minutes . . .

Her whole body started to move. Still being doused by the hose, she slowly rolled over and pushed herself up to her hands and knees. She stayed that way, head drooping toward the ground, while Jeff, walking along the top of the wall, sprayed her back and buttocks and the backs of her legs.

They were shiny – but red with dozens of contusions, scuffs, welts and scratches.

Jeff turned the hose away from her. Twisting the nozzle, he shut off the water until it only trickled out. Then he pulled more hose toward him. Nozzle still in his hand, he leaped off the wall. He climbed toward the woman, dragging the hose.

She remained on her hands and knees, head low.

Jeff looked at Pete. 'You believe this?' he asked.

Pete shook his head.

'We thought you were dead, lady.'

She didn't respond.

'Did you get through to the police?' Pete asked.

Looking annoyed, Jeff said, 'Busy signal. I tried a couple of times. Then I figured it wouldn't hurt to grab the hose on the way back – clean her off.'

'Sure,' Pete muttered.

You didn't even try to call, did you? Figured you'd pull a sneak attack. Once you've hosed her down, we can't call the cops.

He glared at Jeff.

'All it would hurt is every bit of evidence about who did this to her.'

'It's cool, man. She's not dead.'

'Yeah, right.'

'You oughta be glad.'

'I am glad.'

Jeff flashed him a strange smile, then knelt beside the woman.

She was breathing hard – her back rising and falling – as if she were trying to make up for all the air she'd missed while lying dead.

Almost dead.

The moisture on her skin glistened and sparkled in the sunlight. Here and there, it trickled downward.

Pete stepped closer to her. He crouched next to Jeff.

The woman on her hands and knees was slightly upslope from him.

He could see the goosebumps on her skin.

He watched a drop of water dribble down the side of her left breast. It slid to the tip of her nipple and stayed there, trembling.

'You're safe now,' Jeff told her. 'You'll be all right. We'll take care of you.'

Her head moved slightly up and down – a nod?

The drop of water lost its hold on her nipple and fell to the ground.

'We need to get her an ambulance,' Pete said.

'Good luck, man. All you'll get is a busy signal.'

'Sure.'

'I'm telling you. But go ahead if you don't believe me. You'll find out.'

He didn't want to go. If he left, he might miss something.

Might?

At the very least, he would lose his chance to *watch* her for a few more minutes. But who knows what else might happen? She might decide to lie down on her back for a little more rest. She might stand up and stretch. She might start talking.

Pete didn't want to miss *anything*.

'Maybe she doesn't *need* an ambulance,' Jeff said.

'Are you kidding? Look at her. She should be in a hospital.'

'We could take her to one in your car,' Jeff suggested. 'It'd be quicker that way.'

'I don't know,' Pete said.

His heart started pounding faster.

We'd have to pick her up. Put our hands on her body. On her bare skin. Touch her. Hold her.

Feel her.

'It probably would be quicker that way,' Pete agreed. 'Yeah. That's not a bad idea. It's worth a try, anyway.'

The woman gasped out a low, whispered word.

'What'd she say?' Pete asked.

'I didn't—'

'*Doh!*'

'Dough?' Jeff asked.

They both leaned closer to her and lowered their heads.

'*Doh-nn.*'

'Don't?' Pete said.

'Don't what?' asked Jeff.

'*Tuh . . . Tuh-ch.*'

'Touch?' Pete asked.

'Don't touch?'

'*Meeee.*'

Chapter Thirty-four

'We just want to help you,' Jeff said.

'*Don't . . . touch.*'

She wasn't unconscious before, Pete thought. She was wide awake and paying attention. Knows everything we said and did. Now she's got us figured for a couple of creeps . . . or perverts.

Burning with shame, he wanted to run away from her.

But he remained by her side.

'We just want to help you,' Jeff explained. 'We want to take you to a hospital.'

'*No.*'

'What do you *want* us to do?' Pete asked.

In the silence following his question, he half expected her to answer, 'Go to hell.' Or, 'Fuck off.' Or, 'Eat shit and die.'

When she finally spoke, she said, '*Waht.*'

'What?' Jeff asked.

'*Waht-urr.*'

'Water!' Pete blurted, vastly relieved.

'I've got the hose right here.'

'*Dring.*'

'I'll go get a glass or something,' Pete said. 'Right back.'

She didn't respond.

Pete stood up and stepped backward down the slope.

'Everybody stay right where you are, okay? Nobody move.'

'We'll be right here,' Jeff said.

'Don't do anything.'

Jeff smirked at him.

Pete whirled around, rushed down to the wall and climbed it. At the top, he looked back. Jeff, kneeling, blocked his view of the woman's shoulders and head. But he could see the rest of her. She was still on her hands and knees, her body gleaming and dripping.

He hated to leave them.

Hated to miss out on even a few minutes by her side.

Envying Jeff, he sat down on top of the wall, pushed himself off, and dropped. He landed on the hot concrete. Instead of running around the pool, he dived in. The cold shocked him for a moment, then felt good. As he glided below the surface, he realized his trunks had been jerked down around his knees. He pulled them up, then swam to the other side. He almost lost his trunks again when he climbed out. Pulling them up, he ran to the back door of the house. He skidded it open and rushed in.

Though dripping wet, he ran straight across the living-room carpet.

By the time he entered the kitchen, his feet were dry but water continued to spill from his trunks and roll down his body.

What'll I get her? he wondered.

She asked for water, but maybe she'd rather have a Coke or a beer or . . .

Just get her a glass! We can fill it from the hose.

What about ice cubes?

'Good,' he muttered.

He grabbed a tumbler down from the cupboard, hurried over to the refrigerator and tugged open the freezer compartment. He reached into the ice-cube container, grabbed a handful of cubes and dumped them into the glass.

Now what? he wondered.

Try the phone?

He stepped over to the wall phone . . . and stared at it.

If I get through and they send an ambulance, they'll take her away.

He picked up the handset. Bringing it toward his ear, he heard a dial tone.

She won't be with us anymore. We might never see her again.

Why *should* I call? he asked himself.

Because she needs an ambulance, idiot.

Jeff and I are perfectly capable of driving her to the hospital.

She needs an ambulance.

She *said* no hospital, he reminded himself. She just wants water.

And I want to get back outside.

He hung up the phone.

Then, feeling a sudden rush of guilt, he grabbed it again.

I *have* to call, he told himself.

He set the glass on the floor to free his right hand, then tapped in 911.

Jeff's gonna kill me.

The ringing started.

I must be nuts, he told himself, throwing away a chance like this. But it's the right thing to do. I've gotta live with myself.

We would've had to lift her up, he thought. Maybe even carry her. Now we won't have any excuse to touch her at all. We'll just have to leave her on the ground and stand around till the ambulance shows up.

One of us will have to wait in front of the house, not even *with* her. And guess who *that*'ll be?

The ringing continued.

'Haven't got all day,' he muttered.

Another ring.

How many is that?

Four or five?

I'll give it five more. If nobody's answered by then . . . He hung up.

Screw them if they can't answer the phone.

He crouched and picked up the glass. It felt slippery and cold from the ice cubes inside.

Should I take her some aspirin? he wondered. Bet she's got a headache.

Might not be such a hot idea, though. Messed up the way she is, the last thing she needs is a blood thinner.

What about Tylenol?

Forget about it, he told himself. Just get out there with the glass and . . .

What else?

Find her something to wear.

Jeff'll kill me.

I'd want to kill me.

But what will *she* think if I don't come back with a sheet or something to put around her?

This is a no-brainer, he thought, hurrying toward the hallway. I take her out something to wear or I look like a total shit.

But what? he wondered.

It's gonna get bloody.

An old sheet? An old towel? Something of Mom's . . .?

I can't go looking through Mom's stuff.

What about *my* stuff?

Let her wear a pair of my trunks.

He had a dresser drawer full of old swimsuits. They would be too big for her. They wouldn't stay up.

All the better.

And his swimsuits didn't come with tops.

Even better.

Just take her out a pair of big, loose trunks . . . It'll look like I tried . . .

He suddenly remembered the swimwear in the guest room. Mom and Dad had collected a variety of suits in different styles and sizes for friends who might drop by the house and want to enjoy the pool.

She doesn't know about them, he told himself. I could still take her a pair of my trunks.

That'd be a dirty trick.

Besides, Pete had occasionally spent some time inspecting the guest suits. There were a couple of very good ones. Especially the black string bikini that Harriet Hanson always liked to wear when she came over.

Harriet looked amazing in it.

If our gal looks half as good . . .

Pete hurried into the guest room, set down the glass of ice cubes and opened the dresser drawer.

In seconds, he found the string bikini.

Holding it up, he looked at the dangling cords and tiny patches of fabric.

What'll she think . . .?

I'll tell her it's all I have, he thought.

Besides, the less there is to it, the less it'll be touching the places where she's hurt.

He shut the drawer. Glass in one hand, bikini in the other, he ran from the guest room and down the hall to the living room. The sliding door was still open. Outside, he used his elbow to shut it. Then he raced alongside the pool, his feet slapping the hot concrete, the ice cubes clinking inside the glass. He took the corners fast. Ahead, he spotted *A Moveable Feast* on top of the cinder-block wall. He ran to it, set the glass near the book, then stuffed the bikini under the waistband of his trunks and leaped at the wall.

Braced up with stiff arms, the top edge pushing against his waist, Pete held himself steady and looked out at the slope.

No longer on hands and knees, the woman was sitting cross-legged, her head down, her hands folded on her lap. Jeff, standing off to the side, was showering her with a broad, fine spray from the hose.

Nobody was supposed to move.

He felt a moment of anger, then noticed hazy bands of blue and yellow and red light floating in front of the woman, wrapping her in an aura of pure colors.

Pete couldn't move.

He could only stare at her.

She looked magical.

Supernatural.

My God, he thought.

He gazed at her, struck with awe and wonder.

I'll never see anything like this again.

With that, though she still sat shrouded in a misty rainbow, the magic vanished. The loss made Pete ache inside.

He knew he would always remember the way she looked and the way it had made him feel for a few miraculous moments. He also knew that he would have to write about it. And that he didn't stand a chance of getting it right.

How could he possibly make his readers see those vivid rainbow colors? Or the way you could look through them to the woman, the girl, sitting under the spray with her short boy-hair matted down against her scalp and the sunlit water sliding down her body?

Can't.

Nor could he possibly do justice to her radiance, her damaged beauty, her innocence and strength.

He wanted to make his readers ache for her the way *he* ached for her.

He wanted them to fall in love with her.

And to be spellbound by the image of such a glorious wounded survivor sitting naked inside a rainbow all her own.

Can't.

But I can try, he thought.

I should make some notes while it's all still fresh in my mind.

Not that I'll ever forget any of it.

Make notes anyway, he told himself.

'What're you doing up there?' Jeff called.

'Nothing,' Pete said.

He climbed over the top, lowered himself to the ground on the other side, then reached up for the glass of ice cubes.

Chapter Thirty-five

On his way up the slope, Pete pulled the bikini out of his trunks.

'Whatcha got there?' Jeff asked.

'Something for her to wear.'

She didn't look up.

Jeff snarled at him, but said, 'Good idea,' in a way that almost sounded as if he meant it. He turned the hose away as Pete approached the woman.

'It's a swimming suit,' Pete told her. 'It's clean and everything. We keep some extras around for visitors.'

She didn't respond. She just kept her head down, maybe staring at her folded hands, maybe at her ankle or the stem of a weed on the ground in front of her crossed legs. Maybe looking at nothing.

'You want to wear it, don't you?'

'Wah . . . ter,' she said.

'I've got that, too. I've got ice, anyway.' To Jeff, he said, 'Shoot some in here.'

'I almost gave her some in the mouth,' Jeff said. 'Scared she might choke on it, though. Comes out pretty hard.' He swung the spray over and flooded the glass.

'You're not kidding,' Pete said. As the glass overflowed, he pulled it away.

Jeff twisted the nozzle and shut off the water.

Without the hiss and splatter of the spray, the morning seemed strangely quiet.

'Did you find out anything while I was gone?' Pete asked.

'Like what?'

'Like *anything*?'

'Found out she doesn't talk much.'

'What about her name?'

'Haven't got a clue.'

Pete sank to a crouch just in front of her. She didn't look up. 'My name's Pete,' he said. 'This other guy is my friend, Jeff. We found you unconscious back here a few minutes ago. We figure somebody must've . . . well, that you were the victim of a crime. Anyway, we're behind my house. My parents are away for the weekend, but Jeff and I are going to take care of you. Okay?'

She didn't respond.

'What's your name?' Pete asked.

After a few seconds, her head moved a bit from side to side.

'Your name?' Pete asked.

Another shake, but this time it was accompanied by a moan.

Pete frowned over at Jeff and asked, 'What did she say?'

'Said it hurts to shake her head.'

'Very funny.

'I don't think she knows her name,' Jeff said. 'Or doesn't want to tell us.'

'Can you remember your name?' Pete asked her.

'*Water*.'

'Maybe that's her name,' Jeff suggested.

'I doubt it.'

'Ever hear of John Waters?'

'Yeah, but . . .'

'We can *call* her Water.'

'*Water*,' she said again.

Pete reached out with the glass and held it under her face. 'Here you go,' he said.

Slowly, she lifted a hand. She took hold of the glass, but almost dropped it. Letting out a soft whimper, she jerked up her other hand and caught it. Some water sloshed out. The ice cubes clinked like wind chimes struck by a gust.

She raised the glass toward her mouth, then stopped without taking a drink.

She *can't* take a drink, Pete realized. Not slumped over like that.

'Want some help?' he asked.

Moaning, she raised her head and straightened her back. Her eyes met Pete's.

The whites were bloodshot, but the irises were pale blue. He thought he could see pain in them. And wariness.

Her eyes lowered. She watched the glass as she lifted it with both hands toward her lips.

Swollen, cracked, bloody lips.

As she drank, she shut her eyes. She tipped the glass higher. Water suddenly spilled from its edges and ran down her chin, but she continued to swallow. The dribbles rolled down her neck, trickled down the center of her chest.

With her arms up, there was nothing in the way of Pete's view. Ashamed of himself but excited, he stared at her breasts.

What if she catches me?

I'll be okay as long as she's drinking.

Quickly, he slid his gaze down her front and stared between her legs.

He ached.

She started to lower the glass, so Pete jerked his eyes up to her face.

Jeff let out a laugh.

Pete scowled at him. 'What?'

'Nothing,' Jeff said.

The woman's left hand fell away from the glass and dropped across her thigh. Her right hand, holding the glass, settled on her knee. The water was gone. A few shrunken pebbles of ice remained at the bottom of the glass.

'More water?' Pete asked.

She looked at him. 'Huh-uh.'

He showed her the bikini. 'Do you want this on?'

Her head moved slightly up and down.

'I don't think she's in any shape to put it on herself,' Jeff said.

'Do you want us to help you?' Pete asked her.

'Blee . . .'

'I think that's a "please",' Jeff interpreted.

'Yuh,' she said.

We have to put it on her!

'She'd better stand up first,' Jeff said.

'Can you stand up?' Pete asked her.

'I . . .' She shook her head a bit.

'Is anything broken?' he asked her.

'How would *she* know?'

'She might know if she has a broken leg or something.'

'What makes you think so? She doesn't even know her name.'

Looking Pete in the eyes, she said, 'Chair.'

'She wants a chair?' Jeff asked.

'Me,' she said. 'Chair. Chairee.'

'Is that's your name?' Pete asked.

She nodded and winced.

'What's her name?' Jeff asked.

'Cherry, I guess.'

'Wow,' Jeff said. 'Cool name.'

She groaned.

'Do you think any of your bones are broken?' Pete asked her.

'Ah . . .' She lowered her head.

'She moved around enough to sit up,' Jeff pointed out. 'I'm pretty sure she hasn't got a broken leg or arm.'

'Do you want us to lift you, Cherry?'

'Yuh.'

Jeff stepped over to her side and squatted down. 'You take one arm,' he said, 'and I'll take the other.'

'Okay.'

Pete stuffed the bikini under his waistband, then crawled to her left side, turned around and crouched. He studied her upper arm, looking for a good place to grip it.

There *was* no good place. Wherever he might take hold, he would encounter bruising or raw, red wounds.

'Be careful where you grab her,' he told Jeff.

'Sure thing.'

Turning toward her, Pete slipped his right hand under her armpit. It went in from behind. Her armpit felt moist and hot and snug. He eased his thumb down against an abrasion on the outer side of her arm.

'How's that?' he asked.

She nodded.

He cupped his left hand under her elbow. She didn't flinch or cry out, so he supposed it must be okay.

'How you doing, Jeff?' he asked.

'Got her.'

They waited while she uncrossed her legs, brought up her knees and planted her feet against the ground.

'Ready?' Pete asked her.

'Yuh.'

'Ready, Jeff?'

'All set.'

'Okay, *up*.'

Pete and Jeff stood, lifting her. She stiffened and whimpered. On her feet, though unsteady, she seemed to be bearing most of her own weight. Pete relaxed his hold.

She flinched. '*Don' leggo!*'

'I won't. I won't. It's all right. We won't let you fall.'

'It'll be all right,' Jeff told her. In a louder voice, he said, 'Let's get her off this hillside before we do anything else.'

'Right.'

Bracing her up between them, they made their way down the slope. They stopped on level ground in front of the cinder-block wall.

'Maybe this'd be a good place to put the swimsuit on,' Pete told her. 'Can you stand on your own?'

'Ah . . . try.'

As they loosened their hold, Cherry raised her arms, leaned forward and put her hands against the wall like a fugitive waiting to be frisked by the police.

Pete pulled the bikini out of his trunks.

'Do you think you can put it on yourself?' he asked.

'Nuh.'

'Okay. Well.' As Pete stared at the bikini, Jeff came over to him.

'Here,' Jeff said, and took the pants. He stepped in close behind Cherry, knelt down, and used both hands to spread the thin elastic waistband. 'Can you lift a foot?' he asked.

She raised her left foot off the ground.

Leaning so close to her that his forehead almost touched

her rear end, Jeff slipped the pants around her upraised foot. 'Now the other.'

A moment later, they were around both her ankles. Keeping the sides of the waistband pulled away from her, Jeff lifted the pants. As the skimpy black seat slid up her buttocks, he eased the elastic in against her hips. 'Wanta keep it loose,' he muttered. Then, as if afraid she might misunderstand, he added, 'Pull it up too much, it might hurt. You know, your wounds.'

He shuffled backward on his knees, then stood up. With a nod toward the bikini top in Pete's hands, he said, 'Want me to take care of that for you?'

'That's all right,' Pete said.

With Jeff watching, he tied the two neck strings together. Then he stepped up to Cherry's side. 'I think I have to get under there,' he said. He ducked beneath Cherry's arm. As he came up slowly between her and the wall, his bare shoulder brushed against her breast. The feel of it shocked him with delight and embarrassment. 'Sorry,' he murmured. Though the touch had lasted only a moment, he could still feel it as he straightened up and faced her.

Her eyes were inches from his.

He tried to smile. 'This is kind of awkward,' he said. With both hands, he slipped the loop over her head and eased it down behind her neck. 'There,' he whispered.

Bending his knees slightly, he saw that the limp black patches draped the tops of her breasts. The remaining two strings dangled toward her waist. He crouched lower, took one string in each hand, and raised them to the sides of her ribcage.

'Jeff,' he said. 'Can you get these?'

'No problem.' He stepped behind Cherry and took the strings from Pete. 'Tie 'em?' he asked.

'Yeah.'

As Jeff drew them backward, the bikini top closed in too high – slightly above her nipples. 'Hold it,' Pete said.

Jeff stopped pulling. 'Problem?' he asked.

'Not really.'

Pete crouched slightly lower, reached up with both hands and hooked his fingertips underneath the bikini. He felt Cherry's breasts against the backs of his fingers. They were hot and slippery, her nipples stiff. He pushed upward gently against them as he drew the bikini downward. It came down easily past the bottoms of her breasts.

'Okay,' Pete said. 'You can tie 'em now.'

To protect the long, curving cut beneath her left breast, Pete kept his fingertips under the bikini while Jeff tied the knot behind her back.

'Got it,' Jeff said.

Pete pulled his fingers out. Then he straightened up and looked Cherry in the eyes. Blushing furiously, he said, 'It's a little loose so it won't hurt you.'

'Good,' she whispered. 'Thanks.'

Thank *you*, Pete thought. But he said, 'You're welcome.'

'Yeah,' said Jeff.

Pete smiled at her. 'Well,' he said. 'Guess that's it.' Then he ducked and sidestepped, passing underneath her arm, this time missing her breast. 'That takes care of that,' he said.

He wished he could do it all over again.

Chapter Thirty-six

'Now what?' Jeff asked.

'Take her to a hospital, I guess,' Pete said.

'How?'

'Drive her.'

'In the 'vette?'

'The Mercedes. Mom and Dad took the 'vette to Palm—'

'No,' Cherry said.

They both looked at her.

She stood just as before, leaning forward slightly, her arms up, her hands on the wall. 'No . . . No hah . . . hospital.'

'You've *gotta* go to a hospital,' Pete said.

'No she doesn't,' Jeff said.

'She's hurt really bad.'

She took a step toward the wall. Shoving at it, she stood up straight. She lowered her arms to her sides, then stood there motionless with her head down. After a few seconds, she lifted her head. Very slowly, she began to turn around. She looked so unsteady that Pete raised his hands, ready to catch her if she should start to fall. But she stayed up and continued to turn ever so slowly until she was facing him. Then she said, 'I'm . . . fine.'

A single, quick laugh burst out of Jeff. Then he said, 'Sorry. Not funny.'

Pete frowned at him. To Cherry, he said, 'You're *not* fine. You're a wreck.'

'She is standing,' Jeff pointed out.

'Yeah. And she looks like she's up for a role in *Beach of the Living Dead*.'

'Not . . . dead,' she said.

Maybe she *is*, Pete suddenly thought.

Yeah, right.

But something in his face must've betrayed his sudden concern because Cherry said, 'I'm . . . not . . . dead.'

He forced himself to laugh. 'I know. Jeez. Of course you're not.'

Grinning, Jeff said, 'Ain't no such thing as the living dead, dude.'

'I know that.'

'Besides, Cherry's breathing. She's got a heartbeat. And she's warm.'

She turned her head slightly toward Jeff and said, 'Thanks.'

'She's also beautiful and brave.'

She groaned.

'Well, you are.'

'But you're *really* banged up,' Pete told her. 'You might have some sort of serious damage that needs to be fixed. You know? Maybe you've got internal bleeding or something. Maybe you need an operation.'

'No,' she said.

'How do you know?'

'She doesn't want to go to a hospital,' Jeff said. 'So why don't we leave it at that?'

'We're responsible for her.'

'Are not. We're not even adults – and she *is*. She can make her own decisions. If she wants to stay away from the hospital, we've got no right to force her. I mean, who knows? Maybe she's got very good reasons.'

'What's a good reason?'

'Hospital's gonna cost her a fortune,' Jeff said. 'Maybe she's got no medical insurance.'

'Even if she doesn't—'

'Or how about this? Maybe getting medical care's against her religion. You know? She might be like a Christian Scientist. Some people, they'd rather *die* than go against their faith.'

Cherry looked into Pete's eyes and nodded.

'You won't go to a hospital because of your religion?' Pete asked.

She nodded more strongly, but it seemed to hurt her. With a grimace, she stopped.

'Okay,' Pete said. 'No hospital. But what do you *want* us to do? Should we phone someone for you? Take you someplace? We'll do whatever you want.'

'In . . . the house.'

'You want to go inside *my* house?'

'Yuh.'

'Okay,' Pete said. He almost smiled, but held it back. 'That'd be fine.'

Fine? he thought. *Fine?*

This is so damn great!

Take it easy, he told himself. She's been through all kinds of hell. I've got no right to feel happy about any of this.

'I think we can forget about going over the wall,' he said. 'We'll have to go around.'

'Kind of far,' Jeff said.

'She can't climb over this.'

'Try,' she said.

'No. You're wrecked up enough as it is.'

'*More* than enough,' added Jeff. To Pete, he said, 'What about getting out a ladder?'

'She can hardly stand up; we don't want her trying to climb a ladder.'

'Then I guess we'll have to hang on to her arms and hobble around to the front of the house.'

'We can't walk three across,' Pete explained, avoiding the word *abreast*. 'It's too narrow back here.'

'Well, maybe just one of us can hold her.'

'I'm . . . fine,' Cherry said. 'Walk alone.'

'It's a *long* way,' Jeff said.

'I'll . . . make it.'

'You sure?' Pete asked.

'Try,' she said.

'I'll go first.' Jeff turned away, took a couple of steps alongside the cinder-block wall, then stopped and looked around. 'This way,' he said.

Slowly, Cherry began to turn toward him.

'Wait,' Pete said. Blushing again, he stepped in front of her. 'If you want, I'll be happy to carry you. I mean, you know, like piggyback? Why don't we try that? Unless you'd rather not.'

'That's a really good idea,' Jeff pointed out. 'I'd carry you myself, Cherry, but as you can see I'm a pint-sized shrimp.'

Meeting Pete's eyes, she said, 'Uh-kay.'

'Great.' He hitched up his drooping trunks, turned away from her, then squatted so low that his rear end almost touched the ground.

Jeff turned around to watch.

Pete heard Cherry stagger up behind him. Her hands lowered onto his shoulders. When her open legs slid against his sides, he reached back with both hands and clutched her under the thighs. Lifting, he straightened his legs.

My God, she's heavy!

Or I'm just weak.

Riding him up, Cherry went rigid and let out a whimper.

'You all right?' Pete asked.

'Fine.' She spoke the word in a high voice that sounded like a hurt little girl.

'Do you want me to put you down?'

'No,' she said.

I'm gonna lose her if . . .!

With a small jump, Pete tugged at her thighs and raised her higher onto his back.

She yelped.

'I'm sorry,' he said.

'Uh. Okay.' She let go of his shoulders and held on to the top of his head.

'You okay?' he asked.

'Yuh.'

'Here we go.'

He started walking quickly alongside the wall. Jeff, several strides ahead, walked sideways and backward so he could keep his eyes on them.

This is so cool, Pete thought.

She seemed awfully heavy for someone so slender, but he liked carrying her. He liked clinging to the bottoms of her thighs. He liked having her legs on both sides of him. Her groin, tight against his back, felt hot through the thin fabric of her pants. Higher, she was bare and slippery. Her breasts, on both sides of Pete's head, bounced and swayed inside her loose bikini top. Sometimes, when he jostled her, they swung and patted his ears.

He carried her to the end of the wall, around the corner, then along a strip of level ground between the wall and a drainage ditch.

As they approached the front corner, Jeff asked, 'How's it going?'

'Okay,' Pete answered, just as a breast bumped softly against his ear.

Jeff grinned. 'Looks like the job has its perks.'

'Up yours,' Pete said. Short of breath, he added, 'How about . . . opening the gate?'

'Gotcha.' He stepped around the corner.

By the time Pete arrived with Cherry on his back, Jeff was standing inside the pool area, holding the gate open for them.

'Thanks,' Pete said. He stopped in front of Jeff. 'Give me a hand?'

'You're about to lose something, huh?'

'Pull 'em up?'

'I don't know, man.'

'Just do it. Please?'

Laughing softly, Jeff ducked and reached for Pete's drooping trunks. He gave them a quick lift by the waistband.

'Thanks,' Pete said. 'Now can you get the back door?'

'Righto.' Jeff hurried ahead, slid it open, then stepped out of the way.

Pete entered, carrying Cherry. After walking over the ground and the concrete, the soft carpet of the living room felt wonderful under his bare feet.

Jeff slid the door shut. 'Gonna put her down?' he asked.

'Where?' Pete asked.

'How should I know?'

'I was asking Cherry.'

'Uh,' she said. 'Bath . . . room.'

'Good idea.'

Though no more gates or doors stood in the way, Jeff hurried ahead of them.

Cherry started to slip.

Pete jumped and hoisted her higher. She whimpered a little

but didn't cry out. 'Sorry,' he said, and hurried across the living room. At the foyer, he turned right and carried her down the hallway.

Jeff was already waiting just outside the guest bathroom. He'd turned the light on.

Pete lurched through the doorway. The moment he felt the tile floor under his feet, he stopped and crouched low. He released his hold on Cherry's legs. She slid off his back.

Though haggard and aching and breathless, Pete suddenly felt nearly weightless. He stood up straight, groaning. Where he'd been feeling the slick heat of Cherry's skin, he now felt cool air.

He felt vast relief to be free of the burden.

But he missed it, too.

I'll probably never do anything like that again.

She patted him gently on the back. 'Thanks,' she said.

He turned around and smiled at her. 'Glad I could help.'

Nodding slightly, she patted him on the chest. 'Now go.'

'Okay,' he said. 'But what . . .? What should we do? Do you need anything?'

'I'll . . . be fine. Just . . . need time. Bath.'

'You want to take a bath?'

'Can't say I blame her,' Jeff said.

'We'd better run the water for you,' Pete told her. 'And we'll help you in. Okay?'

Patting him on the chest again, she said, 'Go. I'm fine. I'll . . . be out . . . in a while.'

'You want us to just wait?'

'Yuh.'

Jeff asked, 'What about your swimming suit? Do you need us to help you take it off?'

'Nah.' She almost smiled. 'Thanks. Go.'

'Do you need *anything*?' Pete asked.

'Bye-bye.'

'Okay. Bye.'

'Bye,' said Jeff.

They left her standing in the middle of the bathroom. Pete, last out the door, pulled it shut.

They headed down the hall.

'How about a Pepsi?' Jeff asked.

'Sure.'

'Man, oh man.'

'What?' Pete asked.

'What do you mean, *what?* Man, we got us a babe.'

'She's really something, huh?'

'She's in-fuckin'-credible.'

'She's awfully messed up.'

'All the better, dude. We can take care of her.'

'I guess so.'

'Just you and me.'

'For now, anyway.'

'Let's *keep* her, man. We've got your whole house to ourselves.'

'Well, we'll see what she wants to do.'

In the kitchen, Pete walked over to the refrigerator and took out two cans of Pepsi. 'I left that glass outside,' he said.

'I'll get it for you.'

'Thanks.'

'Let me rest for a minute.'

'What do *you* need to rest for? You didn't carry her around on your back.'

'It was hard work watching, you lucky stiff.'

Smiling, Pete handed a can to him.

Jeff popped it open. 'Sure wish *I* could've carried her.'

'She's heavier than she looks.'

Jeff shook his head, then took a drink, then sighed, then said, 'Man.'

'What?'

'Is this the coolest thing that's ever happened, or what?'

'I don't suppose *she* feels that way.'

Chapter Thirty-seven

Toby woke up to find himself shivering. He was stretched out on his own bed – on top of the covers – and wearing only the Winnie the Pooh nightshirt that he'd taken from Sherry's apartment.

Somebody must've boosted up the air conditioning.

He rolled onto his side and saw the clock on the nightstand.

10:20.

Sid and Dawn were probably up by now.

Stores would already be open. Sid could get the duplicate keys made.

I don't wanta ask him.

Toby didn't want to *see* Sid, much less remind him about the car keys.

Maybe I should just go back to sleep, he thought.

But he couldn't fall asleep unless he got warm, so he crawled under the covers.

Feeling cozy, he sighed and shut his eyes.

So much to do. I shouldn't be going back to sleep.

I *need* more sleep, he told himself. After last night . . .

In his mind, it was last night again. He was in Sherry's bedroom, on Sherry's bed, on top of Sherry.

I should go through it from the start, he thought, so I won't miss anything.

But starting where?

How about in the car when I pulled her down on my lap?

No, start when I got her on the bed. That was when all the best stuff happened.

No, how about a little earlier when she was up on the window sill and I stuck my hand under her skirt?

Yeah.

So he started there.

Soon, the covers felt too hot and heavy on top of him. He shoved them out of the way, keeping only the top sheet. Lifting his head off the pillow, he saw that the sheet was jutting up like a tent over his groin.

I'll never fall asleep thinking about this stuff.

What *should* I think about? he wondered.

AIDS.

The word leaped into his mind as if it had been lurking nearby, waiting to pounce.

It landed on him hard.

Knocked his wind out.

You're gonna die, he heard Sherry say. *You fucked me. You bit me. You got my blood in your mouth. You got AIDS now.*

Stomach hurting, Toby went cold all over. He felt as if he were shriveling.

He rolled onto his side and curled up.

She *didn't* have AIDS, he told himself. It was a lie. She was just trying to get at me.

And man, did *she!*

And man, did she pay for it!

The numbing terror loosened its grip as Toby found himself reliving what he'd done to Sherry – payback for scaring him like that.

Oh, yes. Got her so good.

He lingered on the way she'd flinched and squealed. On how she'd jerked rigid. On how she'd thrashed and whimpered. On how her whole body had shuddered just before the end.

Oh, did she pay!

Toby moaned in pleasure, remembering.

If only she'd lasted longer . . .

Best night of my life, anyway. Especially there on the bed. Especially the payback. If she did give me AIDS, it was worth it.

Did she?

Probably not, he told himself. It was probably just a lie. And even if *she* had it, doesn't mean *I'll* get it.

But what if I do?

He felt the terror beginning to creep into him again.

I'll still have a good ten years, he told himself.

Maybe not so 'good'.

Fucking bitch. I oughta . . .

Oughta what, kill her again?

No, but I can kill her whole fucking family for her.

Even if she didn't give me AIDS, he thought, I told her I'd nail them all if she gave me any shit – and she went for the gun. I owe her for that.

Besides, he thought, I *want* to.

First, I'll take care of her mom and dad. Get them out of the way, then take my time with Brenda.

An image of Brenda filled his mind.

Oh, man.

She'll be even better than Sherry, he thought. What I've gotta do is figure a way to keep her. Maybe take her someplace where we can live together.

That'd be so cool.

Keep her as my prisoner for as long as I want.

Do everything with her.

To her.

That'll be so great!

But where do I keep her?

How about here?

I can do her right here on my own bed! That'd be so incredibly great*! Tie her down . . .*

Sure, he thought. That'd be great, all right. Except for one thing.

Sid and Dawn.

That's two things, he corrected himself.

Well, not really. Two people, but they're both the same problem.

Not really. They're different problems. Dawn, she'd be shocked and go ballistic. Sid, he'd muscle in and take over Brenda for himself.

I can't do it with them in the house.

Chapter Thirty-eight

Some of the others had stripped down to their swimming suits. Not Brenda, though. She had kept her sneakers on, and she still wore her Piglet T-shirt and cut-off jeans over her bikini. She was glad of it, too, when she saw her parents' car pull into the school parking lot.

'Is that your mom and dad?' Fran asked, and wiped her face with a sleeve of her sweatshirt.

Fran, like Brenda, was barefoot and wearing cut-offs. Instead of a T-shirt, however, she wore a large, bulky gray sweatshirt. Brenda had rarely seen her friend *not* wearing such sweatshirts. Fran seemed to like the way they disguised her hunky torso, never mind how they made her sweat in hot weather.

'It's them, isn't it?' she asked.

'Yep. They probably came over to check up on me.'

'As if,' Fran said. 'They're *nice*.'

'They're okay.' She turned away from the car she was washing and tossed her sponge into a bucket. 'Guess I'd better see what's up.'

'Maybe they want their car washed.'

'Wouldn't surprise me.'

As Brenda walked toward the car, the driver's side window slid down and her father smiled at her. 'How's it going?' he asked.

'It's going.'

'Hi, dear,' Mom called from the passenger seat.

Brenda bent over and put her hands on the window sill. 'So how was breakfast?' she asked.

'Great,' Dad said. 'We went to Coco's.'

'Ah, for the famous cinnamon bread French toast?'

'That's what *I* had.'

'Big surprise. What about *you*, Mom? Corned beef hash and eggs?'

'Not today.'

'You were wrong!' Dad blurted. 'I can't believe it!'

'I get a second try,' Brenda said. 'Country fried steak and eggs.'

'There you got it,' Mom said.

'I never fail.'

'Not if we give you enough tries,' Dad pointed out.

'So what're you guys doing here?' she asked.

'You mean you don't know?'

'You came to get the car washed.'

'Not bad,' Dad said. 'First try, too. I'm impressed.'

'Are you sure it *needs* a wash? It hasn't been a year yet.'

'That's what *I* said,' Mom said.

'We just want to support your endeavor,' Dad explained.

'Has Sherry come by?' Mom asked.

Brenda shook her head. 'Not yet. But it's still early. If she spent the night shacked up with Duane or someone, she might not get the message for hours. Anyway, it's no biggie if she doesn't show. I'm glad you guys came by, though. Some of us are thinking about going for pizza after we get done here. Okay if I go along?'

'Sure, honey,' Mom said. 'I don't see any problem with that.'

'Where're you planning to go?' Dad asked.

'It's not definite. Shakey's or Pizza Hut, probably.'

'Do you have plenty of money?' he asked.

She rolled her eyes upward and said, 'Yes. My money situation hasn't taken any dramatic turns since we discussed it earlier this morning.'

'As a matter of fact,' Dad said, 'when we discussed the situation then, you weren't planning to go anywhere for dinner.'

'I suppose that's true.'

'Thank you.'

'*Do* you have enough?' Mom asked.

'Yes.'

'How'll you be getting to the pizza place?' Dad asked.
'In a car, I imagine.'
'In *whose* car?'
'We're not sure yet.'
'*We* could drive you and your friends over.'
'That's all right, Dad. We don't have a shortage of drivers.'
'How about *responsible* drivers?'
'I'm not going to let some *jerk* drive me around.'
'Do be careful who you ride with,' Mom cautioned her.
'I will, I will. I'm not a moron.'
'So then,' Mom said, 'we won't pick you up at five and we won't expect you home for supper.'
'You got it.'
'What time *will* you be home?' Dad asked.
Brenda grinned. 'In time for bed. *I'm* not the daughter who stays out all night.'
'You're the daughter who's a smart-ass.'
'Mom, you gonna let him talk to me that way?'
'You *are* a smart-ass.'
Laughing, she said, 'I try.'
'What time *can* we expect you?' Mom asked.
'I don't know. Nine? Ten?'
'You're planning to spend five hours eating pizza?' Dad asked.
'We might wanta do something later. Take in a movie, go to a mall . . . have a drunken orgy, rob a Speed-D-Mart.' She shrugged elaborately.
'Ten will be fine,' Mom said. 'If anything comes up and you won't be back by then, call us.'
'Okay.'
'And call us if there's a change of plans,' Dad added.
'Sure, why not?' She held out her hand. 'You got five bucks?'
'Ah, you *do* need more money!'
'Ah, I don't. It's for the car wash.'
'Ah,' he said.
'Ah.'
He leaned away, pulled out his wallet, fingered its bill compartment and drew out a ten-dollar bill.

'You're gonna make me make change?'

'Keep the whole thing. It's for a good cause.'

'Just five'll be fine. That's all we're charging. Don't you have some ones?'

'Take the ten, okay?'

She shook her head, rolled her eyes upward, sighed, and took the ten. 'Happy?' she asked.

'Overjoyed.'

'It'll be about a five-minute wait,' she said. 'That okay? I know how you love to wait.'

'No problem,' Dad said.

'Okay. Well, you'll be next after we get done with that red car. Why don't you pull in behind it? We'll get to you as soon as we can.'

'No hurry,' Dad said.

'Better put your windows up,' Brenda told him.

'How about if we leave them open until you're ready to start?'

She rolled her eyes. 'Suit yourself. See ya.' Stepping backward, she pointed toward the red car.

'I know,' Dad said.

As he started backing up, Brenda turned away and hurried over to join the rest of the crew.

When they were done washing the car, Dad started the engine and rolled down his window.

Oh, please. Not in front of everyone.

But all he said was, 'Have a good time.' Then he smiled and drove off.

No last-minute interrogation or advice.

Thank you, thank you, thank you.

As Quentin waved a Land Cruiser forward, Brenda nudged Fran's arm. 'How about going out and having some fun after we get done here?'

'Huh?'

'We'll get a few of us together and go someplace. You know? I was thinking maybe the Third Street Promenade or the pier or something. I don't have to be home till ten.'

Fran smiled, but she looked wary. 'I don't know,' she said.

The Land Cruiser pulled forward and stopped in the midst of the washing crew.

Knowing what was coming, several students backed away from it.

Ralph stepped toward the front of the vehicle and opened up with the hose. The water shot out and exploded off the windshield. Spray flew. Brenda saw how it sparkled in the sunlight. She felt cold sprinkles on her legs.

Turning to Fran, she asked, 'What do you say?'

'Huh?'

'Tonight,' she said, raising her voice. 'Santa Monica.'

'That'd sure be pretty cool. Only thing is, my folks are supposed to pick me up at five.'

'Give them a call.'

'I guess I *could*. But I don't think they'll let me go anyway. I mean, you know.'

'Oh, do I ever.'

Ralph started circling the Land Cruiser with his hose.

'My parents,' Brenda said, 'are so overprotective it hurts. Thing is, nobody has to know what we're really up to. Just tell your folks that the whole group's going out for pizza afterward. Tell them *everyone's* going, and you don't want to be the only one left out.'

Fran grinned. 'You're so devious, Brenda.'

'It's one of my many charms.'

'If they let me do it, though, they'll insist I be home by . . . like seven.'

'Tell them you're invited over to my place afterward.'

'I hate to lie.'

'You *are* invited. That's no lie. You can actually spend the night if you want to.'

'You mean for real?'

'Sure. It'd be a kick.'

'What about *your* parents?'

'I didn't ask, but they wouldn't have any problems with that. Half the time, they're *begging* me to make friends and bring them over. They're afraid I've got recluse potential.'

Fran laughed. 'You do.'

Done with the preliminary hose-down, Ralph backed away

from the Land Cruiser. 'Have at it, gang,' he called.

Brenda hoisted her bucket of sudsy water. Flanked by Fran and Baxter, she moved in. Baxter carried a sponge in one hand, a stool in the other. As they reached the Cruiser, Baxter said, 'Excuse me,' and plunged his sponge into Brenda's bucket. Then he planted his stool on the pavement, stepped up and started to wash the vehicle's roof. Brenda set the bucket down. She and Fran took out their sopping sponges and split up to wash the Cruiser's side.

Baxter climbed down. He gave his sponge another dip. As water spilled out of it, he said to Brenda, 'I've got a cell phone in my car.'

'Glad to hear it,' Brenda said.

His face went crimson. 'No, I mean you can *use* it if you want. *Fran* can use it. What I mean is, I happened to hear you talking about . . . you know, tonight. I wasn't *trying* to listen. It's just that you were talking pretty loudly and I was just standing there, and . . .'

'That's all right, Bax. Don't worry about it.'

'I'm just saying she can use my phone. I mean, my car's right here and everything.'

'Okay. I'll ask her about it. Thanks.'

'Sure.' He flashed a wild, frightened smile, then dipped his sponge again and mounted his stool to resume washing the roof.

Brenda hurried over to Fran. Crouching beside her, she said, 'Baxter says you can use his cell phone.'

'Huh?'

'To call your parents about tonight. He told me you can use the cell phone in his car.'

'Baxter?' She looked up at him.

'Yeah. He was eavesdropping on us.'

'Eavesdropping? Ha! You know why?'

'Why what?' Brenda asked.

'Why he was *listening*.'

'Sure I know.'

'Sure you do. You know everything.'

'Precisely,' Brenda said. 'It's one of my many charms. I'm legendary for—'

'So tell me.'

'I'm not big on quizzes.'

'That's because you don't know.'

'I *do* know.'

'Prove it.'

'Why do I have to prove it?'

'Ha! You *don't* know.'

'Yes, I do.'

'Wanta bet?' Fran asked. 'Betcha five bucks you can't tell me why he was listening.'

'No way. Betting's for suckers.'

'You just don't know.'

Smiling with exceeding sweetness, Brenda said, 'Ah, but I do. He was listening because he's madly in love with me.'

Fran beamed at her. 'You *do* know everything.'

'Damn betcha, baby.'

Fran laughed. Then she knitted her eyebrows. 'If it works out and we can really go, why don't we ask Baxter to come along with us?'

'Get real.'

'Come on, Brenda.'

'He's a twerp.'

'But he's a *nice* twerp, and he's crazy about you.'

'All the more reason *not* to ask him.'

'He's got a car,' Fran pointed out.

'Hmm. Let me think about it.'

Chapter Thirty-nine

Jeff looked over his shoulder at the kitchen clock. Again. He'd been checking the clock ever since they sat down to drink their Pepsis. A while ago, he'd taken a break from his vigil to hurry outside. He'd returned with the empty glass and Pete's copy of *A Moveable Feast*. Dropping into his chair, he'd resumed watching the clock.

Now, he grimaced at Pete. 'She's been in there an awfully long time.'

'My mom disappears for at *least* an hour every time she takes a bath.'

'Mine, too,' Jeff said. 'But this is almost an hour and a half, and Cherry's messed up. You know? I think we oughta check on her. Make sure she hasn't passed out, or something.'

'Maybe we oughta give her a little more time.'

'So she can drown?'

He didn't add, *Like my sister*. He didn't have to. Pete saw it in his eyes.

'Okay,' Pete said. 'I guess it won't hurt anything to knock on the door.'

They hurried out of the kitchen and down the hallway to the guest bathroom. Their heads almost touching the door, they stood motionless and listened.

Pete heard nothing from the other side.

Jeff shook his head.

Pete knocked gently on the door. No response came, so he called, 'Cherry? Are you all right?'

Nothing.

He met Jeff's eyes.

'We'd better go in,' Jeff whispered.

'I guess so, but . . .'

'Now.'

'Okay.'

As he reached for the doorknob, it turned and the latch popped with a sudden thump. Startled, he flinched. Jeff gasped. The door swung inward and warm, moist air drifted out. Standing in the wispy steam, a towel spread out on the floor beneath her feet, was Cherry.

'Hi guys,' she said.

She no longer wore the black, string bikini. Her naked body, clean and shiny, was dripping onto the towel.

Pete and Jeff gaped at her.

She made no attempt to cover herself.

Doesn't she know what she's doing to us?

Trying to keep his eyes on her face, Pete said, 'Uh . . . We were getting worried. We wanted to make sure . . . Are you okay?'

'Better,' she said. 'Thanks.'

'You look better,' Pete said. Blushing, he added, 'I mean like more alert.'

'Guess you didn't drown,' Jeff told her.

'No.'

'Glad of that. We'd hate to lose you.'

'Can you help?' she asked.

'Sure,' Jeff said.

'What do you want us to do?' Pete asked.

'Antiseptic. Bandages. I don't want to . . . get infected.'

'We've got all kinds of stuff,' Pete said.

'Should we dry you off first?' Jeff asked.

She shook her head slightly. 'No. It'd hurt. I'll be dry . . . pretty soon.'

'Not in this steamy place,' Pete said. 'Maybe we should go to a different room.'

'Yeah,' she said.

'If we go outside,' Jeff said, 'the sun'll dry her off. The wind, too.'

Pete frowned. 'I don't know. Might be better to stay in the house. Somebody might see her back there.'

'Nobody's gonna see her.'

'Probably not, but . . .'

'Outside,' Cherry said.

'Sure,' Pete said. 'If that's what you want.'

'Yeah.'

Trying to smile, he could feel his lips trembling. 'Want me to carry you out?'

'Thanks. Don't want to break you. I'll—'

'*I'll* carry you,' Jeff offered, his red face grinning. 'I'm a *strong* shrimp.'

'You'd drop me.'

'Nah!'

'I'll walk. But thanks.'

'We'll need to take some stuff out with us,' Pete said. He entered the bathroom, turning sideways to slip past Cherry.

She turned, too, and stepped backward toward the counter.

In front of Pete, the bathtub was empty. The string bikini was draped over its faucet handles. He wondered how she'd managed to take it off.

Probably easier to take it off, he thought, than to put it on.

He turned toward the medicine cabinet. Its mirror was fogged except near the very bottom. There, the glass had already gone clear. It showed a reflection of his belly and swimming trunks. The trunks, though loose and baggy, jutted out enough to be fairly obvious.

He wondered if Cherry had noticed.

How could she not?

Blushing, he swung the cabinet open. He took out a plastic bottle of hydrogen peroxide, a tin of bandages, and a small box containing packets of Neosporin. He held them in one hand and took down a clear plastic box full of cotton balls. He set the cotton container on the edge of the sink, then reached up for a roll of gauze.

'Need a hand?' Cherry asked.

She was leaning back against the counter, her knees bent slightly, her head turned toward him. Her right arm was down at her side, her hand flat against the tile surface. The edge of the counter was pushing into her buttocks. Pete lifted his eyes to her face. 'Jeff can help me,' he said.

'Sure. What do you want? More than happy to oblige, old bean.'

Cherry, almost smiling, turned her head toward Jeff.

'Come on over and help me carry some of this stuff.'

'On my way.' Hurrying past Cherry, he smiled and said, 'Excuse me, please.'

Pete saw the way Jeff's trunks were sticking out.

Oh Lordy, he thought, we've *both* got boners. This is insane.

What's so insane about it? he asked himself. We're a couple of horny teenagers and she's standing around without a stitch of clothes on. And she's *gorgeous*.

Or she *would* be gorgeous if she weren't so banged up.

Shit, she's gorgeous anyway.

'Here, take this stuff,' he said. He handed Jeff the container of cotton balls, the roll of gauze, and a dispenser of adhesive tape. 'That should do it.'

'What about scissors?' Jeff asked.

'Oh, yeah.' He stepped past Jeff and cast a nervous smile at Cherry. 'They're over here.'

'Am I in the way?' she asked.

'No. No, huh-huh. You're fine. They're just in this drawer here.' He glanced at the drawer. It was below the counter top and dangerously close to the side of Cherry's right buttock. As he approached it, he tried not to let his gaze stray.

Still a long stride from the drawer, he halted and bent forward and stretched out his arm. He pulled the drawer open. Though he kept his eyes on it, he couldn't avoid seeing Cherry's belly. Still wet, her skin was shiny.

Don't look, he told himself.

I'm not!

But rummaging through the drawer, keeping his eyes off Cherry, he saw how her pubic hair was matted down, curls clinging to her pink skin.

He found the scissors and raised them high. 'Got 'em!' He shoved the drawer shut.

'Ready?' she asked.

'All set.'

She pushed herself away from the counter and turned toward the bathroom door. She had a red crease across her buttocks from the edge of the counter. It looked deeper and darker than the cuts and scratches and scrapes scattered up and down her back and rump and legs.

As Pete turned, he met Jeff's eyes.

Jeff raised his eyebrows.

Pete scowled and shook his head.

Hands loaded with first-aid supplies, they followed Cherry into the hallway. Jeff hurried out in front of her. Sidestepping, he smiled and said, 'I'll go first and get the door for you.'

'Thanks,' she said.

But Jeff didn't hurry off to open the door; he stayed a few paces ahead of her. 'How you doing?' he asked.

'Better.'

A lot better, Pete thought. She limped and held herself stiffly, but she seemed much steadier on her feet than she'd been before her bath.

After the gloom of the hallway, the living room seemed very bright.

For the first time, Pete noticed a pattern among the injuries on her back. Hidden like a secret code in the midst of random abrasions and scratches and bruises were ten or twelve long, narrow streaks as if someone had marked her back with a tube of lipstick. But the streaks looked raw and shiny.

Pete felt his throat tighten.

'Jeez,' he muttered.

Cherry's head turned slightly, but she didn't look back at him.

'Somebody *whipped* you?'

'*What*?' Jeff blurted.

'Looks like she's been *whipped*.'

Jeff, almost at the door, hurried back for a look. He stood by Pete's side and shook his head. After a few seconds, he muttered, 'Shit.'

'What'd he whip you with, Cherry?'

Turning around, she glanced from Pete to Jeff and said, 'Shhhh.'

They went silent.

Did she hear something? Pete wondered.

He listened carefully.

'What?' Jeff whispered to her.

'Shhhh-erry. Not *Ch*erry.'

'Huh?' Jeff asked.

'Oh!' Pete blurted. 'I get it! Your name's *Sh*erry!'
'Yeah.'
'Not Cherry?' Jeff asked.
'*Shhh*erry,' Pete told him.
Sherry nodded, almost smiled, the turned away from them and limped toward the glass door.
'I'll get it,' Jeff said. He rushed ahead of her, shifted the cotton container to his left hand and slid the door open.
Sherry stepped outside. Pete and Jeff following her, she limped over the hot concrete to the table.
'What should we do for you?' Pete asked.
She shook her head. Then she dragged one of the chairs away from the table. Turning her back to it, she bent her knees, gripped the aluminum arms, and lowered herself gently onto the plastic seat. Perched near its front, she didn't lean back.
'Bring the stuff,' she said.
They came over to her.
'Start with the . . . hydrogen peroxide,' she said. 'On cotton. Get me . . . every open wound.'
We can't get them *all*, Pete thought. Not while you're sitting down. But he decided not to mention it.
'No problem,' Jeff said.
'Then Neosporin,' Sherry said.
'Okay,' Pete said.
It's a *goo*, he suddenly thought. We'll have to put it on with our fingers!
'Then . . . I don't know. We'll see about bandages. Some, I guess. Anyway . . .' She looked from Jeff to Pete. 'You guys . . . you're so nice.'
Pete felt himself blush. Again. 'We just want to help,' he said.
'We're here to serve you,' said Jeff.
'I know . . . it's tough on you. I'm sorry.'
'Nothing to be sorry about,' Pete said.
'Nothing at *all*,' Jeff said. 'Our pleasure.'
Pete scowled at him.
'Well, it is.'
'I just . . . don't let all this . . . embarrass you. Okay?' said Sherry.

'Nothing embarrasses Jeff.'

She met Pete's eyes. 'Don't *you* be embarrassed. Okay? It's okay for you to . . . you know, *see* me like this. And touch me. Hell, you haven't got much choice.'

He tried to smile. 'Not under the circumstances, I guess.'

'So don't . . . worry about it. Or, you know, about being aroused.'

Pete blushed so fiercely that he wondered if smoke might be rising off his face.

'It's okay,' Sherry said. 'Okay?'

'Okay,' he murmured.

'Ready to go?' she asked.

'Who gets the front and who gets the back?' Jeff asked.

Rising to her feet, Sherry said, 'Share.'

Chapter Forty

After taking a long, hot shower, Toby got dressed and went looking for Sid.

In the den, the curtains were shut across the glass wall, keeping out most of the daylight. Toby found Sid reclining in the glow of the big screen television, a Bloody Mary in one hand, his eyes on the TV where an oiled, shiny guy was posing on a stage, showing off his enormous muscles in time with the song, 'Macho Man'.

The guy on the TV wore skimpy white bikini pants.

Sid wore leopard skin.

Though Toby felt a sickening tightness in his stomach, he asked, 'What're we gonna do about the car?'

'Fuck off,' Sid told him.

'But—'

'I'm busy.'

'We just gonna *leave* it there?'

'Not gonna have my whole day fucked up 'cause of you.'

'How about if I just borrow your keys? I'll walk over and get the car and—'

'The hell you will. Get out of here and leave me alone.'

'You promised.'

'I didn't promise shit.'

'*Sid!*'

'You say one more word, I'm gonna get up and rip you a new asshole.'

Toby kept his mouth shut and started to walk away.

'Fuckin' tub of lard,' Sid muttered.

Toby felt as if he were crumbling inside. But he kept his mouth shut and left the room.

He went looking for Dawn.

This time of the morning, if she hadn't gone off on an errand, she could usually be found poolside working on her tan.

Toby entered the living room. The curtains were open, the room full of sunlight. He walked over to the glass door and looked out.

Dawn was face-down on one of the loungers by the pool.

Toby eased the door open and stepped outside. He slid it shut with barely a sound, then walked silently toward Dawn.

She had untied the strings of her bikini top so they wouldn't leave lines on her back. All she wore was a lime green thong. Sid must've spread the suntan oil on her back. Her tawny skin glistened all the way down to her feet. She looked spectacular except for her bruises. They looked like dark smudges on her arm, on the side of her ribcage and on her left buttock.

Toby crouched down beside her.

Dawn's head was turned in his direction. He could only see her right eye, and it was shut.

'Dawn?' he said quietly.

The eye opened. 'Go away, Toby,' she said, her voice a husky growl as if she were half asleep.

'Didn't Sid say he'd go and get duplicate keys made this morning?'

'I don't know. Don't drag me into this. Go away. You're not supposed to be out here.'

'It's my house, too.'

'Sid catches you out here, he'll pound us both.'

'He can go to hell.'

'*You* go to hell. Okay?' She raised her head off the mat and scowled at him. 'I mean it, Toby. I'm supposed to have my privacy when I'm out here sunning. You know that. He doesn't want you looking at me. And I don't, either, frankly.'

'I'm not hurting anyone,' he said.

'I'm not *here* for your benefit. I'm Sid's gal, not yours. So go on and get out of here.'

'I thought you liked me.'

She frowned at him in silence for a few seconds, then said,

'You'd better get going before he catches you back here.'

'He isn't gonna. He's watching some muscleman thing on the TV.'

'I don't care. Go away.'

'You're the one who oughta leave. What do you want to stick around here for when he's always beating you up?'

'He isn't *always* beating me up. Besides, it's none of your business.'

'If you were *my* girl, I sure wouldn't hit you.'

'Yeah, well, I'm not. So . . .'

'I'd treat you right.'

'Sure you would. But I'd never *be* your girl, Toby.'

'Why not?' he asked, cringing inside, crushed by the answer before she'd even spoken it.

'Look in a mirror sometime,' Dawn said.

'Real nice,' he muttered.

'*Now* will you go away?'

'Yeah. Sure. Sorry I bothered you.'

Not saying another word, Dawn sank down onto the mat and shut her eyes.

'See ya later,' Toby said.

She didn't answer.

Early that morning, Toby had left Sherry's pistol in the van so he wouldn't have to walk into the house with it. He'd parked the van on a quiet street a couple of blocks away.

He didn't feel like walking that far.

Besides, he didn't want to take the risk of neighbors hearing gunshots.

So he stepped back inside the house just long enough to grab a ring of keys. He took the keys outside, unlocked the side door of the garage, opened the door, and entered. He flipped a light switch. An overhead fluorescent came on, buzzing and filling the garage with bright pale light.

There were no cars in the two-car garage.

The day of their parents' funeral, Sid had banished the Mercedes and Mustang to the driveway. Soon, he'd converted the garage into an exercise room with all the latest muscle-building equipment and a wall of mirrors.

But he'd allowed the workbench to stay.

He liked to build things other than his own muscles now and then.

And he prided himself on his collection of tools.

Toby saw himself in the mirrors as he made his way toward the workbench. He hated what he saw.

I'm a tub of lard, all right. No wonder everybody hates me.

But I can fix myself up, he thought. I'll have all this stuff to myself, and I can work out every day and pretty soon I'll look like one of those guys on the TV.

I'll do it, too. I'll look great. All the babes'll throw themselves at me.

Sid's new Black & Decker cordless drill with a twelve volt battery pack was standing upright on top of the workbench. It had a stubby little screwdriver attachment sticking out of its chuck.

Toby turned the chuck and slipped the screwdriver out.

He inserted a drill bit that was about a quarter inch in diameter and maybe four inches long. He twisted the chuck tight. Then he tried to wiggle the bit. It felt good and firm. He smiled.

He set down the power drill.

Hands trembling, he removed all his clothes.

A box cutter was hanging from a hook above the back of the workbench. He took it down and thumbed out an inch of razor-sharp blade.

He set it on the workbench beside the drill.

In a nearby cupboard, he found several pairs of gardening gloves. Most had belonged to his mother. They would be too small for Toby's hands. But there were larger gloves, too. Gloves that his father sometimes wore when digging holes for new bushes – and that Toby had worn, himself, on several occasions when Dad had ordered him to bury animals.

You killed it, you sick fuck, you can bury it.

Sick fuck, Toby thought. Nice thing to call your son.

'Well, guess who got the last laugh,' he muttered, and pulled on a pair of large, cloth gloves.

Naked except for the gloves, he picked up the box cutter and the power drill.

On his way toward the front of the garage, he turned his

head and watched himself in the mirrors.

'Sick fuck in action,' he muttered. Though he smiled, he felt his lips trembling. He seemed to be trembling all over, though none of it showed in the mirrors. He didn't look nervous at all.

'Just nuts,' he said, and chuckled.

When he entered the house, he heard music and voices from the television. On shaky legs, he walked to the den. Before stepping through the entryway, he put his hands behind his back.

Sid was reclining in the easy chair, the same as before. He still wore his leopard-skin bikini pants and still held a Bloody Mary in one hand. His eyes slid away from the television, settled on Toby, then suddenly grew wide. They darted down Toby's body, then up to his face.

'What do you think you're doing?' Sid demanded.

'Figured you might wanta blow me,' Toby said.

'WHAT?'

'Come and get it, honey.'

'I'm gonna kill your fat ass!' Sid roared. He slammed his glass down on the TV tray beside his chair, leaped to his feet and rushed Toby.

Toby waited for him.

He saw a flicker of doubt in his brother's eyes.

Must be wondering how come I'm not running away. And maybe wondering what I've got behind my back.

But the doubt only lasted an instant before the rage came back to Sid. The rage and the confidence. Because, after all, what could this repulsive little puke do to *him,* a wonder of strength and agility?

Charging and growling, Sid reached out for Toby with both hands.

Toby swung up the power drill from behind his back and pressed its trigger. The tool whined into action. He put the four-inch bit into Sid's left eyeball.

Sid squeaked and crashed into him and took him down backward.

Toby slammed against the floor, Sid on top of him.

The drill still in Sid's eye.

Toby's finger still pressing the trigger.

The pierced eye, inches above Toby's face, jittered and squirted and shriveled as the drill whined.

The way Sid was thrashing about, Toby couldn't hold the tool steady. It twisted this way and that, reaming out the socket. In seconds, the eye seemed to be gone. Blood was gushing out of the hole, drenching the power drill and Toby's hand and face.

The blood made the trigger slippery. Toby's finger slipped off it. The tool went silent.

Sid, still on top of him, was whimpering and shuddering.

Toby lowered the drill. The bit slowly emerged from the cavity of Sid's socket.

'How'd you like *them* apples?' Toby asked.

Sid didn't answer.

'I asked you a question,' Toby said.

Sid said nothing. He just whimpered and jerked.

'What's the matter, your ears plugged?'

Not waiting for a response, Toby inserted the four inch bit into his brother's left ear. He pulled the trigger. As the tool whined, he pushed gently. The bit sank in.

Sid twitched and squealed.

Chapter Forty-one

Sherry had remained seated while Pete dabbed hydrogen peroxide on the side of her head. 'What happened here?' he asked.

'Got clobbered.'

'I'll say.'

'Thought he'd shot me . . . guess not.'

Pete stepped out of the way, and Jeff moved in with a gray gob of Neosporin on his fingertip.

Sherry winced as he spread the salve on her wound.

'Take it easy,' Pete warned him.

'It's okay,' Sherry said.

Crouching in front of her, Pete dampened another cotton ball and stretched his arm toward her face.

'I'll stand up,' she said. 'Make it easier.'

'Probably a good idea,' Pete said, backing off.

Sherry clutched the arms of the chair. She pushed herself up slowly, wincing and shaking, then let go of the chair and hobbled forward like an old woman. After stopping, she straightened herself up. 'Easier said than done,' she said.

'You all right?' Pete asked.

'Fine. Ready when you are.'

'I'm all set,' Jeff said. He stood nearby with a foil pack of Neosporin in his hands.

That's not fair, Pete thought. 'Hey Jeff,' he said, 'why don't we *both* do the hydrogen peroxide?'

'Why don't *you* take care of that and I'll follow along after you with the goop? Like an assembly line.'

Bastard.

We can't argue about this, he thought. Sherry'll figure out *why* I want to smear the stuff on her.

'It's a two-step process,' he said.

'You do the first step, I'll do the second.'

Shit!

On the other hand, Pete told himself, this way I'm sure to work on all the good places.

'Okay,' he said. 'No problem.'

Pete stepped up to Sherry and began to dab her facial wounds with cotton balls soaked in hydrogen peroxide. Each time he finished an area, Jeff moved in with a glob of Neosporin on his fingertip.

From her face, Pete worked his way downward, slowly circling her, Jeff coming along in his wake.

Touching her with his finger.

Pete tried not to resent it.

Jeff doesn't even live here. If he hadn't barged in this morning, I could've had her all to myself.

Yeah, right. Only thing is, he's the one who found her. If he hadn't come along – and started screwing around with my book – I never would've known she was back there. She might've stayed out on the hillside and died.

Pete suddenly found himself crouching slightly, facing Sherry's left breast. In addition to the bruises, it had numerous raw, red scratches.

'What about . . . uh, here?' Pete asked.

She looked down. 'Yeah.'

'You sure?'

'Yeah. Go ahead.'

Chuckling, Jeff said, 'We sure don't want *that* to get infected.'

Pete scowled at him.

'Want *me* to do it?' Jeff asked.

Not answering, Pete poured some hydrogen peroxide onto a fresh ball of cotton. He dabbed at the scratches on the top and sides of the breast. Where the clear liquid touched the wounds, it fizzed. Some of it trickled down her breast and dripped off. Pete swabbed the nipple, feeling its stiffness through the wet gob of cotton.

Crouching lower, he looked at the curving slash below her breast. Though it wasn't bleeding, it looked deeper than her other wounds. 'The guy use a razor on you?' he asked.

'Knife.'

Jeff crouched beside him and looked at the wound. He muttered, 'Man.'

'It isn't very deep, though,' Pete pointed out.

'He just wanted to . . . get my attention.'

'Fucking bastard,' Jeff muttered.

Pete gently drew a cotton ball along the length of the slit. Then he moved sideways and began to work on Sherry's other breast. 'Who did this to you?' he asked.

'A guy.'

'We figured that,' Jeff said.

'Someone you know?' Pete asked.

'Sort of.'

As he patted her scratches, his eyes strayed over to Jeff. Jeff was stroking her nipple with a fingertip, smearing it with the greasy salve.

Man!

'I'd sure like to get my hands on him,' Jeff said.

'You and me both,' Pete said.

Sherry said, 'Me, too.'

'We'll rip him a new one,' Jeff said.

Pete worked his way downward, pouring hydrogen peroxide, patting her wounds, littering the concrete around his feet with used cotton balls as he crouched lower, following the scratches and scrapes and gouges down her body.

'Do you know the guy's name?' Jeff asked.

Pete stared between her legs. She had a few raw places.

Should I ask permission?

You know what the answer'll be, he told himself. Just do it.

He poured the fluid onto a fresh ball of cotton, then reached out and gently patted the wound. Sherry flinched.

'I'm sorry,' he said. 'You've got cuts or something.'

'He . . . bit me.'

'Here?'

'Yeah.'

Pete moaned.

Jeff muttered, 'Oh, man.'

'Go ahead,' Sherry said.

Pete glided the dripping wad along the soft, fleshy edges, thinking, *Oh my God. I can't believe I'm doing this. I can't believe she's* letting *me.'*

Done, he began swabbing the wounds on her right thigh.

Jeff moved in with the salve on his fingertip.

Pete watched.

Sherry squirmed a little, then said, 'I can't . . . can't remember his name.'

'Whoever he is, I wanta kill him.'

Bending over slightly, Sherry reached down and rubbed the top of Jeff's head. 'Thanks,' she said. 'But that's . . . my job.'

Chapter Forty-two

Toby stood under the shower just long enough to rinse off the blood. Then he shut off the water and climbed out of the tub. He didn't bother with a towel. Water running down his body, he stepped over to the counter. He frowned at the bloody power drill, then at the box cutter.

The cutter was still fairly clean.

He snatched it off the counter and walked through the house. On his way past the den, he noticed Sid on the floor. There was a nasty puddle under his head.

What'm I gonna do about that?

'First things first,' he muttered.

In the living room, he went to the glass door and slid it open. He stepped outside.

Dawn was still stretched out face-down on the poolside lounge. Her arms, no longer against her sides, were folded underneath her head. As before, her face was turned to her left – toward Toby.

He figured her eyes must be shut.

If they'd been open, she would've yelled by now.

Probably asleep, he thought.

Cutter behind his back, he walked slowly toward Dawn.

Her right eye was definitely shut.

They've both gotta be shut or she'd be raising hell.

The top of her string bikini was still untied. The way her arms were raised, Toby could see her bare side all the way down to the lime green waistband of her thong. Her left breast, its side bare, seemed to be resting loosely on the limp pouch of her top.

He squatted down beside her for a better view.

Her smooth, tanned skin glistened with oil and sweat.

From the way her ribcage slowly expanded and contracted, Toby figured she must be asleep.

He reached down to her hip with the cutter, eased the tip of its razor-sharp blade underneath her waistband, and gently lifted. The strip of fabric parted.

Her side was now bare all the way down.

Dawn slept on.

Toby stood up, stepped around to the other side of the lounge, then crouched and severed the right side of her waistband.

He stood up. Holding the cutter in his teeth, he bent over her and gently drew the thong downward, easing it out of the crevice. She didn't seem to notice. He let it fall into the space between her thighs.

Then he stepped back and took a deep, shaky breath.

Fantastic, he thought.

His heart was pounding quick and hard. His mouth was dry. His rigid penis ached.

Now what? he wondered.

He stepped around to her left side. Crouching, he clamped the cutter between his teeth.

Dawn still seemed to be sleeping.

He caught the dangling string of her bikini top and slowly, carefully, tied it to the aluminum tubing at the side of the lounger.

Then he took hold of the aluminum frame with both hands.

Ready . . . Set . . .

He lurched upward, jerking the lounger off the concrete, tumbling Dawn off the other side. She let out a cry of alarm. Her lime green top stayed with the lounger. The pad started to go with her, but Toby grabbed it. Dawn smacked the concrete and grunted.

Toby hurled the lounger and pad out of his way.

Dawn was sprawled on the concrete, naked, the rag of her ruined thong draping her right thigh, a look on her face as if she didn't know what was going on but knew she didn't like it. Blinking, she turned her face toward Toby. Her eyes suddenly grew wide.

Toby took the box cutter out of his teeth.

She stared at it.

'Hey,' she said. 'Hey.'

'You're my girl now,' Toby said. 'For the next hour or so, anyhow.'

'SID!' she shouted.

Toby stomped her breath out, stopping the shout.

Then he sat on her belly.

Wheezing for air, she writhed and thrashed. Toby liked how the rough movements made her oily body rub against him. And he *really* liked how her breasts lurched and swung.

Chapter Forty-three

When they finished with Sherry, every exposed scratch and abrasion gleamed with a layer of Neosporin and her body was a patchwork of bandages.

'That it?' Sherry asked.

Pete and Jeff slowly circled her, looking her over.

'I think we got everything,' Pete said.

'And then some,' Jeff added.

'Thanks.' Sherry hobbled over to the chair, turned her back to it, grabbed its plastic arms and eased herself down. 'Can somebody . . . run and get the bikini for me?'

Pete and Jeff looked at each other.

'You get it,' Jeff said.

'I got it last time.'

'Whoever brings it,' Sherry said, 'gets to put it on me.'

Before Pete could speak a word, Jeff blurted out, 'Me!'

Sherry laughed, then winced.

Jeff ran into the house.

Pete looked at Sherry. She smiled. 'Wanta do me a favor?' she asked.

'Anything.'

'I'm hurting.'

Pete grimaced. 'I'm sorry. I know you must be . . . in awful pain.'

'Can you get me something for it?'

'Aspirin? I thought of that earlier, but it's a blood thinner.'

'I was thinking more like . . .'

'Tylenol?'

'Booze. Do your parents keep any around?'

'Sure. I'm not supposed to fool around with it, but . . .'

'I don't want to get you in any trouble.'

'No, that's all right. This is sort of an emergency.'

'Is for me,' she said.

'We've got just about everything. My dad believes in keeping a well-stocked bar. So what'll it be?'

'Know how to make a Bloody Mary?'

'Sure. I've seen Dad do it.'

'I could sure use something like that.'

'Fine. Do you want to come in the house or stay here?'

'Here's good.'

'Okay. I'll be right back.'

He smiled and nodded. As he backed away, he realized she would probably be wearing the bikini by the time he returned.

Might never see her like this again.

But he couldn't just stand here and gape at her forever, so he turned away.

'Wait,' she said. 'Pete?'

He stopped and looked back at her.

'Do you have a phone I can use?'

'Sure. I'll bring it right out.'

'Thanks.'

Nodding and smiling, he again turned away. The glass door was still open. He stepped into the living room. As he picked up the handset of the cordless remote phone, Jeff came striding in, swinging the bikini by his side. He had a spring in his step. He seemed hugely cheerful. 'What's up?' he asked.

'Getting her the phone.'

Jeff halted. 'Oh really? Whoops.' Leaning sideways, he peered out the door. Then he whispered, 'Conference,' and waved for Pete to follow him.

They hurried into the hallway.

'What?' Pete asked.

'Who does she wanta call?'

'How should I know?'

'And you're just gonna *give* her the phone?'

'She wants to make a call, not take it home with her.'

'Well shit, man. She's probably gonna ask somebody to come and pick her up.'

'Maybe.'

'That happens, we *lose* her.'

'Yeah, so?'

'What do you mean, "yeah, so"? You don't want her leaving any more than I do.'

'She has every right to leave.'

'I know, I know.'

'What do *you* want to do, keep her prisoner?'

'I'd *love* to.' He leered. 'Ooooo, yes.'

'Well, forget it.'

'I know, I know. What do you think I am?'

'A horny pervert.'

'Fuckin'-A right, and so are you. *Man!* Wouldn't you just *love* to . . .'

'Knock it off, Jeff. Don't even think about it.'

'How can I not *think* about it. I can't think about anything *else*. Bet you can't, either.'

'Yeah, well . . .'

'Oh, man, I'm *achin'*.'

'Yeah, well, so am I.'

'We can't let her *leave*.'

'We don't even know she *wants* to leave yet. Or who she wants to call. All I know is she wants to use the phone and I'm taking it to her.'

'You're gonna blow it, man.'

'I'm gonna do whatever she asks me to do. As far as I'm concerned, she's the boss.'

'Sure, fine. But right now, you know, she's *all ours*. Your mom and dad won't be home till tomorrow night. Nobody knows she's here. There's just the three of us.'

'Yeah, but . . .'

'We could *at least* keep her overnight.'

'Not if she wants to leave.'

'I don't say we use force or anything, but if we can get her to stay somehow . . . Wouldn't it be great? Just imagine. You'd *really* have something to write about.'

'Let's just see how it goes,' Pete said. 'If she wants to stay here, fine. If not . . .' He shrugged. 'It's up to her.'

'Just remember this, man. When she *does* go, we're never gonna see her again. It'll be "thanks for the help" and *adios* forever.'

'Maybe.'

'No maybe about it.'

'I don't care.'

'You'll care when it happens.'

'I don't mean that,' Pete said. 'I just mean we have to do whatever she wants, no matter what. We do everything we can for her. If she wants to leave, we help her leave. Even if we *don't* ever see her again.'

A smile flickered across Jeff's face.

'What?' Pete asked.

'By George, I do believe the boy's in love.'

Blushing, Pete said, 'Get real.'

'You *are*.'

'What, because I don't want to take her prisoner and *molest* her?'

'Ha! Because you *do* wanta take her prisoner and molest her, but you won't do it because you're wildly, madly in love with her.'

'Maybe I won't do it because it'd be a shitty way to treat someone.'

'Nah, that ain't why.'

'And highly illegal.'

'Nope. You're in love, man. Admit it.'

'Screw you.'

Jeff laughed.

'Let's get out there. She's gonna wonder what's going on.' Not waiting for a response, Pete turned away and headed down the hallway. As he stepped into the living room, he glanced back at Jeff and said, 'Keep your mouth shut about all this.'

'My lips are sealed.'

'They better be.'

He hurried to the door and stepped outside. Sherry was still seated in the lawn chair. He waved the phone, smiled and said, 'Got it.'

'And I've got your duds,' Jeff announced, waving the bikini.

'Let me call first,' Sherry said.

'I got no problem with that,' Jeff said.

She almost smiled. 'You're sort of a troublemaker, aren't you?'

'Moi?'

'He's a pain in the butt,' Pete said, approaching with the phone. 'Would you like me to dial for you?'

'I can probably . . . maybe you'd better. Yeah.'

Sherry told him the number. He pushed the on/off button. As the dial tone sounded in his ear, he thought about entering the *wrong* number.

Can't do that to her.

Besides, it wouldn't accomplish anything unless they lucked out and got no answer at the other end.

Call this *number and she'll get a busy signal.*

I can't do that!

But he did.

Not waiting to hear the result, he handed the phone to Sherry.

'Thanks,' she said. Grimacing slightly, she raised it to her ear. Then she moaned. 'Damn,' she muttered. 'Busy.'

It worked!

He felt pleased, but rotten.

How could I do that to her?

'Who were you trying to get?' Jeff asked.

'My folks.' She frowned at the phone, then thumbed the button to turn it off.

'Might try them again in a few minutes,' Pete said.

She lowered the phone and rested it on her thigh. 'They're probably okay,' she said. 'The guy who did all this to me . . . he said he'd go after them . . . to pay me back.'

'Pay *you* back?' Pete asked.

'I . . . caused him troubles.' A smile lifted the swollen, discolored corners of her mouth. 'And I gave him AIDS.'

Pete's stomach turned to ice.

'That's what he *thinks*, anyhow. Thinks I killed him, the bastard. That's . . . that's when he tried to kill me.'

'So you *don't* have AIDS?' Jeff asked.

'Nah. Just said it to freak him out.'

After the plunge into shocked horror, the sudden relief made Pete's throat go tight. He turned his head away as his vision went blurry with tears.

'Anyway,' she said, 'I don't know. He might go after my

family. Said he would. But he's gotta be worn out after last night. Can't imagine he'd do anything today. Or at least not till later. Maybe tonight.' Turning her eyes to Jeff, she said, 'Ready to dress me?'

'I'm never gonna be ready for that.'

'Can't get enough of me, huh?'

'You said it.'

'Oughta see me when I'm *not* a wreck.'

'As if *that's* ever gonna happen.'

'Never know,' she said. She handed the phone to Pete, then grabbed the arms of her chair and pushed herself up.

'You *sure* about this?' Jeff asked. Not waiting for an answer, he sank to his knees in front of her and spread open the bikini pants.

Sherry put a hand on top of his head. She carefully stepped into the leg holes and Jeff raised the pants. Just before the crotch panel met her body, he stopped and eased the sides of the waistband in against her hips. 'Wanta keep it loose, right?'

'Yeah,' she said. She looked at Pete. 'I could sure use that drink.'

'Sure. Fine.'

He backed away.

'No,' she said. 'Wait a minute. Let's try calling again.'

'You wanta dial this time?'

'I'm awfully shaky . . . messed up. Guess I can manage to hit redial.'

Jeff stood up in front of her. Leaning in with bikini strings in both hands, he reached behind her neck and started to tie a knot.

'Might be better if we do the whole number again,' Pete said. 'Just in case, you know? Maybe I screwed it up last time.'

Looking at him over Jeff's shoulder, she said, 'You'd better do it.'

'What's the number again?'

She told him.

Very carefully, he entered the correct numbers.

Jeff glanced back at Pete, then stepped out of the way. The bikini top hung from Sherry's neck, its limp pouches drooping between her breasts, its back strings swaying in front of her belly.

'Ringing,' Pete said.

Glad to see the relief on Sherry's face, he handed over the phone.

She held it to her ear.

While she listened, Jeff stepped behind her and moved the chair out of the way.

Sherry began to frown. 'Geez, they were just there.'

Jeff tried to reach around her sides, but he had trouble so she raised her arms. Reaching underneath them, he blindly groped for the dangling bikini. One of his hands rubbed against her right breast, but she didn't seem to mind.

Into the phone, she said, 'Hi, it's me. Anybody home? If you're home, please pick up. It's important. Mom? Dad? Brenda?'

Jeff found the bikini. He fumbled with it, pulling it open and trying to fit its limp cups over her breasts.

He's feeling her up, the bastard!

After a pause, Sherry said into the phone, 'I don't want to upset anybody, but . . . there's this guy who, uh . . . I made him mad and he threatened to go after my family. That's you. He's been following me around. He knows where you live. Probably followed me when I came over last Sunday. I don't know if he'll really try anything, or when, but . . . he's very dangerous. I think he's killed some people. So watch out for him.'

Her breasts now filled the flimsy pouches, so Jeff pulled the strings toward her back. When his hands were out of the way, Sherry lowered her arms.

'Dad, you oughta keep your gun handy, just in case. He's a chubby guy, about eighteen years old. Long brown hair. He's sort of scruffy, but has this innocent-looking face. A baby face, you know? And it might be a little bruised.'

Done tying the bikini behind her back, Jeff came around to the front.

'If you see him, call the cops. Or shoot him. Just don't let him *get* you. Okay? He's a very bad guy. He had ideas about . . . doing stuff to all of you, but especially Brenda. Maybe you should all play it safe . . . get out of the house and go to a motel or something. Just till tomorrow, maybe. By then, the cops'll probably have him. Okay. That's about it. I'll be in touch. Love you. Bye.'

She lowered the handset, looked at it and thumbed the on/off button.

'Was all that true?' Pete asked.

'Not all. Mostly, though.' She handed the phone to him, then used both hands to adjust the front of her bikini top.

'Did I get it on okay?' Jeff asked.

'Not bad.'

'Had a little trouble.'

'I noticed.'

'Sorry.'

'No problem.' Looking at Pete, she struggled to smile. Then she said, 'I could sure use that drink now.'

'Sure. Bloody Mary, right?'

'That's it.'

'Make me one, too,' Jeff said.

Chapter Forty-four

In the kitchen, Pete took three glasses out of the cupboard and began making three Bloody Marys.

Why not? he thought.

He felt daring but guilty.

No problem giving a drink to Sherry. Dad would've done the same thing. She was over twenty-one and a guest. But Dad and Mom would be shocked if they ever found out he'd also made Bloody Marys for himself and Jeff.

He could just imagine their reactions.

Mom: *How* could *you?*

Dad: *I thought we could trust you to use better judgement than that.*

Mom: *What on earth were you* thinking?

Dad: *I'm really disappointed in you, Pete.*

They don't have to know, Pete told himself. If it comes up, I'll say I made a Bloody Mary for Sherry and we had Cokes.

He pulled out a 2-liter jug of vodka. It was about half-full.

Dad'll never notice any's gone.

The tomato juice was a different story. It took an entire 12 ounce can to make the three drinks.

No problem, Pete thought. I had to use the stuff for Sherry's drink, anyway. Just say we used it all up. If they ask. Or I could go to the store and replace whatever gets used.

All I've really gotta do is make sure I wash all three glasses.

Then lie through my teeth.

Pete *hated* to lie.

But he really wanted to sit out by the pool and sip cocktails with Sherry. It would be something he would always remember. It would be something to write about.

Just like Hemingway, he thought.

The girl and I sat by the pool that day, talking and drinking. Our Bloody Marys were deep red, and the ice cubes flashed in the sunlight.

When the drinks were made, Pete placed them on a serving tray and carried them outside. Sherry and Jeff were both on chairs near the table.

'Do I see *three* drinks?' Jeff asked, beaming.

'Yep.'

'Don't tell me you came through. Two of 'em must be *Virgin* Marys, right?'

'Nope.'

Jeff slid the notebook, pen and coffee mug to the other side of the table and Pete set down the tray.

'They're all real?' Jeff asked.

'Yep.'

'My man!'

Pete handed one of the glasses to Sherry. 'Thank you,' she said.

'You're welcome. Is it all right?'

She took a drink, lowered the glass and sighed. 'It's great,' she said.

'I can add more of something.'

'It's perfect. Sit down.'

He took a chair from the other side of the table, carried it past Jeff, and turned it toward Sherry. Then he picked up his drink. He sat facing her.

She raised her glass. 'To you guys,' she said. 'Saved my life.' She stretched out her arm, reaching toward them with her glass.

They both rose from their chairs, leaned in, and clicked their glasses against hers. Then they sank back into their seats and drank.

Pete had to squint because of the glare on his ice cubes. They bumped together, not with musical clinks, but with soft clacks, the sounds muffled by the heaviness of the tomato juice.

To you guys. Saved my life.

This is so great, he thought.

The Bloody Mary tasted strange and wonderful. He didn't

usually like tomato juice. But this had the vodka in it. And the Worchestershire and Tabasco and the slice of lime and the ground pepper. It was tart and made his eyes water.

'Hey,' Jeff said, 'This is pretty good.'

'Yeah.'

'So this is a Bloody Mary. You sure there's booze in it?'

'A big shot of vodka.'

'No kidding?' Jeff drank some more. 'Whew! Good stuff!'

'You gonna get in trouble about this?' Sherry asked.

'About what?' Pete asked.

'The drinks.'

'Only if my parents find out.'

'And they don't get home till tomorrow night,' Jeff told her. He grinned as if already looped.

Can't be, Pete thought. Not yet.

'How old *are* you guys?' Sherry asked.

'Sixteen,' Pete said.

'Going on seventeen,' added Jeff.

Sherry winced. 'Got a couple of minors here. Getting corrupted.'

'Lovin' every second,' Jeff said and drank some more.

'Yeah,' said Pete. 'This is great. I mean . . . you know . . . except for what happened to you.'

'Which, if it *hadn't* happened,' Jeff told her, 'you wouldn't be here having a wonderful drink with a couple of terrific guys like us.'

'True,' she said.

'Are you hungry?' Pete asked. 'I can get us some lunch.'

'Later. Let's just enjoy the drinks.'

'Okay.'

'Fine by me,' Jeff added. 'This sucker's *good*. I could drink 'em all day. Yummy in the tummy!'

Maybe he *is* already feeling it, Pete thought – beginning to feel a little strange, himself. There was a peculiar, buoyant sensation behind his forehead. And his cheeks felt slightly numb.

Is this what booze does to you? he wondered.

I could get to like this.

'So, Sherry,' Jeff said, frowning now as if determined to be serious. 'Do you really think the cops are gonna nail this guy today?'

'Huh?'

'Like you said on the phone . . . Told your parents it'll all be over by tomorrow. What makes you think so? Or *do* you think so?'

She took another drink, then lowered her glass and rested it on the yellow plastic arm of her chair. 'I don't know. The cops might get him. Maybe they've already got him. He . . . did a lot of stuff last night. Killed some people.'

'*Killed* people?' Jeff blurted. 'In that apartment building? The one over in west LA?'

'It was . . . yeah.'

'Where they found that *head?*'

Her face twitched. 'Yeah.'

'Holy shitski!' Jeff gaped at Pete. 'This is all part of that weird shit I was telling you about, dude! On the news? Where they found this severed head, and there was this woman got stabbed like about a zillion times!'

'My God,' Pete muttered. To Sherry, he said, '*You* were in on that?'

'Tried to get away from him.'

'*He* did all this to you?' Speaking, Pete realized his tongue felt a little sluggish. His words seemed to come out all right, though.

'Yeah. But . . . there was another guy. Jim.'

'Huh?'

'Jim Starr. He was there, too. He got stabbed.' To Jeff, she said. 'Do you know anything about him?'

'The *other* guy? Yeah. They took him to the hospital.'

'He's alive?'

'I think so. Pretty sure. They said he was cridigle . . . critical . . . but stable.'

Sherry's chin began to tremble. She raised her glass and took a drink.

'He a friend of yours?' Jeff asked her.

'Shhh,' Pete said. 'Leave her alone.'

Sherry lowered her glass. She sniffed. With one hand, she wiped her eyes. 'He . . . Jim? I met him last night. He was trying to help me. And I almost got him killed.'

'What about the others?' Pete asked.

'The woman . . . she heard stuff and came to the door. The other . . .'

'The head?'

She nodded. 'That was Duane. We . . . went together.'

'He was your boyfriend?' Pete asked.

'Yeah.'

'Oh, my God.'

'Ooooo,' Jeff said, looking extremely pained.

'Really sorry,' Pete said.

'Yeah. Man, that sucks. Truly blows.'

'And that's why Toby killed him. Cut off his head. To get Duane out of the way. He did it *all* because he wanted me.'

'Jeez,' Pete said.

'The killer's name is Toby,' Jeff announced. 'Right? Am I right?'

Sherry frowned. 'Did I say that?'

'Yeah, you did. Toby.'

'Oh. Okay. His name's Toby.'

'Toby what?' Jeff asked.

'Never mind.'

'Come on, tell.'

'Forget it,' Sherry said.

'What?'

'His name. Forget it, okay? I don't want you guys knowing who he is.'

'I'd *love* to know who he is,' Pete said, and drank some more.

This stuff really is *good.*

'Cough up his name, lady,' Jeff said. His smile looked a little crooked.

'Huh-uh. No.'

'Vee haff ways of making you talk.'

'Cut it out,' Pete said.

'*Dat's* how vee make you talk!' His eyes gleamed as he grinned. 'Vee *cut* it out of you!'

'Knock it off,' Pete said. 'I mean it.'

'It's all right,' Sherry said.

Dropping his act, Jeff leaned toward her and said, 'Make you a deal. You tell us who he is and we'll kick his ass.'

'I wanta *kill* the bastard,' Pete said.

'I don't want you guys anywhere near him. You're nice guys. Jim was a nice guy. He tried to help, and he almost got killed.' She closed her eyes, took a deep breath and winced. Then she drank some more of her Bloody Mary. Done, she said, 'The cops can take care of him.'

'Maybe they've already got him,' Pete suggested.

'Last I heard,' Jeff said, 'they didn't have any idea who done it.'

'Let's check the news. Hang on.' Pete stood up and set his glass on the table. It landed somewhat harder than he'd expected. Jeff and Sherry flinched at the quick noise. 'Sorry,' he said. Then he headed for the house. He felt light and a little wobbly.

This is so *cool*, he thought.

Just don't fall down.

I'll have to write about all this later, he told himself. My first bout with booze.

In the kitchen, he grabbed the portable radio. As he lifted it off the counter, it slipped. Gasping, he caught it. Then he clasped it to his bare chest. With his other hand, he pulled up his sagging trunks. Then he ran outside.

Sherry looked worried as he approached.

Jeff was finishing off his Bloody Mary.

Pete turned on the radio, listened for a moment to the cheerful, confident voice, and said, 'It's "The Best of Rush Limbaugh".'

'The Rush-man,' Jeff said. 'All right!'

Pete placed the radio on the table, picked up his drink, and sat down. 'There'll be news pretty soon. They have reports on the hour 'n' half hour.'

'Wha' time is it now?' Jeff asked.

Pete shrugged. He saw that nobody was wearing a watch.

'No hurry,' Sherry said. 'I can wait.'

'Is Rush okay with you?' Pete asked her. 'A lot of people think he's awful.'

'You're talking to a ditto-head,' Sherry said.

Jeff let out a whoop. 'Makes three of us! The Three Rushkateers!'

Smiling, Pete shook his head. This is *so great*! he thought.

'What?' Sherry asked.

'I don't know. It's just weird. I mean . . . I don't know.'

'I do,' Jeff said.

'What?'

'Pete's smitten with you,' he explained, nodding sagely.

'Hey,' Pete said.

'Head over heels.'

'Knock it off, huh?'

'Madly in love.'

'I'm gonna kill you,' Pete said, blushing furiously.

Grinning, Jeff held out his empty hand as if to ward off a blow. 'Take it easy, dude. You kill me, how'm I gonna be your best man?'

Sherry laughed, then winced and said, 'Ow.'

'Only hurts when you laugh?' Jeff asked her.

'Hurts *all* the time. But *more* when I laugh.'

'Jeff's such an asswipe,' Pete said.

Oh shit! Did I say 'asswipe'?

'Just tellin' the truth,' Jeff said.

'Damn it!'

Sherry met his eyes. 'Don't be embarrassed, Pete. Okay? It's all right. Whatever you're feeling. It's fine. Hell, it's great. I've got no problems if you like me. Or even if maybe you feel . . . something stronger. You're a good guy.'

'How 'bout me?' Jeff asked.

'You're a blabber-mouth,' Sherry said.

Pete glimpsed a hurt look in his eyes, but it quickly vanished. Grinning strangely, Jeff asked, 'But would ya kick me outa bed?'

'Hey!' Pete snapped.

'Jus' kidding.'

'Kidding aside,' Sherry said, 'you're a good guy, too. Even if you *are* a troublemaker.'

'Does that mean you would or wouldn't kick me—'

'*I'll* kick you in the nuts,' Pete warned.

'No kicking allowed. You're my heroes. You're both great

guys and my friends forever. So no fighting. How about another drink, Pete?'

'Sure.'

'Me, too,' Jeff said.

'I don't know about that.'

'Come on.' Grinning, he held out his glass. 'Like my old man says, "Can't fly on one wing." '

'I don't know.'

'Can't let Sherry drink alone, can we?'

'Well . . .' He looked at Sherry.

A corner of her puffy mouth lifted. 'Why stop now?' she said. 'One more won't hurt you. Not much, anyhow.'

Chapter Forty-five

With three fresh Bloody Marys on the tray, Pete stepped outside. Sherry and Jeff were both staring at the radio. Pete said nothing as he approached. He walked carefully, worried he might stumble but *more* worried that his trunks might suddenly drop around his ankles.

Through the sounds of the wind, he could hear a female voice. But he couldn't make out what she was saying. Her words were like bits of nonsense.

Sherry and Jeff quit listening at the same moment. Their heads turned toward Pete.

'You just missed it,' Jeff said.

'The news?'

'Yeah, man. It was the top story.'

Pete held the tray toward Sherry. 'Thanks,' she said, and lifted her glass.

With the other two drinks still in place, he eased the tray down on the table. Then he hitched up his drooping trunks, took his glass off the tray and stepped over to his chair. As he sat down, he said, 'So what's going on?'

'Well,' Jeff said, 'looks like Sherry's friend is doing okay so far. He's off the cridigle list.'

'Glad to hear it.'

Sherry nodded, her eyes glistening.

'Other two, still dead.'

'That's not very funny,' Pete said.

'Ah, I know.' Jeff lifted his glass off the tray and took a sip. 'Mmmm, good.'

'What about Toby?' Pete asked.

'They didn't mention him,' Sherry answered. 'I don't think they know anything about him. How would they? I'm the only one who . . .' She frowned. 'Actually, *Jim* probably knows his name.' She took a sip of her Bloody Mary. 'Maybe he hasn't been able to talk yet.'

'Jim knows the last name?' Jeff asked, raising an eyebrow.

'I think so.'

'What was it again?'

'Trying to trick me, Jeffrey?'

'*Moi?*'

'I'm not going to tell.'

'I'd tell you.'

'But I already know,' Sherry pointed out.

'If I *did* know 'n' you didn't, I'd tell. You bet I would. Wouldn't I, Petie?'

'Sure.'

Jeff took a couple of swallows, leaned toward Sherry and said, 'What do *you* wanta know? You ask, I'll tell.'

Looking him in the eyes, Sherry asked, 'Do you have a girlfriend?'

'Sure do.'

'What's her name?'

'Mary Jane Thatcher.'

Pete had never heard of Mary Jane Thatcher. He supposed Jeff must've pulled the name out of nowhere, just for an answer.

'Now my turn to question *you*,' Jeff said. 'What's Toby's name?'

'Toby.'

'Toby what?'

'Give it up,' Pete told him.

'I wanta *know*.'

'I don't *want* you to know,' Sherry said.

'Why not?'

'Come on, Jeff, leave her alone.'

'If you know who he is,' Sherry explained, 'you might try to find him.'

'Durn tootin',' Jeff said.

'Yeah,' Pete said. 'I wouldn't mind that, myself.'

'This isn't a game, guys.'

'We know that,' Pete said. 'Look what he did to you.'

'You want to get revenge on him for that, don't you?'

'Sure do,' Pete said.

'Fuckin'-A.'

'I could use a little vengeance, myself,' Sherry said.

'We'll take care of it for you,' Pete offered.

'No, you won't. You might end up like Jim. Or worse. I've already gotten two people killed. So far. That I know of. Maybe there're even more by now. I don't want you guys added to the list.'

'We'd wipe up the floor with him,' Jeff said.

'You won't get the chance. What I'll have to do . . . I guess I'll call the cops and tell them everything. Give *them* his last name.'

'What is it again?' Jeff asked.

'Very funny.'

'Not really,' Pete said.

'If you call the cops,' Jeff explained, 'they're gonna show up and haul you off to the hospital. That what y'want?'

'Not much.'

'Know what else? They're gonna know we all been drinkin'. Me and Pete'll be up the ol' Shit Creek without the ol' paddle.'

Pete muttered, 'Oh, man. If my parents find out . . .'

'They'll find out, all right. They'll have to bail your ass outa jail.'

'Nobody's going to jail,' Sherry said. 'And nobody has to find out you've been drinking. I can hold off on making the call.'

'Good idea,' Pete said.

'I'm all for that,' Jeff said. 'Let's wait till tomorrow.'

'Afraid not,' Sherry said. 'But I can wait a couple of hours. Why don't we all have a bite to eat and then take a nap? An hour or two of sleep, we'll probably all be good and sober.'

'You saying we oughta sleep together?' Jeff asked.

'Cut it out,' Pete told him.

'Chill, man. I'm just kidding around.' Grinning at Sherry, he said, 'It's da booze talkin'.'

'I know what it is. Don't worry about it.'

'I'm not such a bad guy, you get to know me.'

'You're a fine guy. You're both fine guys. I'm really lucky

I was found by a couple of fellas like you two.'

'Thanks,' Pete said, feeling a warm mixture of delight that she appreciated them – and guilt.

She wouldn't feel so kindly toward them if she knew the truth.

But she doesn't, he reminded himself. Thank God.

'So what's for lunch?' Jeff asked.

Pete looked at Sherry. 'What do you feel like having?'

'Just about anything. Don't go to a lot of trouble, though. Maybe sandwiches, or . . .'

'How about grilled cheese?' Pete suggested.

'Sounds great.'

'Yeah,' Jeff said. 'I could go for that, too.'

'Why don't you come in and give me a hand?'

'Why don' I stay out here and keep Sherry company?'

'Why don't you not?'

'I'll be fine,' Sherry told him. 'Go on in and help, okay? It isn't fair to make Pete do all the work.'

'Yeah, well . . . if you say so.'

'Anything I can get you from inside?' Pete asked Sherry as he stood up.

'No thanks. I'm fine.'

'Another Bloody Mary?' Jeff suggested.

'Just started this one.'

'How 'bout one for the other hand?'

'No thanks.'

'Okay. Well, don' go away.'

'I'll try not to.'

'We'll be back in a few minutes,' Pete said. 'If you need us for anything, just yell.'

'I will.'

He set his drink on the table, then muttered, 'See ya,' and headed for the house. Jeff followed him inside.

In the kitchen, Jeff said, 'Soon as she gets that nap, man, she's gonna call the cops.'

'She *should*.' Pete took a skillet out of a cupboard and set it on the stove. 'She probably should've called 'em a long time ago.'

'Fuck that. We gotta stop her.'

'We're not gonna stop her.' He opened the refrigerator.

'They'll take her *away*!'

'I don't want her to leave, either, but . . .'

'The cops take one look at her, they'll have an ambulance out here. Presto-zippo, man, that'll be the last we ever see of her.'

A tub of butter and a pack of cheddar cheese in his hands, Pete stepped back from the refrigerator and kneed its door shut. 'If she *doesn't* call the cops,' he said, 'that Toby guy might go after her family.'

'They'll be okay. She warned 'em, right? Told 'em to get outa Dodge.'

'She left a message, that's all.' Pete set the cheese and butter on the counter. 'Who knows when they're gonna come home and *listen* to it? Hell, maybe they'll *never* hear it.'

'They'll hear it. Why wouldn' they hear it?'

'I don't know,' Pete said, 'but it's not like a hundred percent sure. Maybe they'll forget to check the machine, or . . .'

'You worry *way* too much.'

'I think we gotta let Sherry do anything she wants. Even like call the cops, you know? 'Cause what if we stop her and then Toby nails her family? It'd be *our* fault.'

'They'll be fine.'

'Sure. If Toby doesn't show up and demolish them. You wanta get some plates down?' He pointed to a nearby cupboard.

'*God* I wish we'd get our hands on him,' Jeff said. He opened the cupboard. 'Three plates?'

'Yeah.'

Jeff reached up for them. 'If we just nail his sorry ass, Sherry hasn't gotta call the cops – she can just stay with us, you know? Like overnight?'

'She doesn't want us getting involved.'

'We're already involved, man! We're *involved* up the Grand Wazoo! *You're* in love with her 'n *I* sorta got the hotsies for her my own self. That's *involved*! Ain't that *involved*!'

'Yep,' Pete said.

'Fuckin'-A.'

Pete opened a drawer and took out a paring knife. 'Bring

the plates over here, okay? I'll cut the cheese and you get the bread.'

'Don' go cuttin' the cheese, dude.'

'Very funny.'

Jeff came over to the counter and set down the plates. 'Where's the bread?'

With the knife, Pete pointed at the loaf. Then he started trying to cut open the plastic wrapper around the cheese.

'We gotta do something,' Jeff said, 'or it's gonna all be over in a couple of hours.'

'What do you suggest?'

'We gotta *make* her tell us Toby's name. Then we gotta find him and take him out.'

Pete looked around at Jeff. 'Take him out?'

'Take him *right the fuck out*. You know?'

'I know.'

'You got a problem with that?'

'Why should I have a problem with a little thing like that? Do it all the time.'

'I mean it, man.'

'You're talking about *killing* a person.'

'You betcha.' Jeff's eyes gleamed. 'The fucker who did that to Sherry. You got a problem with that?'

'Like murder him?'

'Whatever. Murder him, kill him, cancel his ticket. Yeah. You betcha. You *said* you'd like to get your hands on him. Did you mean it?'

'I meant it.'

'So let's do it.'

'I don't know about actually *killing* someone, though.'

'He damn near killed Sherry. You saw what he did to her, man. And he *raped* her. You saying you don't wanta kill him for that?'

'I want him punished, that's for sure.'

'How you think he's gonna get punished, the cops get him? Only way they're gonna kill his ass is if he goes up against 'em with a gun or something. You know that. Chances are, he won't get a scratch on him when they bust him. *If* they bust him.'

Pete groaned, then turned away and tore the remains of the

wrapper off the cheese. He placed the block of cheese on one of the plates and started to slice it. 'How about buttering the bread?'

'Sure.' Jeff stepped up to the silverware drawer, opened it and took out a dinner knife. 'So the cops, they nab Toby, right? *If* they nab him. Then what happens?'

'A trial,' Pete said, and cut another slice.

'Right. Maybe like a year or two down the road. All that time, he's in jail – if we're lucky. And Sherry, she hasta wait and worry and be the center of addenshun. News people all over her like the fuckin' vultures they are. Then comes the trial and she's gotta testify against the asshole. And she's probably on the TV all the time so everybody ends up knowing every damn thing about her and every single shitty thing Toby did to her. They'll rip her life apart. Y'know? She's the *victim*, 'n they get crucified every fuckin' time there's a trial. 'N for what? For *nothin'*! Know what I mean?'

'This being Los Angeles,' Pete said, 'the jury acquits Toby and he goes free.'

'You better fuckin' believe it. They let Toby go and he gets to play golf the rest of his fuckin' life – or maybe he goes on a little spree 'n takes out Sherry just for the fun of it.'

'On the other hand,' Pete said, 'they probably *would* find him guilty.'

'*Might*. Not problee.'

'Okay, might.'

'So he goes to the slammer. Big whoop.'

'Killing all those people is "special circumstances",' Pete pointed out. 'So he might get the death penalty.'

'So they maybe kill him fifteen years down the road. If at all. And meanwhile, back at the ol' ranch, Sherry has to keep *dealing* with it.'

Pete smirked and shook his head. 'You oughta be a lawyer.'

'No way, man. Gonna be an assassin.'

Pete laughed. 'Sure.'

'Waste bad guys.'

'This isn't the movies, you know.'

'Tell you what. You *write* about my eggsploits. Forget them wimpy-ass novels. You be my Roswell.'

'Boswell.'

'Fuckin'-A! And we'll start it all off with how we wiped *Toby Asshole* off the face of the earth.'

'You're nuts. Anyway, we can't do *anything* to him unless we can find him.'

'Eggzackly.'

Chapter Forty-six

With Sid's key in the ignition, Toby drove the Mercedes to the house at 2832 Clifton Street.

As he approached, he slowed down.

There was no car in the driveway.

He saw no sign of Sherry's parents or Brenda.

What if nobody's home?

He started to feel angry and cheated.

Take it easy, he told himself, driving past the house. This could turn out really good. Maybe Mom and Dad took off in the car and left Brenda alone. Or maybe Brenda's the one with the car.

Any way you slice it, he thought, this'll be fine. Things'll be a lot easier if I don't have to handle all three at once.

At the end of the block, he turned the corner and parked his car. He pocketed Sid's keys, climbed out, and went to the sidewalk.

Sherry's pistol was heavy in the right-hand front pocket of his shorts. With each stride, it swung and brushed against his thigh. Anyone watching him would see the swinging, but the pocket was very deep and the shorts were loose and baggy. Nobody should be able to tell that the pocket held a gun.

Or that he had a folding Buck knife with a four-inch blade in the left-hand front pocket of his shorts.

Or that he carried a screwdriver, its handle hidden beneath the hanging front of his shirt, its eight-inch shaft underneath his belt and shorts, cool against the side of his right leg.

Or that he had a pair of rubber gloves stuffed inside his right rear pocket.

Or that his left rear pocket held a pair of pliers.

Or that he was bare underneath his big, floppy shorts.

So much that nobody could tell by looking.

People *did* look, but he knew they weren't seeing *him* with his hidden truths.

An elderly couple walked by. They glanced at him, nodded and smiled. He nodded and smiled back. A dapper fellow came along carrying a white poodle. He gave Toby a curt nod and kept going. Across the street, a woman gliding along beneath a white turban didn't seem to be aware of him at all. Neither did the gawky, darkly tanned gal who jogged by on the street. She looked wizened and breastless and carried a water bottle on her hip.

None of you see me, Toby thought.

All they saw, if anything at all, was a shaggy-haired, hefty teenager strolling along with a smile on his face and a song in his heart.

What song in my heart? he wondered.

He began to sing to himself, very softly, 'Stuck in the Middle with You'.

And smiled, picturing the scene in *Reservoir Dogs*.

And wished *he* looked like Michael Madsen.

If I looked like him, Toby thought, the babes'd be all over me.

Oh, well. Who needs good looks when you've got weapons?

He stepped up to the front door and rang the bell. He heard chimes, but no other sounds came from inside the house.

Anybody home? Come on, come on.

He rang the bell again.

Nothing.

He shrugged for the benefit of any neighbor who might be watching, then turned away from the door, stepped down from the stoop and went to the driveway. Its iron gate was shut.

He smiled toward the gate, raised an arm in greeting, and said in a cheerful voice, 'Oh, there you are. I'll come through.'

He walked to the gate, lifted its latch and swung it open. On the other side, he pulled it shut. The latch fell into place with a quiet clank.

Though his heart pounded hard, he had to smile at his performance.

Ahead of him, the driveway was empty all the way to the

closed door of the garage. Just to the left of the driveway was a redwood fence. It must've been six feet high, but the neighbor's house stood just beyond it. From where he stood, Toby could see the upper regions of several windows. The curtains seemed to be shut, but that was no guarantee that the neighbor wasn't peering out near the top, keeping an eye on him.

So he moved on.

At the rear corner of the house, he said, 'Ah, there you are. Sorry I'm late. Want some help with that?'

He saw no one.

The back yard had a concrete patio with a padded lounge, lawn chairs, a white-painted picnic table, and a gas barbecue grill. Some T-shirts and nightshirts, hanging from a clothesline, were being lifted and flapped by the wind.

Toby stepped behind the house.

He turned around slowly, scanning the garage, the fences and trees.

Plenty of privacy back here.

He stared at the faded green pad of the lounge.

I bet Brenda sunbathes on that.

He pictured her lying there, the back of her bikini top unfastened, her skin agleam with oil. Like Dawn, only younger and prettier. He imagined himself rubbing her back. It would be hot and slick in the sunlight.

He imagined himself pulling down the skimpy pants of her bikini. Rubbing her buttocks.

But then she turned over and she was naked, all right, but she was Sherry, not Brenda. Smiling, she said, 'Hi there, dead boy.'

Toby felt his scrotum shrivel, his penis shrink.

I'm not dead yet, you rotten bitch. Too bad I killed you deader than shit so you can't watch what I do to your precious family.

He stepped up to the back door of the house and peered through its window.

On the other side was the kitchen.

He took the rubber gloves out of his back pocket and put them on. Powdered inside, they fit easily over his hands.

He tried the knob. It wouldn't turn. He tugged it, but the door stayed shut. So he drew the screwdriver out of his shorts. With the butt of its handle, he punched the window. Glass broke and fell inside the house, shards clinking and clattering as they struck the floor.

'I'm such a klutz,' he said. 'Let me clean that up for you.'

For a while, he stood motionless and listened.

He heard a gust of wind rushing through the nearby trees, heard the *whop* of flapping clothes, heard the distant sounds of an airliner and a lawnmower and a door thumping shut and even a bright, faraway laugh that sounded like a girl startled with delight.

But no sounds came from inside the house.

Or from the house next door.

Toby eased the screwdriver down the side of his shorts. Then he plucked a few large pieces of glass out of the window frame and set them down silently on the concrete at his feet. When the hole seemed large enough, he inserted his arm. Careful to keep away from the jagged edges, he reached down. He leaned against the door. Shoulder inside the broken window, glass tickling the hair of his armpit, he reached lower, felt around, and found the inside doorknob.

He caught the button between his thumb and forefinger and gave it a twist.

Then he carefully withdrew his arm.

Not a scratch.

He turned the outside knob, pulled the door open and stepped into the kitchen. After shutting the door, he stood motionless and listened to the house. He heard a quiet buzzing from the kitchen clock, the hum of the refrigerator, a few creaking sounds of the sort that houses often made, especially in strong winds.

Nobody home, he thought.

Can't be sure of that.

Though the place *felt* deserted, Toby knew he'd better be careful.

Play it like they're all home.

Who knows? he thought. Maybe they *are* all home. Car might be in for repairs.

They're all home, he told himself, and somebody heard me break the glass.

He stepped quietly over to the wall phone, lifted off its handset, and heard a dial tone.

Nobody was calling the police.

And nobody's gonna.

He tapped in a random set of seven numbers, got a busy signal, and lowered the handset to the floor.

Then he took off his sneakers.

He reached into his pocket for the pistol, but changed his mind and left the weapon where it was. Why wander around with a gun in his hand? It would just upset people . . .

Not that anyone's here.

Besides, he could get it out in half a second if he needed it.

And he didn't really want to shoot anyone. That'd be too noisy. Not much fun, either. The pistol was for emergency use only.

He pulled the knife out of his pocket and opened its blade.

Holding the knife behind his back, he walked through the kitchen. The tile floor was a little slippery under his crew socks. In the dining room, the carpet felt thick and soft.

He found nobody there.

Nor in the living room.

In the living room, on a lamp table next to an armchair, he found a telephone with an answering machine. On the machine, a red light blinked.

Someone had left a message.

Another clue that nobody was home.

But not proof. Some people didn't *like* to play their messages. Himself, for instance. And Sid. It used to drive Dawn crazy. She'd whine, *What's the matter with you two*?

To which Sid would say, *I don't happen to give a shit who called. Wasn't you, right? You're here. So who gives a rat's ass?*

Or something like that.

But that wasn't the real reason. Toby didn't think so, anyway. Because he had his own good reasons for hating telephone messages, unexpected calls, strangers showing up at the door, and even the daily arrival of the mail.

Any of them could mean that someone had *found out.*

It has recently come to our attention that your parents were deceased prior to the motor vehicle accident and fire that was previously believed to be the cause . . .

Toby went squirmy and cold inside.

Forget it, he told himself. It never happened and it's never *gonna* happen . . . talk about water under the bridge!

He let out a laugh.

Great! What if somebody heard it?

Nobody heard it. Nobody's home.

Maybe, maybe not.

Bounding up the stairs toward the second floor, he called out 'Hello! Anybody home? This is the police! We're evacuating the neighborhood! Fire's on its way! Your house is right in the path!'

No response.

He rushed from room to room. They were tidy and sunlit and deserted.

He returned to the upstairs hallway.

Nobody *is* home.

He felt relieved. He could relax. There would be no need for urgent action to save himself or take captives. But he felt disappointed, too.

As if the home had been a beautifully wrapped box – a gift. Expecting a wonderful surprise inside, he'd opened it and found it empty.

But it won't be *staying* empty, he realized. This is where they *live*. Sooner or later, they'll be coming back.

And I'll be here waiting.

He entered Brenda's bedroom. Like the master bedroom across the hall, its front two windows had a view of the street. He stepped over to one of them and looked down.

This'll be great, he thought. I'll know when they show up.

From where he stood, however, he could also see into the upstairs windows of the house across the street.

Though he saw nobody, he realized that he could be seen from over there if anyone happened to look.

He took two quick backward steps.

I'll just look out if I hear something.

'In the meantime,' he whispered.

He turned in a circle, giving the room a quick inspection: desk, bed, bookshelves, closet, dresser . . .

He smiled.

'Ah, yes,' he said.

He folded his knife, dropped it into his pocket, then wandered over to the dresser. He opened a few drawers until he found Brenda's bras and panties.

'Here we go.'

One at a time, he lifted the garments out. He held them open and tried to imagine Brenda wearing them. The white, flimsy bra and nothing else. The skimpy pink cotton briefs and nothing else. The black lace bra and nothing else. He caressed his face with them. He sniffed them. They all seemed freshly laundered.

Leaving the dresser, he went to the clothes hamper. He opened its top.

Yes!

Bending down, he reached inside and picked up a pair of panties.

Chapter Forty-seven

With his spatula, Pete flipped the sandwiches. Their buttered tops hit the skillet and sizzled.

'Man, they smell great,' Jeff said.

'Yeah.'

'Don' let 'em burn.'

'I don't plan to.' He pressed each of them down with the spatula. 'Gotta wait for the cheese to melt.'

'Just don' burn 'em.'

'I'm *not* gonna burn 'em.'

'You all set with the plan?' Jeff asked.

'I don't know. It's a pretty stupid plan.'

'It's only stupid if it don' work. You wanna nail the bastard, don' you?'

'I guess so.'

'You only *guess*?'

'I wanta nail him.'

'My man.'

Rich yellow cheese leaked out the side of one sandwich, rolled down a narrow crust and puddled on the skillet. It bubbled and turned brown around the edges.

'Plate,' Pete said.

As Jeff reached a large plate toward him, Pete knifed his spatula under the nearest sandwich and lifted it off the skillet. In seconds, all three were safe aboard the plate. Pete turned off the burner. Then he hefted the skillet, carried it to the sink and propped it under the faucet. He turned the water on. Hitting the hot iron surface, the water sizzled and steamed. He shut the faucet off. 'Let's go,' he said.

'You're gonna play along, right?'

'Sure. Right.'

Jeff leading the way with the plate of sandwiches, they hurried outside.

Sherry nodded to them. She still sat in her chair by the table.

The radio was still on the table where they'd left it.

'Sorry it took so long,' Pete said. He saw that she had finished her drink. 'Can I get you a refill?'

'I don't think so. Thanks.'

Jeff stepped in front of her and held out the plate. 'Here y'go,' he said.

Sherry picked up one of the sandwiches. 'Looks good,' she said.

Jeff eased the plate down onto the table.

'Get you something else to drink?' Pete asked. 'A Pepsi or a beer or something?'

'No thanks. Sit down, you guys.'

Jeff took a sandwich, picked up his Bloody Mary, and sat in his chair.

As Pete took the last sandwich and reached for his own drink, he realized he could hear the radio. But just barely. Though someone seemed to be speaking, he couldn't make out any words.

More than likely, neither could Sherry.

Maybe it'll work.

He sat down and took a swallow of his Bloody Mary.

'You heard the news,' Jeff said. He sounded as if she *must've* heard it.

Chewing, Sherry shook her head.

'No?' Jeff sounded surprised. 'It was on the radio. We heard it in the kitchen.'

She shook her head some more.

'They caught 'm,' Jeff explained. 'Toby. The cops picked 'm up about half an hour ago.'

She stopped chewing.

'Ran a red light. The cops, they went t'pull him over, but he took off 'n then they had one a those high-speed chases till he got stuck in traffic. Then he bailed out, only he din get very far.'

Sherry looked at Pete as if seeking confirmation.

He nodded, felt rotten, and took a bite of his sandwich. The grilled bread crunched. The cheese inside was soft and hot and tangy.

'Anyway,' Jeff continued, 'he was all bloody when they god'm. They found a bloody knife in his car. Next thing y'know, they busted him for the killings. The ones last night.'

'How'd they know it was him?' Sherry asked.

'He musta said something,' Jeff said. Shrugging, he looked at Pete.

'I'm not sure they told how.'

'Fuckin' reporters,' Jeff muttered.

'Cops don't always tell 'em everything,' Pete said.

'But they busted his ass, all right,' Jeff said.

Pete nodded.

'And you're sure it was Toby?' Sherry asked.

'Thas what they said,' Jeff told her.

'Toby Bones?'

It worked!

Pete's heart slammed.

'Bones?' Jeff asked. 'I thought they said *J*ones.'

'Bones,' Sherry said. 'With a B.'

'Ah. Well, that was him. They god'm, all right.'

'My God,' Sherry murmured. Tears shimmered in her eyes. Her chin began to shake. As tears spilled down her cheeks, she lowered her hands. Wrists resting on her thighs, she held the glass and sandwich between her legs as she wept.

How could we do this to her? She'll hate us!

Not if she doesn't find out, Pete told himself.

How's she not *gonna find out? I must've been nuts to go* along with this!

After a while, Sherry calmed down. She sniffed a few times. With the back of her sandwich hand, she gently wiped the tears from her face. Then she exhaled loudly. 'I can't believe it,' she said.

You shouldn't.

'It's all over?'

'All over,' Jeff told her.

'God.' She sniffed again. 'That's . . . great.'

'You'll problee hafta testify 'n shit,' Jeff threw in.

'Yeah. Sure will. God.'

'Would you like another drink now?' Pete asked.

'Yeah. Yeah, okay.'

Pete stood up. Leaning toward the table, he set down his glass and sandwich.

'Turn it up, okay?' Sherry said.

'Sure.' He raised the radio's volume.

A commercial for Taco Bell.

He took Sherry's glass and hurried into the house. In the kitchen, he quickly made her a fresh Bloody Mary. Then he pulled out a drawer near the wall phone and hauled out the telephone directory.

He flipped through its pages.

Did she say Bones? Weird name, Toby Bones.

Spelled like body bones?

Goddamn dirty rotten trick.

Hard to believe it really worked.

Pete wondered if the booze had helped loosen her tongue.

Probably.

He stopped turning pages when he came to the heading BOLOTNICK-BOORN. The first column ended with Bonaz. Half the next column showed listings of people named Bond.

He looked for James Bond and found two.

Which is double-oh seven? he wondered.

Quit fooling around.

He continued down the column. After a couple of Bondys, he found the Bone Density Center. This was followed by several people named Bone, no 's'. Then a Bonel, then a Boner.

Shit! There's a Boner in here!

First name Randy.

Pete laughed.

Oh, man, how can somebody have a name like that? Randy Boner? How'd he survive grade school?

Still grinning, Pete shook his head looked at the name under Boner.

Bones BD. Then came Bones George, then Bones James & Sally, Bones Jill, Bones Norman, Bones Sidney and finally Bones Thomas.

After Bones Thomas came Bonette Darren.

Just to make sure he hadn't overlooked Toby, Pete studied the listings again.

He hadn't missed it.

Bones Toby wasn't there.

He counted. There were seven different numbers for people named Bones.

Toby probably lives with his parents. Or parent. Or a relative of some sort.

Only way we're gonna find him, Pete realized, is to start calling the numbers.

Seven. Not bad.

But he couldn't do it now, not with Sherry waiting for her drink.

Have to go by Jeff's plan and wait for her to conk out.

He tucked a paper napkin into the phone directory to mark his place, then shut the book and returned it to the drawer.

Before heading outside with Sherry's Bloody Mary, he added another generous splash of vodka.

Chapter Forty-eight

Where the hell is everyone?

Take it easy, Toby thought. Just relax. They might not get back for hours.

What if they're gone the whole weekend?

He roamed Brenda's room, scowling.

I can't wait forever. When the cops find Sherry's body, they'll *come over. They could show up any minute.*

They won't, he told himself. Even when they do find her – and that might not be for days or even weeks – they won't know who she is. She hasn't exactly got her driver's license on her. And she doesn't exactly *look* like herself, either. More like how she'd look if she went a few rounds with Mike Tyson.

Thinking of Tyson, Toby remembered Sherry's fingertips.

He'd intended to chew them off, but the AIDS had changed his mind about that.

He'd done his nibbling on Sherry *before* finding out she was infected. He'd bit her and fucked her and sucked her and swallowed some of her blood . . .

But that doesn't mean I caught it!

Maybe he'd been lucky.

Anyway, he'd figured why take the extra risk of biting off her fingertips?

I should've chopped 'em off with a knife and put 'em down the garbage disposal.

Should've, but didn't. Didn't even think of it.

Doesn't matter, he thought. There's no way in hell anybody's gonna identify her body today. After today, who cares? Let 'em. I'll have Brenda, the rest of the world can take a flying fuck.

He stepped closer to one of the windows.

Down on the street, a car rushed by.

Maybe they went to the movies. A Saturday matinee.

He sat on an edge of Brenda's bed and looked around.

I gotta find something to do. Can't just sit here.

He supposed he could mess around some more with her clothes, but the idea of it didn't seem very appealing.

Been there, done that. Time to hold off for the real thing.

He turned his eyes to her desk. She had her own computer.

That might be pretty interesting. Maybe she keeps a diary or something.

Then he noticed her bulletin board. The large cork board was attached to the wall just to the right of her desk. Pinned to it were post cards, notes, all sorts of—

A calendar! It hung near the center of the bulletin board. The large kind of calendar that shows a month at a time. Its top half was an illustration of Winnie the Pooh, twig in hand, standing on a bridge over a creek.

These gals sure like their Pooh, Toby thought.

The bottom half of the calendar had rows of dates, a square for each day. Some of the squares were blank. From where he sat on the bed, however, Toby could see handwriting inside most of them. He stood up and went to the calendar.

He found the square for today's date.

CAR WASH 9–5 was scribbled in red ink.

'Ah-*ha*!'

But what does it mean? he wondered. Is it just a reminder to get the car washed? Who in their right mind would put *that* on a calendar? If you wanta get your car washed, you just go . . .

She's working *at it from nine till five!*

It's probably some sort of fund-raiser, he realized. A bunch of kids get together and spend the day washing cars 'cause they need money for some dumb-ass project – like they want to buy a new set of hymnals for the church or maybe uniforms for the school marching band.

He pictured Brenda stretching herself over the hood of a car, swabbing it with a sudsy sponge, her skin wet and glinting in the sunlight.

Where the hell *is* this car wash? he wondered.

Probably somewhere nearby.

If I drive around, maybe I can find it.

He left Brenda's bedroom and hurried downstairs. In the foyer, he turned his gaze to the telephone answering machine.

Maybe someone had left a message about the car wash. Might at least be *some* sort of clue about where she is.

Couldn't hurt to give it a try.

He stepped over to the table and pressed the new messages button. After a couple of clicks, the tape began to rewind, quietly humming. More clicks. Then came a female voice.

'Hi, it's me. Anybody home? If you're home, please pick up. It's important. Mom? Dad? Brenda?'

Holy shit, is that Sherry?

Sure is.

After a moment of alarm, he realized she must've made the call *before* he got his hands on her.

Of course.

Should be interesting, he thought.

'I don't want to upset anybody, but . . . there's this guy who, uh . . . I made him mad and he threatened to go after my family.'

That's me! Oh, shit! When did *she call?*

'. . . where you live. Probably followed me when I came over last Sunday. I don't know if he'll really try anything, or when, but . . . he's very dangerous.'

Legs going numb, Toby sank into the easy chair and kept on listening.

After the message stopped, the machine beeped three times and went silent.

She's alive.

How can she be alive? I killed *her.*

Apparently not.

Toby felt as if he'd been bludgeoned.

I've gotta get out of here!

He pushed himself out of the chair and staggered toward the kitchen.

Hold it, he thought. If she's alive – *if?* – how come this place isn't crawling with cops? She figured I'd come after her family, so the cops would've been *waiting* for me.

Wouldn't they?

And where's Sherry? he wondered. Where did she make the call from, the police department? A hospital?

She oughta be in a morgue!

He returned to the answering machine.

He stared at it for a few seconds, then picked up the handset.

Busy signal.

Why the hell . . . ? Oh!

He let out a wild laugh, ran into the kitchen and hung up the wall phone. Then he raced back into the living room. Again, he lifted the handset. This time, there was a dial tone. He tapped the star button, then six-nine.

The feature was supposed to work just like redial, except that it called the last person who phoned *you.*

Maybe they don't have it, but if they do . . .

He heard the quick beeps of a phone number being activated.

Yes!

From the earpiece came the sounds of a ringing telephone.

Chapter Forty-nine

Pete flinched when the telephone rang. He was confused for a moment, then saw the cordless remote phone on the table beside the radio.

'Gonna get it?' Jeff asked.

'Maybe I'd better.'

As Jeff reached over to pick it up, Pete wondered who might be calling.

What if it's Mom and Dad and they're coming home early?

Jeff handed the phone to him.

Pete put it to his ear, but it sounded dead. It rang again. Then he realized he needed to push the on/off button. Embarrassed, he smiled at Sherry and said, 'Woops.' Then he thumbed the button and said, 'Hello?'

'Hey, man, how's it going?'

Pete didn't recognize the voice, but it sounded like a kid about his own age.

And the kid seemed to know him.

'Pretty good,' Pete said. 'How about you?'

'Can't complain.'

Who is this?

'What're you up to?' the kid asked.

'Not much.'

'Me either.'

Gonna tell me who you are?

He looked at Sherry and shook his head.

'Who is it?' Jeff whispered.

He looked at Jeff and shrugged. Then he asked into the phone, 'Who is this, anyway?'

The kid laughed. 'It's *me*, man.'

'Me who?'

'John.'

John? Oh, that narrows it down.

'Which John?'

'Give me a break. You don't remember me?'

'I don't *know* if I remember you. I don't exactly know who you are.'

Frowning, Sherry lowered her glass and rested it on the arm of her chair.

'John from the eighth grade.'

'Eighth grade?'

'Yeah. I looked you up, man. I'm in town for the weekend and figured maybe we could get together, talk about the old days.'

'I still don't—'

'You still living at the same place?'

'No, huh-uh, we moved the year I started high school.'

'Really? What's the new address?'

Pete felt his stomach tighten.

Sherry and Jeff were both staring at him, looking worried.

'I'm not gonna be around,' Pete said into the phone. 'I'm leaving in a few minutes. For the day.'

'Well, maybe I can drop in tomorrow. It'd be really cool to see you again, know what I mean? Anyway, I've got that money I owe you.'

'You owe me money?'

'Yeah. Fifty bucks.'

'Why do you owe me fifty bucks?'

'The bet, man. The bet. Don't you remember?'

'I don't remember any bet.'

'You don't have much of a memory, do you?' He laughed. 'Anyway, you want the money, don't you?'

'I'm not gonna be around the house, so . . .'

'Guess I can always *mail* it to you.'

'That might be better.'

'Really like to see you, though.'

'But I'm leaving in a few minutes. You'd better just go ahead and mail it to me.'

'Okay. If you're sure. Wanta give me your address?'

'My address?'

'Don't give it to him,' Sherry whispered.

'Maybe you oughta hang up,' Jeff whispered.

'Just a second,' Pete said. 'Can you hang on? Someone's at the door.' He leaned forward, rose out of his chair, took a step toward Sherry and handed the phone to her.

She raised it to her ear. Then she sat motionless, listening.

Pete watched her.

She was breathing hard. Her shoulders and chest were moist, shiny in the sunlight. He stared at the tops of her breasts. They were bruised and scratched like the rest of her, but so . . . She looked up at him and shook her head.

Pete bent down. With his face close to the side of Sherry's face – so close he thought he could feel her heat – he said toward the phone, 'Back. Sorry about that.' Then he stepped away.

A moment later, Sherry's face seemed to go slack. She reached toward Pete with the phone.

As he took it, she whispered, 'It's Toby.'

'Holy shit,' Jeff muttered.

Pete pressed his hand against the mouthpiece. 'What'll I do?'

Sherry just looked at him. 'I . . . I don't . . . You said he'd been *caught*!'

Pete grimaced.

'That was a little fib,' Jeff explained. 'Sorry.'

'A fib. Great.'

'I'm sorry,' Pete said. 'We wanted to know his name, that's all. It was a dirty trick, but . . .'

'Tell him to come over,' Jeff said. 'We'll waste his fuckin' ass.'

'No!' Sherry gasped.

Pete took his hand away from the mouthpiece. 'Sorry about that,' he said. 'My ride's here, so I guess I've gotta get going.'

'Wait, man. You want the fifty bucks, don't you?'

Heart suddenly thudding wildly, Pete said, 'Yeah, go ahead and send it to me. Got a pen and paper?'

'Hang on.'

'*Don't!*' Sherry whispered, leaning forward and looking frantic. '*Are you nuts?*'

'Okay,' Pete said into the phone. 'You can send it to 835 Chandler Court.'

'Oh, my God,' Sherry muttered.

'That's LA.' As Pete gave the zip code, he turned his head and saw Jeff grinning at him like a maniac.

'All right there, man,' Toby said. 'I'll get that check in the mail to you right away. Oughta be showing up in a couple of days.'

'No hurry,' Pete said.

'Hey, it's been great talking to you. Too bad we can't get together.'

'Maybe some other time.'

'Right. Next time I'm in town, I'll look you up.'

'Great. Good talking to you.'

'Same here.'

'So long.' He thumbed the on/off button and the phone went dead.

Jeff chuckled and shook his head.

Sherry, gazing at Pete with shock and disappointment, muttered, 'I can't believe it! First you guys lie through your teeth and say the *cops* got him . . .'

'That was so *we* could go after him,' Jeff said.

'*Now* you told him where we *are*. He knows *I'm* here. Somehow, he figured it out and now he'll be coming over.'

'Fuckin'-A,' Jeff said, grinning.

'I gave Toby the wrong address,' Pete explained.

'You're kidding!' She looked appalled. 'That's even *worse!* He'll go to *that* house looking for me and . . . God help whoever's there.'

'Nobody's there,' Pete said.

'It's the house next door,' Jeff explained. 'It's up for sale, been empty for *months*.' Beaming at Pete, he said, 'Brilliant work, dude. We'll fuckin' ambush his ass!'

Sherry slumped back in her chair. Looking exhausted, she said, 'We'd better call the cops right now.'

'No cops,' Jeff said. 'No way. *We'll* take care of him. Me and Pete.'

'Or he'll take care of you,' Sherry muttered. 'And after he gets done with you guys, he'll take care of *me*.'

'That isn't gonna happen,' Pete said.
'You just *hope* not.'
'Just in case, you shouldn't be around. I'll give you the car keys, and . . .'
She let out a soft, tired laugh.
'Are you okay to drive?'
'I'm not *going* to drive. *God!* How could you give him that address?'
'It's next door,' Jeff reminded her.
'I *know* it's next door, but Toby isn't stupid. If you think he'll walk into some kind of trap . . .'
'I had to tell him *something.*' Pete said.
'No you didn't.'
'He didn't just call here by accident, you know.'
Sherry stared at him. 'I know that.'
'How do you think he found out you're still alive? How did he know where to call?'
'Oh, God,' Sherry murmured. 'He's at my parents' house. He heard me on their answering machine . . . and they've got some kinda call return thing on their phone.'
'Star sixty-nine?' Jeff asked.
'Yeah, that's it. That's how he called here.'
'Oh, man.'
'We've gotta get over there,' Sherry said.
'He'll be on his way *here*,' Jeff said.
'But my mom and Dad . . . Brenda . . .'
'Maybe they're okay,' Pete said. 'Maybe they weren't home.'
'I've gotta find out.'
'One of us could drive over and look around,' Pete suggested.
'Not me,' Jeff said. 'I'm not gonna go off 'n leave you guys here. *He's* gonna show up. Anyhow, I'm a little tanked. I'd problee get pulled over by the cops.'
'I guess we could *all* go,' Pete said.
'Who drives?' Jeff asked. 'We *all* been boozin' it up.'
'I'm okay to drive,' Sherry said.
'You're hardly okay to *stand*,' Pete told her.
'My head's pretty clear. I can manage.'
'We'll miss our chance at Toby,' he said.

'How long'll it take to get there?' Jeff asked.

Turning her head, Sherry stared up at the bluff beyond the back wall. 'That's Mulholland?'

'Yeah,' Pete said. 'About a mile from Coldwater.'

'Guess it'd take twenty minutes, half an hour. To get there.'

'Then the whole thing'll take like an hour,' Jeff said. 'We're gonna *miss* him.'

'We'd better do it,' Pete said, meeting Sherry's eyes. 'Make sure your family's okay. We can worry about Toby later.'

'Thanks.' She handed her half-finished Bloody Mary to Jeff.

'Done?' he asked.

She nodded. 'Had enough for now.'

He set her glass on the table.

Sherry grabbed the arms of her chair, leaned forward and started to push herself up.

Pete lurched out of his chair and hurried to her side. He gently took hold of her left upper arm.

'Thanks,' she said as he helped her up. On her feet, she said, 'Let me see if I can get along on my own. I'd *better*, huh?'

'Okay.' He let go of her arm, then watched her. She swayed slightly, but stayed up.

'Might be a good idea to put away all this stuff,' she said. 'Toby might come snooping while we're gone.'

'Snoopin' at the house next door,' Jeff pointed out.

'For five minutes, maybe,' Sherry said. 'Then he'll notice it's empty and figure out somebody pulled a fast one. Then maybe he'll come looking over here.'

'Let's get everything inside,' Pete said.

'I'll go on in,' Sherry said, and started hobbling toward the glass door.

'Y'all right?' Jeff asked her.

'Peachy.'

She made it into the house.

It took two trips for Pete and Jeff to carry everything in from the table. Then Jeff picked up his clothes and brought them inside. While he stepped into his jeans, Pete shut and locked the sliding door.

'You going like that?' Jeff asked.

Pete closed the curtains. 'Guess I'd better get dressed.'

'How about me?' Sherry asked from where she waited by the front door.

Pete hurried over to her.

'Maybe you can find me a shirt to wear.'

'You wanta come along and pick something?'

'I'd better wait here. Just grab me anything. We've gotta hurry.'

'Yeah.' He gave his trunks a pull, then started down the hallway toward his bedroom.

'Do you have any guns in the house?' Sherry called.

'Yeah.'

'We'd better take something with us, 'cause I know Toby's armed.'

Chapter Fifty

Standing in the kitchen to put on his shoes, Toby noticed a pink sheet of paper fixed by an Eeyore magnet to the refrigerator door. In both top corners were cartoonish drawings of cars. The car on the left looked filthy, while the car on the right seemed to sparkle – lines like sunshine rays radiating off it.

Toby stepped into his shoes, then rushed to the refrigerator. The message was hand-lettered, large and bold:

DIRTY CAR?
YOU WANT A CLEAN CAR
WE WANT A NEW COMPUTER
FOR THE SCHOOL NEWSPAPER!
COME TO US!
IT'S A WIN WIN SITUATION!!!
WHEN: SATURDAY, 9 AM TO 5 PM
WHERE: PARKING LOT, FAIRVIEW HIGH SCHOOL
8321 FAIRVIEW BOULEVARD, LOS ANGELES
HOW MUCH: $5.00 DONATION
IF NOT COMPLETELY SATISFIED,
WE'LL REFUND YOUR DIRT!

In blue ink, someone had scrawled, 'Too cute!' underneath the comment about refunding dirt.

Did Brenda do that? Toby wondered. Probably.

He liked the idea that she'd scribbled a smart remark on the thing.

Perky kid. She'll be a scrapper. It'll be great.

Toby plucked the paper off the refrigerator, sending Eeyore flying. He watched the magnet hit the floor. It bounced but didn't break.

He read the announcement again.

Fairview High. That won't be hard to find. Can't be too far away, either.

But should he go for Brenda? Or forget about her and go after Sherry?

A hard choice.

There'd *been* no choice before listening to Sherry's message. It had been simple then; take down the parents, grab Brenda and drive her to his house for fun and games.

But he'd given up that plan after hearing Sherry on the answering machine. For one thing, there was no guarantee he'd be able to find Brenda at all. The car wash might be miles away in any direction. He could spend hours searching for it and maybe *never* find it. For another thing, it'd be crazy to go chasing after Brenda now that Sherry was alive.

How the hell did she live through all that? he wondered. She's gotta be in *awfully* bad shape.

She didn't sound so bad on the phone.

Keeping the flier, he left the house and headed for his car.

It all keeps changing, he thought as he walked along. Now I *know* where to find Brenda. I can go straight there. Can't be all that far away, either. But Sherry's alive. She knows who I am. She can send the cops after me.

Why *hasn't* she?

'Good question,' he muttered.

Realizing he'd spoken out loud, he looked around. He was at the bottom of the driveway. He saw no one nearby, just a couple of Sikhs walking along on the other side of the street. They were paying no attention to him. He looked down at himself. The fly of his shorts was open, he had the car wash announcement in one hand and he still wore the rubber gloves.

Not breaking stride, he clamped the paper between his teeth, pulled off the gloves and shoved them into the right rear pocket of his shorts. After glancing around again to make sure he wasn't being watched, he pulled up his zipper.

He checked himself again.

'Lookin' good,' he muttered.

Where was I?

Gotta decide between Brenda and Sherry.

He sure knew who he *wanted*. Brenda. She was fresh and beautiful and unused.

He'd already done everything he'd ever dreamed of with Sherry. She was used up.

Oughta be dead.

Needs to be dead, he told himself. That's the thing. She knows my name. All she has to do is tell the cops who I am . . .

But she hasn't.

Not yet, anyway. If she'd told, I'd be busted by now.

Or dead.

As he approached his car, the notion scurried through his mind that maybe he shouldn't let himself be taken alive. Might be better to have a shoot-out with the cops, go down in a blaze of glory.

It's either that, he thought, or spend the rest of my life dying of AIDS in prison.

Feeling a little sick, he climbed into his car. He tossed the pink sheet of paper onto the passenger seat, then started the engine. And sat there.

Who *says* I've got AIDS? he thought. Just because *Sherry* has it . . . *if* she does . . . Who says she wasn't lying? And even if she was telling the truth, you don't have to necessarily catch it just because you mess around a little.

A lot. I messed around a lot.

He started remembering, reliving in his mind all that he'd done to her. He could see her slim, naked body under him; feel her hot slippery skin and her snug suction; taste her flesh, her juices; hear her grunts and whimpers; hear the thuds and smacks and whipping sounds of the beating; hear the wet sounds their bodies made together.

As he dwelled in the vivid memories, his sickening fear quickly faded away. His penis pushed upward against the front of his shorts.

Good thing I zipped up, he thought. It'd be sticking out.

He smiled.

Who do I want to stick it *in*? That's the real question.

'Brenda,' he said, 'here I come.'

He started the car and pulled away from the curb.

Just forget about Sherry, he told himself. I've had her.

Oh, God, yes! Best night of my life.

Now it's time to move on and nail her kid sister.

Pretend I never heard that damn message.

But I know where Sherry is! I could go over there right now, fuck her all over again, eat her up!

The thoughts made him ache.

I'd end up with AIDS for sure.

Anyway, she isn't alone. She's got that guy with her. The one on the phone. Who the hell is he, anyway?

A cop?

No way. They'd have me by now.

She said they'd have me tomorrow, though. What was that about? They wouldn't wait till tomorrow, would they?

She hasn't told them who I am. Simple as that.

What's she trying to pull?

Maybe nothing, he thought. Maybe it's something really simple – like she can't remember my name.

Is that possible?

Possible, maybe, but not likely. She'd sounded awfully coherent on the answering machine. Not at all like someone with a memory problem.

But she didn't say my name.

'Everything *but* my name,' he muttered.

She has to know it, he thought. Toby Bones? Who could forget that?

Let's say she does remember my name, he thought. She's alive and okay enough to make that call. She remembers everything about last night, but she hasn't sicced the cops on me. What does it mean?

She doesn't want the cops picking me up?

Why?

Makes no sense at all.

Maybe it has something to do with where she is now – and the guy on the other end of the phone.

Maybe he won't let *her call the cops!*

Toby let out a laugh.

Wouldn't that be rich? It's a miracle I didn't kill her – me or the fall – and somehow she lives through it all and ends up in the hands of another guy just like me.

Laughing again, Toby shook his head.

'Far out,' he muttered.

Such things *did* happen. He'd heard stories of gals making narrow escapes – and fleeing straight into the arms of strangers who end up raping them.

The more Toby thought about it, the more likely it seemed. Somebody found her. A guy, obviously. There she is, naked and helpless – maybe even out cold. He gives her a good looking over, sees she's a great-looking babe under all the blood and stuff. Maybe he fucks her right on the spot. Or else he holds off till he can take her someplace safe.

Like his house on Chandler Court.

'Ah, yes,' Toby said.

Where he cleans her up, patches her up and keeps her for some fun and games.

'My kinda guy,' Toby said.

It would explain everything.

Whoa. Maybe not everything. What about the call she made to her parents?

That's easy, Toby thought. He let her do it as part of a deal.

The sneaky bitch probably talked him into it.

He could just hear her. *'Let me call my parents so I can warn them about Toby, and I'll cooperate with you. Okay? Just let me make the call and I'll do anything you want.'*

That's *gotta* be how it went down, Toby thought.

This is great!

If Sherry's being held prisoner, she won't be making any calls to the police. Not in the near future, anyway. Probably never, because the guy almost has to finish her off eventually.

If I don't get to her first.

But there's no big hurry, Toby told himself. The guy might keep her alive for days, maybe even weeks.

I can take all the time I want with Brenda, then go on over to Chandler Court.

And rescue Sherry.

At first glance, he didn't see Brenda. But there were eight or ten people gathered in the parking lot at the far end of the school. Some didn't seem to be wearing much. Most were surrounding a couple of cars. He glimpsed buckets, rags, and a hose shooting a long flashing stream of water at a car.

This has to be it.

Eyes on the car wash, Toby hadn't caught the name of the school. But how many schools on Fairview Boulevard would be having car washes today?

He slowed almost to a stop before turning. As he drove into the parking lot, he reached over to the passenger seat and grabbed the pink flier. He glanced at the inked-in remark, 'Too cute!' Smiling, he crumpled the paper and stuffed it into the right front pocket of his shorts.

Chapter Fifty-one

'Their car isn't here,' Sherry said, and steered into the driveway.

'I bet they aren't home,' Jeff said from the back seat.

I sure hope you're right, Pete thought. If they *are* home, they're probably dead.

Sherry stopped the car and shut off its engine.

'Why don't you wait here?' Pete suggested. 'Jeff and I can run in and make sure everything's okay.'

She turned her head toward him, wincing as if the movement hurt her neck. 'I've gotta go in.'

'But *he* might be inside.'

'All the more reason to stay together.'

'She's right,' Jeff said. 'We can't just leave her sitting alone out here. Toby might sneak out . . .'

'We could leave her the gun.'

'She might use it on us.'

'Cut it out,' Sherry said.

'See?'

'I don't *care* about your stupid little lie right now, okay? Forget about it. Let's just pretend it never happened.'

Looking at Sherry, Pete said, 'Why don't you stay here and we'll leave the gun with you?'

'I'm going in,' Sherry said. She handed the keys to Pete, then opened her door.

Pete pocketed the keys. Bending down, he reached under his seat and pulled his revolver out of a towel. He set it on his lap while he opened his door. Then he reached inside his half-unbuttoned shirt. Holding the weapon out of sight against his ribcage, he climbed from the car.

Jeff shut the door for him.

Pete looked around. He saw nobody nearby.

Sherry waited in front of the car, her loose shirt fluttering and flapping in the wind. It was a Hawaiian shirt that Pete's parents had brought back to him from Maui last year. He'd hardly ever worn it. Though he liked the slick, lightweight feel of it, it was just too gaudy for him. Bright red. All those flowers.

It sure looked great on Sherry.

You couldn't tell she was wearing anything under it. Only when the wind picked it up could you glimpse her bikini pants.

'Jeff,' she said, 'why don't you run up and check the front door? Just see if it's locked. Then come back. Don't go in.'

'You got it,' he said and hurried off.

'I have a feeling they aren't home,' she told Pete.

I sure hope they aren't, he thought. He said, 'Me, too.'

'They almost always *do* go someplace on Saturday afternoons. Mom and Dad have this real *thing* about sitting around the house.' She grimaced. 'Only thing is, Brenda likes to stay home.'

Jeff came hurrying back. 'Door's locked,' he said.

She seemed glad to hear it. Nodding slightly, she said, 'Let's go around back.'

They followed her to the driveway gate. There, she started to reach for the latch. Before her arm was halfway up, she let out a groan of pain.

'I'll get it,' Pete said.

'I'm fine.' She strained, writhing slightly, and reached the latch.

They followed her through the gate. Jeff eased it shut. Then they walked slowly up the driveway, Sherry in the lead.

To their left was a redwood fence. Music came from the neighbor's house. It sounded like Enya, but might've been the *Titanic* soundtrack. No sounds came from the house of Sherry's family.

God, what if they're all dead inside?

They're probably not even home, Pete told himself.

Then he imagined finding them dead, Sherry bursting into tears and throwing herself into his arms. He held her gently as she cried. Her face was hot and wet against the side of his neck. Spasms wracked her body, shaking her shoulders and back, making her breasts move against his chest.

Terrific, he thought. Have Toby butcher her family so I can hug her.

He shook his head.

'What?' Jeff whispered.

'Nothing.'

What if wishing makes it happen?

Don't be an idiot, he told himself. I could wish till hell freezes over and it wouldn't . . .

I don't want it to happen. Do not. That was not a request. If anybody's listening out there, I'm not *wishing them dead. Got it?*

What if they don't let you take it back? he wondered.

Bullshit.

'Uh-oh,' Jeff said.

Pete turned his head, saw the back door of the house and realized that its window was broken. He felt as if a hand had suddenly clutched his heart.

What's the big shock? We knew he got inside. This is how. Calm down.

Sherry hobbled toward the door.

What if he's still inside?

'Wait,' Pete said, his whisper loud.

She stopped and glanced over her shoulder at him.

'I'll go first.'

She nodded.

'I'll guard the rear,' Jeff whispered.

Pete pulled the revolver out of his shirt. It was one of his most prized possessions. Though it still legally belonged to his father, it had been presented it to him on his thirteenth birthday. *You've got a good head on your shoulders*, Dad had told him. *This is yours now. Keep it near your bed in case of intruders. Just make sure you don't shoot the wrong person – like me or Mom.'*

The handgun was a Ruger Single-Six, a Western style single-action .22 with six rounds in the cylinder. Not much stopping power compared to Sherry's .380 – which Toby was probably carrying. Before leaving home, however, Pete had switched cylinders. Now it was equipped with the magnum cylinder and loaded with the extra-powerful .22 rounds.

He'll still have me outgunned, Pete thought. I'd damn well better shoot first and nail him good.

God. I hope he's not here.

Holding the Ruger behind his back, he stepped up to the door. With his left hand, he tried the knob. It turned. As he pulled the door open, he pressed his thumb against the hammer of his revolver, ready to cock and fire.

Broken glass on the kitchen floor.

He saw nobody.

He stepped in, bits of glass crunching under his shoes.

No one seemed to be in the kitchen.

Sherry came in, careful to avoid the glass with her bare feet. Then Jeff entered and shut the door.

'Wait,' Sherry whispered. She limped over to the counter and pulled two large carving knives out of a wooden holder. She handed one to Jeff. 'Okay. Let's go. But let's go fast. I can't stand this.'

Pete looked her in the eyes.

Bloodshot eyes, the surrounding tissues swollen and discolored. But Pete saw in them the dread that her family had been slaughtered.

Though his own heart was slamming with fear, he knew how hers must be aching.

What if it was my parents . . .?

'I tell you what,' he whispered. 'Stay here.' To Jeff, he said, 'You, too.'

They both looked ready to argue, but Pete didn't wait for it. He swung the revolver out from behind his back, whirled around and ran from the kitchen.

'Come on,' he heard Sherry say. 'We've gotta cover his back.'

They'll have to catch me first.

He raced through the dining room, across the foyer and into the living room, looking for bloody corpses or Toby but finding no one, alive or dead. Sherry and Jeff were just coming out of the dining room when he reached the foot of the stairway. 'Okay so far,' he gasped. Then he charged up the stairs, taking three at a time.

Nobody at the top of the stairs.

He rushed from room to room, checking behind furniture, dropping to his knees to glance under beds, throwing open closet doors. In the two bathrooms, he threw aside the shower curtains and looked in the tubs.

No bodies. No blood. No Toby.

No sign of Toby, either. If he'd been up here at all, he'd left behind no obvious traces.

Huffing for breath, Pete returned to the top of the stairway. Sherry and Jeff stared up at him. 'It's clear,' he called, then started to descend. On his way down, he lowered his revolver. It still wasn't cocked. He switched it to his left hand, wiped his sweaty right hand on his jeans and looked at his thumb. The pad of it had a red, corrugated dent from being pressed so hard against the hammer spur.

'Nobody's here?' Sherry asked.

'Doesn't . . . look like it.'

'Any sign of Toby?' Jeff asked.

'Huh-uh.'

'Might be hiding.'

'Possible. Go up and look around if you want.'

Jeff shook his head. 'That's okay.'

As Pete stepped off the bottom stair, Sherry turned away. He and Jeff followed her into the living room. She stopped beside a lamp table. 'Here's where he must've played my message,' she said.

The new message light wasn't blinking.

Sherry bent over and lowered a finger toward the rewind button.

'Wait,' Pete said. 'You'd better not touch it in case he left fingerprints.'

'Doesn't matter,' she said. 'There won't be a trial.' She pushed the button, but nothing happened. 'That's . . .' She opened the top of the answering machine. It raised like the hood of a car.

Pete expected to see a tape cassette inside.

Apparently, so did Sherry. 'Shit,' she muttered. 'He took it.'

'Why would he do that?' Jeff asked.

'Just to make sure nobody gets to hear what I said about him.' She pushed the lid down. Then she looked at Pete. 'He probably took off the minute you gave him that address.'

'He'd be there by now,' Jeff said.

Sherry nodded. 'Maybe we can still catch him. If he hangs around for a while . . .'

'You wanta leave a note for your parents?' Pete asked her.

'Toby won't be coming back here. Let's just get going.'

'You could stay here,' Pete said.

Jeff glared at him.

'You'll be a lot safer here. Your parents'll probably be home pretty soon, and . . .'

'No way,' she said. 'I don't *care* to be safe. Let's use the front door. It'll be quicker.'

As they headed for the door, Jeff asked, 'Do you wanta grab your father's gun?'

'What'll *he* use?'

'If Toby's not coming back, anyway . . .'

'Not gonna take my dad's gun. He might need it. You never know.'

With his left hand, Pete opened the door. After Sherry and Jeff were outside, he hid his own revolver under the front of his shirt. Holding it against his chest, he left the house and pulled the door shut.

'Besides,' Sherry said, 'We've already got a gun.' She smiled at Pete. 'That's all we oughta need.'

Chapter Fifty-two

The window of the Mercedes slid down and the driver smiled out at Brenda. He looked embarrassed. 'Hi,' he said. 'I guess I'd like to get the car washed.'

'You came to the right place.'

Blushing, he fumbled with his wallet. 'Five dollars?' he mumbled.

'That's right. We're trying to buy a new computer for journalism.'

He held a five-dollar bill out the window and Brenda saw that his hand was trembling. 'You okay?' she asked.

'Sure. Fine.'

'Afraid we'll scratch your car?' she asked, though she knew that wasn't it.

She knew exactly what it was.

This guy was a male version of Fran. All his life, he'd been ignored or belittled by every good-looking gal he saw. He blushed and trembled because he was afraid of Brenda.

'It's my dad's car,' he said. Blushing again, he said, 'You can scratch it if you want.'

The others were still working on one of those enormous Suburbans, so there was no hurry.

'You don't go to Fairview, do you?' Brenda asked.

'Nah.'

'I didn't think so. I was pretty sure I hadn't seen you around.'

'That's why.'

'Are you still in school?' she asked.

'Yeah. I'm a senior at Foster.'

'Really? My sister teaches at Foster a lot. She's a substitute.'

'Foster *High School*?' he asked.

'Right. She mostly teaches English.'

'Gosh, maybe I've had her.'

'Maybe so.'

'That'd be a kick, huh? What's her name?'

'Gates. Sherry Gates.'

'Hmmm.' Frowning, he shook his head. 'What does she look like?'

'Like me, sort of. But taller and prettier. She's twenty-five.'

The frown lifted into a smile. 'Know what? I think I *have* had her. She subs for Mr Chambers?'

'Oh, I don't know who she's subbed for. I just know she talks about working a lot at Foster.'

'It's gotta be her. She *did* look a lot like you.'

'Probably *was* her.'

'It's a small world, isn't it?'

'Sure is,' Brenda said. 'I'll have to tell her I ran into one of her students. She'll get a kick out it.'

'Yeah. Tell her I said "hi." '

'What's your name?'

'Jack. Jack Bundy.'

'Nice to meet you, Jack,' she said, then heard the Suburban rumble to life. 'I'm Brenda.' Turning her head, she watched the gleaming blue vehicle roll slowly forward and stop. The drying crew – four girls in bikinis – swarmed around it with rags in their hands. 'Looks like we're ready for you now,' Brenda said. 'Why don't you pull on forward?'

He nodded. 'Then should I get out or stay in the car?'

'Either way. Doesn't matter. But you'd better roll your window up or you'll get a snootful of water.'

He chuckled. 'Thanks for the warning.'

Stepping backward, she waved him ahead. Then she walked alongside the Mercedes. The moment it stopped, Ralph began to blast it with the hose. Water exploded off the windshield, spraying those who stood too close. Nobody tried to get out of the way.

Jack remained inside.

Brenda wondered if he wanted out.

Doesn't matter, she thought. He's got air conditioning in there.

'Know him?' Fran asked.
'Not really.'
'You sure talked to him a long time.'
'Not *that* long.'
'Pretty long.'
'He knows my sister.'
'Really?'
'He goes to Foster High . . .'
'A rich kid.'
'Guess so. Anyway, he's had Sherry for a substitute.'
'He's kinda cute,' Fran said.
Jack did have a big, puffy face that made him look like an overgrown infant, but Brenda would hardly call him cute.
It's all in the eye of the beholder, she told herself.
To Fran, she said, 'He seemed pretty nice.'
'What's his name?'
'Jack. Want to meet him?'
Fran's eyes widened. 'Uh-huh. No way.' She shook her head. Brenda supposed she was probably blushing. Her face was certainly red, but it had been flushed and shiny all day from the sun and heat.
Ralph stopped hosing the car.
Brenda crouched and picked up her bucket. 'You oughta do his windshield,' she suggested.
Fran laughed. 'No way!'
'Come on, do it. Worst case scenerio, he ignores you. On the other hand, maybe he'll be smitten.'
'Smitten my ass.'
Side by side, they walked toward the Mercedes.
'If you're gonna do it,' Brenda said, 'lose the sweatshirt.'
'I *am* awfully hot.'
'Doggone right you are. Don't hide it under a—'
'That's not what I meant and you know it.'
Brenda laughed. Then she said, 'Do it,' and turned away. She carried her bucket toward the rear of the car. Baxter was already swabbing the lid of the trunk, so Brenda crouched and began to sponge the rear quarter panel.
Fran, standing near the hood, started to pull up her sweatshirt. Brenda saw the white skin of her midriff.

What's she wearing, a bikini?

Maybe this isn't such a terrific idea.

Why not? Jack's tubby, too. Maybe they're made for each other.

Instead of pulling the sweatshirt off, Fran lifted its front just high enough to wipe her face with it . . . and high enough to expose the bare white undersides of her breasts for a second or two.

Brenda felt her stomach go funny.

Holy cow!

Had Fran done that on purpose? Right in front of the whole world?

What is she, nuts?

Either that, or desperate. Or she *really* likes the looks of this Jack guy. Or she didn't realize she was lifting her sweatshirt *that* high. Or maybe she forgot she wasn't wearing anything underneath it.

How do you forget that?

Brenda wondered if anyone else had gotten a look at Fran's breasts.

Had Jack seen them?

Funny if he of all people happened to be looking the other way.

Fran crouched, reached into her bucket and lifted out a dripping sponge. Then she bent over the side of the car, leaned against the windshield and stretched out an arm . . . pushing her right breast against the glass directly in front of Jack's face.

What's gotten into her?

Brenda felt a little scared.

Maybe she's just finally had it with being ignored.

Done with the windshield, Fran started to use her sponge on the hood. Brenda stood up to see her better. Fran didn't expose herself or writhe on the hood. Nor did she glance in Jack's direction.

Probably really embarrassed.

Jack seemed to be watching her. Brenda couldn't tell where he was looking, but his head was straight forward.

Of course he's watching her. She showed him her boobs.

He's hoping for a repeat performance.

But Fran didn't give him one. She scrubbed her side of the hood while Quentin worked on the other side. Then she crouched to work on the front quarter panel.

Soon, they all stepped back and Ralph brought his hose into action. Sudsy water streamed down the car. When the water stopped being white and frothy, Ralph turned the hose away. He waved Jack forward.

The Mercedes drove ahead. When it stopped, the drying crew rushed in with their rags. They scampered around Jack's car, talking and laughing among themselves, hanging over his hood and trunk, leaning against his windows.

'Look at them,' Fran muttered. 'That's me being erased from Jack's mind.'

'I don't know,' Brenda said.

'Not a lard-ass in the bunch.'

'Take it easy.' Brenda patted her on the back. 'He won't be erasing you any time soon.'

'Think not?'

'Guys don't forget that sort of thing.'

Fran frowned at her. 'What sort of thing?'

'You know.'

'I do?'

'This?' Brenda reached down, lifted the front of her T-shirt and wiped her face with it. 'Minus the bikini top?'

'What?'

'You showed him your boobies.'

'I did not.'

'Maybe not on purpose, but . . .' Brenda shrugged.

Fran gaped at her. 'You're kidding.'

Brenda shook her head.

'Oh, my God.'

An accident?

Brenda laughed.

'It's not funny.'

'Sorry.'

'It happened when I wiped my face?'

'Right after I said you should take your sweatshirt *off*.'

'I couldn't take it off. I've got nothing on under it.'

'We know that now.'

'Oh, God.' Lowering her head, Fran muttered, 'I think I'm gonna be sick.'

'Hey, it's okay. I don't even think anyone was looking except me. I'm probably the only one who noticed.'

'What about Jack?'

'Even if he *did* see them, he'll be gone in a couple of minutes.' Brenda looked over at the Mercedes. All the girls except Traci had already wandered away from it. Traci was wiping its rear window. 'Look. They're almost done.'

Fran didn't bother to look. 'How much showed?' she asked.

'Not that much. You shouldn't worry about it, okay? Even if Jack saw *everything*, it's no big deal. He doesn't know who you are. You'll probably never even see him again.'

Fran turned toward the Mercedes.

Traci, done with it, twirled her rag as she ambled over to join her friends.

The driver's window slid down.

'All done,' Stephanie called out. 'So long, handsome.'

'Bitch,' Fran muttered.

'Yep,' Brenda said.

As they both watched, the gleaming black Mercedes drove forward to the nearest exit. It stopped and waited for a while, then turned right onto Fairview.

When it passed, Brenda saw Jack through the open passenger window.

'Oh, my God,' Fran said. 'He's looking at us.'

'At you.'

Then he slowed down, turned right, and entered the parking lot.

'He's coming back,' Brenda said.

'Oh, my God.'

'Maybe he wants another look.'

Fran elbowed her.

Ralph, Quentin and Baxter looked at them, glanced at the approaching car, then eyed each other.

Baxter was frowning.

Quentin was chuckling.

Ralph, hose by his side, grinned at Brenda and sang out, 'Somebody's got a boyyyyfriend.'

Smiling, Brenda pointed her thumb at Fran.

Fran grimaced. 'Not me,' she said.

The guys turned away and tried to look uninterested as the car eased to a stop in front of Brenda and Fran.

Chapter Fifty-three

Jack smiled out the driver's window. First at Brenda, then at Fran. Eyes shifting back to Brenda, he said, 'Hi, I'm back.'

'Hi. This is my friend, Fran. Fran, this is Jack.'

'Hi, Jack.'

'Hi, Fran.' He nodded and blushed. 'The thing is, you did such a good job . . . What I'm wondering – you don't make house calls, do you?'

'What do you mean?' Brenda asked.

'We've got three other cars back at home.'

'Three?'

Smiling, he shook his head. 'My folks . . . we've got cars up the ying-yang.'

Fran laughed.

'They could *all* use a wash,' Jack explained. 'I mean, if you're interested in raising some extra money. It'd take me all afternoon if I tried to bring 'em over here, but it occurred to me, maybe if a couple of you came out to my house . . .'

'I don't think so,' Brenda said.

'Oh, okay. Just thought I'd ask.'

'We really have to stay here. We can't go running off to people's houses.'

Especially not strangers, she thought.

He's probably harmless, but you never know.

'I'd pay extra,' Jack said. 'How about fifty dollars?'

'For three cars?' Fran looked at Brenda. 'That's a *lot*. And things *are* sort of slow right now.'

'Hang on, Jack.' Brenda took hold of Fran's sleeve and led her away from the car. When she figured they were well beyond Jack's hearing range, she stopped. 'Forget it,' she said. 'We're not going over to his house. We don't know anything about him.'

'I think he kind of likes me.'

'Maybe he does.'

He *oughta*, Brenda thought.

'I know I like him.'

'Guess so.'

'The thing is, if we say no and he goes driving off, I might never see him again.'

'There's an easy remedy. Give him your name and number.'

Fran grimaced. 'I can't do *that*.'

'You'll lift up your sweatshirt but you won't give him your . . .'

'I didn't *do* that.'

'Maybe you didn't *mean* to, but you did.'

'It was an accident.'

'Well, accidentally give him your phone number.'

'I can't. I mean, it'd be too obvious.'

'Unlike lifting your . . .'

Fran elbowed her. Again.

'Hey, hey. Easy on the merchandise.'

Fran leaned close to her and whispered, 'The thing is, if we go and do his cars, it'll like give me a chance to talk to him and stuff. You know? We can get to know each other. Maybe he'll even *ask* for my number.'

'Let me introduce you to a concept: Shallow grave by the side of the road.'

'Let me introduce *you* to one, Miss Know-it-all: Nothing ventured, nothing gained.'

'It's not worth the risk,' Brenda said.

'Not for *you*.'

'Not for you, either. I know he *looks* like a nice guy, but you can't tell by looking. For all we know, he might be a nutcase.'

'He isn't any nutcase. He's perfectly normal. Except for the fact that he might actually be *interested* in me. Come on, Brenda. This could be my big chance.'

'Let's try something,' Brenda said.

'What?'

Not answering, she turned around. Jack smiled out of his car window as they walked toward him. 'What's the verdict?' he asked.

'I don't know yet,' Brenda said. 'Where do you live?'

'You know where Foster High is?'

'Yeah.'

'Our house is just a few blocks from there. But I'll drive, so you don't have to worry about finding it.'

'And you'll drive us back here when we're done?'

'Sure.'

'Three cars for fifty dollars?'

'Yep.'

'Sounds pretty tempting.'

'So it's a deal?' he asked.

'Only thing is, three cars will take a long time if just Fran and I try to do them. Suppose we have a couple of the guys come with us?'

Jack seemed pleased by the idea. 'Sure, why not? It'll make it easier for everyone.'

'Guys!' Brenda called. 'Come here a minute.'

Ralph, Baxter and Quentin hurried over to them.

'What's up?' Ralph asked.

'Anybody wanta make a house call? Jack has three other cars at home. He'll give us fifty bucks if we wash 'em.'

'You mean like *all* of us go?' Baxter asked.

'Somebody'd better stay and hold down the fort,' Ralph said.

'You're the hose man,' Brenda told him. 'You wanta stay?'

'Sure.'

'How about you guys?' she asked, glancing from Baxter to Quentin.

'Count me in,' Baxter said.

'Me, too,' said Quentin.

'So the four of us?'

'What about *them*?' Baxter asked with a nod toward the drying crew.

'*They're* not coming,' Fran said. 'No way.'

To Ralph, Brenda said, 'Maybe you can get a couple of them to help with the washing.'

'If any more customers show up,' Ralph said.
'There'll be more,' Brenda assured him.
'Sure hope so. We haven't exactly made a killing so far.'
'Well, we'll get fifty bucks out of this.'
And maybe Fran'll get a boyfriend.
She stepped closer to Jack's window. 'I guess it's all set. Can you fit four of us in there?'
'Sure.'
'Wanta open the trunk? We'll throw in some buckets and sponges.'
'You don't have to bring any of that stuff. I've got everything at home.'
'You sure?'
'Sure. Just hop in and we'll be off.'
Fran hurried around to the other side and opened the passenger door. 'Okay if I sit up here?' she asked.
'It's right where I want you,' Jack told her.
'Okay. Great. Thanks.' She sank into the seat.
Brenda opened the back door, climbed in, and scooted to the middle of the seat. While Quentin followed her in, Baxter hurried around the car. He came in from the other side.
Jack smiled over his shoulder. 'Everybody ready?'
'All set,' Brenda said.
Quentin and Baxter nodded.
'You'd better put your seat belts on. I don't want anybody getting hurt.'
He watched as they strapped themselves in. Then he turned his eyes to Fran in the passenger seat. 'How are you doing?' he asked.
She beamed. 'Oh, fine.'
'You must be awfully hot in that sweatshirt.'
She laughed softly and the flush of her face seemed to deepen. 'It's okay.'
'I'll crank up the air for you.'
The car already felt plenty cool enough for Brenda, but she wasn't wearing a sweatshirt. Neither were Baxter or Quentin. The boys, sitting rigid on both sides of her, wore nothing but swimming trunks and sneakers.
Jack leaned forward to adjust the air conditioning. As a

sound like blowing wind filled the car, he settled back in his seat and started to drive.

Quentin waved out the window at the drying crew. Several of the girls, laughing, gave him the finger. 'Charming ladies,' he said.

'I'm sure glad *they* aren't coming,' said Baxter.

Jack waited at the parking lot exit, then turned onto Fairview Boulevard.

'You've got the cream of the crop here,' Brenda said.

'Those others are student council,' Fran explained. 'The car wash was supposed to be just for the school newspaper . . .'

'That's us,' Quentin said.

'And Ralph,' Baxter added.

'But the student council always has to butt in,' Fran continued.

'The bikini brigade,' Quentin said.

'Hey,' Brenda said, and gave him a gentle punch on the leg. '*I'm* in a bikini.'

'You're not like them,' said Baxter from her other side.

She turned and met his eyes.

He blushed and shrugged.

'Thanks,' she said.

'The thing about the student council,' Fran continued, 'is that they've gotta stick their noses into everything that happens on campus. They have all these awful *rules* you've gotta follow.'

'I hate rules,' Jack said.

'Yeah, me too. But what I *really* hate is how they get to take half of everything we earn.'

'That isn't fair,' Jack said.

'Sure isn't. But they make the rules.'

'Stinks,' Jack said.

'Doesn't it? That's why we don't like those girls. They're all student council.'

'That's *one* of the reasons,' Brenda said.

'Plus they're foxes,' Quentin added.

'They're not so hot,' Baxter said.

'Oh yes they are.'

'Bull.'

Brenda smiled at him.

He thinks I'm foxier than they are, but he can't say it.

She patted his leg.

His bare skin felt moist and cold.

She looked at him. He had goosebumps. His shoulders were drawn up. His chin was trembling.

Quentin seemed to be in much the same shape as Baxter.

Wearing her Piglet T-shirt and cut-off jeans over her bikini, Brenda was better off than them. But she, too, had gooseflesh and shivers.

'Hey, Jack,' she said. 'I wonder if you could turn down the air a little. We're freezing back here.'

Fran looked around at her, then glanced from Baxter to Quentin. To Jack, she said, 'You'd better turn it down.'

'What'll *you* do?'

'I'll be fine.'

'Are you sure?'

'Yeah. It isn't fair to freeze everyone else just because I have a sweatshirt on.'

Nodding, Jack reached forward. A moment later, the blowing sound diminished.

'Thanks,' Brenda said.

Jack looked at Fran. 'Let me know if you get too hot. I can boost it back up for a while.'

'No, don't. I'll be fine.'

'You get too hot,' Quentin advised, 'just take it off.'

'Thanks,' she said, 'but I don't think so.'

'You'd be *amazed* at how nice the summer feels when you're not suffocating inside a sweatshirt.'

'I'll keep it in mind.'

'Well, it's crazy. Nobody in their right mind goes around in a *sweatshirt* on a day like this. You wear 'em *all* the time. It's insane.'

Brenda frowned at him. 'It's not insane.'

'It's ape-shit crazy is what it is.'

Leaning forward against his chest strap, Baxter frowned past Brenda and said, 'Leave her alone, Quent.'

'Don't give me that. *You've* said the same thing.'

In the front passenger seat, Fran stared straight ahead.

'She can wear whatever she wants,' Brenda said. 'And she doesn't need anybody riding her about it.'

Jack turned his head toward Fran. On the half of his face that Brenda could see, he was frowning. He reached over and put a hand on Fran's shoulder. 'There's nothing wrong with what you're wearing,' he said.

She looked at him and almost smiled.

'There's nothing wrong with *you*,' he added.

'Thanks,' she murmured.

'I think you look great.'

'She'd look better if she lost the stupid sweatshirt,' Quentin said. 'She'd feel better, too. And the rest of us wouldn't have to freeze.'

Fran looked back at him. 'I can't take it off. I've got nothing on underneath.'

Quentin's eyes widened. 'Whoa!' he said. 'All the *more* reason.'

Fran laughed and faced the front.

Chapter Fifty-four

'It's the next street,' Pete said. 'But maybe you'd better stop.'

'Here?' Sherry asked.

'Yeah. If we go on into the cul-de-sac, he might see us.'

'If he's still hanging around,' Jeff said.

Sherry pulled over to the curb and stopped.

'I don't think Toby'd drive over here,' Pete said, 'then just take a quick look around and rush off. You know? He went to all that trouble to get the address and . . .'

'He *has* to kill me,' Sherry said.

'Has to *try*,' Pete corrected her. 'What kind of car does he drive?'

'I don't know. Last night he was in a Mustang, but he lost the keys and had to leave it on the street. Then he had Duane's van. I guess he might still be using the van, but that'd be awfully stupid. The cops must be looking for it. He probably ditched it somewhere. Maybe he's picked up the Mustang by now.' She shook her head again, very slightly. 'I don't know. He could be driving just about anything, I guess.'

'That's what I'll look for,' Pete said. 'Wait here, okay?' He reached under his seat and pulled his revolver out of the towel. 'Why don't you guys hang on to this till I get back?'

'I'll take it,' Jeff said.

'Are you sober yet?'

'Hey, dude, I didn't drink any more than you.'

Sherry looked at Jeff in the rear-view mirror. 'Do you know how to use it?'

'Does a moose poop in the woods?'

'His parents don't allow any guns in the house,' Pete said, 'but he's gone shooting with my family a few times. He knows how to handle it okay.'

'*Okay?* I'm a regular Wild Bill Hickok.'

'In your dreams,' Pete told him.

'He can take it,' Sherry said. 'I'll deal with the car.'

'Sounds good.' Pete opened the passenger door.

'Be careful,' Sherry said. 'Just take a look and come back. Don't go *searching* for him.'

'I'll just check out the cars.'

He shut the door, then walked to the corner. Turning his head to the right, he stepped off the curb. Instead of stopping to take a long look up the road, he strolled slowly toward the other side.

There were two houses on each side of the straightaway leading in, plus three around the circle. Most of them had vehicles parked in their driveways and along their front curbs.

The driveway of his own house was empty. So was the driveway of the deserted house next door. But a car and a pick-up truck were parked along the bend of the curb.

He saw no Mustang.

The only van in sight, parked in a nearby driveway, was a bright new Chevy that his neighbors had bought a month ago.

Pete stepped onto the curb, kept walking until he passed a redwood fence, then crossed the street and looped back to his car. He stepped up to the driver's side.

Sherry looked up at him from the open window.

He bent toward her. 'I didn't see anything obvious,' he said, 'but there're a lot of cars parked around. He could be anywhere.'

'I'm the only one he can recognize,' Sherry said. 'Why don't you and Jeff get in the front? I'll lie down on the floor in back.'

'Good idea,' Pete said.

'I've got a better idea,' Jeff said. 'You come back here, Sherry, and I'll hide you under me.'

'Give it a rest,' Pete said.

'Just a suggestion.'

'Thanks anyway,' Sherry said, and climbed out.

In a matter of seconds, they were all in position. 'Ready?' Pete asked.

'Let's do it,' Sherry said, her voice sounding a little muffled.

Pete glanced at Jeff to make sure the revolver was out of sight. Then he drove around the corner and up the road. He used the remote control to open his garage door.

And to lower the door after they were inside.

He shut off the engine. 'We're back,' he said.

Behind him, Sherry grunted and moaned as she struggled to push herself off the floor. He looked over the seat back. So did Jeff.

'You okay?' he asked.

'It was easier . . . getting down.'

'Need help?' Jeff asked.

'No, that's . . .' She flopped onto the back seat and let out a yelp.

'You okay?' Pete asked.

She was slumped crooked, propped up with one elbow. Pete's big Hawaiian shirt, half unbuttoned, drooped off her shoulder. Face contorted, she said, 'I'm not feeling so good.'

'What is it?' Pete asked.

'I think the painkiller wore off.'

'There's more in the house.'

'Let me just . . . I don't want to move for a minute.'

'I could go in the house and get you something.'

'No. Huh-uh. Let's all stay together till we know where Toby is.'

'You don't think he's in *this* house?'

'I wouldn't bet against it.'

Pete jerked his head toward the door to the kitchen.

Jeff turned forward on his seat, swung the Ruger through his open window and aimed at the door. 'Here, Toby-Toby-Toby,' he chanted softly as if calling a nearby cat.

'You'd better hope he doesn't come,' Pete said.

'I hope he *does*.'

'You with a six-shot .22 single-action, him with a seven-shot .380 semi-auto. I wouldn't want to be sitting beside you if that happens.'

'I'll put the first one in his face.'

'From your lips to God's ears,' said Sherry.

'I bet he's not in there anyway.'

'He might be,' Sherry said. 'And if he *is* inside, he has

to know a car just drove into the garage.'

'What do you think we should do?' Pete asked her.

'I don't know, but . . . Wait. How about hitting the remote again? Get the door back open and start the engine. That way, if he comes out blasting we'll have a chance to get away.'

Nodding, Pete opened the garage door. Then he started the engine. Keeping his foot on the brake pedal, he put the car in reverse.

'That's better,' Sherry said.

'Except now he can get us from behind,' Jeff said.

'You watch the kitchen door,' Sherry told him. 'Pete, you keep an eye on the rear-view mirror. If Toby pops up back there, maybe you can run him down.'

Both hands tight on the steering wheel, Pete watched the mirror. Jeff kept the revolver aimed at the kitchen door.

Nobody appeared in the mirror.

Nobody opened the kitchen door.

'How long do we keep this up?' Jeff asked.

'I think he'll make a move pretty soon if he's here,' Sherry said.

They waited.

And waited.

Finally, Pete said, 'He isn't coming.'

'Starting to look that way,' Sherry agreed.

'Maybe I oughta go in,' said Jeff. 'He's probably not in the house, but if he is . . .' He looked at Pete. 'Keep the car running and get ready to take off.'

'I don't know . . .'

'Somebody *has* to go in sooner or later.'

'It's my house. I'll do it.'

'But I've got the gun,' Jeff said, flinging open his door and lunging out.

'Jeff, get back here.'

He looked over his shoulder, grinning. 'Don't worry, man. I'll blow his head off.'

'Be careful,' Sherry called to him.

'If I get out of this alive, do I get a kiss?'

'Sure.'

'A good one? Not just a peck on the cheek or something?

A big old juicy one right on the smacker.'

'You got it,' Sherry said.

'I'll risk my ass for that any day of the week,' Jeff said, then faced the kitchen door.

'Will he be able to get in?' Sherry asked softly.

'Yeah. We don't normally lock . . .'

He didn't bother to finish because Jeff was already swinging the door open.

Before entering the kitchen, Jeff looked back again. He waved with his left hand, made a mock-terrified face like a kid about to pull a daredevil stunt, then looked forward and stepped over the threshold.

'He thinks it's a game,' Sherry said.

'I'm not so sure,' Pete said, speaking softly, half expecting gunshots to interrupt him. 'It wouldn't surprise me if he knows *exactly* what he's doing. He's kind of a strange guy.'

'I've noticed.'

'He comes across as sort of a goofball, but he's awfully intelligent. I think he knows he might get killed in there.'

'Wants that kiss,' Sherry said.

'Sure he does. Who wouldn't?'

'How did I get so lucky, running into a couple of guys like you?'

'The luck of the drop,' Pete said.

'God, I hope he's all right.'

'We'll hear shots if . . .'

'Not necessarily,' Sherry said. 'Toby used knives on the others.'

'I'd better go in.'

'I'll go with you.'

Pete shut off the engine, then thumbed the remote to start lowering the garage door. He climbed out. By the time he could get to Sherry's side of the car, she was already on her feet. She was breathing hard and grimacing.

'You okay?'

'Tip-top shape of my life.' She reached out and gripped his arm. 'Let me hold on, okay?'

Side by side, they made their way toward the open door to the kitchen.

'Don't call out,' she whispered.

At the doorway, she let go of his arm. He stepped into the kitchen. She came in after him and put a hand on his back. It felt good through his shirt.

They stood motionless.

Pete realized he was sweaty all over. They hadn't been using the air conditioning in the car, and it wasn't on in the house. The house was warm, but not stifling. The sweat, he supposed, was mostly nerves.

'I don't hear anything,' he whispered.

He heard *plenty*: his own pounding heart, Sherry breathing behind him, the hum of the refrigerator, the clicking clock, birds chirping and twittering outside, a lawn mower that sounded very far away. But no sounds of anyone else in the house.

I've got to remember all this, he thought. What I hear and don't hear. The way the sweat tickles running down my sides. And how Sherry's hand feels on my back.

Especially that.

She's probably just using me to hold herself steady.

But it feels personal.

When I write about this, I'll turn her into my girlfriend.

No, have her be who she is. It'd be stupid to change her. She's better than anything I could make up.

But I can't write about some of this. Like how we found her. People might read it. Like Mom and Dad. Everybody'll say I write dirty stuff . . .

The hell with what they say.

But what would Sherry think?

I can't have *her* read it!

But maybe she'd like it.

She'd probably want to kill me.

I can't believe I'm thinking about this, Pete suddenly thought. Jeff might be dead . . .

That'd make the story even better.

Oh great, he thought. Real nice. Now I'm hoping my best friend'll get killed.

I am not!

His heart lurched at the sudden thudding sounds of someone

rushing through the house. Sherry's fingers twitched against his back.

Then Jeff ran into the kitchen and smiled when he saw them.

He's all right!

'Coast is clear.' He grinned at Sherry. 'You owe me a kiss.'

Sherry's hand went away from Pete's back. She stepped out from behind him and said, 'Come and get it.'

On his way to her, Jeff wiggled his eyebrows at Pete. Then he handed over the pistol. 'Stand guard while I collect,' he said.

'Just take it easy,' Sherry warned him. 'Try not to hurt me.'

Jeff barely touched her at all when he put his arms around her.

She leaned toward him. Her lips were puffy and cracked.

Jeff brushed his lips against them.

Sherry leaned closer, pressing her injured lips a little more firmly against him. The way her shirt looked, Pete was sure that her breasts must be pushing at Jeff's chest.

It could've been me, he thought. I should've done the searching.

Too bad Toby *wasn't* here.

I don't mean that.

But it could've been me. Now Jeff's the damn hero. With *my* gun! And Toby wasn't even *here*! He's getting to kiss her and feel her and all he did was go on a wild-goose chase.

Shit!

Next time, I'll be the hero.

Chapter Fifty-five

For the past few minutes, Jack had been steering the car up narrow, shadowy roads in the hills. The woods on both sides looked green and peaceful, but Brenda had a jittery feeling in her stomach.

'Where *do* you live?' she asked.

'It's not much farther,' Jack said.

'It's already pretty far.'

'I'd rather be here,' Fran said, 'than back at the car wash.'

'Does anybody else smell smoke?' Quentin asked.

Brenda sniffed. She detected a very faint, tangy aroma of wood smoke. 'Yeah. A little.'

'Nothing to worry about,' Jack said. 'The fires are *miles* from here.'

'The wind must be blowing this way,' Baxter said.

'Maybe we'd better turn back,' Brenda suggested.

'We're almost there. Anyway, I don't see any cops or firemen. They'd have the streets blocked off by now if there was any real danger.'

'Guess so,' Brenda admitted.

Jack turned onto a sideroad. The heavy forest was soon replaced by driveways, lawns and sprawling, stucco houses.

'It's just up here.' Jack drove past several homes, then slowed in front of a peach-colored house. Though only a single story, it was spread out like a hacienda. It had white trim and a roof of red Spanish tiles.

'This your place?' Quentin asked.

'Yep.'

'Not a bad-looking joint.'

'It's *fabulous*,' Fran said.

'Nice,' said Brenda.

Baxter, sitting beside her, nodded in agreement. He seemed tense.

Maybe he's just nervous about being stuck in the back seat with me, Brenda thought.

Though they'd been working together on the school newspaper for more than a year, Baxter had always been shy around her. She supposed it must be agony for him to be sitting this close to her, especially since he wasn't wearing anything except his swimsuit.

And me in my bikini, she thought. But at least I've got a T-shirt and cut-offs on.

What would he do if I took them off?

Not about to find out. That's Fran's department.

Jack drove up the driveway to an iron gate and stopped. 'The other cars are in back,' he explained. He swung open his door. 'Let's go through the house.'

They all climbed out.

Brenda felt as if she'd escaped from a refrigerator. The heat felt wonderful. She took a deep breath. Smelling smoke on the wind, she looked all around. The air seemed a little hazy.

Jack and Fran were already heading across the front lawn. Quentin walked a few strides behind them, while Baxter waited beside Brenda.

'Worried about the fires?' Baxter asked.

'A little.'

'I think they're pretty far away. You know, you can smell the things for miles.'

'Yeah.'

'And there *aren't* any cops or firemen around. Or helicopters. If nothing else, there'd be news choppers all over the sky if this area was threatened.'

'That's for sure.' She started walking after the others, Baxter by her side but walking in the grass. 'I just wish we'd stayed at the car wash. This was a lousy idea.'

'Fifty bucks is a lot,' Baxter said.

'I'm not so sure about this guy.'

'He seems okay.'

'Fran likes him. That's the thing. She hasn't had very good luck with guys.'

'I know how that goes.' He laughed and shook his head. 'I don't mean with guys.'

'I know.' She smiled and watched him blush.

They caught up with the others on the front stoop. Jack was just opening the door. 'Come on in,' he said.

Everyone followed him into the house.

The air was warm and pleasant. It carried a smoky odor that frightened Brenda for a moment. Then she recognized the scent as balsam. Somebody had apparently been burning incense.

Jack shut the door.

The others stood mute in the foyer, looking around.

'You don't have to worry about my parents,' Jack said. 'They're gone. Nobody's here but us, so we can just like relax and have a good time.'

'Sounds cool to me,' Quentin said.

'It's a *gorgeous* house,' Fran said.

'Thanks.'

'How about showing us around?'

'We'd better get to the cars,' Brenda said.

Fran gave her a peeved look. 'I think we could spare two minutes.'

'I'm game,' Quentin said.

Jack shook his head. 'I don't know. The place is a real mess.'

From where Brenda stood, she could see that he wasn't kidding; straight ahead, what looked like several days' worth of newspapers were scattered over the carpet in the middle of the den.

'Why don't I show you the kitchen?' Jack suggested.

They followed him to the right.

'It's sort of a mess, too, but we can get some drinks.'

'We'd better get started on the cars,' Brenda said. 'Maybe when we're done with them . . .'

'I could use a drink,' Quentin said.

'Yeah,' said Fran. She gave Brenda another look. 'Me, too.'

Turning to Brenda, Baxter said, 'I'm not thirsty. If you want, we could go ahead and get started on the cars. They could come out when they're ready.'

'I'd have to open the garage,' Jack said.

'Okay,' Brenda said. 'Why don't you do that, and we'll . . .'

'What's the big hurry?' Fran asked.

They entered the kitchen.

'We shouldn't even be here,' Brenda said.

'Nobody'll know the difference.'

'*I* know the difference. We were supposed to stay at the car wash, not go traipsing off somewhere.'

'That's a good one coming from you.'

Jack opened the refrigerator. 'We've got Pepsi, Diet Coke, and beer.'

'*Beer?*' Quentin asked.

'Coors, Corona, and Bud Lite.'

'No beer,' Brenda said.

Fran smiled at Jack. 'I think *I'd* like one. How about a Bud Lite?'

'Jesus H. Christ,' Brenda muttered.

'I'll have a Corona,' said Quentin.

'Me, too,' said Jack. He reached into the refrigerator, handed a can of Bud to Fran, then took out two bottles of Corona. The glass of the bottles was clear. The beer inside was pale yellow and looked to Brenda a lot like urine.

'How about you, Baxter?'

'No thanks. I don't drink.'

'Go ahead,' Quentin told him. 'Have a brew. Live a little. I know you want one. You're just scared of going against Brenda.'

Baxter's face went crimson. 'I am not. But we're not here to have a party. Besides which, you're all under age.'

'Big fuckin' deal,' Quentin said. 'Gonna be a pussy all your life?'

At the counter, Jack pried off the Corona tops with a bottle opener. Then he handed a bottle to Quentin.

'*Gracias*,' Quentin said.

Smiling at Brenda, Jack said, 'I guess *you* don't want a beer.' He had a funny look in his eyes.

Bastard, she thought.

'No thank you,' she said.

'Pepsi? Diet Coke?'

'No thanks.'

Fran popped open her can. Some beer fuzzed out of the top. She sucked it off. Then she said, 'Why don't you just *have* something, Brenda?'

'Like Baxter said, we didn't come up here for a party.'

'Couldn't hurt,' Quentin said, and took a drink. 'Never hurts to party.'

'That's what you think.'

Glaring, Fran said, 'You just have to always control everything.'

Brenda stared at her, shocked.

She's just showing off for Jack.

I could put her down so hard. But she's still my best friend, even if it has slipped her mind.

'I'm obviously not in control of *this*,' Brenda said, pleased to hear herself sounding so calm. 'You want to have a party, have a party. I'm not the boss. Do whatever you want.'

'You always have to be so superior.'

That's because I am.

'It's all right,' she said, shrugging. 'Enjoy yourself. You're free to do whatever your heart desires.' She watched the three of them take drinks of beer. Then she said, 'So am I,' and walked out of the kitchen.

'Where are *you* going?' Fran asked.

'Out,' she called back.

'I'll come with you,' Baxter said.

She paused to wait for him.

He hurried toward her, an embarrassed look on his face. 'Is it all right if I come?'

'Maybe you'd better stay here. You're not wearing any shoes.'

'Where you *going*?'

'Back to the school.'

'Now?'

'Nobody's interested in washing cars around here.'

'But you're *walking*?'

'Looks that way.'

'I'll go with you.'

'You're barefoot and it's a long hike.'

'That's okay.' Hurrying ahead of Brenda, he pulled open the front door. 'I'm going, too. Unless you don't want me around.'

'I'd be glad to have you.'

His eyes lit up as if magic had entered his life.

'No, wait,' Jack called.

Brenda looked back. Jack was frowning at her from just outside the kitchen entrance. 'You can't walk all the way back to the school. It's *miles*.'

'Ten at the most. Probably less. So long.'

'Hey, don't.'

Fran and Quentin came out of the kitchen and stood behind Jack. The three of them stared at Brenda and Baxter. Fran looked disgusted. Quentin, apparently amused, smiled and shook his head.

'What's so wrong with having a beer?' Fran asked.

'It's the principle of the thing.'

'Why do you have to be such a tight-ass?' Quentin asked.

'Just my way. Have fun, everyone.' She stepped past Baxter, who was holding the door open for her. 'You sure you want to come with me? It'll be a hard walk.'

'Oh, I don't care. I'm with you.'

'Good man.'

'Don't go,' Jack said, walking toward them.

Brenda ignored him.

She turned toward the bright afternoon daylight outside the doorway and took a step and jumped at the sudden hard blast of noise that crashed through the house. She jerked her head sideways.

Wisps of pale smoke drifted from the muzzle of the pistol in Jack's hand.

It looked like the same kind of pistol Sherry liked to use.

It was pointed her way.

She didn't feel that she'd been hit, but then Fran was squealing and Quentin was standing motionless with shock on his face and Brenda whirled around in time to watch Baxter drop toward the floor as if all the muscles had been chopped out of his legs. His face was all bloody and he had a hole in the middle of his forehead.

He sat down hard, hitting the marble floor with an impact that seemed to jar his entire body.

Then he fell backward. His head whapped the floor with such a loud *thock* that Brenda heard it through the ringing in her ears.

'Don't try to run!' Jack yelled.

Brenda lurched for the doorway.

Jack fired and his bullet took her down.

Chapter Fifty-six

Quentin was tanned and had a pretty good build. Though not nearly as powerful-looking as Sid had been, he looked as if he wouldn't have much trouble overpowering Toby in a fight. But he just stood there hanging on to his bottle of beer, an astonished, vaguely amused expression on his face.

Fran was the problem. She was screaming and she'd already dropped her can of Bud so she could wave her hands at the sky like a gospel singer.

Toby slammed her across the face with the side of his pistol. The screaming stopped. Blood started to spill out of her split cheek. She clutched her face with both hands and sank to her knees, sobbing.

That wasn't so hard, was it?

He'd been worried. *Four* of them, after all.

He aimed his pistol at Quentin's bare chest. In spite of his muscles, the guy was sweaty and gasping for air. With a twitchy smile at Toby, he raised the Corona to his lips. He drank. And tipped the bottle higher and drank some more, gulping down the beer.

Wants to finish it off before I kill him.

Maybe just wants to show me how macho he is.

Toby looked over at Brenda. She lay curled on her side, half out the doorway. From where he stood, he could only see her up to the waist. Her right hand was clutching the back of her thigh where the bullet had torn through just below the faded denim of her cut-off jeans. Her hand was all shiny and red. She squirmed as she held the wound.

'I'll drag her in for you,' Quentin said. The bottle was empty. He had an excited look in his eyes.

'Go ahead.' Toby aimed the pistol at him.

'It's cool,' he said. He set the bottle on the floor, then strolled sideways into the foyer. 'I'll help you with Bax, too. The fuckin' pussy.'

'Just get Brenda in here.'

'You got it, pal.' He stepped past Brenda, crouched and grabbed her by the ankles. When he pulled her legs straight, she cried out and rolled onto her back. He dragged her the rest of the way into the house.

'Stop there and shut the door,' Toby said.

Quentin didn't lower Brenda's feet to the floor, he dropped them. The heels of her sneakers bounced. Brenda yelped, then rolled onto her side and curled up and clamped her hand to the bullet's entry wound near the back of her thigh.

Quentin grinned down at her.

This guy's okay, Toby thought. *Or trying to fake me out.*

Turning toward Toby, Quentin brushed his hands against the sides of his trunks. 'What's next?' he asked.

'Maybe I'll put a bullet through your face.'

'I got a better idea.'

'Bet you do.'

'Let's strip Brenda. Know what I mean?'

Toby laughed.

'I mean it. Get her naked, you can have all kinds of fun with her. I'll hold her for you.'

Fran, still on her knees, was sobbing and whimpering.

'Shut up,' Toby told her.

She hunched over and buried her face in her hands.

'Okay, Quen,' Toby said. 'Mind if I call you Quen?'

'Call me anything you want.'

'Get the T-shirt off her.'

'*All right!*'

'And tie it around her leg. Real tight. Make the bleeding stop. I'm gonna keep her around for a while and I don't want her crapping out.'

'My pleasure,' Quen said. He sank to his knees and tugged the T-shirt up Brenda's torso. When he had it rucked above her bikini top, he said, 'Raise your arms.'

She did as told and Quen got to work again. The T-shirt turned inside-out. It took on the shape of her face and then it hid her arms and then it was off.

'Want me to take off the rest?' Quen asked.

'Want me to shoot you?'

'Not much.'

'Just do the bandage like I said.'

Quen spread the shirt on the floor, rolled it lengthwise, then wrapped it around Brenda's thigh. He looked back at Toby. 'I can't tie it. It's too short.'

'Hold it a minute.' He looked around for something that would serve to fix the makeshift bandage in place.

Maybe a lamp cord . . .

His own leather belt would be perfect. He unbuckled it and stripped it out of its loops.

His loose, baggy shorts, weighted by heavily loaded pockets, dropped around his ankles.

With a laugh, he stepped out of them.

Quen said, 'Cool,' and caught the tossed belt. He wrapped it twice around Brenda's shirt-wrapped thigh, then fit the end of the strap into the buckle. As he pulled it tight, she jerked rigid and gritted her teeth. He fastened the buckle.

'Good job,' Toby said.

'Now what?'

'You get a treat.'

Worry flickered in Quen's eyes.

'Take off your trunks,' Toby said.

He looked as if he didn't know whether to be delighted or terrified. With a trembling smile, he pulled down his swimming trunks and stepped out of them. Toby saw that he was partly aroused.

Can't fake that.

'She's all yours,' he said.

Quen's face lit up. He looked down at Brenda.

'Not *her*. You gotta be kidding me. She's mine, you dumb shit.'

'Oh. Okay.' Quen managed a feeble smile. 'Sure.'

'You get Fatso.'

Fran let out a whine.

'That okay with you, Quen?'

'Sure.'

'Better a lard-ass than no ass at all, right?'

'You bet.' He stepped toward Fran.

'Leave her alone,' Brenda said from the floor, her voice shaky.

Toby grinned at her. 'She'll love it.' He turned to Fran. 'Won't you, Porky?'

Still on her knees, she sobbed into her hands.

'You're gonna love it, right?' Toby asked.

'No,' she gasped. 'Please.'

'Hopin' it'd be me, huh? I know. I saw how you been looking at me. Only one problem, I don't fuck fat ugly cows like you. That's how come I'm givin' the job to Quen.'

'Leave her . . . alone.'

'I *am* leaving her alone. Think I'd *touch* her? No way.' He nodded to Quen. 'She's all yours.'

'Quentin,' Brenda said. 'Don't.'

'Fuck you.'

'Please.'

'Gotta do what I gotta do,' Quen said. 'It's not like I'm exactly looking *forward* to it.'

'Oh, I think you are,' Toby told him.

Quen looked down at himself and chuckled. 'Oh, that. Has a mind all its own.'

'Don't do it, Quentin.'

'Gotta.'

'What's Fran . . . ever done to you?'

'Offended my eyesight?'

Toby burst out laughing.

'Anyhow,' Quen said, 'this'll be the best thing ever happened to her. Bet she's never gotten it from a handsome dude like me.'

'Or from anyone else,' Toby threw in.

'She's lucky I'm not making her *pay* for it.'

'Don't,' Brenda said again. 'You wanta mess around . . . mess around with me.'

Quen glanced at Toby.

'No can do,' Toby said. 'Now just shut up and lay there before somebody gets hurt.' To Quen, he said, 'I think Fran's ready for some lovin'.'

'I do believe you're right, Jack.' He stepped in front of her, clutched her short brown hair and pulled her head back. She looked up at him, her eyes red and wet and bulging. 'Where do you want it?' he asked.

'No!' she blurted. 'Please!'

He jerked her head forward and prodded her in the eye.

She squealed.

'There?'

'No!'

Brenda, looking fierce, rolled onto her back and shoved with both arms at the floor.

Toby decided not to warn Quen.

Pulling Fran by the hair and snarling, 'Stand up, stand up,' into her face, Quen dragged her to her feet. He let go and she stayed up. 'Take it off,' he said, 'or I'll rip it off.'

She pulled her sweatshirt over her head, tossed it aside, and quickly folded her arms across her breasts.

Quen shoved her arms down. 'Nice set a knockers,' he said.

'Not bad,' Toby agreed.

Quen slapped Fran's left breast sideways. Then he slapped the other. Each time he smacked one, Fran yipped and flinched. He soon had both breasts swinging, bumping against each other. Then he seemed to sense trouble. He turned around just as Brenda, hobbling on her good leg, her mouth twisted in agony and tears spilling down her face, hurled herself at him.

'Shit!' he gasped.

Snarling, she reached for his throat.

He caught her in the cheek with a hard right that knocked her head sideways, made her lips go rubbery and sent a shower of spit into the air. The blow turned her body toward Toby.

Toby stepped in against her, put his arms around her and drove his knee up into her belly so hard she was lifted off her feet.

She crashed hard to the floor.

'That oughta take some of the get-up-'n-go out of her,' Toby said.

'I'll say,' said Quen. 'Wow.'

'Now let's see what you can do with Fatso.'

Grinning, Quen clamped Fran's nipples between his thumbs and forefingers.

'Please,' she whispered.

He squeezed and lifted. Whimpering, Fran went up on her tiptoes.

'Keep her like that,' Toby said. He stepped behind her, took hold of her shorts with one hand and jerked them down to her bare feet.

She wore baggy white cotton panties.

Weird, Toby thought. All sexy without any bra on, then come to find out she's wearing old-lady drawers.

'Go figure,' he muttered. He dragged them down with his left hand.

She was still on her tiptoes.

'Step outa your stuff,' Toby said.

Whimpering, she stepped out of the shorts and panties and kicked them away.

Toby snatched up the panties, wadded them into a ball and stuffed them into her mouth.

The fabric muffled her noises.

He grinned at Quen. 'Better?'

'A lot.'

'Have at her. She's all yours. Entertain me. If you're *really* good, I might even let you have a crack at Brenda after I get done with her.'

Quen beamed.

Chapter Fifty-seven

Leaving Sherry at his own house with Jeff and the revolver, Pete had made a solo trip to the house next door. He'd wandered completely around it, looking for any sign that Toby might be lurking on the grounds or inside. He'd peered through windows into its empty rooms. He'd checked the doors.

Back in the kitchen of his own house, he explained, 'It's all locked up. There's no sign of a break in. So unless he managed to *pick* a lock . . .'

'Somebody might've left something open,' Jeff suggested.

'It's possible. But I looked around the best I could without breaking in, myself. I don't think he's there.'

Sherry, sitting at the kitchen table, took a sip of her fresh Bloody Mary. 'We figured we'd miss him. We were gone when he showed up and he had the address of a vacant house. He's not stupid. One look inside, he knew something was wrong. There'd either been a legitimate confusion about the address – or he'd been tricked. Either way, he would've hit the road fast.'

'If he ever came out here at all,' Pete said.

She nodded. 'That's possible, too. Can't imagine why he *wouldn't*, but . . .'

'He might've been afraid it was a trap,' Jeff suggested.

'I doubt it,' Sherry said. 'He thought he was being so damn clever about getting the address . . .'

'That stupid story about being an old school pal,' Pete added.

'He's real big on stories,' Sherry muttered. Shaking her head, she drank some more Bloody Mary. 'You know what? Maybe after he got the address he realized how phoney his story must've sounded. That could explain why he decided not to come over.'

'*If* he decided not to come over,' Pete said.
'Anything's possible,' Jeff threw in.
'But some things,' said Sherry, 'are more likely than others. Now that he knows I'm alive, he *has* to get his hands on me. Has to finish the job, for one thing.'
'For *one* thing?' Pete said.
Jeff huffed. 'That oughta be enough.'
'Not for Toby. I imagine he has big ideas about what he'd like to do to me. So if he didn't come over here, he must've had an awfully good reason.'
'But maybe he *did* come.'
Sherry let out a short laugh. 'How much have *you* been drinking?'
'Not as much as you.'
'I have an excuse.'
'Just seems to me,' Pete said, 'that we've got no way of knowing *where* he is. He probably isn't here in the house with us and he probably isn't next door. But he might be here *or* there or just about anywhere. We just won't know till he makes a move. And if he *is* around here someplace right now, that move's gonna take us by surprise.'
'You're right about that,' Sherry said. 'If he's here and we don't know it, we're screwed.'
'We oughta be the ones screwing *him*,' Jeff said.
Pete nodded. 'Hit him before he hits us.'
'Fuckin'-A, dude! Preemptive strike!'
'Can't strike him if we can't find him,' Sherry said.
'What if we pay a visit to his house?' Pete suggested. 'He's bound to show up there. No matter where he is right now, he'll go home sooner or later. And we could be waiting for him.'
'And screw *his* ass.'
'But we don't know where he lives,' Sherry reminded them. She had a strange, intense look in her eyes.
'I bet we can find out,' Pete said. He shoved his chair away from the table, stood up, and walked around the end of the counter. 'I did some checking.' He removed the telephone directory from the drawer. 'After we found out Toby's last name, I looked it up.' He carried the phone book to the table, plopped it down, and opened it to the napkin he'd used as a

marker. 'There're only seven listings for people named Bones. No Tobys, but I figure maybe he lives with his parents. All we've gotta do is find out which . . .'

'He lives with his brother,' Sherry explained. 'Sid.'

Pete felt a jump of excitement in his chest. '*Sid?* Oh, man, I think there *is* a Sid in here.' Bending over the book, he slid his fingertip down the listings. 'Bones,' he muttered. 'Come on, come on, I know you're here. *Bones!*' he hunched lower and studied the first names. '*Sidney!* Here it is, right here! Bones, Sidney.'

'That's Toby's brother,' Sherry said. 'That's where he lives.'

'Only thing is, it doesn't give an address.'

'They hardly ever do,' Jeff said.

'Not anymore,' added Sherry.

'Too bad we're not cops,' Pete said. 'They have reverse directories. All we'd have to do is look up the phone number . . .'

Jeff gave him a skeptical glance. 'Where'd you get that?'

'Reading Ed McBain. But I suppose that stuff's all computerized by now.'

'You can bet on it.'

'Which means zilch to us,' said Sherry. 'Unless one of you just so happens to be some sort of fabulous hacker who can bust into the police computer . . .'

Pete and Jeff looked at each other and shook their heads.

'Know anybody who can do that?' Sherry asked.

They both shook their heads.

'That mostly just happens in books and shit,' Jeff explained.

'Yeah,' said Pete. 'They always know *somebody* who can hack their way into *anything*.'

'Convenient,' Jeff said.

Pete nodded. 'Hell, I don't know *anybody* who can pull that sort of stuff.' He frowned. 'Unless maybe Kate. I heard she got into some trouble last year hacking into *some* sort of computer system. They almost threw her in jail.'

'Yeah, I'd forgotten about Kate.'

'She's a computer whizz.'

'But what's her last name?' Jeff asked.

Pete shrugged. '*I* don't know. Do *you* know?'

'No idea. Have you got her phone number?'

Pete shook his head.

'Know where she lives?'

Pete shook it again. 'Not really.'

'So how are we supposed to find her?'

'Forget about it,' Sherry said. 'Sounds like she'd be harder to dig up than Toby.'

'So how'll we get Toby's address?' Pete asked.

'Let's just call the number,' Jeff suggested. 'Maybe *Sid*'ll answer the phone.'

'Yeah,' Pete said. 'Great idea. And I can tell him how I owe Toby fifty bucks from an old school bet . . .'

'We should be able to do better than that,' Sherry said.

'We'd need an *awfully* good story before someone's gonna cough over a street address.'

'Unless he's a moron.'

'Toby said a few things about Sid,' Sherry told them. 'The guy doesn't sound like a moron. He might be cooperative, though. Sounded like he and Toby aren't exactly the best of buddies.'

'But what if *Toby* answers the phone?' Jeff asked.

Sherry shook her head. 'The one thing we *don't* wanta do is lose our element of surprise.'

'That's right,' Pete said. 'If Toby's home, we're totally shot down.'

'So how *do* we find out his address?' Jeff asked.

'Maybe we don't,' Sherry said.

Pete scowled. 'There's *gotta* be a way.'

'Not necessarily,' Sherry said. 'There *isn't* always a way. At least not a *good* way. Sometimes no way at all.'

'Maybe we oughta just call the number and take our chances,' Jeff said. 'Know what I mean?'

'I don't know,' Pete said. 'That might be worse than doing nothing.'

Sherry drank some more of her Bloody Mary. Frowning, she set down the glass. Then she looked from Jeff to Pete. And sighed.

'What?' Pete asked.

'I know how to find the house,' she muttered. 'No phoning involved.'

'How?' asked Jeff.

'I'm not sure I wanta tell.'

'Come on, Sherry.'

'If *we* knew,' said Jeff, 'we'd tell you.'

'Are you guys looking to get killed?'

'We're gonna kill *him*,' Jeff assured her. 'If we can *find* his sorry ass.'

She shook her head again. 'How about this? How about loaning me the car and the pistol? You guys wait here and I'll go over to his house and . . .'

'No way!' Pete blurted.

'I was hoping . . .' Her voice died away.

'Hoping what?' Pete asked.

She took a deep breath, but it must've hurt. She winced, then exhaled slowly. 'I wanted to take care of this alone. I *still* do.'

'You mean like take down Toby?' Jeff asked.

'Yeah.'

'It isn't gonna happen,' Pete told her. 'You're too messed up to go after someone like him. And even if you weren't, we wouldn't let you.'

'Yeah. I know. I know how much you guys . . . care about me.'

'Actually, we just wanta get in your pants.'

'*Jeff!*' Pete snapped.

Sherry made a quiet laugh and said, 'I know. But it's a little more than that. A *lot* more. I've been at the mercy of you two guys since you found me. You've seen every inch of me . . . and *touched* most of them. It must've been pretty tempting.'

'Nah,' Jeff said. 'What could've been tempting about that?'

'But you never let yourselves . . . well, you held back. All you ever did was try to help me. You're a couple of damn nice guys and I think you'd probably do almost *anything* for me. But I won't have you die for me. So far, things have gone okay. You've risked yourselves, but we've been lucky. We haven't run into Toby yet.'

Pete felt a chilly tingle on the nape of his neck.

'Eventually,' Sherry went on, 'I'm gonna find him or he's

gonna find me. I don't want you to be around when that happens.'

'*We* want to be around,' Pete said.

'How you gonna stop us?' asked Jeff.

She almost smiled. 'I had me a little plan. Didn't exactly work out, but almost.'

'What sort of plan?' Jeff asked.

'I came up with it after you guys got done patching me up and I left the message for my parents. You'd already offered me a Bloody Mary,' she reminded Pete. 'When I told you I was ready for it, Jeff said he'd like one, too. I didn't think it'd happen. I'd already pegged you as a straight-arrow . . .'

'Thanks a lot.'

'Nothing wrong with that, for God's sake. If I had my way, *everyone* would be that way.'

He felt himself blush.

She just *thinks* I'm a straight-arrow, he told himself. If she knew what was really going on . . .

'But then you came out with *three* Bloody Mary's,' she continued. 'I couldn't believe it. But that's when I got the plan. It was simple – I'd drink you guys under the table. You're sixteen and you've probably never taken more than sip or two of liquor in your entire lives.'

'Oh,' Jeff said, 'I wouldn't be so sure . . .'

'Yeah, right,' said Pete. 'You're a real booze-hound.'

'Anyway, I've been drinking maybe a little more than I should for a few years, so I've built up some tolerance. I knew I could handle a few Bloody Marys, no trouble at all. But not you guys. Pretty soon, you'd either pass out or fall asleep. I think I even said something about how we oughta all take naps after lunch.'

'Oh yeah,' Pete said. Amazed by her revelations, he felt a grin starting to spread over his face. 'To sober us up before you called the cops.'

'Right. But I never intended to call the cops. Soon as you two zonked, I was gonna borrow the car and go after Toby alone.'

Jeff suddenly let out a wild laugh. 'Shit!' he blurted. 'Soon as *you* were zonked, *we* were gonna take off after the bastard.'

'Without you,' Pete added.

'That's how come Pete kept feeding you more drinks.'

'And that's how come I looked up Bones in the phone book.'

'My God,' Sherry said.

'Great minds,' said Jeff.

'So much for great plans,' Pete said.

'Too bad Toby called,' Jeff said. 'Now we'll never know who would've passed out first.'

'I still don't want you guys going after him,' Sherry said. 'With or without me.'

'And we don't want *you* going after him,' Pete told her.

'We won't *let* you,' added Jeff. 'Not without us, anyhow.'

She sighed, then drank the rest of her Bloody Mary. 'Okay,' she said. 'If you won't let me go after him by myself, I guess there's only one way to do it.'

'How's that?' Jeff asked.

'Together.'

'Good enough,' Pete said.

'How do we find his house?' asked Jeff.

'Last night, I helped him lose his keys so he had to leave his car behind. I've got a pretty good idea where he left it. If he hasn't moved it yet, maybe we can get Toby's address off the registration slip.'

'What if it doesn't *have* a registration slip?' Jeff asked.

'Then it doesn't,' Sherry said. 'But it might.'

'Let's go find out,' said Pete.

[illegible]

[illegible] Toby. 'Can we stop [illegible]'

[illegible] the automatic at him.

[illegible] He dragged [illegible] body with [illegible]

[illegible] said. 'It's your big idea [illegible] you into this [illegible]'

[illegible]

Chapter Fifty-eight

Quen climbed off Fran. She was sprawled on the foyer floor, sweaty and panting for air but no longer crying.

'I think she liked it,' Toby said.

'I *know* she did,' said Quen. He grinned at Toby, then bent down and picked up Fran's sweatshirt. 'Gave her just what she always wanted,' he said. He started mopping the sweat off his body. 'Man, you got air conditioning in here?'

'Yeah, but I like it like this. Everybody all wet and slippery.' He smiled down at Brenda. She was sitting on the floor, leaning back against the front door, her bandaged leg straight out, her other leg drawn up with the knee in front of her chest.

She'd been that way for a while, watching in silence.

Watching Quen with Fran.

Watching Toby watch.

Sometimes glancing over at the body of her wimpy pal, Baxter.

'You want the air on?' Toby asked her.

She met his eyes, then looked down again.

'What *do* you want?'

'You to drop dead. Both of you.'

'Gutsy,' Toby said. 'Just like your sister.'

She stared at him, but said nothing.

'*Love* your sister.'

'Go to hell.'

Quen looked at Toby. 'Can we strip her now?'

Toby aimed the automatic at him.

'Never mind.' He resumed wiping his naked body with Fran's sweatshirt.

To Brenda, Toby said, 'It's your big sister got you into this. I *told* her what'd happen if she tried to pull any shit with me.

So you know what she does? She goes for her gun. This one right here.'

That got Brenda's attention. Her wide eyes fixed on the weapon.

'The bitch wanted to shoot me with it. But now *I've* got her gun and I shot *you* with it. And your little snot-munching friend there.' He nodded toward Baxter's body. 'How do you like getting plugged by your own sister's gun?'

'What'd you do to her?' Brenda asked, her voice low and steady.

'Well, now, that's a long, long story. Easier to tell you what I *didn't* do to her.'

Tears started to leak out of Brenda's eyes. Her chin trembled.

'Aw, don't cry.'

She sniffed. 'Did you . . . kill her?'

'Would I do a thing like that?'

'Did you?'

'Maybe, maybe not. How bad do you want to know?'

'Tell me.'

'Don't tell her,' Quen said.

Through her tears, she gave him a fierce look. 'Shut up,' she said.

'I'll shut *you* up.'

Toby aimed the pistol at him.

'Sorry,' he said. 'I'm just thinking, hold back the information till she does what you want. Make her work for it.'

'I already figured that out.'

'Oh. Okay. Sorry.'

'Just stay out of this.' He looked down at Fran. She was still on her back, but she no longer gasped for breath. Her face was smeared with blood from the gash on her cheek. The rest of her body was pale and shiny, running with sweat. Her gaze was fixed on the ceiling. She seemed uninterested in it, though. She looked as if she might be daydreaming about something vaguely pleasant.

'Just watch Fran,' Toby said. 'Make sure she doesn't try nothing.'

Quen chuckled. 'She won't try anything. She's just

lying there hoping I'll fuck her again.'

'*Watch* her. And keep your mouth shut.'

'Aye-aye, sir.' Quen snapped to attention and saluted Toby.

Toby had to smile. Turning to Brenda, he said, 'So you wanta know if your sister's alive?' he asked.

Her head moved slightly up and down.

'Gotta do something for me first. Do what I say, and I'll tell.'

'Okay.' With the back of one hand, she wiped the tears from her eyes. Her face still glistened with shiny wet streamers. Not all tears, Toby realized. Had to be sweat there, too, because she sure didn't have tears running down her neck and chest and belly.

We're *all* dripping like crazy, he thought, and me and Quen haven't been crying at all.

Correction, he thought. *Baxter* ain't dripping.

Oh yes he is.

Toby laughed.

Brenda stared up at him.

'Ready?' he asked.

'Sure,' she muttered.

'Take off your top.'

A corner of her mouth twitched. 'Why am I not surprised?'

Toby laughed.

Brenda sat forward, grimacing – maybe because of the bullet hole in her leg? – then reached behind her back with both hands. Watching her, Toby felt himself grow heavier in the groin – stiffening and rising under the front of his loose, hanging shirt.

Its back strings untied, the bikini went slack. Its pouches no longer held her breasts, but draped them like a pair of tiny rags. She brought her arms forward, slipped her left arm underneath the limp garment to cover her breasts, then plucked at the neck strings with her left hand. The bikini top fell away and came to rest on her lap.

'It's off,' she said. Toby heard a tremor in her voice. 'Happy?' she asked.

'Put your arms down.'

She lowered both arms.

Her breasts were small, smooth mounds, pale as moonlight, tipped with nipples the color of a baby's lips.

The front edges of Toby's shirt brushed against the sides of his rising shaft.

Brenda looked at him sticking out, then quickly raised her eyes to his face. 'Tell me about Sherry,' she said.

'I killed her,' Toby said.

And watched her face, already wet and red, contort with agony. Slumping back against the door, she covered her face with both hands and wept.

'Just kidding,' Toby said.

Quen brayed out a harsh laugh.

'She isn't dead,' Toby went on. 'Not yet, anyway.'

Brenda kept on crying.

'But I've got her,' Toby explained. 'She's my prisoner. So if you don't want me to finish her off, you're gonna do everything I tell you. *She* was supposed to follow orders but she blew it. That's how come all this is happening to you and your pals – because big sister tried to screw me over. Now it's up to you. I've got her. I can nail her any time I want. And that's what I'm *gonna* do if you give me any shit. All you've gotta do is listen to me and do everything I say. Be real friendly and nice and no funny stuff, and it'll stop here. How's that grab you?'

Brenda wiped her face and jerked her head up and down. 'Yeah,' she blurted. 'I'll . . . I'll do it. Anything.'

'That's what Sherry said, but then she fucked with me.'

'I won't. I'll be good. I promise.'

'We'll see about that.'

He looked over at Quen. The guy was gaping at Brenda, his mouth hanging open, his hands pressed flat against his thighs, his rigid penis aimed at the ceiling.

'There's a knife in my shorts,' Toby told him. 'Take it out. I wanta see you slice those jeans off her. And whatever she's got on underneath.'

Quen cast him a feverish glance. 'You got it, boss.' He sank to a crouch over Toby's shorts. Searching the pockets, he found a pair of pliers. He held them up. 'Want 'em?'

'Maybe later. Just get the knife.'

'Yes sir.' He resumed the search.

'I can *take* my pants off,' Brenda said. She sniffed and wiped her eyes. 'Nobody has to cut them.'

'Quen does.'

'Why?'

' 'Cause I told him to.'

'Screwdriver?' Quen asked.

'Just get the knife.'

'Here we go.' Quen removed a folding Buck knife from a pocket of the shorts. He pried open its blade, stood up and stepped over to Brenda.

'Scoot down and lie on the floor,' Toby told her.

She eased herself down, gritting her teeth, a couple of times flinching with pain.

Toby watched drops of sweat dribble down her body. He watched how her small breasts jiggled ever so slightly as she moved. When she was flat on her back, she almost seemed to have no breasts – might've been a boy except for the very subtle slopes and the size of her nipples.

Quen spread her legs, stepped between them and squatted down.

Fran, still on the floor, pushed herself up to her elbows and raised her head to watch.

Quen slipped the knife blade underneath the frayed denim high on Brenda's left thigh. Then he looked over his shoulder at Toby. 'Can I cut her?'

'You want to?'

'Maybe a little.'

'No skin off my nose.'

Brenda pushed herself off the floor and braced herself up with her elbows, like Fran only slim and beautiful. Looking Quen in the eyes, she hissed, 'You just dare cut me, you shitty pervert, and I'll shove that knife up your ass.'

Laughing, he started to work the knife back and forth, sawing his way up her thigh.

Toby watched the denim split open, a V widening its way up the top of her leg.

Fran watched, too. She had a strange look on her face. It looked almost like a smile.

Brenda also watched the knife's progress. She didn't flinch

or cry out, so apparently Quen was avoiding her skin.

She scared him off.

She wasn't wearing a belt. When Quen sliced through her waistband, the side of her cut-offs slid from her hip and fell to the floor. With a quick flick of the blade, Quen severed the side of her bikini pants.

Then he began to cut a slit up the right side of her shorts.

He sawed through the waistband. The right side fell away.

When he slashed the side of her bikini pants, she jumped and yelped. Blood started to spill from a gash near her hip. 'Woops,' he said. 'Sorry about that.'

With his left hand, he grabbed the front of her waistband and pulled downward. The shorts, loose at both sides, lifted away from her like a large denim flap hinged by the narrow strip of fabric at her crotch. He jerked hard. The strip broke and he flung the panel away. Then he tugged off her severed bikini pants. She grunted as the seat was jerked out from under her rump.

On his knees between her legs, Quen gazed down at her wispy golden curls and cleft.

Toby stared, too. And moaned softly with the ache of wanting her.

Quen turned his head and smiled at him. 'What do you want me to do now, boss?'

'What do you *want* to do?'

'You kidding?'

'Wanta stick it to her?'

'You kidding? But . . . it's not my turn. You'd better go first. You wanta go first, don't you? I mean, if you don't, it's fine with me, but . . .'

'No, you can go ahead.'

'*Really?*'

'Sure. But first you have to give her the knife.'

'*What?*'

'You cut her. See that blood?'

'Yeah, but . . .'

'She *told* you what she'd do if you cut her.'

'But she's our *prisoner!*' He let out an odd laugh. 'Doesn't matter what she says.'

'Does to me. Brenda and me, we're working out a deal. We're *co-operating*. So give her the knife.' Toby aimed the pistol at his face.

'You serious?'

'I *feel* serious.'

'She said she'd stick it up my ass!'

'Well.' Toby grinned. 'Should've thought of that before you cut her.'

'Shit.'

'It's the knife from her or the bullet from me. Take your pick.'

He looked at Brenda. She was still braced up on her elbows. 'You won't really do that to me, will you?'

She just stared at him.

'I mean . . . we're friends. I *had* to do this stuff, you know?'

'I know,' Brenda said.

'You gonna stick it up my ass?'

She shook her head. 'No.'

'Promise?'

'I promise. None of this is your fault. Jack made you do it.'

'Right,' Quen said. 'I was forced.' Though he looked worried, he handed the knife to her.

She sat up fast – very fast – grabbed Quen's erection like a handle to stop him as he tried to lurch away, and slashed the blade across his throat.

Chapter Fifty-nine

Quen squealed.

Blood erupted from his ripped throat, spraying Brenda.

Fran screamed.

Toby, delighted, called out, 'Thata way to go, Brenda baby!'

Releasing her hold on Quen, Brenda slumped back down on the floor. Blood still flew at her, falling like thick red rain on her face and chest and belly.

Quen clapped a hand against his slit throat and lurched to his feet. His other arm reaching out, he staggered toward Toby. 'Help,' he gasped. 'Ambulance.'

Toby grinned and nodded. 'Good idea. I'll get right on it.'

'Please!'

As Quen lurched closer, Toby pranced backward.

'*For God's sake help him!*' Fran yelled.

She was on her feet.

Toby aimed the pistol at her face.

She cried out, '*Yeee!*'

'Get down!'

'*Don't! Don't! Please!*'

Quen grabbed the front of Toby's shirt and looked at him with pleading eyes.

Toby kicked a leg out from under him. Quen went down, still clutching Toby's shirt, ripping some buttons loose, then letting go but leaving behind a bright red handprint. He landed hard on the marble floor.

Toby checked Fran. She was on her knees, sobbing, her bulgy red eyes jumping from Quen to Toby to Brenda to Quen to Toby.

He checked Brenda. Spattered with blood and dripping with sweat, she was stretched out on her back, her eyes toward the ceiling, her chest rising and falling as she took quick breaths, her arms down by her sides, her legs slightly apart.

'Guess you took care of *him*,' Toby said.

She ignored the comment.

Quen was twitching a little.

Leaking a *lot*, Toby thought, and chuckled.

'Why'd you *do* that?' Fran shouted at Brenda, her voice shrill. 'You didn't have to do *that!* My God, that was *Quentin!* You killed him!'

Brenda kept staring upward.

'You goddamn bitch! You always *were* a goddamn bitch! He was a *good guy* and you *killed him!*'

'I know what I did,' Brenda muttered, her gaze still fixed on the ceiling. 'Just let it go.'

'*Let it go?*'

'Let it go,' Brenda said, sounding very calm. 'He was worthless.'

'*Worthless! How can you say that! He was a human being!*'

'Worthless garbage. The world's now a better place.'

'*No!*'

Brenda turned her head and calmly met Toby's eyes. 'Just like it'll be a better place when *you're* dead.'

A grin spread across Toby's face. 'You're *fabulous*! You're a *gem*! You and Sherry . . . Wow! You two are *so much* alike. Course, she has bigger tits. I'm not saying they're *better* tits, just bigger.'

'Whatever you're gonna do, why don't you just shut up and do it.'

'Good idea.'

With his free hand, he undid the lower buttons of his shirt. Then he slipped the shirt off each of his shoulders. It fell down his back, slid down his arms and floated to the floor.

He took a step toward Brenda.

'What about *me?*' Fran asked.

'Oh yeah. You.' He aimed the pistol at her face.

'*No! Wait!*' She put out a hand as if she thought it might stop the bullets. '*The knife!*' she blurted. '*Brenda's still got the knife!*'

His guts went cold.

He whirled toward Brenda.

She still lay stretched on her back just like before. No sign of the Buck knife she'd used on Quen.

'Okay,' he said. 'Where is it?'

Her blood-flecked eyebrows lifted. 'Where's what?'

'You know damn well what. The knife.'

'Thanks for opening your yap, Fran.'

'Fuck you, Brenda.'

'He'd *forgotten* about it till you opened your mouth.'

'So what?'

Brenda frowned up at Toby. 'Friends like this, who needs enemies?'

Toby chuckled. 'You've got me.'

'Guess I'll be getting you whether I want you or not. Which I don't, by the way.'

'Now let's have the knife.'

'I haven't got it.'

'I thought you were gonna cooperate.'

'I *am* cooperating. I don't know where it is. It flew out of my hand after I cut Quentin.'

Toby looked over at Fran. 'Did it?'

She shook her head. 'No. I was watching. She still has it. I think it's *under* her.'

'Thanks,' Brenda muttered.

'Wanta do me a favor, Fran? Go over and get it for me.'

'Yeah, Fran. Come and get it.'

She shook her head. 'Huh-uh. No way. You'll nail me like you nailed Quentin.'

'Why would I do that?' Brenda asked.

' 'Cause you're a bitch.'

Brenda stared at her, then said, 'God, Fran, I thought we were friends.'

'Yeah, well.'

'I thought we were *good* friends.'

'Yeah, well. So maybe you were wrong. You're not *always* right. I know you *think* you're always right, but you're not. You think you're so perfect and everybody else is some sort of worthless loser.'

'Most people are,' Brenda said. 'But I didn't think *you* were.'

'Oh girls, girls, girls,' said Toby, grinning and shaking his head.

'*Baxter* wasn't a loser,' Brenda muttered. Then she said very softly, 'Good old Baxter.' And Toby saw her start to weep.

He turned to Fran and pointed the pistol at her forehead. 'Go over and get the knife.'

'But . . .'

'Or do you want me to put a slug through your ugly face?'

She pushed out her lower lip as her chin began to tremble.

'Who knows?' said Toby. 'Maybe Brenda *won't* slash your throat.'

As Fran struggled to her feet, she said, 'You won't let her, will you?'

'Why not?'

'Because. Because I *warned* you. I *told* you she had it. If I'd kept my mouth shut, she might've killed you. I saved your life.'

'Yeah, maybe so. Thanks.'

'So you like owe me. Right?'

'Sure. I tell you what, Fran. You go over and take the knife away, and I'll let you leave.'

'Really?'

'Sure he will,' said Brenda.

'You shut up,' she snapped. 'You don't know everything.'

'I promise to let you go,' Toby told her.

'Reality check,' said Brenda. 'You're an eyewitness, Fran. You aren't going anywhere. Not alive, anyway. Not if *he* has any say in it.'

Toby walked up to Fran and pushed the muzzle of the pistol against the tip of her nose. 'Go get the knife.'

'Okay.'

He lowered the weapon and moved aside. Fran wiped her eyes, then stepped past him. He watched the fat, dimpled cheeks of her buttocks wobble and shake as she walked toward Brenda.

'Now *that's* a lard-ass,' he said.

She glanced back at him, a pouty look on her face. Then she stopped in front of Brenda's feet. She held out her hand. 'Just give it to me.'

'I don't have it.'
'Yes, you do. I know you do.'
'Where'd you say it is?' Toby asked.
'Under her back.'
'Well, reach under and grab it.'
She started to squat.
'You're blocking my view.'
'Sorry.' She straightened up and stepped around to Brenda's other side. 'Here?' she asked Toby.
'Perfect.'
She knelt down close to Brenda's hip. Resting her hands on her own thighs, she frowned and said, 'Roll over.'
Brenda latched her eyes on Fran. A corner of her mouth twitched slightly, but she didn't roll over. 'Don't think so,' she said.
'Please.'
'I would've had him, Fran. I would've *had* him. But you had to open your big mouth.'
'He was gonna shoot me.'
'You didn't have to tell him about the knife. It was our only chance.'
'Not *much* of a chance,' Toby said. 'Knife versus gun? I don't think so.'
Brenda looked at him. 'You feel that way, just let me keep it.'
'Take it, Fran.'
'Roll over,' Fran said.
'Make me.'
Fran jutted out her trembling chin. 'You better not try something.'
'*Do* it!' Toby snapped.
'I'll just reach under,' Fran explained. She placed her left hand on Brenda's hip, then bent lower and started to shove her right hand into the crevice between Brenda's back and the floor.
Brenda sat up fast.
Her elbow smashed against Fran's face.
'*YES!*' Toby cried out.
Fran tumbled backward off her knees, blood rushing from

her crushed nose. Her naked back slapped the floor, followed a moment later by the *thonk* of her head. Followed by the quick *toot* of a fart.

Toby laughed.

Brenda, twisting her torso, let fly with the knife.

It flipped end over end toward Toby.

He took quick aim. Just as the knife struck him in the forehead, he fired.

Chapter Sixty

The noise of the gunshot blasted Brenda's ears and she felt a strange, quick stir in the air by her cheek. Even as she realized the bullet must've missed her, Jack's head jerked backward from the impact of the knife.

It had struck him, handle first, in the middle of the forehead, then bounced off.

He still held out the pistol as if he hoped to fire again, but now it seemed to be pointing way too high and he was taking a wobbly step away.

He took just the one step. Then he fell backward onto the carpeted hallway. Brenda felt the floor shake. His head bounced. The pistol hopped out of his hand and scooted over the carpet, stopping almost a yard beyond his curled fingers.

She had lost track of the knife after it caromed off his brow.

She looked around quickly for it, but couldn't see it.

Maybe it had fallen out of sight behind one of the bodies.

Better to have the gun, anyway, she thought.

Get it and I'll be fine.

She would need to make her way past Jack, but he seemed to be out cold.

How long's *that* gonna last? she wondered.

The sound of a groan sent a gust of fear through her belly, but then she realized it had come from Fran, not Jack.

The girl was sprawled on her back, her knees in the air, both hands holding her face.

God, I did that to her.

It made Brenda feel sick.

Why didn't I just push her away? I didn't have to hurt her.

Worry about it later, Brenda told herself. She went against me and I had to hurt her and now she's useless and I have to get the gun before Jack wakes up.

Brenda clenched her teeth, put her weight on her straight left arm, turned her body and rose onto her left knee. Shuddering and sweating, she held herself up with both hands on the cool marble floor.

This doesn't feel too good, she thought.

The pain from her gunshot right leg seemed to be everywhere.

Screw it, she thought. Screw the pain. Get the gun and worry about it later.

Letting her wounded leg slide along behind her, she crawled toward Jack on her hands and one knee.

He seemed very far away.

This is so awfully jolly.

It didn't seem that it should be so difficult to crawl a few yards on one knee. She wondered if she should try to stand up.

Just what I'd need, she thought. Get way up there on one foot and hop along and *fall*. I sure don't need to fall again. I've had enough of that.

This'll be fine, she told herself. I'm getting there, I'm getting there.

But her whole body was trembling form the effort and the pain. Sweat seemed to be pouring out of her, stinging her eyes and blurring her vision, sliding down her body like run-off in a storm, dripping from her ear lobes and the tip of her nose and her chin and her breasts. It ran down her arms and made her hands wet.

Once, her right hand slipped on the marble and plained forward and she bashed her elbow hard on the floor and cried out.

Braced up on her elbow and knee, she wiped her right hand on the T-shirt bandage around her thigh. But she couldn't think of a way to dry her left hand.

I'm almost to the carpet. Then I'll be all right. It'll be good and dry . . .

She would have the carpet for traction, but she would also have Jack beside her.

Hope he isn't faking.

She pushed herself up. The marble felt cool and dry under

her right hand, but slick under her left.

Be careful, she told herself, and resumed crawling.

Blinking because of the sweat in her eyes, she watched Jack. He lay sprawled on his back, shoes big on his feet, his bare legs straight out and apart. His penis, rooted in a nest of curly brown hair, drooped sideways against his left thigh. It looked small and soft, not at all like the big, stout shaft it had been a while ago.

He can't hurt me with that thing, Brenda thought.

Not unless it gets big again.

She suddenly thought about Quentin shoving his into Fran and how Fran had cried out in pain, then wept and begged him to stop, but then how later she'd been embracing him, moaning, moving her own hips to meet his thrusts almost as if she'd *liked* it.

How could she like it?

It's supposed to hurt like crazy when it's your first time and that had been Fran's first time unless she'd been lying and unless the blood afterward had been for a different reason. And you're *never* supposed to like it when they rape you. You're supposed to hate that, no matter what it might feel like.

But Fran had been fond of Quentin before. She'd thought he was cute and she'd admitted to daydreams about being with him. So maybe it makes a difference if you *like* the guy.

Or maybe she just lost her damn mind.

I sure wouldn't want a thing like that getting stuck into *me*, Brenda thought. If that's what it takes to make babies, I'll pass, thank you very much.

Her hand came down on the good dry mat of carpet a few inches from Jack's right foot.

Now I'll be fine, she thought. Long as he doesn't wake up.

The broad, low hill of his belly was rising and falling slightly as he breathed. His head was turned sideways, his mouth drooping open, his eyes shut. In the center of his forehead was a shiny red dome as if half a ping-pong ball had been shoved underneath his skin.

I got him good, she thought. He's out like a light.

Doesn't mean he'll stay that way.

But Brenda was making quicker progress now that she had the carpet under her.

I'm gonna make it!

Unless he wakes up in the next few seconds.

He isn't going *to wake up in time because I got him good with the knife and he's out cold and this isn't some crappy movie where the bad guy* always *grabs the gal just at the last second.*

Besides, she could see his eyeballs shifting back and forth under the lids.

He's still out, and I've made it.

The pistol, now, was almost within reach.

If he wakes up, dive for it.

It was Sherry's pistol, all right – or at least the same *kind* of pistol.

What'd he do to Sherry?

Soon as he wakes up. I'll make him talk.

Slide forward, hammer back, the pistol looked loaded and cocked and ready to fire.

Don't kill Jack unless you have to.

Bracing herself up on her left knee and right hand, she leaned forward and reached for the pistol and squealed with alarm and pain and despair when her right ankle was grabbed and jerked. Pain smashed through her body. She fell onto her side – onto Jack's arm and shoulder and face.

He's still down!

She twisted herself over.

Fran was hunkered low, both hands wrapped around Brenda's ankle, lumbering backward, dragging her.

'What're you *doing*!'

Fran didn't answer, didn't look up, just kept waddling backward, her breasts hanging toward the floor and swinging from side to side as she towed Brenda by the ankle.

'Let *go*, you idiot!'

'Fuck you,' Fran grunted.

'What's the *matter* with you?'

'You. You're the matter.'

Carpet no longer under her body, Brenda slid along on the cool marble floor.

'He's gonna wake up!'

'Good.' Fran flung Brenda's foot straight down at the floor.

Her shoe absorbed some of the impact, but pain exploded from her wound. Wracked with agony, she flinched rigid, arching her back, shoving her belly into the air.

Fran straddled her and dropped, buttocks slapping against her belly, driving her down, mashing her.

Brenda felt as if she'd been caved in. She fought for a breath but made squeaking sounds and seemed to get no air.

'How ya like it?' Fran asked. Cords of wet hair clung to her bloody, sweaty face.

Brenda had no breath for answering.

'Who's the loser now, huh? Huh?' Her open hand smacked Brenda hard across the face. 'How about a quip? How about a snappy rejoinder?' She slapped Brenda again. 'Who's on top, now?'

She clutched Brenda's breasts.

'What d'ya call these, huh? They're *nothing*! You got tits like a guy. A *skinny* guy. You got no tits at *all*, you emaciated fucking *twerp!* And everybody calls me *fat*! I'm fat and ugly and worthless and you're some sorta stunning *beauty* for godsake but you look like a fucking *guy*! But all the guys *want* you and I'm some sort of ugly fucking *cow* they don't wanta touch with a ten-foot pole. They don't wanta *kiss* me and nobody's *ever* gonna fall in love with a cow like me and the one time I get lucky maybe for the only time in my whole stinking life, you go and *kill* him.'

She pinched Brenda's nipples and twisted them hard.

Brenda jerked stiff and cried out and was surprised to find that she *could* cry out.

Could breathe again, though not very well.

'Stop it,' she gasped. 'Please.'

'You *killed* him.'

'He *raped* you!'

'So what!' She let go of Brenda's left nipple and smacked her across the face again. 'You killed him and you were gonna let Jack kill *me* so you could keep the fucking *knife*.'

'He's *out cold*, Fran. We can take him! We can survive this but you've gotta get off me.'

'Who *wants* to survive?' asked Fran.

'I do.'

'Well, you aren't gonna!'

'She happens to be right,' said Jack.

Brenda went cold inside. 'Now you've done it,' she muttered.

Fran's bloody face grinned down at her. 'Good,' she said.

'Don't let me stop the fun and games,' said Jack. 'Both of you stay where you are. Fran, let's see you hurt her some more.'

Chapter Sixty-one

'It has to be around here someplace,' Sherry said, slowing as they neared the Speed-D-Mart. 'This is where Duane's van was parked last night. Toby switched over to it, so he must've parked *his* car fairly close to here.'

'What kind of car?' Pete asked.

'A blue Mustang.'

Sherry turned right onto Airdrome.

'Like that one?' Jeff asked.

'Where?'

'Other side of the street. Near the corner.'

Sherry leaned closer to the steering wheel and turned her head to the left. 'Looks like it,' she said. She drove past the Mustang, then made a U-turn and pulled to the curb behind it. She shut off the engine. Bending down, shoulder against the wheel, she reached to the floor. She came up with the Club. 'Mind if I borrow this for a minute?' she asked.

'Help yourself.'

She pulled at the steering wheel locking device, lengthening it until the two steel bars came apart in the middle. She set the smaller piece down on the floor and kept the other. 'Both of you wait here, okay? Pete, why don't you get behind the wheel? Pull on ahead of Toby's car and wait. And keep your eyes open. If any cops come along, just drive on as if you don't have anything to do with me.'

'Sure,' Pete said. 'Just leave you.'

'I mean it. I don't want you guys getting busted for any of this.'

'We aren't gonna *ditch* you,' Jeff said.

'For all I know,' Sherry explained, 'the car isn't even locked. But it probably is, and Toby said it has an alarm. If it does, busting the window'll trigger it. Might get real noisy around here. But nobody pays much attention to car alarms. And cops . . . the only way they'll show up is if they happen to be passing by. So I don't think there *will* be any trouble. If there is, though, take off without me. Maybe drive around the block, keep an eye on things from a distance.'

'Let's see if the coast is clear *before* you go busting in,' Pete suggested. 'We can at least make sure there aren't cops at the Speed-D-Mart.'

'Cops are *always* at Speed-D-Marts,' Jeff added.

'Not always,' Pete said. 'Anyway, when I pull forward I'll have a good angle on the parking lot. I'll honk if I see any cop cars.'

'Good deal,' Sherry said. She smiled at Pete, gave him a pat on the thigh, then said, 'Be careful, you guys,' and climbed out of the car.

She left the driver's door open. As she walked toward the Mustang, Pete hurried around the front, scurried in and shut the door. He started the engine.

Limping, Sherry walked slowly alongside the Mustang. She looked straight ahead as if not at all interested in the car. At its front, she hobbled toward the curb.

Pete drove slowly by. As he neared the corner, more and more of the Speed-D-Mart parking lot slid into view. There were about a dozen vehicles in the small lot, a couple of them trying to exit. Several people milled about, including customers on their way to the entrance and a beggar waiting in ambush. A big white delivery truck was turning in from Robertson Boulevard.

Pete saw no police cars.

'Looks good,' he said, and eased over to the curb.

'Looks great,' Jeff agreed. 'I don't even see any rent-a-cop cars.'

'We'd better keep an eye on the intersection.'

'*You* keep an eye on it. I got better stuff to watch.'

Pete glanced over his shoulder. Jeff was twisted around on the back seat, staring out the rear window.

'Check her out, dude.'

Facing forward, Pete gave the intersection a quick scan.

Then he turned his attention to the right side mirror. It gave him a small but clear reflection of Sherry by the passenger side of the Mustang.

She bent and peered through the window, then straightened up. Keeping the steel bar low by her side, she looked toward Pete's car. The wind was blowing in her face, sweeping her short hair backward, flapping and filling her mostly unbuttoned shirt. Inside the gawdy shirt, she seemed to be wearing more bandages than swimsuit. The skimpy top was black against her tanned skin, the bandages white as rainless clouds. Lower, a patch of white on her thigh was larger than the black triangle of pants between her legs.

She nodded toward their car, then turned around slowly as if scanning the entire area.

'If she's trying to be inconspicuous,' Jeff said, 'she's failing miserably.'

'Yeah.'

'God, look at her.'

'I know.'

'And just think, she's with *us*.'

'Hard to believe,' Pete admitted.

'And she *likes* us.'

'Yeah.'

'Wow.'

'Yeah.'

'We might never have another day like this one, good buddy. Hope you're taking notes.'

'I'll take notes later. Wouldn't wanta miss a single—'

'There she goes.'

Sherry's image in the side mirror bent over and swung the bar, smashing the Mustang's passenger window. The noise of the alarm made Pete shrivel inside. Sherry reached through the broken window. A moment later, the door swung open.

Pete forced his eyes away from the mirror.

He scanned the traffic for police cars.

So far, so good. But all it'll take is one.

He looked across the street at the Speed-D-Mart's parking lot. People wandered about, but nobody seemed to pay any attention to the alarm.

'Shit shit shit,' Jeff said.
'What?'
'Why doesn't she *hurry*?'
'We're okay so far.'
Returning his eyes to the side mirror, Pete saw that the Mustang's door was shut. 'Where *is* she?'
'Inside. She's in the passenger seat.'
'Good idea.'
The door suddenly swung open. Sherry climbed out. She stood up, a purse now hanging at her hip, a paper in her right hand. She stepped past the door. With her bare left foot, she shoved it shut. Then she made her slow, limping way to the sidewalk.
'God, she's taking her time!'
'Maybe she *can't* move any faster,' Pete said. 'A few hours ago, she could hardly move at all.'
'Shit, yeah. We thought she was dead.'
'Nice recovery, huh?'
'Man, I sure hope we get to see her when she's *really* recovered. Preferably naked.'
'In your dreams,' Pete said.
'Yours too, good buddy.'
Pete leaned over the passenger seat and shoved the door open for her.
A few seconds later, Sherry ducked through the doorway and eased herself down in the seat. 'Let's go,' she said, pulling the door shut.
Pete checked the traffic, then stepped on the gas.
He reached Robertson, stopped for a moment because of the red light, then turned right. As he picked up speed, the beeping of Toby's car alarm faded and died out.
'By George,' said Jeff, 'I do think we made it.'
Pete turned his head and grinned at Sherry. 'Did you find the address?'
'You bet. *And* my purse.'
'Great.'
She held open the registration slip and studied it. 'Okay,' she said. 'The car's owned by Sidney Bones, Four Eight Nine Two Shawcross Lane.'

‘Where the hell is that?’ Jeff asked.

‘Up in the hills,’ Sherry said. ‘It’s a few miles from a school where I’ve done a lot subbing . . . Toby’s school.’

‘You know how to find it?’

‘I think so. I’m pretty sure I ran into Shawcross last year when I was trying to find a faculty party. It’s up there someplace. I know I’ve seen it. Might take a little hunting . . .’

‘That’s what we’re here for,’ said Jeff.

Chapter Sixty-two

'Okay,' Toby said. 'That's enough.'

Fran, grunting and groaning as she worked on Brenda, ignored him.

'Stop it,' Toby commanded.

She gave Brenda a last quick slap, then crawled off her. She lowered herself onto the floor and rolled onto her back, huffing for air.

Brenda, spread-eagled, wet all over, sobbed and writhed as she struggled to breathe.

'Having fun yet?' Toby asked her.

She didn't answer.

'I know I am. I haven't had this much fun since . . . last night with Sherry. And I haven't even touched you yet. This is gonna be great.'

Fran braced herself up with her elbows. 'What'll you . . . do with her?'

'What do you think?'

'I'll . . . help.'

'Bet you will.'

'Just . . . name it.'

'Sure,' he muttered. He supposed Fran would probably do anything he asked of her. She had nothing to lose, after all. And she obviously held some very strong, strange feelings about Brenda – a wild mixture of envy and hatred and desire. She'd seemed to *enjoy* inflicting pain on her so-called friend.

I can use her, Toby thought, but I'd better watch out. No telling *what* she might try.

'I want Brenda in the bedroom,' he said.

'Okay.' After struggling to her feet, Fran scowled down at Brenda. 'How'm I spose to—?'

'Pick her up, drag her, I don't care. Just—'

Someone knocked hard on the front door. Toby jumped. His heart lurched and he felt as if his breath had been knocked out.

From the other side of the door came a loud voice. 'This is the police. Please open the door.' More pounding.

Fran darted her eyes toward the door.

Toby aimed the pistol at her face.

Brenda, squirming on the floor, seemed wrapped up in her own misery.

The doorbell rang several times quickly. Then came more knocking. 'I know someone's in there,' the police officer said. 'Please open the door. We're evacuating . . .'

Toby stepped up to the door, opened it and shoved his pistol into the cop's face and pulled the trigger. The bullet socked a hole through the bridge of the man's nose.

Before the cop had time to fall, Toby reached out and grabbed him by the shirt and jerked him forward. The threshold stopped his feet. Toby scampered aside as the cop toppled into the foyer. A moment after he slammed face first against the marble floor, Toby hopped over him.

Leaning out the doorway, he looked around.

The air smelled like a campfire. It was yellow with blowing smoke, snowy with gray ashes.

Toby saw no flames, though.

Nor did he see any other cops.

There gotta be more around, he thought.

Who gives a hot shit? Any more show up. I'll blow their fucking faces off.

He shoved the dead cop's feet clear of the doorway, then shut the door and locked it.

Brenda remained on her back, still sweaty and writhing and out of breath, a wounded and beaten and beautiful naked female surrounded by three dead guys.

Fran stood over Brenda's feet, gazing down at the dead cop.

'Grab her,' Toby said. Not waiting for Fran to respond, he crouched over the cop. Holstered at the man's side was a pistol that looked larger than the one Toby had been using.

Anyway, he thought, mine's gotta be low on ammo.

He set Sherry's pistol on the floor, unsnapped the cop's holster strap, and removed the weapon. It was a boxy-looking thing.

He supposed it must be fully loaded and ready for action. But did it have a safety on?

He pointed it at Fran.

'*No!*' she squealed, turning her back, hunching over and hugging her head like a kid afraid of a snowball.

'Take her in the bedroom,' Toby said.

Whimpering, Fran straddled Brenda and bent down and grabbed her arms.

Toby swung the pistol toward Quen, aimed at the dead boy's head, and pulled the trigger. The pistol fired, bucking in his hand, its blast slapping his ears. The slug missed Quen and hit the marble by his head, throwing dust and chips into the air.

'Cool,' Toby muttered.

This was a better gun than Sherry's – bigger and more powerful.

With Brenda in a sitting position, Fran scurried around behind her, squatted and reached under her armpits. She wrapped her arms around Brenda's chest and struggled to lift her. 'Stand up,' she gasped. 'Come on.' She tugged. 'Get up or he'll kill us.'

Brenda made no effort to stand.

Fran couldn't lift her.

'Shit,' Toby muttered. 'Wait a second.'

He picked up the smaller weapon he'd taken from Sherry. Now that he had the cop's gun, he no longer needed it. He certainly didn't want to drag it around with him. But he didn't want to leave behind a weapon that someone might use on him. So he studied the pistol, worked a lever that didn't seem to do anything, then pressed a button that released the ammo magazine. He slid the magazine out of the pistol's handle and looked at it. It seemed to have only one round in it.

He worked the cartridge loose and hurled it into the living room. A moment after it vanished in the shadows, he heard it *thunk* against a wall.

He gave the empty magazine a toss. It landed on the

newspapers that he'd spread over the carpet to hide the bloody mess left behind by Sid.

Then he dropped Sherry's pistol. With the cop's weapon in his right hand, he stepped toward the girls.

'You take that side,' he instructed Fran. 'I'll take this.'

Keeping the cop's pistol in his right hand, he crouched and used his left hand to grab Brenda's upper arm. He clutched it just below the armpit. The skin was hot and wet and slippery. 'Okay, lift,' he said.

Together, they hoisted her off the floor.

It was easier than Toby had expected. Brenda seemed to be helping, pushing at the floor with her good leg – maybe afraid of being dropped.

Starting to move, Fran tripped over Baxter. As she stumbled, they all lurched sideways and Toby almost lost his grip on Brenda. But Fran recovered. Nobody fell. Toby adjusted his grip.

'Watch where you're going,' he warned.

'Sorry,' Fran said.

Leaving the foyer behind, they started up the carpeted hallway toward Toby's bedroom.

'What about the fire?' Fran asked.

'What about it?'

'It's coming, isn't it?'

'Maybe.'

'I mean, isn't that what the cop was about?'

'Guess so. Who cares?'

'I don't wanta get burnt up.'

'Soon as Brenda's on my bed, you can leave.'

'Really?'

'Sure.'

'What about you?'

'I'll be okay.'

'Not if the fire comes.'

'Screw the fire. I give a shit. It burns me, it burns me. I've had it, anyhow. All I wanta do is have my fun with Brenda before it gets me.'

'It doesn't have to get you. Why don't we leave? Why don't we leave right now? Just you and me. When the fire gets here, it'll burn up all the bodies and evidence and everything, nobody'll ever know you did all this stuff.'

'You'll know,' Toby said.

'I'll never tell.'

'Sure.'

At his bedroom doorway, they halted. They turned Brenda sideways and Toby entered first.

'I *won't*,' Fran insisted.

Toby said nothing as they hustled Brenda over to his bed. There, they turned her around. They sat her on the edge of the mattress, then eased her down onto her back. Her legs hung over the edge, shoes on the floor.

Toby stepped away. 'Take her shoes off,' he said. 'Then put her legs on the bed.'

Fran squatted in front of Brenda's knees. As she pulled off the shoes, she said, 'Know what? I just thought of something, Jack. A wife can't testify against her husband. All we'd have to do is get married . . .'

'That's an idea,' Toby said.

She cast a nervous smile over her shoulder.

'I'd make you a really good wife,' she said. 'I'd do *anything* for you, and I'd never tell on you. I wouldn't be *allowed*, even if I wanted to.' She straightened up, lifting Brenda's bare feet, and swung her legs onto the mattress.

'Thanks,' Toby said.

'What do you think?'

'I'd rather be dead than married to an ugly fat load of shit like you.'

She thrust out her lower lip. Her chin started to tremble.

'Even if I *wanted* to marry you, we're too young.'

'Maybe not if our parents . . .'

'*My* parents are toes-up, babe. I made 'em that way. Me and my asshole brother, Sid. They ain't gonna give permission for shit.'

'You killed your parents?'

'They were a pain in the ass. And rich.'

Sobbing, Fran blubbered, 'But we can *still* get married. We can . . . go away someplace. Another state, or . . .'

'Besides which,' Toby said, 'you've got it wrong about

wives. In this state, they *can* testify against their husbands. Can't be *forced* to do it, but they can do it if they want.'

'How do you know?'

'I read.'

'Anyway . . .' She sniffed and wiped her eyes. 'It doesn't matter. I *wouldn't* testify. They couldn't *make* me.'

'You're already made, and what a mess.'

She looked stunned. She blinked at him, tears sliding down her cheeks.

Toby laughed.

He heard the faint, sputtery hum of a distant helicopter.

'Can *I* go?' Fran asked.

'I said you could.'

'Okay.' She turned toward the door and started to walk.

The sound of the helicopter grew.

'Hey, Fran?'

She turned around and raised her eyebrows.

'Know what I'm gonna do? I'm gonna stay right here and hump the living daylights outa Brenda and have the time of my life. And when the house burns down, I'll be right on top of her, fucking her, and we'll burn up together. We'll *melt* together, and be like one big clump. They won't even be able to take us apart. Cool, huh?'

Blinking her wet red eyes, she nodded slightly and said, 'Yeah.'

'Get outa here.'

'You won't . . . shoot me, will you? When I turn around?'

'Nah.'

'Promise?'

'You're too fuckin' ugly to kill.'

She turned around and resumed walking toward the door.

Toby watched her fat ass shimmy with each step.

She lowered her head and raised her shoulders as if getting ready for a bullet.

'Tub of lard,' Toby said.

He aimed at her back.

She cowered and hugged the back of her head and trotted for the door.

Toby intended to shoot her down.

But his finger stayed light on the trigger.

A moment later, she was out the doorway and out of sight.

He thought about hurrying into the hallway and popping her.

It'd be easy.

It was a long hallway and the fat slob was so out of shape it'd probably take her forever to reach the front door.

Just let her go, he thought. She's such a fucking loser. Give her a break. What's she gonna do, anyway? Tell on me?'

He laughed.

Then he remembered the cop he'd just killed.

And wondered if maybe the cop had a partner nearby, a partner wondering where he'd gone.

If Fran runs into him . . .

Toby rushed to his doorway.

Fran had already reached the foyer. She was squatting down beside the dead cop, picking up Sherry's pistol.

'Good luck, you dumb twat,' he called out. 'Didn't you see me empty it?'

She pointed the pistol at him.

It fired!

As the blast resounded through the house, Toby felt as if his left hand had been struck by a hammer.

But I emptied *the gun!*

And I let her go!

You don't shoot a guy who lets you go!

Fran let the gun fall and lurched for the front door.

Toby opened fire.

He pulled the trigger fast.

He missed and missed.

She got the door open.

But then a round caught her shoulder and spun her around, away from the door, and as she pranced backward, arms flapping for balance, Toby fired and missed again but then hit her in the middle of the chest, then missed, then hit her in the stomach and in the right breast, missed again, then put a slug through her right eye.

She slammed her back against the foyer wall, bounced off it, and fell forward.

Chapter Sixty-three

As Pete drove toward the barricade, the police officer raised a hand, signalling him to stop.

'Looks like we've had it,' Jeff said.

'I don't know,' Pete mumbled.

'They probably closed off the road for the fires,' Sherry said. 'Try to talk him into letting us through.'

'How do I do *that*?' Pete asked.

'Come on, dude,' said Jeff. 'You're supposed to be a writer, right? Make up a story.'

With the back of her bare foot, Sherry nudged the towel-wrapped revolver a bit farther under the passenger seat.

The cop came to Pete's door, ducked and looked in the window. 'I'm afraid the road's closed,' he explained. 'The area's being evacuated.'

'But Brett's grandma lives up there,' Pete said, and nodded toward Sherry.

The cop looked over at her. 'Is that so?' he asked.

Sherry nodded. 'Her house is on Sunshine Lane.'

'We'll take care of her,' the cop said. 'We've got people going door to door.'

'She's bedridden,' Sherry explained. 'And she's alone. She won't be able to *get* to the door. She's also hard of hearing, so she won't even know if someone's ringing the bell.'

The cop frowned as if considering the situation.

'Can't we just drive up there real fast and grab her?' Sherry asked. She sounded as if she were trying to control her growing worry. 'I've been staying with her, but I had to go to the emergency room this morning.'

'How'd you get those injuries?'

'Just lucky. I fell down the hillside behind grandma's house.

Anyway, when I left the emergency room, I heard on the radio that the fire was moving this way so I went to get a couple of my friends. They're gonna help me carry her out. If you'll let us go up.'

'Just in and out?' the cop asked.

'Quick as we can pick her up,' Pete assured him.

'All right. I'll let you through. But keep your eyes open. The fire's closing in at a pretty good clip, so you don't have a lot of time.'

'How long do you think?' Pete asked.

'Half an hour? Hard to say. Just make it quick.'

'Thank you, officer,' Pete said.

'Thank you *very* much,' Sherry added from the passenger seat.

'Be careful,' the cop said, then hurried over to the barricade and lifted it out of the way.

Pete gave the officer a grateful smile as he started forward.

After they'd passed the barricade, Jeff said, 'You're pretty tricky, dudes. Good job.'

'What was that about Sunshine Lane?' Pete asked, glancing at Sherry. 'Toby's place is on Shawcross.'

'Sunshine's just a couple of streets away from Shawcross. That's where I went for the faculty party. Thought it'd be better not to mention Shawcross under the circumstances, you know? In case we *do* find Toby and . . . commit an illegal act.'

'Like kill his ass?' suggested Jeff.

'Or whatever,' said Sherry.

Chapter Sixty-four

Shaking badly, Toby sank to a crouch and set his pistol down on the hallway carpet. Then he picked up the middle finger of his left hand. Where the bullet had blown it off, it was a bloody mess. Some shreds of skin and tendon and muscle hung from it, swaying.

They can probably sew it back on, he thought.

Yeah, sure. If I get over to a hospital fast enough.

I'd have to leave now.

What's it gonna be, my finger or Brenda?

Hand trembling, he eased the finger toward the raw place on his hand where it used to belong.

It seemed to be about half an inch too short.

Muttering, 'Fuck it,' he threw his finger away. It hit the wall. He heard the quiet thunk through the sounds of helicopters.

Must be a shitload of news choppers out there.

But they weren't roaring overhead. Not yet, anyway. So the fire must still be a somewhere else.

Plenty of time.

He snatched up the pistol and rushed into his bedroom.

Brenda was stretched out on the bed. Above her, all along the length of the bed, the curtains were blowing, rising away from the window, letting smoky golden daylight fall on her body. Her eyes were shut. She was breathing hard, her sweaty chest rising and falling.

Toby stepped closer.

Her skin was blotched with ruddy places where she'd been hurt. She was also spattered and smeared with blood. Blood from her gunshot leg, he supposed. The T-shirt belted around her thigh had leaked plenty. But she probably wore blood from everyone else, too – Baxter and Quen and Fran, even some from the cop.

How many of *them* have HIV? he wondered.

'Who cares?' he muttered. *I already got it from her sister. I can wallow in blood till hell freezes over, won't mean shit to me.*

'Your fucking sister gave me AIDS,' he said. 'Did I already tell you that?'

Brenda just kept her eyes shut, kept panting for breath.

But she jerked and gasped and looked up at him with eyes full of fear and pain when he jerked her legs apart.

He crawled onto the bed.

Knelt between her legs and jammed his gunshot hand against her groin.

She cried out. So did he.

She reached for his wrist.

He slammed the pistol against the side of her head.

Though the blow didn't knock her unconscious, it seemed to knock the fight out of her. She lay limp, staring off to the side.

'That's better,' Toby said.

He took his hand away. Her pubic hair, no longer downy and golden, was painted red. So was the area below.

'I bet I just gave it to you,' he said. 'Think so?'

She didn't answer.

'Doesn't matter anyhow,' he said. 'None of us're gonna die from AIDS, you can bet on that. I'm gonna hump you to death.'

Her eyes opened slightly.

Her gaze slid toward his groin.

She muttered, 'Reality check.'

He looked down, himself.

How'd that happen?

Getting my finger shot off maybe had a little something to do with it. And ramming my stump into her twat.

'I'll be fine,' he said.

'Sure.'

Toby set the pistol on the sheet by Brenda's left hip. He slid her arm up until her hand disappeared under the pillow, then placed his hand on her breast.

It felt like a soft, springy pad. The skin was warm and slick. As he caressed it, he felt the nipple stiffen and rise.

He felt himself stiffen and rise along with it.

He squeezed her nipple, making her flinch. Making himself harder.

'Check again,' he said.

Brenda lifted her head off the mattress and looked. 'Big whoop,' she said.

'Big enough. Your sister sure thought so.'

Her eyes opened a little wider. 'Want me to suck it?' she asked.

The suggestion gave him a sudden ache of desire. 'No,' he said. 'You'd bite.'

'Huh-uh.'

He suddenly remembered last night, sinking his teeth into Sherry.

That had only been a little nip. He'd tasted some blood, but not much flesh.

Nothing really to chew on, like he'd gotten from Duane.

I can eat Brenda! Bite her all over, taste her skin, drink her blood, chew her and swallow!

Right hand against the mattress, he eased himself lower. He licked her nipple. It felt big and rubbery in his mouth.

Eat it and work my way down.

As he licked and sucked, he realized that Brenda was moaning under him. Squirming, too.

She likes this?

He lifted his mouth off her breast.

'Don't stop,' she murmured. One of her hands went to the back of his head. Fingers pushing through his hair, she guided his head back down until his mouth latched onto her breast.

He sucked.

She moaned.

She's faking.

It's her left hand, he realized. Maybe she's planning to work her way down and grab the pistol.

Long as she's fooling with my hair, nothing to worry about.

'Yes,' she gasped. 'Suck. *Suck.*'

She was thrashing beneath him, hand pushing at the back

of his head, mashing his face against her breast.

'Oh, yes!'

She clenched his hair.

'Yes yes *yes*! Now the other.'

Why not?

Her hand remained on the back of his head, clenching his hair as he moved his mouth to her right breast and tongued the nipple.

It tasted fresh and somehow made him think of Santa Monica beach early in the morning before the crowds arrive . . . a mild breeze coming in from the ocean, gulls squealing and circling.

He could feel the ocean breeze on him now, blowing down gently from the windows alongside the bed.

If only she was my girlfriend, Toby thought. And we were at the beach right now . . .

Get real, he told himself. She wouldn't *go* to the beach with a guy like me. Never in a million years. She wouldn't be caught dead with a guy like me. Sherry, either.

None of them – none of the good ones – would *ever* go to the beach or to a movie or anything else with a tub of lard like me.

Maybe a pig like Fran. She's the best I'd ever be able to get.

But I sure got Sherry last night.

And I've got Brenda now.

This is as good as it's ever gonna get.

He slipped his lips down over Brenda's nipple and rubbed it with his tongue. Flicked it. Thrust at it.

She moaned and writhed.

He sucked hard, drawing more of her breast into his mouth.

She bucked under him in a frenzy.

'*Yes!*' she gasped. *'Oh!'*

She clenched his hair and pushed his face more tightly against her breast.

He squeezed her breast with his teeth.

'Ah! Jack! Yesssss!'

I'm gonna come! Better stop this and . . .

Something stabbed Toby in the left eye.

Squealing, he flung himself up.

'You fucking bitch!' he shrieked. *'What've you done to me?'*

Brenda glared at him.

His own leather belt dangled from her hand. She was clutching its buckle. The steel prong jutted out from between two fingers.

He glanced at her leg.

The bloody T-shirt bandage hung loose around her wound.

'I'LL KILL YOU!' Toby shouted.

As she tried to strike at him again with the prong, he caught her by the wrist with his shot hand. Pain flashed up his arm, but it wasn't much compared to the pain from his eye. He held on.

With his right hand, he slapped the mattress by her hip, trying to find his pistol.

'TOBY!'

He jerked his head toward the sound of the voice.

Lurching through his bedroom doorway was a woman. A woman with a bandaged head and battered face. She wore a bright flowery shirt as if she'd just come back from Hawaii. She didn't seem to have any pants on. Her bare legs were scratched and bruised and patched with many bandages.

Sherry?

She came into the bedroom with a guy on each side.

They looked like they were about sixteen.

A shrimp and a clean-cut looking jerk who probably made straight As . . . and had a revolver.

The revolver was aimed at Toby.

'Hands up,' said the kid.

The hole in the muzzle of the revolver looked very small, as holes go.

'Shoot him,' said the shrimp.

Ignoring him, gun-boy said, 'Stick your hands up and get off the girl.'

Toby found the pistol by Brenda's hip. He snatched it off the mattress and swung it toward the trio.

Take 'em all down, the fuckers!

SHERRY FIRST!

Before he could bring the pistol around far enough, however, two things happened.

Brenda caught hold of his wrist.

And a bullet from the kid's .22 knocked into his chin and turned his head sideways.

Feeling as if his jaw had been blown apart, he spun away from the impact. His head pounded against the bedroom wall.

Brenda was twisting under him, trying to throw him off.

Then someone grabbed the hair on the back of his head and jerked as if trying to rip his scalp off. He fell backward, off Brenda, off the edge of his bed.

His back slammed the floor.

Sherry stood over him.

She had pants on, after all. Even with just one eye, he could see the thin strip of black fabric between her legs.

Too bad.

But I bet that teeny weeny fuckin' bikini won't stop a bullet.

He brought his right arm up off the floor to shoot her with the cop's big pistol.

But the cop's big pistol was no longer in his hand.

She stomped his face with her bare foot.

Through the daze of pain, he heard her say, 'Brenda. You okay?'

Brenda said, 'Fine.'

'Guys,' said Sherry, 'get her out of here. Wait, take this. She can wear this.'

A few seconds passed. Then he heard Brenda say, 'Thanks.'

'I'm Pete, by the way,' a guy said.

'Hi.'

'I'm Jeff.'

'I'm Brenda. Nice to meet you.'

'Chit-chat in the car,' Sherry said. 'I'll be right with you.'

'You'd better come now,' one of the guys said.

'Yeah,' said the other.

'Take Brenda out to the car,' Sherry said. 'I'll just be a minute.'

'The fire . . .'

'I know. Don't worry. We've still got time.'

'Not much.'

'*Go!*'

Chapter Sixty-five

'We meet again,' Sherry said.

Toby, sprawled at her feet, his chin ruined, his nose mashed, his left eye gone, looked up with his right eye.

'You never should've messed with me,' she said. 'You shouldn't have messed with my friend, Jim. And you *really* shouldn't have messed with my sister.'

He coughed, spraying blood from his mouth.

'They'd probably execute you for all the shit you did,' she said. 'But maybe not. Hell, this is Los Angeles. Maybe they'd just set you free. You never know. I'd better go ahead and kill you, just in case.'

He shook his head, blood spilling from his mouth.

'You don't want me to kill you?'

He grunted and shook his head some more.

'Should I turn you in to the cops?'

He nodded.

'Okay,' Sherry said. 'I guess that's what we'll do, then. I mean, you've probably suffered enough. Lost a finger, lost an eye, not to mention your chin's messed up. We'll get the cops and they'll take you to a hospital. Maybe you can even have your finger reattached.'

He nodded some more, somewhat eagerly.

'By the way, I didn't give you AIDS. Just said that to mess with your head.'

He almost looked relieved.

'So you'll have plenty of time to enjoy Death Row – like about fifteen years – before they put the needle in you.'

He nodded and grunted and coughed out some blood.

'Just kidding,' said Sherry.

'Huh?'

'Not about the AIDS. About your future on Death Row.'

She showed Toby's single eye what she'd been holding behind her back.

A Buck knife she'd found on her way into the house – near one of the bodies on the foyer floor.

'Does this belong to you?' she asked.

He shook his head.

'Doesn't matter,' Sherry said. 'Because I'm gonna give it to you anyway.'

He made little whimpery noises as Sherry crouched over him.

Chapter Sixty-six

'Was that a scream?' Pete asked, looking over his shoulder.

Jeff, in the back seat with an arm across Brenda's shoulders, shrugged and said, 'I don't know, man. All I can hear are choppers and sirens.'

'Me, too,' said Brenda. She was slumped sideways against Jeff. Sherry's gaudy shirt was buttoned almost to her throat and Jeff's shirt draped her lap and thighs. 'Who *are* you guys?' she asked.

'I'm Pete.'

'I'm Jeff.'

'Reality check. I *know* your names. I mean, who *are* you?'

'Friends of your sister,' answered Pete.

'Yeah,' said Jeff. 'Just a couple of friends.'

'Well, you're my friends now,' Brenda said. 'Now and forever.'

'All *right*!' Jeff blurted. 'Cool.'

'Yeah,' said Pete. 'But you might change your mind once you get to know us.'

'Real smart, dude. Cripes! He's just trying to be funny, Brenda. We're *swell* guys.'

'I can tell,' said Brenda.

'Sherry's sure been in there a long time,' Pete said.

'Long as we get out of here ahead of the fire,' Jeff said, 'she can take all the time she wants.'

'Yeah, but I wouldn't wanta be sitting here if more cops show up.'

'Hey, *we* didn't kill anyone.'

'Maybe not, but . . .' Pete suddenly saw Sherry hobble onto the front stoop of the house. 'She's out,' he said.

'All *right*! And the fire nowhere in sight!'

Leaving the shadows behind, Sherry limped into the smoky sunlight.

The black bikini, little more than strings and tiny patches, looked great on her. Its loose top wobbled and bounced a bit with the motion of her walking. Her tawny skin glistened. Though Pete could see numerous bandages, her scratches and abrasions and bruises were mostly invisible in the distance.

The way she looked made him feel good all over.

Even in his heart.

Especially in his heart.

He leaped out of the car and ran to her.

'Everything okay?' he asked.

'Can't complain.'

Walking beside her, he put a hand low on her back. He felt the slickness and heat of her skin.

She met his eyes. A corner of her mouth tilted upward, trembling slightly.

'Did you take care of Toby?' he asked.

'Oh, yeah. Been keeping an eye out for the fire?'

'Hasn't come over the ridge yet. We oughta be fine.'

'Great.' She put her hand on Pete's back. He felt it just below his shoulder blade, but its touch seemed to spread all through him as they walked the rest of the way to his car.

The First Official Gathering

by

Peter Hanford

It was midnight at the Nacho Casa restaurant. We picked up our food and drinks at the counter, then sat around a large, U-shaped booth.

Jim Starr, Sherry, me, Brenda and Jeff.

Everybody had pretty much recovered from the Toby Bones ordeal.

So we'd succeeded, after all – in spite of Jeff's early predictions to the contrary – in seeing what Sherry looks like without the injuries.

All I can say is 'WOW!'

And Brenda looks pretty good, herself.

As for Jim, he ain't beautiful but he seems to be a real cool guy. He's nice. He's also tough as nails.

I guess we're all a lot tougher than we used to be.

Tougher and, in some ways, happier.

Because we'd worked together and helped each other through a hairy situation.

Because we'd put down a bad guy.

Because we now had each other.

There was a lot to be happy about.

Not to mention, the district attorney's office had decided, once all the investigating was done, not to press charges against any of us. Though we'd broken a few laws, we'd done it for pretty good reasons.

My shooting of Toby Bones was considered self-defense.

They overlooked the illegal carrying and discharging of my firearm.

They never did find out whatever Sherry had done to Toby, there at the end, because the house burnt to the ground about twenty minutes after we'd fled. All the bodies got pretty badly messed up. Tough to do a good autopsy on a crispy critter.

Anyway, here we were at the Nacho Casa.

Midnight, one month later.

We all sat around and chatted and laughed and generally had a great time while we ate our tacos and burritos and enchiladas and stuff.

Finally, we finished eating.

'So what now?' Jeff asked.

'Just sit around and keep our eyes open,' Jim explained.

'Is that all?'

'That's about all,' Jim said. 'Maybe something will happen, maybe not.'

'Sooner or later,' Sherry said, 'a damsel in distress is sure to come along.'

I nodded, smiling. Even though I'd been seeing Sherry almost every day, I still couldn't get over how wonderful she looked.

Tonight, her short blonde hair seemed to float around her face. She wore a glossy, royal-blue blouse that seemed to be made of silk. It had short sleeves. The buttons were undone halfway down her front, and the blouse was untucked. It hung past her waist and draped her white shorts like a small, airy skirt.

I felt like the luckiest guy in the world to be sitting beside her.

Not just because she's so beautiful, either.

Mostly, it had to do with how great she was: brave and funny and smart and sweet.

'Even if no distressed damsels do show up,' I said, 'it'll be nice just sitting here.'

Sherry looked into my eyes and smiled.

It was as fine a smile as I had ever seen.

'Exactly,' she said.

'It's kind of fun,' Brenda said. She cast a smile at Jeff, who blushed.

'What could be better than this?' Jeff asked.

'Too bad we can't do it every night,' Brenda said.

'I think Saturday nights will be as much as we can handle for the time being,' Sherry told her. 'At least while school's in session.'

'I think you're right,' I said. 'It'd be pretty tough to keep this from our parents if we did it *very* often. Mine think I'm spending the night at Jeff's house.'

'And I'm supposedly staying with *him*,' Jeff said.

'I'm having a sleep-over with Sherry,' Brenda explained.

'Bunch of sneaky rotten kids,' said Jim.

'And proud of it,' Jeff said.

Leaning forward with an eager look in her eyes, Brenda glanced from Sherry to Jim to me. 'We oughta give ourselves some sort of name.'

Jim looked amused. 'If you want.'

'Like what?' Sherry asked her.

'I don't know,' Brenda said. She shrugged. She was wearing a *South Park* T-shirt with several versions of Kenny meeting demises. 'How about "The Avengers"?'

'Been done,' I said. 'What about "Sneaky Rotten Kids"?'

'That leaves out me and Jim,' Sherry said.

' "The Rescuers"?' Brenda suggested.

'That was a mouse cartoon,' Sherry complained.

'Come on,' Brenda said. 'Let's have some ideas. What do you think, Jeff? Give us a name.'

His smile going broad, Jeff said, 'How about "Three Bad-Ass Dudes and Two Great-Ass Babes." '

She whapped his shoulder with the back of her hand.

'*Ow!*' He quickly added, 'Got another one. "Death Defying Dudes and Dudettes Dealing out Justice in the Mean Streets of Los Angeles." '

'A little wordy,' I said.

'Why not just, "The Dealers"?' Sherry suggested.

'Not bad,' Jim said.

'I mean, if we really *want* a name.'

' "The Dealers," ' Brenda said, frowning slightly and nodding. 'Pretty decent.'

'I like it,' I said. 'A lot.'

'I can always count on you,' Sherry said, and patted me on the thigh. After she got done patting, her hand stayed there.

'I like it, too,' Jeff said.

Looking very pleased, Brenda gave her head a brisk nod. ' "Dealers" it is. Now, how about getting some T-shirts made up?'

We all laughed.

Except Brenda. She straightened her back and raised her eyebrows. 'I'm serious,' she said. Then she cast a glance at Jeff.

'T-shirts?' Jeff said. 'Great idea.'

'Heads up,' Jim said, a quiet urgency in his voice.

I glanced at the door just as three guys in camouflage jackets swaggered in.

'Remember,' Jim said, 'we're just customers here. We don't do anything unless someone starts trouble.'

'But if they *do* start trouble,' Sherry added, 'we *deal* with it.'

Brenda chuckled softly. ' 'Cause we're the "Dealers".'

'Kill 'em all,' whispered Jeff. 'Let God sort 'em out.'

The Midnight Tour

Richard Laymon

'The Beast House – legendary site of ghastly murder! See with your own eyes where the bloody butchery took place!'

The sales pitch hasn't changed much over the years – except now you can listen to it on earphones. But the audio tour of the house only gives a sanitized version of the horrific events that made the Beast House infamous. If you want the full story, you'll have to take the Midnight Tour. Saturday nights only. Limited to thirteen courageous tourists. It begins on the stroke of midnight.

You'll be lucky to get out alive . . .

'If you've missed Laymon, you've missed a treat' Stephen King

'No one writes like Laymon and you're going to have a good time with anything he writes' Dean Koontz

'In Laymon's books, blood doesn't so much drip drip as explode, splatter and coagulate' *Independent*

'A gut-crunching writer' *Time Out*

0 7472 5827 9

Among the Missing

Richard Laymon

At 2:32 a.m. a Jaguar roars along a lonely road high in the California mountains. Behind the wheel sits the beautiful wife of Professor Grant Parkington. In spite of the night's chill, she wears only a skimpy nightgown. She has left Grant behind. She's after a different kind of man – someone as wild, daring and passionate as herself.

The man she wants is waiting for her near the road. Mrs Parkington stops for him. 'Where to?' she says. He suggests the Bend, where the Silver River widens and there's a soft, sandy beach. With the stars overhead and moonlight on the water, it's an ideal place for love.

But no love will take place there tonight. In the morning a naked body will be found – a body missing more than its clothes . . .

'If you've missed Laymon you've missed a treat' Stephen King

'No one writes like Laymon and you're going to have a good time with anything he writes' Dean Koontz

'A brilliant writer' *Sunday Express*

0 7472 6072 9